Fredrick Wentworth, Captain

A Novel in Two Parts

Book 1

NONE BUT YOU

by
Susan Kaye

Wytherngate Press
2007

2007 Wytherngate Press

Cover photograph
Veer/Westend 61 Photography
WFP0006393

Cover art direction: Margaret Coleman
Cover design: Galina Vishnevski

ISBN 0-9728529-4-8   ISBN 13 978-0-9728529-4-4
LCCN 2007920282

Wytherngate Press website: wytherngate.com

The principal text of this book was set in a digitized version of 10 point
Baskerville. Title appears in Edwardian Script.

Printed in the United States of America on acid-free paper.

Kaye, Susan.
   None But You/ Susan Kaye.
   252 p.; 21 cm.
   Series: Fredrick Wentworth, Captain; 1.
   ISBN 978-0-9728529-4-4
   1. Regency—England—Fiction. 2. Regency fiction. I.
Austen, Jane, 1775-1817. Persuasion. II. Series:
Fredrick Wentworth, Captain; Book 1.

   813.54   2007920282

—&—

This book is dedicated to
Mom, who gave me my love of words,
Bill, who has loved me regardless how messy the house has been,
Will and Emily, who have been patient all these years,
Laura and Pamela, who have supported me in writing and other things,
Linda and Sue, who remembered to ask.

—&—

Chapter One

C"aptain Wentworth, thank you for inviting Anne and me. There is no honour quite like taking dinner in the Great Cabin of a frigate." Admiral Hammond pumped the Captain's hand and then dropped it to move to the side, admonishing the men manoeuvring his niece in the boson's chair, "Carefully there, carefully, you grass combers."

Wentworth was glad to be released from the man's sweaty grasp but bristled at the remark. His men were gentle as a gaggle of nannies with the fair Miss Hammond. The Admiral's remarks were uncalled for, though it was only natural, as Hammond had no good reputation amongst seagoing men. Stories from his active service were punctuated with instances of cruelty and barbarism, and the Captain took this into account.

Nodding to the smiling Miss Hammond as she disappeared over the side, he noticed a little wave. He hoped the Admiral did not see it, as it was meant for his friend, Gilmore Craig, who kept a vigilant watch just next to the accommodation ladder. They were on the verge of carrying off another successful meeting between the two youngsters, and he wanted nothing to go wrong at the very close of it.

With the niece safely stowed, Hammond insisted on another round of handshakes. "Thank you, again, Captain. There are few men whose invitation don't make me wince and whose company I can abide so well. I wouldn't mind having more of it." The man's meddling was always off-putting, particularly that having to do with his niece, but Wentworth would endure for the sake of his friend.

"Thank you, sir. I too look forward to our next meeting, but as you leave for India inside the week, I fear it will be delayed some."

Still grasping Wentworth's hand, Hammond pulled him closer. "Yes, but with enough warning and depending on the time of year, I can be back in country in two months time." Brushing past Craig, he growled,

"Good evening," then gingerly picked his way down the accommodation ladder.

Wentworth and his guest watched them row out and away. Craig finally said, "As much as I would have liked to be in Miss Hammond's company, I am quite glad the Admiral's boat is too small to safely accommodate three passengers."

Wentworth smiled. "Yes, but I'm certain there would only have been two passengers by the time the shore was reached." Turning, he headed to his cabin.

"Just what did you mean, Captain? Captain?" Gilmore Craig followed.

The marine opened the door to the Great Cabin and the hot air met them full on. At nearly six on a July day, even with skylights and stern windows wide open, the room was oppressive. Fortunately, only in summer was the closeness a nuisance to him. In other seasons, Wentworth took comfort in the closeness of the two rooms. They held minimal furniture—a desk, table and chair with side table in the outer room. His sleeping chamber held a shaving stand, dresser and his cot. He could not think that any accommodations on land could compare, and he was satisfied to endure a few months of discomfort in exchange for such a snug place to call home.

Craig acknowledged the heat with a muttered, "By God," and continued to press his question about Wentworth's comment. "And what exactly did you mean by that curious remark?"

Their entry interrupted Michaelson, Wentworth's steward, who was in the process of carefully removing the china and crystal onto a tray. The man was as meticulous as any woman about the Captain's personal possessions, and it was always amusing to watch him titivating and fussing after such things. After tucking the last of the linen in a basket, he poured the gentlemen each a glass of port.

Wentworth took a drink, unsure his friend would appreciate the humour. "I suppose I meant that, considering Hammond's disapproval of you and your understandable dislike of him, one of you was sure to hove the other over the side and been done with the whole battle of wills." He hesitated in taking another drink. "Poor Miss Hammond. To witness such a thing would be a frightful end to an enjoyable evening." Taking the drink, he awaited Craig's response.

Gil opened his mouth, then closed it, looked puzzled, then spoke. "It would answer, would it not? The old boy over the side and I get Annie."

The Captain turned and watched a gull perched on a beef barrel, floating past *Laconia's* stern windows. His friend's bloodthirstiness was not so disturbing as Craig's pet name for the Admiral's niece.

Holding out his glass to be refilled, Wentworth said, "Let us put that all aside and play. Michaelson, you may set up the table and then leave us."

"If we are to play, then I am taking off this bleedin' coat. I don't mind telling you, when there is no breeze; your cabin has all the appeal of playing chess in Hades."

Michaelson divested the Captain of the heavy, dress uniform coat. With the removal, Hades cooled considerably. Since it was just the two of them, he followed Gil's lead and unbuttoned his cuffs, rolling them up.

"I must say, that is a very apt analogy of what it is like playing chess with you, my friend."

"How so?"

"When it is your turn, there is very little to do and the wait is an eternal one," said Wentworth with a smile.

Craig began unrolling his sleeve. "I could leave you alone with your sparkling wit, you know."

Taking his seat, the Captain said, "No, no. I shall behave and watch my tongue."

Michaelson filled their glasses one last time and departed.

An hour or so later, the evening gun sounded. Soon after, he heard the arrival of the shore party. The summer of 1814 was overseeing the end of the war and an enormous number of ships being called back to home port. This being the case, he endeavoured to keep his men in some sort of decent order by granting them a day's leave by gun crews. With only eight men ashore at a time, it reduced the chances of fighting with other ship's crews and having to fill his brig for such foolishness.

The board was a strategic mess with only ten turns accomplished. Playing chess with Craig was more an exercise in patience than a lesson in tactical thinking. "Gil, please. Have mercy on my nerves and make a move."

He slid a pawn forward, which Wentworth immediately captured with his King's knight. There was no satisfaction in the seizure, but it could be thought of as progress, of a sort.

"You know, I've been wondering something." Craig made a move towards his Queen's knight, but thought better of it.

"And what might that be?"

"The Admiral makes no secret that he wants Anne to marry a navy officer. You particularly." He moved another pawn.

"That is the rumour." It was only one of the rumours in which the clacking tongues of Plymouth engaged. They also had her going to India and being married off to a maharajah so that the Admiral could establish

7

himself a sort of colony of which he would be the undeniable head. The reliability of such talk was suspect at every turn.

"Have you ever thought about her that way? I mean marrying her. Annie is certainly beautiful. I cannot imagine a man not liking those blue eyes and fair hair. And she is educated and has a wonderful sense of humour…"

Taking a deep breath, Wentworth settled in for another lecture on all the graces of Miss Anne Hammond. Ever since Gil met her ten months earlier, whenever her name was mentioned he would, unbidden, set about listing her fine qualities. To be sure, she possessed many, but the list was becoming longer with each recitation, and the recitations were becoming more frequent.

The fact was, early in Wentworth's life he nearly broke himself over a woman named Anne, and ridiculous as it might be, he would rather be hanged than face another over the table, in his bed, or anywhere near his thoughts for the rest of his life. However, with the lectures being more frequent, Wentworth might consider marrying the inestimable Miss Hammond, despite Gil's obvious feelings, just to shut the man up.

"Well, have you?" There was almost an accusatory quality to his question.

The Captain was both amazed and amused. His friend now seemed angry that he harboured no romantic interests in the woman. The absurdity of the human heart would never cease to amaze him. "No, Gil, I have never thought of Miss Hammond in that way. She is obviously in love with you."

Gilbert brightened. "Do you really think so?"

"Yes. There is a look about her when you are around. Women in love have a look about them."

"They do?"

"Yes, they do. Now make a move."

He watched Gil scrutinise the board and realised the words had an ironic double meaning that seemed quite suited to his friend's situation. Before he knew it, he was contemplating a summer long gone and someone who had said the words to him.

~ ~ ~ ~ ~ ~ ~ & ~ ~ ~ ~ ~ ~ ~

"Now make a move," the girl said.

"I cannot." He sat up and tossed his hand of cards into the waste pile. "You have an unfair advantage."

"How can I possibly have an unfair advantage? You have just taught me this abominable game. And I am losing!" She held out an ill-arranged mass of cards to prove her point. All he cared for was her smile and the way her eyes welcomed his gaze.

"I can see nothing but you." Gently taking her cards, he tossed them down with his and moved closer. "There. Now it is a draw. Your beauty is no longer an advantage."

"Not in the game at least." He was delighted with her mortified expression when the full meaning of what she said burst upon her. "I didn't mean I am–"

"Yes, you meant every word," he teased. Looking deeply into her startled brown eyes caused the cards, the picnic, and the quiet country-side to disappear. It also caused the already warm temperature to rise markedly. "You are beautiful."

"And you are a flatterer."

"Ah, but you see, flattery is merely a seed of truth stretched to its uttermost. To say you are beautiful is no exaggeration. It is a truth with no limits."

She looked away.

It was touching that his comments could embarrass her so easily. "What have I said?"

Turning back, her eyes were bright. "In our family, it is Elizabeth who is the beauty. Not I." Taking up the cards, she began to sort and straighten them.

"She is beautiful, by definition. However, there is no attraction there for me. Since my arrival, there has only been you. I have set my course and will not change it." He felt panic when the words returned to his ears, but in almost an instant, their meaning was perfectly analogous to his feelings.

"And what is your course?" Her voice was barely audible.

"To make you my wife."

The thought had been uppermost for days, and when waking that particular morning, he had made no plan to ask the question. However, there was something about her that day, that hour, that minute that made him want her more than he wanted anything else in the world.

Her expression remained quizzical, and she rose to walk a little. He followed.

"What have I done? You do not like the idea of being my wife." Again, he felt panic, but this time there was no immediate consolation.

He could hear the wind in the plane trees that made up the small grove where they met. He could hear the sound of her picking at a bit of loose bark.

She finally turned to him, she leant against the tree and said, "Look at me, and tell me what you see."

He took advantage of the circumstance to draw closer than he had ever dared. He too leant against the tree, taking the opportunity to stare at her openly. "I see a woman who takes my breath away, and I see that she loves me as well, and that she wishes to marry me." After his answer, she smiled and said her feelings were just that. He moved closer for a kiss, but she drew back a little.

Anne Elliot was intelligent and beautiful and her acceptance of his proposal made him feel the world open more widely that he had ever dared consider, but she was still a country girl with country sensibilities. He would not pursue the issue though he wished mightily for more than smiles and the occasional holding of hands.

~ ~ ~ ~ ~ ~ ~ & ~ ~ ~ ~ ~ ~ ~

It was unfortunate that his memories of such a tender moment were polluted by his knowledge of their future. In the past, when he would allow himself to think about her, scenes such as this had been charged with emotion to the point they brought on a rapidly beating heart and the sweats. Now, the memories had lost their edge. Even what he saw in his mind's eye had dimmed. The face was fair and the hair was deep brown. Her eyes were brown as well and he remembered that she was smiling. Nevertheless, it was like gazing through a fog. It was unfortunate that he had fooled himself into believing she loved him. He learned a few days after the impromptu proposal that her loving him was not the truth. If she had truly loved him, she never would have sent him away.

"Wentworth."

Opening his eyes, he was mortified to find his friend reaching over the chessboard to shake his arm.

"That's better. It's bad enough that you take advantage of my poor tactical skills and goad me into playing you, but the least you could do is put a good face on it and stay awake as I humiliate myself."

"Sorry, Craig, I was just going over a list of minor repairs that we now have the opportunity of doing. I have to reach to find things to keep my men occupied."

"Do you think they will take *Laconia* from you?"

"Can't see a reason why not. With Napoleon no longer on the rampage, there is no reason to feed and clothe most of us. I've had no official confirmation, but I expect it any day."

"Damn rotten luck. But surely something will come up."

"Thrown ashore with half-pay is not ideal, though I don't come away from my service exactly poor." Wentworth was known throughout the navy as one of the luckiest captains afloat. There was wild speculation as to his worth, most of it grossly exaggerated, but the truth was, with judicious living, he could be very comfortable for the rest of his life. This was no mean feat considering that he was self-educated, the son of a struggling merchant, and, aside from having a rear admiral of the white for a brother-in-law, unconnected to any real power in the Admiralty. He had done well for himself, but there was still more he wanted–much more.

Craig looked out the window and then checked his watch. "Ah, time to be off. You know I hate being on the water in the dark." Rising, he put on his coat and cast about for his hat. Wentworth donned his coat and looked over the chess pieces; the win was his in less than five moves. It was true Gilmore Craig did not care for being on the water after dark, few landsmen did, but he had to wonder if the loss of yet another game might have as much to do with his desire to be ashore.

"Thank you for inviting me to dine with Miss Hammond and her uncle. This subterfuge is wearing thin, I know."

"Not at all. One sort of chase is as interesting as another," Wentworth said. "Though I do expect, once the Admiral leaves Plymouth for India, the two of you will find your own ways to meet."

"Unless, of course, he is able to convince you to marry her before he sails. That's what he really wants. Blast it, Wentworth, I am what I am. I own a warehouse. I own *five* warehouses and make a very good living. Nevertheless, because I do not wear that blue and gold coat like you, he refuses to acknowledge I exist. Really, you have no idea how grinding it is to have a man despise you for not being good enough."

Better than most, the Captain knew precisely what such a humiliation was like, though he said nothing to Craig. "As I said, once he is departed, the two of you will find your own way in this."

"But she is a good girl, Captain. I don't know that she will go against what she knows to be his wishes, even if he's thousands of miles away."

"Then you will convince her, Gil. She is of majority; you said she has some money of her own. I understand very well the claims of authority, but I also think the heart is its own authority. You must not let her put you aside for a misplaced notion of obedience."

Craig hesitated and studied Wentworth. "That sounds strange coming from you." He headed to the door, and then stopped. "Just out of curiosity, what do you think of elopements? She has no close family other than Hammond; so who would be the wiser?"

Wentworth picked up his scraper and gave it a brush as Craig worked out another fantastical plan to have her for his own. He opened the door and the marine stationed outside snapped to attention, Gil prating on as they came up on deck.

"Thank you for a good evening. I appreciate all the arrangements you make."

"As I said, in a few days you will be able to make your move."

Craig smiled and shook his head. "You should be a politician, Wentworth. You have a knack for choosing the most advantageous strategy."

The Captain watched him descend into the small boat assigned to row him ashore. Taking a turn on the quarterdeck, the Officer of the Watch gave him a report while a procuress came alongside, offering a bargain price for several of her girls. When she was sent on her way without making a sale, she pronounced a pox on *Laconia* and all her crew. Wentworth mused that she was too late for some of the men had already obtained their own curses in their own ways.

He turned away from the activity of the quarterdeck and walked along the waist, the men giving their obediences and making a clear path for him. Letting them think he was observing the nightly rituals, he watched the sun set behind the western hills. As the last of the orange radiance slipped behind the black mounds, he saw the glass turned and bid the officers a good evening.

Michaelson was just clearing away the chessboard and glasses when he entered the Great Cabin. He dismissed the steward, removed his coat, and loosened his neck cloth. Leaning out the stern window, he enjoyed a cool breeze that kicked up. He had no wish to dive into ship's daily paperwork or to read. Too early to turn in for the night, he dragged a chair before the windows, took a seat, kicked off his boots, and put his feet on the stern lockers. It was an ungracious pose, but at this time of night, short of a skylarker falling from the rigging or a fire breaking out, only Michaelson would dare to interrupt him.

It felt good to be alone, an uncommon occurrence on a ship of war, but considering where his thoughts had strayed earlier in the evening, it was also dangerous. He'd given no thought to Anne Elliot or his engagement to her for some time. As he recalled, the last miserable go round with his memories had been the previous summer. Obviously there was something about the hot weather of July that wrung such oppressive thoughts out of him.

~ ~ ~ ~ ~ ~ ~ & ~ ~ ~ ~ ~ ~ ~

His acquaintance with the second daughter of Sir Walter Elliot of Kellynch Hall, Somersetshire, had not happened quickly. Wentworth was a newly made commander in the navy when he arrived but only the visiting brother of a local curate. Social manoeuvring of any consequence took some time. Summer gatherings in the country were few, and the heat dictated the activities. Dinners, cards, and the occasional dance allowed for only a gradual acquaintance. But, the acquaintance, once made, burst into full-blown love on both sides and only intensified after his proposal. They were everything to one another and being apart was agony. For a man whose only example of marriage was his parents' unhappy union, he was shocked how the thought of her brought him such peace. That peace, as it turned out, was short-lived.

When he arrived at Anne's home, Kellynch Hall, to speak with her father, he had every expectation of a warm acceptance. Looking back, he knew his expectation to have been foolhardy. How could it have been otherwise when his very first meeting with Anne had begun with an apology for her father and sister's scarcely hidden disregard of him? Eventually, others in the neighbourhood began to solicit his company—after all, he was an officer of the Crown and fresh from a very successful, highly profitable, and well publicised battle in the West Indies—and the Baronet seemed happy to join the train and to entertain him as though he were welcome and accepted into the man's intimate circle. He later found that he was not genuinely welcome into any circle of the Baronet's—particularly not into the family circle.

The interview itself had been short and comparatively silent. After informing Sir Walter that Anne had unreservedly accepted his proposal of marriage, he waited for a reply. There had been a look of astonishment, silence, and a general atmosphere of contempt. Other than making it plain that he was disinclined to do anything financial for his daughter, nothing was said. Wentworth sat for some time, unsure what should be his next move.

He would not beg. It was clear his suit was distasteful to the head of the family. All that was left to him was to make a bow and thank the man for his time, then clear off.

Fortunately, Anne had arranged to be away, visiting her godmother, when he came to the Hall. Both had been hopeful of a positive outcome, and they had agreed to meet later in a secluded grove that lay between Kellynch and his brother's tiny house in Monkford.

The Baronet's conduct left him enraged, and he was glad for the walk. It gave him time to think and see the situation more clearly. By the time Anne arrived, he was rational again and had a plan.

"Frederick?"

Just hearing her voice and knowing she was near made his breath catch. Such raw, though tender feelings strengthened his determination to outwit her father and make her his very own.

"I'm here."

Anne came around a large tree and looked relieved. "I was worried you would not come."

"And miss an opportunity to be alone with the loveliest young woman of my acquaintance? Never." She was such a pretty, gracious little thing and he was determined he would not lose her.

"I have been worried that things might not go well between you and Father."

To lie was useless. Soon enough she would know how things stood between the two men. "It went very badly." Holding his anger in check, he said it with a smile. Ease and humour were all a part of the plan that was beginning to take shape in his mind.

Her colour drained away and her posture slacked; everything about her diminished markedly. Clearly he should not have been so blunt. He gave her the remaining details laced with hearty self-assurance.

Perhaps he had taken unfair advantage of her when he held her hand and stood closer to her than he had ever dared before. He kissed her fingers and said, "It's all right though. I have come to believe the old boy was only testing me. He wants to see what I do when laid low; do I crawl away and lick my wounds, or do I stand like a man and pursue what I want."

Her gaze eventually met his, and though her countenance was still pale, she gripped his hand like iron. "I do not think my father is the sort of man who would test you. I think he cares little about understanding the character of other men." The tears were pooling in her eyes and threatening to spill down her cheeks. He suspected this had little to do with admitting her father's disinterest in the moral quality of the man offering for her hand. Removing a handkerchief from his pocket, he was tempted to wipe her tears, but instead put the cloth in her hands. At his touch, she smiled. This tiny respite from the pain was comforting. Now, relieving her internal agony was his only concern.

"Come, have a seat here and let me explain."

Nearly carrying her to a fallen tree, he seated her. "Annie, I have learnt over the years that when a man is dressing you down, it is best to listen very carefully since they generally say as much by the words they do not use as those they do." He could tell she only partly comprehended him. Her eyes struggled to stay with his as she blinked to keep the tears at bay. "While your father did not precisely say, 'I give you my blessing to marry my daughter, Anne,' he also did not expressly forbid us marrying. All he said outright was that he had no intention of giving us any sort of settlement."

"I do not understand how you can be pleased with any of this," she said, trying to pull away.

Drawing her down next to him, he continued. "Don't you see? He wants to know that I am not after your settlement money. All I need do is stay around here and prove myself. Show myself to be constant to you and your family. I know I can change his mind. He's only looking out for your good."

Even as he spoke the words, he only half believed them. While it was true the old goat had not forbidden the marriage, he knew the Baronet had no interest but his own at heart. Regardless, he would grasp at anything to keep Anne's hopes afloat. He was flooded with his own ridiculous sort of hope, and even as he spouted the bilge about changing the Baronet's mind, he came to think it a real possibility. He even considered help from another, untapped quarter.

"Perhaps your godmother would help us. Lady Russell is forever saying your happiness is her chief concern. When you tell her how much we love one another, I am sure she will be glad to use her influence with your father on our behalf."

~ ~ ~ ~ ~ ~ ~ & ~ ~ ~ ~ ~ ~ ~

At this long-forgotten piece of history, he muttered, "Good God, Frederick, could you have chosen a worse person in which to place your faith?" After many years, he had determined that, had he kept Anne from rushing to her godmother, their engagement might have been saved. Perhaps she had not loved him as deeply as he loved her, but when she broke the engagement it became clear that Lady Russell had worked on her, had used her considerable influence against him, and convinced her that a marriage with him would only bring her grief. If he had not been so eager to use every means at his disposal to win over the father, he might not have lost the daughter. However, half measures were not his way, and, though it was maddening, he long ago forgave himself the blunder. Anne Elliot had made the choice to break the engagement. To lament it now was only a momentary disturbance in his exceptionally ordered life.

Determined to break the hold of such dreary memories, he rose and filled his glass, then settled back in the chair. The freshening breezes were pleasant but brought along the disagreeable smells of the rotting garbage dumped overboard by the numerous ships crowding the channel. In any case, the gentle winds were more welcome than the heat.

The stirring gusts also brought the show of the gulls weaving, screaming, and diving to pick at the leavings of this nautical civilization. The inelegant amusement of watching them would be denied him after he was thrown ashore. Unless he chose to live on the bottom floor of a very busy boarding house, he would no longer have the sound of many feet shuffling, pounding, dancing or skipping above him, as they did now. Even if he found quarters in a basement, landsmen wore shoes and the sound would not have the softness of bare feet. Moreover, no matter where he lived, the floor of a land home would never creak and heave or faintly sway, as did the deck of his ship. Overall, being thrown ashore would be abominable.

Suddenly, he was angry that such melancholy thoughts would choose this time to attack him. Did he not have newer, more pressing worries to override his old, worn griefs? With his usual matter-of-factness, Gil had touched on it earlier. It was certain that *Laconia* would be taken from him. He had had her for six years – a miraculously long time in the navy for one man to command a particular ship–and she was getting old. At best, a merchant would buy her at auction and she would begin a new, though less dignified, life. At worst, she would go to the knacker's yard, and be stripped of all useable parts, then broken down into scrap and firewood. The very thought of it was painful. *Laconia* had taken him further than he had ever expected to go in life. A truer and more trusted friend would have been hard to come by. It was bitter to think about her future, nearly as bitter as his thoughts of his past. Draining the glass and regretting his choice of water, he nonetheless remained seated. The heat and the memories were taking their toll, and he thought it perhaps time to retire. Having no energy to make a change of scene in the present and judging the cruel little history to have no power to harm him, he allowed himself to return to the grove and study the past.

~ ~ ~ ~ ~ ~ ~ & ~ ~ ~ ~ ~ ~ ~

After ignorantly urging Anne to do the single most destructive thing possible in consulting with her godmother, she pulled away from him and, covering her face with her hands, began to shake.

Thinking he had sunk himself completely, he whispered, "What is wrong? Why do you cry? I told you that I shall convince him, never fear–"

Lowering her hands, he could see the colour had come back, and she was now a lovely shade of pink. She was not crying, but laughing. "You have cast a spell on me, Frederick, and I am thoroughly bewitched. I truly believe you are capable of changing Father's mind." She paused and, with some hesitation, touched his brow. "What sort of hold is it you have over me?" Her eyes were bright with tears and her breath was quick. She looked intently at him. Finally, she said, "When I first saw you, the warmth of your confidence persuaded me that there was nothing you could not do. And now, now that my heart is hopelessly entangled, I know that my father has no choice but to see your reasoning."

Joining her in laughter, he said, "You make me sound like those fellows in India that charm animals to do their bidding." It was then he realised it was he who was being charmed. She moved close to him once more.

"No, I just know that all your future plans and hopes of which we've spoken will come to pass. You will see to it that they do. In addition, once we are married, there is no freedom I shall not feel. No joy we will not share. What stirs me is the only thing you ask is that I give you my love. It is a small thing for all that I receive."

The heat of the day was nothing compared with the heat of his passion. Her words fired every masculine instinct dwelling in him, and all he wanted to do was take her in his arms and follow Nature's course. But he would not. They would be together soon enough. Regardless, he would have to leave her. The isolation of their meeting place indeed sheltered their trysts, but such seclusion offered nearly irresistible temptations.

"No, it is I who come out the best in this bargain. I never harboured a hope in the world of a woman such as you giving me a second glance." Wentworth had been confident he would marry a beautiful woman, one with sense and intelligence, but to have a well-born woman so naturally elegant and refined as Miss Anne Elliot look his way, much less consent to be his wife, was miraculous.

"It would seem we both have been given our heart's desires."

Again, she reached up, this time touching his hair and then caressing his jaw. The velvety fire of her fingertips made breathing impossible. Closing her eyes, she moved close. He supposed she meant to kiss his cheek, but missing her mark, her lips came painfully close to his. It was only natural that he should make a course correction. To begin, as he gently teased her mouth, she was tense, but almost immediately, she relaxed and accepted his kiss.

~ ~ ~ ~ ~ ~ ~ & ~ ~ ~ ~ ~ ~ ~

The fog, which clouded the past, lifted and he was able to clearly see this Anne, still as bright as anything. This was the Annie he loved the most. This Annie had haunted his dreams for years. This was the little brown-eyed ghost he cursed when the occasional black mood settled in.

One hot summer exchanged itself for another and his thoughts shifted abruptly to the bumboat offering reasonably priced female company. He would not boast, but there had certainly been other women in his life. All they knew of him was his rank and that he possessed enough coin to buy an allotted portion of their time. However, such encounters were a two-edged sword; the physical release was welcome, but they left his soul empty. He knew his Annie was the woman he longed for in all those previous encounters. It was the only kiss that ever mattered–the only kiss that mattered still.

"Enough for this night," he muttered. Rising, he shoved the chair out of his way with his knee and headed to his bed. Though agitated, he stopped and listened to the sound of several sets of feet above. They were unhurried, there seemed to be no emergency, but it was late enough that all should be quiet for the night. A single set of steps moved to the gangway, and he readied himself for the business as hand.

At the obligatory knock, he called in the messenger. It was the youngest of his midshipmen, Mr. Guy. The boy did his duty well enough, but was still overawed by those of superior rank and stuttered dreadfully when required to speak.

"B-beggin' your pardon, sir. There's a f-fella come on board who requests to see you. Says his name is Captain Harville, sir, but he's got no uniform. Mr. Cranmer tried sendin' him on his way, but then Mr. Eyerly said you knew him and would be right pissed was he denied." The boy made a face. Wentworth suspected the dust-up between his first officer and coxswain was not intended to be part of the announcement.

"Which you have done, Mr. Guy. Please show Captain Harville to me." The boy touched his forehead and bobbed, then shot out of his presence as if blasted from one of the forward guns.

The hour was too late for a social visit. They had only been anchored two days, and it had been his intention to visit Harville as soon as matters concerning *Laconia* had been settled. Though Harville was a good friend and had served on Wentworth's first command, the *Asp*, he could still observe courtesy and come on board at a decent hour. He knew the man well and only something dire would bring him aboard at such a late hour. He could hear Harville's approach. It was slow, but his friend suffered from less-than-perfect health. Though he had time to gather himself, he was not prepared for Eyerly lurching through the door, with Harville clinging to his shoulder, searching for some place to put the man. Bringing them to the chair he'd just vacated, Wentworth saw his friend gently placed.

"There you go, sir." Looking about, the coxswain spied the water and fetched a glass. "Here you are, Captain. The heat can be right taxin' in here."

"Thank you, Eyerly. That will be all." The man made a little gesture, requesting Wentworth to join him at the door.

"He had a deuce of a time makin' it up the accommodation ladder, sir. I feared for 'im every step."

"I can see he is extraordinarily unwell. Thank you for informing Cranmer of my desires."

Eyerly touched his forehead. "Aye, sir. Captain Harville saved my young arse a time or two. It's only right I help 'im when I can."

Before the coxswain left, Wentworth requested the surgeon be fetched.

"No, please, I don't need a doctor." Harville's voice was strong enough and firm in its resolve. Wentworth cancelled the order.

Harville struggled up and offering his hand said, "Captain Wentworth."

Getting a good look at his friend, Wentworth was shocked. The man's face was as white as Dover's cliffs and thinner than he remembered. Taking Harville's hand, he was equally disturbed to find the grip weak and tremulous, the skin clammy. Without letting loose, he carefully pressed him back into the chair. "Harville, I will not allow such formality between us." Pulling another chair close, he took the seat. Not yet ready to launch into a conversation, he saw the empty water glass and said, "I think you need something stronger."

He called out the door for Michaelson and ordered a decent wine be brought. Pouring Harville another glass of water, he handed it over. "You look as though you could use this."

Harville took it gratefully.

"So, what brings you to me? This is a beastly hot night to be taking your ease below deck on a ship at anchor."

Harville's lips thinned and he set the glass down. He turned to look out the window and Wentworth could not help but notice that his eyes blinked furiously. The man was spared answering when Michaelson entered and poured each a glass of a robust red wine. As he left, the Captain snagged the bottle from him. His steward's thrift and hawkish supervision over his private stores was an advantage at times, but this was not one of them.

The door closed and Wentworth straddled the chair next to his friend. Time passed and the only sounds heard were of the bells and calls from other ships, and the lapping water outside the window. Occasionally, a puff of what might be considered a breeze could be felt, but only occasionally.

Life above deck on the *Laconia* went on apace while Wentworth contemplated the various scenarios that might be the cause of Harville's surprising visit and undisguised grief. Immediately it came to his mind that one of the man's children was dangerously ill. The only thing that might be worse was the loss of his wife, Elsa. The thought of such an evil nearly took his breath away. There were things in life one took for granted. It was a fact indisputable that Wentworth would always be an officer of the Navy; it was just as sure that Elsa Harville would be alive and well to care for her husband and family. She had always been the more robust of the two, and the one who buoyed the man's spirits when his injury brought him low. Nevertheless, there were no real certainties in life anymore. He himself was now thrown ashore with no sign of a ship...

Harville thumped his stick on the floor. No doubt it was a sign of resolve. He turned to face Wentworth. The expression on his pallid face was one of puzzlement and surprise. "It's my sister, Fanny. She's dead." His eyes, and tone of voice, begged for an answer to an unasked question.

For a few seconds, Wentworth could not comprehend Harville's anguish. There was no mention of his wife or any of his several children. What was the crisis? It was merely his sister—

Thankfully, before he could say anything rash, he clearly saw their positions reversed and it was he whose dear sister, Sophia, was dead. They had not seen one another for years, but the knowledge that her thick, gossip-filled letters would follow him to whatever part of the world he found himself, was a comfort that was vital to his happiness.

"It was a fever—in June—she was only sick for less than a week and then she was gone." The statement was of few words, but he might just as well have recited the Articles of War in one breath. He was gulping air and his chest was heaving; his face was growing rosy. All the life was rapidly draining from him.

Chapter Two

Ignoring propriety, the Captain stood, pushed the chair away, and began to strip off Harville's coat. He hadn't the strength to fend off the onslaught and made no attempt to do so. "You should really have something a little lighter for summer, Timothy. You know how stifling this cabin gets in the heat..." One of the buttons popped off and skittered across the floor as they were viciously undone. "And yet, you came calling wearing your sturdiest wool."

"You're right, of course." He refused to look at Wentworth. "But I must be prudent about spending these days," he said between ragged breaths. He was limp as a damp rag and allowed his friend to remove his coat and unwind his neck cloth.

Retrieving a wet towel from the washstand, Wentworth handed it to him. Harville finally glanced up as he dabbed the towel around his neck. "Well, if I must humiliate myself, I suppose it is best done before a good friend." Their eyes met for a moment. He continued, "Please do not allow it get around that I came very near swooning like some agitated woman."

He was relieved Harville was not offended. Unwinding his own neck cloth, he said, "Aside from the excitement, I'm glad you did. As the host, it wouldn't be proper for me to make myself comfortable in the presence of a guest."

"I'm not really a guest, now am I?" Harville refolded the towel and placed it against his neck.

"No, and you never will be *just* a guest. Besides, this cabin is Hades' lower deck, and I suspect that you've not been much concerned about taking care of yourself since Fanny..." He stopped. Her name was now dangerous to utter.

"I have been bearing up manfully for Elsa. She has not taken it well." He took another glass of water mixed with some wine. Looking intently into the reddish liquid, Harville continued. "You know she did not wish

Fanny to live with us. She complained that we were too many in too little space to be taking on anyone extra."

When Wentworth had brought the three women from Portsmouth in the spring, nothing would have led the casual observer to believe there was anything but perfect harmony among them all. But, he knew from experience that the female of the species was highly skilled in making a show of possessing tender emotions when, in truth, there were none.

"She came to us in Portsmouth and Elsa was resentful. But being a Christian woman, she was determined to be kind. Before long they were closer than most genuine kin."

"Your wife has always been a good and generous soul. I have always been treated well when I come to impose."

He smiled. "She likes you very much. Besides, she is a clever girl who knows that wisdom dictates treating men of great influence with great esteem."

Wentworth laughed aloud but felt slightly guilty for an expression of levity at such a wretched moment.

"The irony is the last time either one of us stepped foot into her room was the day she died. The bedding was stripped after they came and took her away, but it now stands empty. Neither of us can bear the thought of anyone in there. All that precious space and no one to use it."

A thought was gaining in his mind, and he was about to ask a question when Harville said, "When she was alive, I took it for granted she would always be with us, even when she married Benwick. There was no great, outward affection between us, but now—" He looked at Wentworth and continued, "I miss her terribly. When you know you will never see someone again, it hurts something awful."

It was a truth he could wholeheartedly embrace. Rather than dwell on it, he asked, "How has James taken the news?"

Timothy's face went blank. "He is on his way from the Cape. Had you heard he was made commander into the *Grappler*?"

"No, I had not."

"We have gotten letters right along. He was making for Plymouth, but then orders were given for Portsmouth."

"I see."

"His last one, the letter that came just before her fever, was very hopeful. He felt he was very close to having the wherewithal for them to marry. He never came out and asked her to think about choosing a date, but he made it clear it would be soon. Very soon." He took a drink.

It was not hard to imagine Benwick savouring his well-deserved step in rank by wetting the swab with the few fellow officers carried by a sloop. It was painful to think of him labouring under the delusion that his promotion now put him and Fanny in the way of marrying soon.

Knowing Benwick's romantic sensibilities, he was no doubt filled with thoughts of Fanny anticipating his return, planning for their forthcoming wedding, and planning a life of perfect felicity and joy for the both of them. Harville's look and lack of explanation on the subject made it clear that their mutual friend was ignorant of his beloved's untimely death.

Wentworth knew Harville's compassionate bent precisely. It had served quite well when a dab hand was needed dealing with the mercurial, sometimes arbitrary nature of a ship's crew. It was also a blade that cut the other way now and then.

Mercy informed Harville's basic nature. In that, he reminded the Captain of his own brother, Edward. While this inclination created a great fraternity amongst the men of his division, it had occasionally forced the two officers to opposite poles concerning discipline of the crew. Wentworth could hardly be called a flogging captain; the cat remained in the bag for weeks on end. He never felt the need to prove his authority with trivial punishments. But, now and then, Harville would take it into his head that the Captain was being too brutal in his dealings with a particular crewman. It was those times he would come to the Great Cabin to plead mercy.

They never agreed in the particular cases, but Harville always presented himself respectfully, always mindful of his position as an inferior officer requesting leniency from his superior. He never presumed upon their friendship. For this, Wentworth was always grateful. Nothing could fuel discontent on a ship like a whiff of partiality. There could be no favourites on a well-ordered ship of war. Loyalty above all things bound them together when they were weeks away from the civility of England. Loyalty to the Captain was fundamental and Harville never failed to give all of his.

That loyalty now touched the Captain's mind and heart. In the same way Harville would always return and, out of respect and duty, administer the proper punishments despite his reticence, it was clear that the duties of friendship required that Wentworth carry out a task that his friend could not. He could not even allow Harville to ask his assistance.

The Captain rose and took a seat at his desk. Pulling out paper and a quill, he began to write. Again, the cabin fell calm and quiet, except for the scratching of the pen.

Finally, Timothy rose, gathered his neck cloth and tossed the towel towards the basin. It missed. He thumped his way across the room to pick it up. "I am sorry I disturbed you. This is a family matter and really isn't your concern."

"Nonsense," Wentworth said, and continued to scratch away. Harville finished the last of his wine and water and made an effort to fold the neck cloth.

Wentworth replaced the quill and blotted the letter. He read it again as he crossed the room to speak to the marine. "Pass the word for Eyerly, Michaelson, and Mr. Lull to come to the Great Cabin." He turned and Harville was standing right before him.

"Thank you for writing this, sir." He reached out to take it. "I just could not bring myself to dash all Benwick's hopes."

Allowing Harville to take the letter, he said, "I suppose I have more experience relaying tragedy than most but this is not the instrument. I am applying to the Admiral for a leave of absence and shall leave for Portsmouth as soon as possible."

A sharp, overlong rapping at the door distracted them. "A moment, please, Mr. Lull." Wentworth took the letter and went back to the desk. As he folded and sealed it, he said, "Why am I not surprised that Mr. Lull is the first? Come," he called.

Lull entered and looked Harville's unkempt frame up and down as he touched his brow. "Sir?"

The Captain pressed his seal into the blood-red wax. "This is to go to the Port Admiral's clerk first thing in the morning. It is a request for leave of absence." He handed the packet to his clerk.

"Might I ask for whom, sir?"

"For me. I must be away immediately. You wouldn't happen to know when the Portsmouth post departs?"

Lull was clearly agitated by this late evening development. "At three, sir. How long will you be gone, sir?"

Leave it to dear old Lull to know something so pedantic as the nightly schedule of the mail coach bound east. He silently thanked God for the man's plodding and tedious ways. Though the question concerning the length of his absence was impertinent, the Captain decided the news of his departure might as well be heralded by a reliable crier as not. "The time is unfixed. I will know more when I arrive in Portsmouth. The business is private." This was said in such a way as to signal an end to the questioning.

"But, sir, what if the request is not approved? How will I explain…"

Wentworth reminded himself he would be thankful for this dull, obtuse little man when he turned over the ship's books. "Mr. Lull, there will be nothing for you to explain. We are merely waiting for the formality of orders to vacate the ship so she might be placed in dry dock. It is unlikely that my request will be denied, but if that does occur, Mr. Cranmer will express me in Portsmouth, in care of the *Grappler*, and I shall return, post haste." He handed Lull a sheet with the information.

"In any case, I will be responsible for explanations, excuses or elaborations."

The clerk took the letter and moved towards the door. Before he left, he turned and asked, "Sir, about the books..."

"You and Lieutenant Cranmer will take care of the books nicely, I am sure." With a quick bob, Lull was gone.

"You are going to a lot of trouble about this," Harville observed.

"No, not really. There's no chance of being sent out again. I've made peace with that."

"Yes. Yes, you are. And I must confess something."

"And what would that be?" Wentworth asked.

"When I came here, I was hoping this would be the outcome–that you would volunteer to go to Portsmouth and speak with James face-to-face. This is not the sort of thing one should learn from a letter."

"There is no need to..." Wentworth wished no more talk of thanks.

"You don't know how I dreaded the notion of going myself, and having to stand before him and tell him that the woman he loves is dead. To be the one who destroys him, with my own heart broken besides."

"Yes, Timothy, I understand. James is, after all, my friend as well."

As though he did not hear Wentworth, Harville continued, "But you are the far better choice for this, I think. You have never known love, and have no understanding of the pain that comes when that love is taken so cruelly from you."

It was all he could do to keep from disabusing his friend of such a notion, to keep from making it clear that he indeed did know what it was to love, what it was to have all your plans and hopes destroyed with a few words from another. A maggot of resentment called up what it was to consume oneself with hopes, then, deciding to put them aside, letting anger have its way with your heart. Feeling the muscles in his face tense, he thought James the lucky one. Fanny was dead. On more than one occasion, Wentworth had to endure the knowledge that the woman he had once loved would undoubtedly be married by now. There was no doubt in his mind; Anne was alive, married, and quite happy without him.

As much as he wished to shake his friend and convince him that he was indeed a brother in the fraternity of heartache, he refrained. No one knew because he never gave away anything concerning his heart. Harville knew nothing because, for years, the Captain had chosen to keep the entire world ignorant of his greatest disappointment. Only two people knew anything about the sad business. Anne knew his anger, and Edward knew his anguish.

He looked at Harville's face. The pain was yet palpable, but somewhat relieved. He could not change what Providence had declared, but he could accomplish this most distressing deed for his friend. There was a rap at the door and it opened, knocking Wentworth into Harville.

"Sorry, sir. You sent for me." Michaelson was obviously just out of his hammock; his eyes were bleary and his jersey on backwards. Before he could answer, Eyerly was also at the door.

"Ready my boat to take the Captain back to shore. After, I shall need you to take me to the three o'clock mail coach for Portsmouth." The coxswain looked curious but said nothing as he tugged his forelock and disappeared. "Michaelson, please assist Captain Harville with his dressing, then you will go with Eyerly." Michaelson began to protest that the Captain needed him to pack his travelling case.

"It will not be necessary, Michaelson. I think I can manage. Now please see to the Captain." He left Timothy to the care of his steward and went above. The air had cooled and the breeze freshened. Short playful gusts lifted his hair and tugged at his damp lawn shirt. A few deep breaths cleared the feeling of the closed, tight cabin.

Eyerly stood near the davit, protecting the small boat as she was hoisted over the side. "Have some grace, you lubbers. I just painted 'er last week." This little scene reminded Wentworth that he was not the only man aboard the *Laconia* who cared for her as though she were a lover. Not that the paint on the little boat mattered now; it would most likely be tossed aside during the refitting, and it was anyone's guess what it might look like after such severe neglect.

Taking a coin from his pocket, he handed it to the coxswain. "Eyerly, take a shag. His leg is as bad as his neighbourhood, so see him right to the door." He stopped as the bell was struck marking eleven-thirty. "Return immediately. And see that Michaelson is not distracted by a late-night cockfight."

"Aye, sir." Eyerly smiled. Both knew Michaelson was a hopeless gambler, and the caveat proved nothing escaped the notice of the Captain.

"When you return, there should be a little time for rest before I have to leave."

Just then, Harville, accompanied by Michaelson, appeared at the side.

"These men will see you home, Captain."

"Captain, I can't tell you how much this means…"

"Yes, we have more than established that I am the most proper man for the job. I will give you a full report when I return."

Harville shook his hand. It was obvious he wished to say more, but they were in public and knew the proprieties. Harville would do nothing to compromise the position of the Captain in the eyes of his crew.

It was indeed painful to watch Harville manoeuvre down the accommodation ladder. Michaelson knew he was being observed and took every care in seeing him settled in the stern of the small boat. Watching them pull away, Wentworth put his mind to the unpleasant task at hand.

~ ~ ~ ~ ~ ~ ~ & ~ ~ ~ ~ ~ ~ ~

"So ya stayin' at the Crown?" asked the driver, Mr. Gordon.

"Yes."

"The Blue Booby's a fine establishment. Close to the docks, and the weemin, if ya knows wha' I mean." The driver gave him the toothless grin the Captain had come to abominate. Three days and nights of bad roads, horrid food, and even worse company had turned his normally sanguine temperament to one of bloody-mindedness. "I'll ship ya right over, free uh charge."

"Thank you for the offer. I am sure the Blue Booby has every convenience, but I am for the Crown." Wentworth was hard pressed to be very angry with the driver. The fellow could hardly be blamed for nearly inedible food at the coaching stations, though he seemed to be on very intimate terms with all the innkeepers. It would be unfair to blame him for the quality of the passengers he hauled, though many of them were his near and distant relations. The roads probably were not his fault, but Wentworth thought it barbarous to place paying customers at the mercy of a carriage whose seats were little more than tanned hides stretched over boards. The springs had long ago lost their temper. The Captain felt as though he had been beaten day and night with a belaying pin. No, for the abominable condition of his carriage, he could be doubly blamed.

As for the Blue Booby, the man undoubtedly had a deal with the keep and would get a bounty for every customer he steered that way. Considering how many family members Mr. Gordon hauled it was more than likely an additional family enterprise. It might also be the sort of establishment where a man woke up sans his money and valuables, or worse. He gave the man a few pence, in hopes he would take himself and his odious smile away.

Seeing he could not deter the Captain from rooming at the Crown, he said, "Suit yaself," and shoved the coins in his waistcoat pocket. He hauled down the Captain's bag and dropped it unceremoniously at his feet. Without a word, he turned, mounted his death machine and drove off.

"An appropriate beginning for my sojourn in Portsmouth," he said under his breath. As he bent to retrieve the bag, a small, young hand reached out and took it.

"Let me get that for ya, sir." Struggling to lift the case with both hands stood a sturdy man-child of indeterminate age, but obvious good humour. "I see you didn't fall for Gordon's offer of the Booby. Might I offer you a place at the Crown?" When he made a sweeping gesture towards the building, the case pulled him off balance. He quickly righted himself, hoisted the case off the ground and waited for the Captain's bidding.

Were he not already bound for that place, the earnest face would have made a refusal nearly impossible. Such good-willed enterprise should always be rewarded. "Lead on, sir." He allowed the boy to struggle, offering no assistance. He had found that honest toil could be the making or breaking of a young man. It was clear from each small grunt issuing from this one; he was improving by the minute.

Setting the case by the bar with as much grace as he could muster, the boy called out and was answered by an older man with cloth over his shoulder and five pints in his hands. "I'll be right wi' ya, sir."

The boy looked up at him, as though the Captain might change his mind concerning the accommodations. "The Crown's the best beds and the best beer in all of Portsmouth."

Wentworth was keenly drawn to the boy. For one so young, he was wonderfully bright and better spoken than most of his officers. Moreover, he was obviously not afraid to step into an advantageous situation. This was just the sort of boy a captain longed to see come aboard his ship. He could help steer him away from foolish mistakes that so often befell a young man with no patronage. This boy could rise as far as he liked in service to the King.

"Now, what might I do fer ya?" the keep asked, glancing up as he began to wipe the bar. At first, he offered Wentworth the customary smile of a man of business looking to please a customer. When his eyes dropped to the Captain's shoulders, his smile widened, and he began wiping his hands on the towel as he gave him his full attention.

"The Captain will be wanting a room, sir. There's one in the back open. Nice and quiet like."

"George." The man was stern of voice and expression. "Let the good Cap'un speak for hisself." His compliment was genuine enough but was also to gently belabour the esteem being paid to a man of his rank.

Glancing at the boy, then looking at the man, he said, "I think George here is right. I would like the room in the back, all nice and quiet like."

The keep gave a slight nod of his head to the boy, and he hared off.

"He'll check and see that ever'thing's sound." As if to punctuate the tranquillity of the room he had rented, a roar of male voices from behind the curtain of a private dining room raised every head in the place. It continued for a time and then sank back to a manageable hubbub.

Fearing the outburst might dampen the captain's enthusiasm for staying at the Crown, the keep said, "Just a few of yer fellows celebratin' their return to the comfort of good English soil." His worried expression begged a reply.

Another roar delayed Wentworth's answer. "No one with a drop of loyalty in him would ever begrudge sailors their celebrations. Besides, I will be out most of the evening."

Relief spread over the man's face. "I figure a little high spirits is in order. As long as they don't break up the furniture, I'm happy to provide the place." Satisfied that Wentworth was not going to take his business elsewhere, he named the room's price.

Wentworth handed over the coins and said, "Your son is quite persuasive. Very well-spoken for one his age."

"Aw, that's the truth. George can talk like a lord to a lord, or better. But George, he ain't mine. He jus' showed up one day and before I could run him off, he made hisself more than a little useful. He's worth his bed and board."

"Has he ever said where he hales from? Does he have a second name?"

"Tuggins. George Tuggins. Other than his given name, he's tight-lipped about ever'thin' else. All I know is, no one's ever come makin' enquiries about him."

Wentworth assured the man that he would not need George's assistance in carrying his case and asked directions to his room. As he made his way down the hallway, he decided if he were ever in Portsmouth again and with a place to put the lad, he would have a word with Master George Tuggins.

The evening was warm. The walk to the docks was longer than he remembered. Having no memory of ever having seen the *Grappler*, he surveyed the ships at anchor. Since there were several sloops from which to choose, he would have to wait until he got aboard to appraise her further.

He began to look for a boat to take him out when fortune smiled. A wiry young man dressed in his finest going ashore clothes was carving on a fist-sized chunk of wood while chatting with a little boy of similar dress. Wentworth continued to survey the ships, but eavesdropped on the animated conversation.

"...now the Post Cap'un's the money-hungriest of 'em all, Billy. Why, most of 'um will sail right into a hurricano without blinkin' a eye if they thinks there's prize to be got. That's why ya want to get onboard a good frigate with one of them crown and anchor fellas. Ya can come away with thirty or forty pounds when they pays ya off." The younger boy was all agape at the idea of such wealth.

Smiling to himself, Wentworth had to agree with the fellow about the greedy nature of men of his rank. There was once a time that description would have fit him very well. But now, he would rather have a hurricano blow up and have to sail precisely into the middle of it than take the short pull out to Benwick's ship. His one consolation was that in a few hours it would all be over, and he would be free of the obligation.

The fellow was going on about a new subject when Wentworth inspected more closely the embroidery on the band of his cap.

"You there, Grappler, I am looking for your captain."

Looking Wentworth over, his eyes took in all the braid of his dress uniform and fixed particularly on his golden shoulders, adorned with the very crowns and anchors he touted a moment before. Motioning for the youngster to stay put, he rose and quickly approached the Captain. He tugged on his forelock and began. "Well, sir, as we've just experienced one of the most unlucky sails of all history, I'll have to ask which captain you might be inquirin' about? We got poor Captain Luden. He made it to Gibraltar and no more. Bad fever took 'im. Then there's Captain Halliwell. He succumbed to an unknown illness just the other side of the Cape. That left our fate to the newly made Master and Commander, James Benwick." He lowered his voice. "The scuttlebutt is that Commander Benwick owes a great deal to the bad moral habits of Captain Halliwell."

Sailors rivalled any group of women for their fondness of gossip. Ordinarily, the Captain would have little to say about this base slander concerning the late Captain Halliwell, but the young boy was listening closely and he wished him to have a lesson.

"What is your name?"

The man's eyes grew large. "Towrey. Henry Towrey, acting coxswain of the HMS *Grappler*, sir."

"Mr. Towrey, it is one thing to gossip among the members of your gun crew while taking your grog. It is quite another to impart such a...delicate communication to strangers. I would hate to see you lose the confidence of your captain when word returns to him that his coxswain might not be the most trustworthy." Glancing at the boy, he hoped the lad had acquired a bit of circumspection that evening. Perhaps Mr. Towrey had as well.

Referring no more to the incident, he said, "It is Commander Benwick that I seek. He is not expecting me, but I come on a matter of some urgency. Please take me to him."

Relief overtook Towrey and he said, "Well, sir, I would most gladly do that, only he's at the Crown bein' feted by his friends. Some of his Portsmouth mates come and insisted they wet the swab good and proper."

"The Crown?"

"Aye, sir. One of the finest houses in the town. The best tap around, as far as Grapplers are concerned. They've been at it a while. Even so, I don't expect him back for quite a spell."

"I see. Well, thank you." He was about to walk away when he turned and said to the boy, "And you, Billy." The boy started at his name. "He's right about a frigate. If you're aching to be rich, find a frigate." The little boy's startled look made him smile as he turned to make the walk back to the Crown.

While he walked, he rehearsed the words, turning them to suit any of the possible responses Benwick might make. The most difficult words had to do with the death itself.

"Miss Harville has died. Miss Harville has passed on. Miss Harville is in a better place. I must certainly say something to the effect that she has left us for a better place."

Dead. Passed on. Gone. Left us. These were the best consolations he could manage concerning a woman. Any others were best left to describing a departed sailor. He determined also to describe for him her lack of suffering and that the Harvilles shared his pain and despair.

With the Crown in sight, he stepped up his pace. He wished to be free of his burden quickly so that he might have a chance at a decent rest. Since Harville's visit, he had had no sleep worth considering.

As he was about to enter, the door burst open and several men came blundering out, hooting and laughing as only drunken men can. He stood aside and hoped that these were the foundation of the loud group in the private room. He had no desire to try to impart such dreadful news in the midst of Bedlam.

Surveying the room, he did not see any sign of Benwick. Perhaps his friends had procured something more private. Despite his grim errand, he could not help but be amused by the idea of Benwick and a few of his studious mates, endeavouring to engage in pleasant, but intelligent conversation while the rout carried on in the next room. The idea was entertaining for only a moment. He knocked on the bar to get the attention of the keep.

"Sir, might you help me? I am looking for a friend."

"Oh, yer back, Cap'n. Who might I find fer ya?"

"I'm looking for a Commander Benwick. James Benwick."

"Ah, yes, Benwick. Well, he's in there with a few of his friends." He pointed to the curtained room. The roar was no quieter than before.

Glancing at the room, Wentworth said, "No, no, you must be mistaken, he would never go in for anything like that mob. He is a very quiet, retiring fellow. Roundish face, dark hair, about this tall."

The man winked as he brought glasses from under the bar. "Well, Cap'n, I know they're wettin' the swab of a James Benwick, who just made Master and Commander. I know the ranks, sir." It was the keep's turn to be amused. "It's amazin' how a little touch o' superiority, not to mention quite a lot o' drink, can make a man so tolerant."

Wentworth smiled. "Very good point, sir. Thank you." He stood for a moment and thought. It would be agreeable to celebrate Benwick's good fortune, regardless of what might come later. It was always agreeable to be in the company of other officers, even those inferior to him.

He pushed off the bar and went to the private room. As he reached to draw the drape aside, an older midshipman came stumbling through. When he extricated himself from the curtain, he caught sight of Wentworth and stuttered to his uniform, "I'm sorry, sir. I didn't see you–" Just then he thought to salute and this sent the glasses he carried down his own front, slopping the remainders of wine and ale over his white waistcoat. The glasses crashed and broke at their feet. He bent to pick up the glass and then straightened to apologize to the Captain. The young man had the look of a marionette bobbing and bending.

"Here, sir, let me help you with that." The keep was in the midst of them, shooing the midshipman away. "He didn't mean no harm, I'm sure." He had no desire that one customer should do anything to aggravate another.

"No, I'm sure he did not." Wentworth agreed.

The keep stood with the glass in his towel. Surveying the Captain, he said, "Beggin' your pardon, sir, but you've got some wine on your fine coat. Let me get ya a towel."

Another burst of laughter came from behind the curtain. After the reaction of the midshipman, the abject fear of facing so much gold braid on one coat, he wondered if his presence might not cause the party to wither and die prematurely. It would be cruel to Benwick to ruin this last happiness for a time.

"Here you are, sir." A towel appeared and began dabbing at his coat.

"Thank you, but might I just take this to my room and return it later?"

"Certainly. There's no hurry, sir." The man then busied himself with a broom, working the remaining glass into a small pile.

In his room, Wentworth wiped at his coat, deciding that the keep's attentions had been an over reaction. There was very little of anything on him, but he did take the opportunity to change.

His undress coat, sans the epaulettes, would lend itself to becoming one of the mob, allowing the junior officers to forget a Post Captain was in their midst. He carefully brought the shoulders together on his dress coat and was about to toss it on the bed, when the dash of red of the crown caught his eye. Drawing it back, he examined the epaulettes more closely than ever before.

"They are beautiful," he said softly. For something made of nothing more than a small sheet of metal, a bit of gold coloured silk, wool and gold thread, they rivalled any work of art. Their beauty was derived from what they represented as much as for how they looked. The gold thread, some woven for the background and the others twisted into the bullions, did not glitter, but had a dignified glow from the light of the lamp. His thumb followed the curving "S" of the rope fouling the anchor. It looked smooth, like silver, but was rough from all the tiny stitches. He then felt the crown, the symbol of his allegiance to his sovereign and country.

These were the objects that proved his worth more than anything else in his life. Not even the generous numbers in his bank accounts meant more. These weighty bits of decoration made most men kowtow. Some, like the innkeeper, gave him due deference; the few that were left gave grudging respect, if nothing else. As for women, this symbol of rank was a prize to be won, and in his experience, most women were not too particular about whose shoulders they rested upon.

However, a woman like Fanny Harville had not cared about epaulettes or rank. She had waited for love of Benwick. Now that she was gone, his new bit of finery would have little meaning. Wentworth feared that the weight of Benwick's promotion would now carry with it the depth of his very great loss.

Perhaps if his own life had been different, he mused, he would not have these beauties now. Perhaps he would have something more. He tossed the coat on the bed, changed, and went down to face Benwick.

Chapter Three

Wentworth's plan was to take Benwick aside as the party broke up. They would bid the others farewell, and with the pretence of a friendly drink, he would take the man to a quiet table and tell him. The plan was set firmly in his mind as he drew back the curtain.

When he looked over the room, he knew the plan was doomed to failure. The party was all ready losing strength; men were weaving and bumping their way around the table to leave. The most obvious difficulty was Benwick himself. Wentworth could not recall ever seeing James Benwick intoxicated. The man had been his First Officer some time ago and he could not think of a single instance of drunkenness. Perhaps the man was so quiet that even when he was in his cups it was not noticeable. In any case, there was no ignoring it tonight.

Two men, helping one another out of the room, lurched into the Captain. He set them on their way and entered. Several fellows were facedown on the table and would be cleared away by the keep. His main concern was Benwick.

"Sir, I think we would do well to go to the ship." A lieutenant prodded Benwick, who was staring at the ceiling.

"Do you require some assistance, Mr..." Wentworth's voice drifted off.

The young man looked up and frowned a little. "Furlong. Acting First Lieutenant Miles Furlong. Of the sloop *Grappler.*"

"And this would be your captain?"

"Yes, sir. Commander James Benwick. Just made."

"He seems to be a bit under the weather."

"Well, yes, sir. He is. But I have to say I ain't never seen him like this afore. Sir."

"No, neither have I. But he does need to return to his ship."

Furlong frowned more deeply and spoke again to Benwick, who started and looked around at the two men.

"Frederick Wentworth, as I live and–," he cried, and struggled to his feet. When he went down it was only by the grace of Providence that Furlong was able to keep him from slamming his chin into the table. Wentworth came around to their side of the table and grabbed an arm.

"I think you could use my help. He's grown a bit stout over the years."

"You have come to wet my swab?" Benwick began to laugh a little.

"Yes, Commander. I've come just to see you." To Furlong he said, "Let's get him to the street and find a cart to take him to the dock."

"It's been a long time, my old friend. Furlong, did you know that I was the first on the *Laconia*? The finest frigate in His Majesty's Navy?" His voice was loud and his speech slurred. Wentworth wished he would just pass out so that they would not have to do this drunken dance while walking him out.

"Yes, sir. You've told me several times."

They now were outside and placed him on a bench next to the door. Looking around, neither saw any conveyances for hire.

"Sir," said Furlong, "I don't know exactly why you've come, but I can assure you that this is not the Commander's customary way. I've served with him for some time and have never seen him like this before."

"As I said earlier, neither have I. He is a man more likely to prose eloquently about the look of firelight gleaming through a glass of wine than to actually drink it."

Furlong reached over and steadied the tottering, giggling Benwick. "I'm sorry if I overstepped meself. It's just that I didn't know what you come about. I mean, the Commander's written orders ain't arrived yet and–"

"You were worried that I might be skulking around for the Admiralty, hoping to find an excuse to deny him his promotion and save Whitehall a pound or two a month, eh?"

"Well, with the peace, sir, there's a lot of frettin'. I wanted to make sure you wasn't, well, you know."

"I assure you, Furlong, I am friend, not foe." It struck him that he might not have the right to claim such a thing after he broke the news.

Around the corner of the building, the rattle of a cart could be heard. Soon an old man driving a bedraggled pony and dogcart passed the inn.

"Sir," Wentworth called out. "Might I have a word?"

The man looked him over and then reined the pony to a stop. "Aye, what do ya want?"

"Just a bit of your time and a little space on your cart." As he approached the man, he made a show of taking out his purse. "My friends here need a ride just to the dock." He clicked some coins together.

The man examined Furlong and Benwick and then asked, "I'm on me way home after a very long trip. Why would I want to go out uh my way for the likes of them?"

Coins glinted in Wentworth's hand. "I just think it would be to everyone's advantage if you were to play the Good Samaritan, that's all."

The man smiled and waved to Furlong. "I think you's right, sir. There is a definite blessin' that come of helpin' your neighbours."

By this time, Benwick was asleep and was no trouble to situate in the cart. Furlong jumped in along side him. "Thank you, Captain."

"Just tell the Commander I am in Portsmouth and wish to congratulate him on his promotion. I cannot trust that he will even remember seeing me. Tell him I will dine aboard *Grappler* tomorrow."

"Aye, sir."

"And Furlong, tell him the dinner is to be private."

"Aye, sir" The young man's worried face disappeared into the darkness.

Wentworth studied the stars for a moment, and listened as Portsmouth quieted for the night. Stuffing his purse back in his pocket, he headed for the door of the Crown. "You are fated to miss another night of sleep, I fear," he sighed.

~ ~ ~ ~ ~ ~ ~ & ~ ~ ~ ~ ~ ~ ~

Though he did eventually sleep, Wentworth was still labouring under the pall of his mission when he walked to the docks the next day. Seeing a group of Grapplers loitering nearby, he looked for Mr. Towrey. The young man saw him first and called the men to order.

"Mr. Towrey, am I correct in assuming you are here to take me out?"

"Aye, sir. Cap'n said to make sure you thought you was glidin' o'er glass, the pull was to be so smooth."

"I'm sure it will be," he said as he took a seat in the stern. The day had been hot from early in the morning and the sun was still a glorious fury in the sky. There had not been a breath of wind all day. Sails not furled hung limp, along with all flags and pennants. It was nearly three; the heat would persist for several hours. As the small boat slid across the water, he saw little activity on the decks of the ships they passed.

Even at the easy pace set by the coxswain, sweat was dripping from the faces of the men rowing. The dark blue baize of Wentworth's uniform was absorbing the heat and becoming uncomfortable. The beaver felt of his cocked hat rested heavily on his brow and gripped like an iron band around his head. A drop of sweat escaped and began a slow, torturous roll down the back of his neck. A lone gusty breeze kicked up and blew across the boat and crew. He focused on the cool of the breeze and the prickling sensation as the bead of sweat moved through the short hairs, and did not allow himself the luxury of wiping it away. Keeping his back straight and hands on his knees was a discipline he required himself to exercise. To give into his physical discomfort and ease it would be a sort of betrayal. He must suffer, even in this trivial way, for the suffering he was to inflict.

"There we are, sir." The coxswain pointed to a sloop just ahead. He was surprised to see a neat, trim, rather large ship-sloop. Her deck was the exception around the fleet as it was alive with activity. He could see Benwick standing at the waist. He could not help smiling; James was a picture with his glass to his eye watching them approach. The man had been as fastidious as a woman when he was Wentworth's First, and it seemed that nothing was changed. The crew would titivate until the moment he planted a foot on the deck. It was Benwick's first real command; he could not disdain the pride and the desire to show off his beautiful *Grappler*.

It was plain to see, as they moved closer, that *Grappler* was, indeed, a true ship with three masts. However, it was also clear she had been stripped down and rebuilt several times to arrive at her present configuration. This was no great shock as the term "sloop" was only a vague notion rather than a precise definition. After examining a few irregularities, he suspected *Grappler* was cobbled together like so many other small vessels. However, it was done with a deft hand and some elegance of design, and Wentworth was glad his friend's first command was one of which he could be proud.

The small boat gently nudged *Grappler's* side and the rope was tossed. It was just a few steps up the accommodation ladder and he was aboard. Unlike a rated ship, the sloop's deck was flush. There was no quarterdeck–that universally acknowledged holy ground on which the captain was high priest and supreme master. Despite this imperfection, *Grappler* was a fine ship. Wentworth counted sixteen four-pounders and an additional pair at both bow and stern. She had pretensions of being a small frigate in her weight and capacity. He estimated her compliment to be between eighty and one hundred men. He quickly counted twelve marines as well. No, unlike his timeworn *Asp*, *Grappler* was a sleek and sturdy ship that could not be disparaged in the eyes of anyone who understood sailing vessels.

"Captain Wentworth, welcome aboard His Majesty's sloop, *Grappler*." Benwick stood ramrod straight as the boatswain's pipe pierced the heat and the assembled men stood taller.

He then ordered Mr. Furlong to weigh anchor. Furlong called to the boatswain and another call sounded, this one sending the men to their stations to raise the anchor. Turning to his guest, Benwick smiled and said, "You have brought us good luck, sir. I watched you as you rowed out, and the wind picked up markedly as you came to us."

Inwardly Wentworth groaned. His hope had been for a quiet visit, a private meal, and the unburdening of himself. Obviously, that was not the plan of James Benwick, or Providence above.

A young man, with a fiddle, mounted the capstan and began to play a shanty to set the cadence for the men exerting themselves on the bars. Employment of the canty tunes was falling out of favour with scientific captains, those more attuned to the *modus operandi* of sailing than giving any place to the romance of her traditions. On this brilliant day, on such an excellent ship, and in the company of his friend, the Captain could see nothing in the world wrong with the practice. Benwick beamed as his men worked, and the familiar tune did much to lighten his own heart.

In just a few moments, he knew the camaraderie of the old days was not lost. In fact, Benwick's newly awarded parity made Wentworth feel their bond more acutely. A man could occupy the position of a ship's first officer and even be the particular friend to the captain, but until such a man had first-hand understanding of command, he could not fully comprehend his friend. Understanding only came with knowing the intense joy of authority and its natural partner, the sharp sting of isolation. Benwick might command a ship smaller than his prized *Laconia*, but the commander was now, in most ways, the Captain's equal.

"We shall haul clear of the shipping lanes and work the guns. The men have fadged up several targets and I am told the wagering is wonderfully heated as to which crew will carry the day." Taking a second look at Wentworth, he said, "Are you unwell? Let us move out of the sun."

He *was* unwell, but heat and sun did not answer for it. However, it was a relief to step into the shade of the canvas stretched over the waist and stern of the ship.

Grappler eased out to open sea. Towrey was at the wheel and did as fine a job as any sailing master. Benwick tried mightily to hide his apprehension, but the occasional widening of the eyes and pursing lips smoked him out. Wentworth assumed this was his first opportunity to show off his crew, and the fellow dreaded any mistakes. He remained expressionless and ignored the few slight errors.

Once they were in unpopulated water, Benwick evidently felt he could divide his attention, and said, "As you can see, we are well equipped with four-pounders. I would dearly love to trade them, even just a few, for sixes, or even twelves, but I am fairly certain those would buckle her knees with the first shot."

Wentworth considered this and said, "You may escape the natural consequences of shooting off larger guns, once, perhaps twice, but after that it is highly likely you would find yourself bursting your seams and having to ask your adversary for a tow into port." They laughed at such foolishness. "No, it is best to exercise with the aim of improving your rate of reload. Sloops in close action, with crack gun crews, are the likeliest to come out the prize-winner."

This observation began an earnest conversation. When Benwick was the First on the *Laconia*, he would never have endured, in part or whole, any comment that gave the slightest superiority to a sloop over a frigate. However, as he was now captaining the first and not the second, his opinion was more elastic. He put forth a suggestion that the Navy might be better served increasing emphasis on the smaller, and more manoeu- vrable sloops than the larger-gunned, more heavily manned, but less responsive frigates.

The good-natured, but deep conversation went on for some time, the two officers weighing the merits of each design, positive and negative and bringing to bear every ounce of their own particular prejudice in favour of their opinion. But it was Wentworth who finally settled the issue, pointing out that regardless of the skill or luck of the gun captain, nearly any sloop could be sunk with one good shot. A frigate, on the other hand, must sustain substantial damage in order for her to sink. Neither was inclined to discuss larger ships and the effect of their weap- onry on the structure of a frigate, so the discussion ended amiably.

Grappler sailed well, not as tightly on the bowline as he would like, but she was completely acceptable. Benwick consulted with his deck officers as the bell struck the hour. Every man was employed, and all was as it should be on a King's ship. Despite a creeping headache and the unfortunate news he must deliver, he felt at home. It was a joy to feel the living deck under his feet and not merely the indifferent drifting in Plymouth Sound that was his present lot. The sounds, the activity and energy of a functioning ship were not to be dismissed because the ship was smaller than he was accustomed.

He could not help but notice Benwick's epaulettes gleaming bright in the sun. As a lieutenant, Benwick had worn only the left shoulder board. Though these new boards lacked the crown and anchor, they communi- cated influence nonetheless. Benwick moved back into the shade of the canvas and his boards maintained their pristine radiance. It stung just a bit that now, with one on each shoulder and a uniform coat as lace- decorated as his own, anyone glancing at the pair of them might mistake them for post-captains.

The ship was as fine as a man could hope for his first command, and Benwick was rightfully proud. If *Grappler* were a scandalous ship and her crew unmistakable slow-bellies who deserved none of his respect, perhaps that would ease his conscience and make telling the news of Fanny's death easier. This was most likely not the case, Wentworth determined. For if the ship were a scandal, and the crew fit for nothing, he would pity Benwick all the more. Either way, his situation was impossible. In short order they arrived at the spot where Benwick intended to show off his gun crews. The anchor was dropped and he ordered they beat to quarters. The men jumped into action, anxious to prove themselves to their captain and his guest and, no doubt, anxious to collect on the wonderfully heated wagers. The targets were towed out and the festivities began.

After several rounds and the sinking of one target, an incongruent tea party was arranged. The heat below deck was too oppressive for human endurance, necessitating the refreshments be brought to the gentlemen at the stern. The beverages consisted of plain grog, for those so inclined, or a rum shrub, which suffered very little for being warm. For those with an appetite, an assortment of sweet biscuits, including an entire plate of arrack biscuits, was part of the offering. Benwick was a canny host and never drew attention to the fact the biscuits were a favourite of his old master. The lemon in the shrub was refreshing, and after several biscuits, Wentworth's headache was on the wane and he felt more like himself.

The tournament required several rounds be shot off, with the eventual elimination of one gun crew. The excitement was high, but the uniformity of the teams in skill and swagger kept either from taking an advantage. The men of Iron Death were a spindly lot but full of skill and purpose. Those manning Bloody Terror were beefy and blustering and determined to prevail, taking the extra rations of tobacco and rum promised the winners.

"Benwick, I am afraid the equality of these men will empty your magazine if this is allowed to go on much longer." The competition, while exciting and acting as a restorative to Wentworth's state of mind, was wearing thin and he wished to see its conclusion.

"And what do you suggest?"

Reaching into his inner coat pocket, he pulled out a hand full of coins and picked out several. "I imagine these are the sort of men who will work double-quick for a sure and generous reward."

Benwick nodded and swept a hand, giving permission for the Captain to address the crews.

The boatswain blew his pipe and the men stopped their cheering, wagering, and murdering of targets to listen. "Gentlemen," he called out as he walked to the larboard rail where the remaining men stood poised.

"I thank you for your exertions on our behalf; we have been greatly entertained by your skill and energy. In gratitude, I offer an inducement." He raised his hand so that they might see the coins. "In addition to the extra ration of rum and tobacco, I offer a guinea for each man on the winning crew with a crown bonus for the gun captain."

Smiles broke out on the dirty, tired faces of the two crews, and the cheers of the others became louder still. He returned to his place next to Benwick, and after much conferring between the crewmembers, the competition began again.

Each crew became more conscientious and each shot took longer to load, tamp, aim, and fire off. The promise of a monetary reward made each man particularly scrupulous concerning his own job, and more so when it came to advising their mates on theirs. Wentworth mused that it would be the crew who could throw caution to the wind and rest on their natural ability who would take the prize. In three shots, the competition was concluded. The men of Iron Death pushed their powder monkey, a thin, pale boy named Herman, forward. After making his obedience, he received the coins, made a leg and hared back to his gun captain.

Benwick said, as the applause for the winners died away, "You are a hero now. This will be spoken of for quite some time."

"Ha! The Greeks would be embarrassed to know they wasted all that blood and life for what I now have at comparatively little cost." Taking out another coin, he handed it to James and said, "I know that Mr. Trent, being a junior officer, should not be accepting what is only a little short of a bribe; but if this were prize money, he would have his share. See that he gets this if you please." He had noticed the stout, awkward midshipman who led the winning gun crew was all eyes as the guineas were handed round. The Captain could not bear the idea that Master Trent's victory would be overshadowed by a slavish devotion to a well-intentioned principle.

"Certainly, Captain. Trent is a good boy. I hope to keep him on my next commission. And what of the *Laconia*? Have you gotten orders as of yet?"

"No, no orders. I am assured she will be placed in ordinary. I gave her copper a terrible battering and it must all be replaced. And there are other repairs that have been ignored for some time. No, I think my dear girl and I are to be separated for good, Captain."

The look on Benwick's face said it all. He was deeply sympathetic that Wentworth's ship should be taken from him, but he was also thankful that he was not the one to endure the loss.

Lieutenant Furlong begged pardon to speak and asked, since the wind had died, did Benwick wish to be underway so as to reach port before dark?

"Aye. Starboard watch to the boats and dismiss the larboard watch to dinner, then join us in the Great Cabin when you are finished."

Wentworth was relieved that they would be returning to their anchorage immediately, but it was also clear that there would be no quiet, private dinner. Rather it would be a full, loud table that was the prerogative of any captain. He clung to the idea that, in but a few hours, he would be free of his burden.

"I know you prefer keeping to the old ways and the old dinner time of six bells, but I could not resist taking her out and remind you what sailing a sloop was like. She's not much, but I know you will excuse the pride. Even the parent of a pale and thin child is wont to show him off." He looked at Wentworth with an embarrassed half-smile and headed towards the gangway.

Entering the Great Cabin, which in a sloop was a term of courtesy and not one of exact description, Wentworth remembered how he struggled to keep the skin on his forehead while living below on the *Asp*. Between the beams, he could just stand to his full height, but still he felt the presence of the decking above. He noticed that Benwick had no trouble standing straight.

The room was obviously James's. Several crates, doubling as bookshelves and containing many nicely bound volumes, were placed neatly beneath the stern windows. There was a small chest of drawers, a dining table laid with serviceable china and pewter, and a small writing desk. Again, the desk reflected its owner. It was tidy and all the writing utensils were placed in neat ranks. This cabin was Benwick's territory to be sure. His exacting mark was everywhere even to the small silhouette of a woman perched on the open desk.

"I have to say, I was quite shocked when Furlong told me you were at the Crown last night. I'm afraid I was..." Benwick said, a look of embarrassment creeping across his face.

Wentworth handed over his hat and said, "You were sated with the fruits of victory, James. As for not knowing I was present, I was quite late to the party. You had no reason to expect me. However, I could not be in Portsmouth and not wish you joy. And so I do. She looks to be a fine ship."

The embarrassment disappeared and pure delight took its place. "She is, sir, I assure you. No man has had such good fortune in obtaining a command. Oh, there are few situations that are not to my liking, but I shall deal with them as I was shown by a former captain of mine." He handed Wentworth a glass of cool water. "I like to think that I learnt at the elbow of a master."

The compliment was crushing. James's shy nature made such a passionate admission all the more agonizing to him. He refused to wonder what Benwick's opinion might be after his mission was accomplished.

"I thank you for the fine words, James, but at the very best, I am a journeyman. No matter what we may call an officer, I am not sure that any one of us can ever truly be a master where the sea is concerned."

Benwick smiled at the deferral. The moment of high feeling was interrupted by the arrival of the other guests. Lieutenant Milsom of the marines looked to be nearly as young as Furlong, but his voice betrayed him as more adult than youngster. Milsom was followed by the ship's Master, Mr. Roderick; a greying man but, like all masters he had ever known, possessing lively eyes and a ruddy tint to his cheeks. Midshipman Trent was introduced after Benwick himself had taken the boy aside and given him the guinea. Lieutenant Furlong came in just as the steward was about to close the door.

"The boats are away, sir."

"Very good, Lieutenant. Shall we all be seated? Captain, you will of course do me the honour of taking the head of the table."

For just a moment, Wentworth considered refusing the seat. However, to do so would go against all tradition and courtesy. Just as on land, it was an honour to give over one's rightful place to a superior. Even more so at the Captain's own table.

"Certainly, Commander. I assure you, the honour is all mine." He took the seat and the rest of the men followed his lead.

The room was stuffed to bursting with the guests, a steward for each, and the men seeing to the removes. It was insufferably hot, but mercifully, the starboard watch was pulling its heart out. A breath of wind moved through the open stern windows and the skylight above.

The food was excellent. Wentworth suspected that Benwick would have taken care with the menu and coins from his own purse to see that the fare was to Wentworth's liking. He was not sure whether the heat and headache were to blame for his lack of appetite or his natural dread of things to come. The reason was irrelevant; the news was to be postponed and nothing could be done for it. He would have to put on a good face and do his utmost to uphold his responsibility as a guest.

The meal progressed wonderfully. All the faces around the table were red with the heat and a few with more wine than was good for them. Furlong and Trent were acquitting themselves well by listening raptly to their betters. The indelicate subject of promotions had come to

43

the fore. Benwick had just told of his own step up from Mid to Lieutenant. It was a laughable circumstance that left all the party saluting the fates and their mysterious ways.

"And I must add, Master and Commander Benwick, had I been apprised of the entire incident, I am not certain I would have allowed you on my quarter deck. A man who can manage to sink the captain's boat, with him in it, is not to be trusted." Wentworth smiled particularly at Benwick and saluted him.

The men all raised their glasses, laughing and calling, "Hear him. Hear him."

The bottle was passed and when the glasses were once more full, Mr. Trent ventured forth into the fray. "Captain Wentworth, might we know how you came to your rank?"

All around the table stared at the child. Squeakers were invited to dine in the Great Cabin so that they might learn to be civilized and behave decently when in company. This training did not include them asking questions of those far superior to them. However, Wentworth was in a benevolent frame of mind. The room was not as stifling as it had been earlier, and the wine had improved his appetite somewhat, though the headache still lurked behind his eyes. To be sure, manners went into the making of an officer and a gentleman, but courage must be counted for something.

Smiling at the boy, he began. "I think my promotion to Commander would be more instructive, Mr. Trent."

He was puzzled as to why he said such a thing. The step to captain had been a great adventure involving a thrilling chase, the first raging storm of the commission, and the sinking of his ship just after delivering an exceptional French frigate into the hands of the Admiralty. It was a story that, at the time, had piqued the interest of more than one high-ranking official in Whitehall. In fact, it was a story he had dined on more than once. Perhaps he looked further into the past because, when he made Commander, his love for the sea and for the navy was still pure and undiluted by anything or anyone. To that point, the most attractive thing he had ever seen was a ship at full sail. He had not yet learnt that the wounds of battle were nothing compared to the pain suffered by the human heart.

"I was told it was the hottest February day in memory, and it was dusk before the French finally surrendered to the superior British forces," he began.

~ ~ ~ ~ ~ ~ ~ & ~ ~ ~ ~ ~ ~ ~

The now 77-gun *Borthwick*, (she had lost one over the side during the action), had taken two captures. The *Petite Fleur*, once the *English Rose*, was a brig-sloop that had been ferrying munitions between the French ships. Her crew was minimal, but it would still put bounty money into the pockets of the Borthwicks.

It was well dark before First Lieutenant Hale saw *Rosie*, as they were now calling the repatriated boat, secured and manned with a prize crew ready to sail. Midnight was sounding and Second Lieutenant Wentworth laid waiting on the surgeon's table. He cursed his luck while he listened to the calls of the men above, wishing Hale well as he pulled away into the darkness. When he had first presenting himself to the medico, there had been talk of malingering. There were few visible wounds. But when he removed his coat, the surgeon became suddenly business-like and nearly tore off his shirt. A deep knife wound near the left kidney was the concern. After probing the wound and finding no broken blade inside, the lieutenant was declared very lucky indeed and told that he should be saying extra prayers for quite some time to come. Stitched up and dosed with a foul tasting tincture, he was sent on his way.

The energy of battle subsided while he had a proper wash. His empty stomach was grinding away even as his exhausted body sank into his hammock. He tried to rest, but the enormity of the day's events crashed in on him. Succumbing to the swing of his bed and the ship's roll, he relived every moment, every stroke of the blade, every man who fell before him.

"You know the Captain is already writing the letters to the Admiralty. Let me be the first to wish you joy at the promotion I know will come of this."

He looked up to see his friend, the *Borthwick's* commander, Patrick McGillvary, holding out cups and a bottle of wine. "I always knew you to be a man of courage. You more than proved it in this engagement, Wentworth, and you will prove yourself even more when the orders for the *Jeanette* are prepared and you sail away with her tomorrow. I inspected her cargo. Your part of the prize will be sizeable."

The news he would be taking the *Jeannette* immediately revived him. "How is this possible? The *Jeannette* is the larger of the two, and Hale has taken the brig. You, by all rights, should be the one to take her." He sat up, cursing the wound.

"Yes, by rights, I should. Nevertheless, as the first officer I must put the good of the ship above personal gain. There are major repairs that require a better hand than yours overseeing them." McGillvary did not smile; there wasn't any softness about him at all.

"But you sent off Hale, who has time and rank all over me. At best, I should have had *Rosie*."

"So, perhaps I misjudged the repairs and the time needed to implement them. Who was to know that Chips would be so deft at repairing the damage to her rudder and making fast the crack in those two larboard knees?" Patrick replied. "Can I help it if we have the finest, most talented crew in this part of the world?"

"When I follow him into Plymouth, just a few days behind, he will bellow so loudly you'll hear him off the cliffs of Dover."

"Lieutenant, do not begin your ascendancy by questioning your superiors." McGillvary's face was as hard set as he had ever seen it. The situation was of his making and to his liking, and it would stand.

He left the hammock and joined Patrick, leaning at the doorway. "Thank you, McGillvary." Nothing more was ever said between them on the subject.

"Well, this is an occasion," Wentworth said, taking the bottle, along with one of the proffered cans. "It takes an event of great magnitude to propel Master and Commander McGillvary into the bowels of the ship to visit an inferior." He poured each of them a bumper of the wine. They drank, and then he said, "As for courage and promotions, I think you exaggerate, Paddy." Nothing was said as they threaded their way farther aft to the table in the gunroom.

It was called a room, but it was really no more than a clearing behind a set of stairs with a terribly abused table and two creaking benches. No one was about; it was the middle watch and little stirred below. The only sounds were assorted snuffings and snortings from various curtained sleeping areas that served as quarters for the inferior and warrant officers. Occasionally, laughter was heard from the duty watch above.

Both men were too worn-out to slide more than a few inches down the seat. They sat shoulder-to-shoulder, drank their wine and picked at a plate of boiled mutton and potatoes left from that afternoon's dinner.

McGillvary shoved the scavenged plate aside and refilled the mugs. Slowly, they drank them away.

"Are you sure about the Captain writing letters, or is this another one of your tricks, Patrick?"

"Me? Tricks? You wound me, Lieutenant Wentworth." He straightened and placed his hand over his heart. "I swear on all that is sacred to me that the Old Man is this minute writing a glowing report, much of it about his valiant Second Lieutenant."

Wentworth took a drink. "That is not much comfort, for you are practically a pagan and a blasphemer into the bargain."

McGillvary's cup came down hard. "I realize I am not the most pious of men, but friend, believe me, I would not set you up for a fall. I had to endure a long homiletic on several of you lower ranking heroes."

He filled his cup and drank it down. "I think he is wonderfully amazed by his talented gaggle of junior officers."

Wentworth snatched the bottle before McGillvary and emptied it into his mug. "You sound almost worried, my friend. Might you be contemplating the day I shall outstrip you?"

Patrick laughed, grabbed Wentworth's mug and drained it. Rising from the table, he said, "Lieutenant Wentworth, I will concede that your moral sense is more acute, owing to that religious brother of yours no doubt, but the day you become my superior officer will *never* dawn." He slammed down the mug and left the room laughing.

~ ~ ~ ~ ~ ~ ~ & ~ ~ ~ ~ ~ ~ ~

The gentlemen of the *Grappler* also laughed heartily and called again for a toast to the latest story. As another took his place telling his story, Wentworth drank his wine and continued in the memories of that all-important year.

~ ~ ~ ~ ~ ~ ~ & ~ ~ ~ ~ ~ ~ ~

"There now, Frederick, have a care." Commander Wentworth had taken up a position next to his brother, bumping his arm in the process.

"Relax Edward, it is only wine. The gloomy uniform of a curate hides a multitude of stains. No one will ever notice."

"Yes, how fortunate for you that my uniform stands in such stark contrast to your glittering blue and gold," he said, as he dabbed a handkerchief at the unseen spots of wine. "But, for all your success, even you cannot change the fact that wine is wet." Before Frederick could reply, he continued. "You're cross all of a sudden. Mission fail?"

Before he could answer, they heard the rustle of a gown and a gentle voice asked, "Mr. Wentworth, might I importune you for an introduction?"

Both men turned to the voice. Mr. Wentworth was all smiles. "Of course, Miss Anne. Miss Anne Elliot, may I present Commander Frederick Wentworth. Frederick, you have met her father, I believe, Sir Walter Elliot of Kellynch Hall."

Wentworth stiffened as he bowed and murmured a greeting.

"Commander. It is an honour to meet you. It is not often we have a genuine hero in our midst. The action was in…"

The slight tilt to her head, as she tried to remember the name of the foreign shore, was breathtaking.

"San Domingo!" she exclaimed, again stifling his reply.

He glanced at his brother. His arrival in the area several weeks earlier had caused little comment. Anne's acknowledgement was, in fact, the first local recognition of his participation in the action against the French. The King's reward had been a step in rank, but no ship had accompanied it as of yet. Tonight, that was of little matter as the Commander found the admiration of a pretty, country girl far more invigorating.

"I am sure my brother exaggerated my importance in the matter, Miss Anne."

Anne smiled at the curate. "He has been the picture of brotherly pride." She glanced around and, lowering her voice, she said, "In fact, there are many who are beginning to avoid his company all together, fearing they will have to endure the story of your exploits for a third, even a fourth time." She smiled at the commander, looked away, and opened a small lace fan. The bit of air stirred by it disturbed tiny curls at her temple. The effect made him swallow hard.

Reluctantly, he looked away, raising a brow towards his brother. It seemed odd that Edward would speak so freely with everyone but him. He had not wished to hoist his own flag; however, the efforts had been great, as had the reward and he wished to share it. To hear that the curate was becoming a tiresome braggart was a surprise and a pleasure.

Edward gave a little laugh. "Thank you for this bit of news, Miss Anne. I was merely riding the coattails of my brother. A curate's life has few luxuries. You cannot blame me for trying to muster a few more invitations to dinner. I shall endeavour to be more judicious in the use of my brother's heroics." He looked into his brother's eyes, then quickly lowered them and took a drink of his wine.

"Mr. Wentworth, I am heartened to see such a humble man as you indulging in a few luxuries. I am sure your brother doesn't feel your weight on his coattails a bit."

"No, not a bit," Wentworth said, leaning his shoulder into Edward's. He had thought his brother did not care about his career, but it would seem he was quite mistaken.

After a few awkward looks and smiles, Edward set his glass aside and said, "I hope you will excuse me. I see a neighbour of mine, and I must speak to him about a small matter." He bowed to Anne and left them.

Wringing her hands through an awkward moment of silence, she finally said, "Commander, while it has been my sincere pleasure to meet you, I have to apologize for my family and for myself."

"I see no need for you to apologise for anything." Apologies were due him but from quite another quarter. He knew that ice would dam the River Styx before Sir Walter Elliot apologized for his contemptuous behaviour. The same was true for his eldest daughter. Wentworth would not allow this lovely girl to make amends for their lack of manners.

"You are very kind, but I heard my father."

He did not remember seeing her anywhere nearby when the introductions to Sir Walter and Miss Elliot were accomplished. Trying not to think how many others might have heard the man's deprecating remarks, he said, "From his comments, I fear your father is not an admirer of the Royal Navy."

"Well, from his comments, I would say you are correct. I cannot explain them. My father can be…capricious. I have never known him to be unsympathetic to the Navy, but, then, I have not lived long enough to hear his views on every subject."

"You needn't worry, Miss Anne, your father's remarks were not sharp enough to cut deeply. This is a very thick hide I wear." Immediately, he regretted his frankness and could not decide whether she coloured on account of the thoughtless comment concerning his person or because the room's temperature was rising markedly.

She smiled. "Might we walk and talk? I would not want the gossips having us in a *tête-à-tête*. Perhaps, if we keep moving, we will escape their notice."

They began a circuit around the room. She pronounced the musicians to be quite good, and he countered with the opinion that the dancing was quite fine. She spoke of the lovely, though warm, weather, and he remarked on the splendid countryside. After exhausting all topics of conversation suitable for strangers, they walked in silence.

Eventually, the quiet annoyed him more than the idea of another discomfiting remark and he said, "Again, I'm sure my brother exaggerated my part in San Domingo." They travelled only a little way before she spoke. "Actually, your brother has been very lavish with his praise of you and your great courage, but when I heard a genuine hero of the Crown was coming to our part of the world, I took it upon myself to learn more about the battle. Our neighbour, Lady Russell, subscribes to the Times and I borrowed her copies until I learnt all I could."

The embarrassment he felt at her revelation was surprising. Suddenly, the room grew warmer and smaller, the music grew quite loud, and the rest of the country party faded away. He looked around the room and then at Anne. Her expression was serious; the light, easy manner was gone.

"Is there something wrong?" he asked.

"Commander," she said, turning to smile at him. "I'm sorry. I can see that either I have put you off with my unrestrained praise, or I have merely bored you silly. For either one, I apologize."

She began to move away, but he reached out and touched her arm. She had no choice but to stop. "No, I am sorry. Now, I owe the apology. I allowed myself to be caught up in memories of the day. I've been at sea far too long, away from the civilizing effect of ladies." He bowed. "Can you forgive this poor, old salt?"

She nodded prettily. "All is forgiven, Commander. I am too sensitive. My rattling on tends to bore the family."

It was no surprise that her blockheaded father and crushingly cold sister would be bored by an intelligent and refined mind. All he could say was, "I am not bored in the least."

~ ~ ~ ~ ~ ~ ~ & ~ ~ ~ ~ ~ ~ ~

"Captain," came an insistent hiss.

He turned to see Benwick offering him his glass. "The toast, sir."

"Ah." He rose and hoisted his glass along with the rest.

"To the King."

"To the King," they cried in unison. They touched glasses, the sound like that of small birds in a tree. They drank the bumpers down and cried their 'Huzzahs.'

He hesitated, fearing he could not continue with the toast. And yet he must.

Chapter Four

T o wives and sweethearts."

Wentworth heard his own voice as he spoke. It never quavered, never faltered in saying the damning words. He raised his glass, knowing Benwick would follow, and forced his friend to toast a dead woman. His eyes fixed on a sconce across the tiny cabin as he raised the glass to his lips.

The laughter oppressed him and his greatest desire was to be free of his burden, but it would have to wait a few moments more. The men crowded up the gangway to a deck alive with activity. Those on watch were preparing to drop the anchor, while those not occupied in the business of the ship were chatting and smoking or playing a few simple instruments. The eventful day was winding down to its natural conclusion.

The officer of the watch reported, "We've arrived at our position, sir. Permission to haul in the boats."

"Yes, Mr. Fields. By all means, haul away."

The Great Cabin party was melting into the crew, and Benwick was speaking with the men at the wheel. The moment had come. He would do it now.

"Benwick, might I have a word." He nodded towards the gangway.

"Certainly, Captain." Out of the hearing of the deck, he said, "I know they are not in fighting form yet, but I have my plans…"

When they were below, Benwick poured them each a glass of brandy. Handing it to Wentworth, he said, "I hope this is to your liking. At the price, it should be to the liking of everyone." The Captain swirled the glass, then took a sip of the amber liquid. He took no pleasure in it.

"There has not been time for news of my promotion to be published. I imagine you heard of my step from Timothy." He took a seat at the table. "And you have seen Fanny, of course." His smile at her name was eager and wistful.

51

"I have seen Harville. He came to call on me just a few days ago." Wentworth took another drink and walked closer to the window.

"Did he say anything concerning Fanny?" Without allowing an answer, he continued, "When I arrived, there was a large packet of mail and, in its midst, were several letters from her. I just sent off an answer yesterday. I must admit to a great deal of pride in telling her I have enough to feel comfortable in performing the ceremony. I am in great anticipation of her response. She had said once she would like a summer wedding above all things. No worry of rain and grim weather I suppose. And that way, if there was to be shift of location, it could be done with little or no trouble. Again, the weather. I have to agree. Bringing her to Portsmouth will be no trouble. That way, whatever happens with the peace, she and I will be together here. So, how is Harville?"

"He is not well to tell the truth. His leg. James…" The moment had come and he still had no notion of what he would say. "James, Timothy came to see me to tell me…it was early in June when Miss Harville…Fanny…took fever. It was very quick and she did not suffer."

Though red-faced from the wine and the heat, James lost all colour. He stopped mid-sip. His eyes were large and staring. They had the same questioning look as Harville's. Wentworth felt as though he had been kicked in the stomach. The room grew close and hot. It was as if a weight were pressing on him, keeping him from moving. Suddenly, Benwick was up and threw himself into a tiny, curtained privy. The sound of retching was all he could hear.

Wentworth took a drink and then slowly, carefully placed the glass on the small table nearby. Perhaps, if he did not move too much, the situation would not be aggravated. He examined his hand and noticed a splinter he picked up somewhere. He worried it with his thumb, grateful for the sharp pain.

The retching ceased and there was silence. He wondered if he should go to his friend. He moved in that direction when there was an explosion of noise from behind the curtain. A sound like the pounding of fists or feet or worse was punctuated by a low moan, strengthening to a scream.

Wentworth's vision narrowed into a tunnel, and all he could see was the curtain jumping and flapping. A pounding at the door distracted him. He turned to see the terrified face of Lieutenant Furlong. Behind him, other faces appeared. The Lieutenant started into the room, but Wentworth stood firm to block him.

"Sir?" Furlong questioned.

"Everything is all right, Lieutenant. Do you understand?" He said it loudly enough that the others behind Furlong faded away.

The man nodded. He tried to look further into the room but could not see past the Captain's shoulder. His expression was doubtful.

"There is nothing here that should concern you or the crew. Do you understand?" The Captain moved a step closer to the door, forcing Furlong back into the gangway.

The Lieutenant nodded. Wentworth could see questions in his eyes, but the young officer hadn't the boldness to ask them.

Nodding to the curtain, he said, "I shall see to him." To buy them some time, he ordered, "Beat to quarters, Lieutenant."

Furlong nodded in acknowledgement and turned to go above.

"Mr. Furlong," Wentworth called. "I shall be conducting the inspection. Do you understand?"

Again, the bob and the frightened look. The young lieutenant turned and hurried up the steps.

Wentworth knew there was nothing to stop the chattering of the crew. A man would have to be deaf not to have heard the pounding and Benwick's desperate cry. Threatening an inspection conducted by an unfamiliar Post Captain would not thwart the idle talk of more hardy gossips aboard, but he hoped it would distract those who feared a severe look and demanding voice.

Slamming the door, Wentworth went to the curtain and threw it aside. Benwick knelt on the floor, slamming his fist into the front of the privy seat. His hand was a bloody mess.

"Benwick," Wentworth said, firmly but quietly. It was his aim to gain James's attention but not startle him. It was not unheard of for men in the throes of extraordinary rage to turn on their fellows. Such anger, coupled with grief, was a particularly volatile mix. "Benwick, let me help you up." He knelt slowly, his sword scrapping the floor.

The curtain fell back in place and darkened the pathetic scene. Benwick heaved one last grunt, gave the boards an impressive blow, and then slumped into the corner. In the dim light, all Wentworth could see was Benwick's sweaty face and a tangle of hair. He was holding the wounded fist close to him.

"Commander, we need to have this seen by the doctor." The heat in the stall was oppressive and the smell of the privy overwhelming. He reached out and touched Benwick's arm. The man did not move. The only sound was heavy breathing, punctuated with sobs. "James, please, let me help you."

As if just waking and realizing he was not alone, the sobbing stopped. A hand reached out of the putrid gloom and tugged on Wentworth's arm.

"Beat to quarters," was the cry from above. Again, an explosion of sound filled the cabin. This time, the thundering was from overhead.

Helping Benwick to a chair, he could not help but see the man's hand was a shambles. Blood covered it and even tinged the cuff of his sleeve. Just a cursory look revealed splinters in and around the knuckles. He fleetingly thought of his own. "I think we should call your medico. That hand may be broken."

Benwick sucked in air through his teeth and said, "No, he's little better than a butcher. See, it moves." He slowly flexed his fingers to prove he needed no aid.

"All right, then do you have something I may use to wrap it? You can't allow the men to see you're injured."

Without moving, he said, "In the bottom drawer there's a few odd things left from Halliwell. There's a shirt that's much too long for me."

Wentworth found the shirt and tore off the old-fashioned ruffle to use to bath the wound. "No sense ruining a good towel," he said, pouring water into the bowl that served for washing up. He carried the bowl to the table and began. "The man was hopelessly out of fashion."

James said nothing, and when Wentworth took his hand, he did not wince or cry out in pain. His expression was fixed in a stare, as if he hadn't the energy to animate the muscles in his face.

"I am not a physician; so you will have to excuse my clumsiness." He thought it best to just set the hand in the basin and dab at it with the ruff. Still, Benwick said nothing.

Wentworth wrapped the hand in the sleeves of the shirt and then tore a longer piece from the body to cover and tie it up. "Not bad, if I do say so myself," he said, tucking the ends under the wrapping.

"You missed your calling, perhaps."

He took the remnant of the shirt and the basin of bloodied water to the chest. "No, I think not. Healing the sick is the providence of better souls than I."

The sound of bare feet running above them and a crash of chains made Wentworth check his watch. "I ordered Furlong to beat to quarters." He snapped the lid closed and tucked the watch away. "I made it clear I would be giving *Grappler* a very scrupulous going over."

"I have no wish to go above."

"Your wishes do not matter at present. Come."

"No, I shall stay here." He was a pathetic sight. He sagged against the table. His hand bandaged, his hair was Bedlam, his face red and swollen. There was no expression on his face or in his eyes.

Wentworth was revolted. It was all he could do to check the growing anger in his breast. "You must come above and inspect the men."

"No."

He leant on the table and spoke into James's ear. "You must, Commander. The men have heard a great ruction, and even now, the rumours are spreading like gangrene. You must go above so they may see you are alive and well."

He didn't move, but replied, "I am not well." Benwick leant back and looked him in the eye. "The only reason to go on has been taken from me." There was blame in his eyes. Wentworth swallowed back his desire to refute his part in the ordeal.

"Regardless, James, your crew needs to see you upright." He couldn't keep the tinge of anger from his voice.

"You do not understand. There is no reason to continue."

Wentworth leant closer and spoke quietly. "I do understand very well. I know it is painful, but you must allow *Grappler* to become your new love. She will save you now, when no others can." His full faith in this sentiment was unmistakable.

"I cannot." The words were barely a whisper.

"You must," was the equally quiet reply.

They looked at one another for what seemed to be ages, each man measuring the devastation of his own heart. Commander Benwick rose of his own accord. Wentworth dipped a cloth in the pitcher of drinking water, wrung it, and tossed it to James. "Wipe your face," he ordered. Finding their hats, he handed Benwick his and said, "You needn't speak. I shall put the fear of God in them, and no one will dare examine either of us too closely. Just stay behind me."

A knock at the door startled them. "That will be your excellent Mr. Furlong, telling me the men are ready." He looked at Benwick. He'd gotten his hat on straight and was examining his bandaged hand. Pulling his coat and cuffs straight, he reseated his own hat and said, "Let us go up, Commander Benwick," and walked to the door.

The inspection was indeed scrupulous and one which the crew would not soon forget. Afterwards, the Captain dismissed all those not on watch to their hammocks. The ship was nearly silent as they returned to the Great Cabin.

Benwick shed his hat and coat immediately and took up a post at the stern windows. Wentworth poured each a glass of brandy. James made no effort to take the glass. Balancing it on the ledge before him, the Captain took a seat at the now cleared table. It was his intention to sit with his friend for a short time and then row back to shore.

He closed his eyes and thanked God for a bit of cool breeze just freshening when Benwick said, "If she took ill in early June, why did Timothy not come to tell me himself? Or at least write?" He turned to Wentworth. "I was to be his brother! At the very least, our friendship would dictate he break the news himself." Grief was all over Benwick's swollen face.

Remembering Harville's wretched expression, the Captain could not allow James to be angry with their good friend who was equally grieved. "He came and told me just a few days ago, but he is not well. His leg refuses to heal, and if you could see him, you would know that Fanny's death has struck him a terrible blow as well."

Benwick's look immediately changed from the passive, blank stare to anger. "*He* was struck a blow! She was his sister! And not all that close until recently, as I have been told. Elsa is not dead. His life and future are in her and their children. He will go on through them. But I have lost everything!"

He had taken the wrong tack. Wentworth could see that now. The waters of grief were treacherous and singular for each sailing them. Charting a course with Benwick would take much care.

"You are quite right; your loss is by far the greater.

"So why you? Why should he ask *you* to bear the news?"

"As I said, he came and told me of Fanny. I saw his health was bad and insisted that I be allowed to come." He would never tell of Harville's immense relief at being so unburdened. "I knew it would destroy him and could not allow that to happen."

"Ah, yes. Of course you would know this. The Captain always knows everything that is best for those beneath him." Benwick turned away towards the window. This bitter wind was beginning to blow in a direction Wentworth did not like. It did not matter; he had done his duty by both his friends.

"At all costs, Harville must be protected. Was that what you were thinking when you came aboard today and allowed me to go on like a fool, prating and preening over my vessel of war? Did I put on a good enough show, firing off my trifling sixteen guns?"

"I never thought that—"

Benwick ignored him and continued. "And what of the dinner, Captain? Grand enough for you? I am sorry my table is not nearly as fine as yours. No silver plate awarded for bravery and devoted service to King and Country. No fine crystal or fine, gilt-edged china. Perhaps, if we are very diligent, my little crew of boys and old men will one day sacrifice themselves and get my name in the Chronicles." He turned a half-turn. "It must have been quite amusing for you to sit and watch me make an ass of myself, knowing all the while that you would—"

"No." He pounded the table and made the glass of brandy splash. "It was not like that James." He rose to his feet and glared. "And I will not allow you to make me out—" Benwick's face was nothing but anger and bitterness. It was clear the recriminations were rabid bile flowing out of shock and grief and deep hurt. There was no sanity in the room on either of their parts. To be offended by the agony of his friend was to be without compassion; to be wounded by James's accusations was ridiculous. There would be time enough to mend this breech and, at present, to be the target and whipping boy was as much a part of the burden as had been the task of giving the evil news.

"I am sorry. This is a task that I am little familiar with. It was my intention to deliver the news with as little torment as possible. I swear, I did not play you. I intended to row straight out here last night, but you were at the Crown and...indisposed. When I arrived onboard this afternoon, you offered so many diversions, and I was reluctant to ruin the day by delivering such wretched news." He leant on the back of the chair for support. "To be honest, my friend, I am a coward. You offered me so many ways out, and a coward always runs and hides when given the chance." There was only the rocking of the ship as they looked at one another. "Please forgive me if, in any way, I have made this worse on you."

Benwick did not reply to this. "As we were returning home, I could feel the miles churning beneath us. I would stand here at night and look at the water. It is as if the sea were black silk." His face brightened. "I have heard tell of rich men who sleep on silk sheets. Imagine that! Such luxury. Decadence, some would say." He turned to the window. "There were nights I could do nothing but think of Fanny. I wanted nothing but to have her here. I craved her and wanted her in every way." He leant against the frame of the window. "To have her here, in my room where I am the master of everything... I suppose God would not abide my corrupt thoughts."

"She was to be your wife. You loved her. It was natural to desire her."

Benwick glanced at him and then back to the water. "It would be wonderful to lie on that silken sea. To rest one's head and just sink slowly away."

His voice was undisturbed, as if he'd just made an observation about the freshening breeze or the need for another drink. Benwick was calm, and the comment contained nothing that should cause the Captain's stomach to tighten. But it did. It would be a frighteningly simple matter for James to slip out one of the windows and never be seen again. Only a fool would engage him with such a suspicion, if it was not there already. To speak of it would be to plant the idea. There was nothing to be said, only things to do.

He quietly walked to the door. To the marine on watch, he said, "Send word for Mr. Furlong." He closed the door and studied James. In an instant, he was back on the *Asp*, his first night of his first command. He, too, had been standing in his shirtsleeves, looking out the stern windows. His thoughts then had not been of self-murder but of white-hot rage from his recent rejection. An army could not have forced him out the stern windows. It was that night he vowed to make himself rich. Money would open every door that birth and lack of connections held shut. Yes, he could well understand the grievous loss Benwick felt, but he could not for the life of him comprehend the desire to die. If for no other reason, James should live so as not to bring shame on his family.

A knock at the door brought him out of his abstraction. "Come," he called.

"Sir, you sent for me?" The young man was bleary eyed and his coat buttoned crookedly.

"Yes, Furlong. Send down your carpenter and have him place a couple of hooks, then find a hammock and have it slung for me. I shall be sleeping in here tonight."

He looked surprised and Wentworth could see he ached to ask any number of questions. He had the presence of mind to ask only one, "The Commander is here," he said, "shall I tell Chips to put you over there?" He pointed at the far wall.

"No, place me before the stern windows."

Again, Furlong looked surprised. "Directly in front of the windows, sir?"

"Yes. I want to be in the way of anything that might make use of them." He looked closely at the lieutenant. Furlong looked over at his captain. "Such as a breeze," Wentworth said in conclusion.

"Aye, sir. I'll see that you're in the way of anything that moves."

Wentworth felt something of a traitor to his friend, but he needed to enlist an ally in keeping Benwick safe. Betrayal aside, it was time the young man learnt that loyalty to your superiors, at times, required nothing more than silent obedience.

Furlong touched his forehead and disappeared.

He also called for James's steward. The room was crowded as the hammock went up and the commander dressed for bed. He watched carefully, seeing that the crush did not set Benwick off again. When everyone was gone and Benwick tucked in, he finally relaxed a bit.

Settling into the hammock, he rested his arm over his eyes. All in all it was a horrific day. He had managed to destroy all hope for his close friend's future. He had demolished his own peace concerning his past. And now, it looked as though the last casualty of the day would be *another* good night's sleep.

Chapter Five

The Captain leant against the mast and watched his friend from the sloop's small fighting top. Benwick did little but stand in the stern and study the water. The crew went out of their way to work around him as they painted, scraped, polished and titivated. Benwick did no more than acknowledge their obediences as they went about their duties. Occasionally an officer would approach, but all conversation looked to be on the other's side. Wentworth reckoned getting Benwick above deck was the best for which he could hope. The shock over Fanny's death was still fresh and the grief was settling securely about James's shoulders. Other than forcing an appearance for the sake of the crew, they did little but sit in the Great Cabin. Benwick pretended to read one of his books while the Captain read dated copies of *The Naval Chronicle* and lost himself in *The Naval Gazetteer, or Seaman's Complete Guide Containing a Full and Accurate Account, Alphabetically Arranged, of the Several Coasts of All the Countries in the Known World.* Reading the name alone occupied a goodly amount of time, for which Wentworth was grateful.

The daily climb to the tops was his only exercise. Even here, he was little more than a gaoler. Though he carried his glass with him, and opened it, most of his time was spent watching James. When Benwick would occasionally glance up his way, he hurriedly raised the glass and began a feigned study of something in another direction, hoping that James would not realize he was being observed. Perhaps he was wrong, thinking Benwick so wickedly vulnerable to grief, but he could neither risk personally losing a good friend, nor a valuable colleague. He knew not when, but he would know when James was on the road to recovery.

Turning to look over the sound, he decided to stop fretting and enjoy what little privacy the tops afforded him. The Isle of Wight looked further away than usual through the heat-induced haze. The sound was so jammed with ships that hardly anything moved. Now and then, a mail packet made its way out, but the only other traffic was small boats going from ship to ship buying slush from the cooks or selling fresh vegetables, fish, or women. It was his wish that if so many were to be thrown ashore it would be done soon. These crowded conditions would accomplish nothing but breed boredom and discontent and cause tempers to flare in the heat. He shut out thoughts of his own *Laconia* in the same condition under the hand of the relatively green Lieutenant Cranmer.

"It is a scandal," he breathed. During the war, most men longed for peace. Now that it was here, all he could feel was dread.

Earlier in the day, he cajoled Benwick into accepting an invitation to dine onshore that afternoon. Though it would be a struggle for James, he looked forward to leaving the tight confinement of the ship. Beating back Benwick's objections had taken a great deal of patience and skill. Nevertheless, it was Wentworth's hope that, in the company of others, the Commander might have a respite from his vigil of mourning. He also hoped for news—truth or rumour, he cared not which. Either would give him a more hopeful outlook for the future. Reluctantly, he ground out the cheroot he smoked and put the butt end in his pocket. His few moments of freedom were over and it was time to go down.

Taking one last look over the sound, he saw a small boat making its way through the traffic. The figure in the stern looked familiar. He closed his glass and said, "Well, I'll be...Mr. Eyerly. You are a sight for these sore, sore eyes." His first feelings were joy at seeing his own coxswain. His second was trepidation at the news the man might bear. Carefully securing the glass in his pocket, he went down the shrouds.

Eyerly haloo'd, acknowledged the Officer of the Watch and requested permission to come aboard.

"Ahoy, Captain."

"Mr. Eyerly. I hope your presence is a harbinger of good news and not ill."

"That must be for you to decide, sir." He tossed up the rope to the boat and in no time was up the accommodation ladder. Taking a brown paper packet from beneath his shirt, he handed it to the Captain and said, "Your mail, sir."

Turning the packet in his hand, Wentworth said, "There's not so much to justify a trip from Plymouth to Portsmouth."

"No, sir, but Lieutenant Cranmer was a bit itchy about a couple of them."

He broke the seal and pulled out four letters. The smallest was from his prize agent in Plymouth. By his calculations, there should only be three captures making their way through the prize courts. The number was small, but they were substantial in what they would bring him in capital. After those were sold and the proceeds dispersed, there would be no more prize money coming to him. With *Laconia* in ordinary, even his monthly pay would be reduced by half.

His stomach tightened. Being thrown ashore was expensive and though he was more than solvent now, he knew from bitter experience that it did not take long to whittle down a decently sized pile to nearly nothing. He had done it in the past, but age and caution had done their work; and he was far less prone to squander the fruits of his difficult labours. However, there was another difference between the present and the past: when coming ashore in the year '06, he had known without a doubt that he would soon command a ship. Even as the *Asp* was giving up the ghost in Plymouth Sound, he knew he would have a better ship and even greater reward. It was a feeling in his gut, an absolute conviction. There was no such feeling now.

Folding the first letter, he shuffled to the second. It was a letter from his brother, Edward. It was only one sheet, and for this he was grateful. One sheet describing the daily life of a country rector was more than adequate. The third letter was from Sophia. At first blush, one would think it was an official communiqué from her husband, Admiral Croft. The name on the Taunton address was his, as was the seal. However, to Wentworth's knowledge, Croft had not written a personal letter in all his married life. An officer of the Navy wrote reports, dispatches, and the occasional set of orders. Letters were a woman's providence in the Admiral's opinion, and any communications with the Crofts came from the hand of his sister.

The last letter was from the Admiral of the Port of Plymouth. He wondered if this might the written confirmation of the end.

"A notice went up several days ago they's convening for Courts Martial in a fortnight or so. They figure that as long as they got so many captains kicking their heels, they'll empty out the brigs and give the sods some justice. That's most likely what this is about, sir."

"Ah, a judicious use of time."

"Aye, sir."

He filed through the letters again.

"By the way, the lieutenant was pretty concerned about the letter from Admiral Croft. I didn't bother tellin' it probably weren't urgent. I figure it's most likely Mrs. Croft usin' the Admiral's seal to keep it from goin' astray when they've gotten in country."

Eyerly's presence was a comfort. However, his statement led to an interesting notion. "It occurs to me Mr. Eyerly, that you and I have been together so long that perhaps you are a bit too familiar with my family and their…practices than is proper."

Without hesitation, Eyerly said, "Undoubtedly, Captain. Too familiar by half." The man nodded at Wentworth as he spoke. His face was a picture in studied openness.

He hated to think how long Eyerly had been with him, going from being a waister on the *Asp* to his coxswain on the *Laconia*. As men, they had seen one another through the best and the worst that life on the sea could offer. For the first time since receiving the news of *Laconia*'s fate, he was beginning to see the future without his ship, his crew, and his purpose in life.

"So, is there any news concerning our girl? Any word about a date for her to go down?"

"No sir. You know how those brutes are, all sixes and sevens. One day it's one thing, and another day it's somethin' else. Then it's nothin' at all. We're back at nothin'. So, we wait and watch all the traffic comin' in the Sound, but little goin' out."

"Same here. The Solent looks like High Street on market day.

Eyerly looked around *Grappler*. "She's a right nice little ship. Though, she's no frigate, mind you."

"No, she's not, but she is a sweet little sailer."

"Not like poor ol' *Asp*."

"No, not like her at all. Speaking of the past, Commander Benwick is just over there, if you would care to pay your compliments."

"I think I will, sir." He walked to the stern, touched his forelock and spoke to Benwick. Wentworth was heartened to see a slight smile come to Benwick's lips. He even extended a hand to Eyerly. It was reasonable that he should make such an effort for someone whose only association was a distant past not connected to Fanny.

Breaking the seal on Edward's letter, Wentworth determined to start with the lightest fare and work his way to the weightier letter from the Port Admiral.

> Frederick, I hope this finds you in health. Things here are
> well. Spring is being coy this year, so we are enduring cold
> and snow even into April. However, that is not so interesting
> to you, I suppose. I do have a bit of news that might be more
> so. Because of this, I am hoping you will come to Shropshire
> when next you are ashore. Surely the *Laconia* and the war can
> be left for a time.

"A new pew for the mayor or some such thing, no doubt," Wentworth muttered. It was obvious the letter was written before the Peace. Edward had never been much for keeping up on the war. Moreover, being in the country, his disinterest put him even further behind the times. Glancing at Benwick and Eyerly, he noted they were still engaged in what seemed to be a friendly conversation. It struck him as odd that someone whom he knew only slightly could engage James. Since telling him the tragic news, they had barely exchanged ten words. Familiarity had bred a certain contempt it would seem.

> Normally I would not be so anxious for you to come, but I
> have done something I never thought I would. I have taken a
> wife....

"So much for pews," he said quietly.

Edward married! For himself, marriage was a forgone conclusion. Regardless of his previous failure, he knew he would have a wife one day, but never Edward. The man was nearly fifty and, as he possessed nothing even approaching a fortune, was hardly an attractive catch for any woman not completely destitute. Perhaps he was marrying for his old age. No one could blame him for taking a wife with a strong back to see him through to the end.

Wentworth felt ashamed at the thought. His brother was not the sort of man who would use the vows of marriage as an indenture. After all, twenty years earlier, Edward had returned to England to care for Sophia and him. His brother, more than most men, understood the cost of freedom.

Twenty years ago, in this very month of August, Frederick had been a boy of only twelve and so could not remember the details of Edward's return. However, he would never forget waking to the presence of his older brother, returned from far away to rescue Sophia and him from the uncertainty left after the death of their mother.

The Wentworth family had not been a happy one. His father was a man whose anger killed the delicate feelings of his wife and found an outlet in his oldest son. When he was older, Sophia told him about Edward's leave-taking. It had come after a brutal thrashing over some work undone in the warehouse his father owned. At sixteen, Edward slipped aboard a ship, which was easy to do in Liverpool, and disappeared. This had lessened the old man's tendency to brutalise the nearest person when things did not go his way, but it did nothing to slacken his vicious tongue. The abuse was decidedly aimed at his mother and occasionally at Sophia, but rarely at himself. His memories of his father were of indifference and the rare pat on the head or sitting on his lap. Nothing more.

There had been no real constancy in his growing up until Edward returned. Though he was only under his brother's direct care for a couple of years, he thought of Edward in a fatherly way. Distant, but fatherly.

And it was in the way of sons and fathers that eight years previous, on one of the hottest August days in memory, he and Edward had quarrelled about his growing interest in Anne Elliot.

Determined to banish thoughts of that summer and Anne, he folded his brother's letter, putting off the details of newly married bliss in favour of his sister and the Admiral's return to the country.

> "Dear Frederick, We have returned from the Indies and miss it already. The farewells were touching and the trip uneventful. We are now back in England and determined to look for property in the country. George is of the mind that we should lease until I am sure I like the more sedate way of country life. We Wentworths being city bred, he prefers to be cautious and not sink a great deal of money into a place I may grow to despise. I have assured him that I will like the country, but you know how he can be. We are in Taunton for the Quarter Sessions and have made inquiries about properties further south. Somerset is a beautiful place and I am certain..."

"Somerset." At every turn there was mentioned people and places he would rather forget. This letter, too, he folded and put away.

The letter from the Port Admiral was indeed about the courts martial. He was being informed that if any in his brig were in need of justice above a flogging or minimal punishment, his clerk was to write up a notice and bring it to the admiral's clerk for scheduling. The letter also notified those captains with no one in need of a hearing that they should prepare to be convened in a fortnight.

Wentworth had no desire to return to Plymouth under such circumstances, but he was grateful the official summons would bring a conveniently timed end to his misbegotten errand of mercy. He folded the letter and thought how justice was an odd business. He had once sat a board hearing the murder of one seaman by the hand of another. To hear tell of a murder was shocking, but it could be spoken of in a dispassionate way, almost as a tale told round the fire. However, to hear all the particulars from those who saw the blows and heard the cries made the crime very real—uncomfortably so.

Having placed the letters safely in his pocket, he joined Eyerly and Benwick. They bid one another good-bye and Wentworth walked to the waist with the coxswain.

"Will we be seein' ya soon, sir?" He stepped down the ladder a step.

"I think it will be soon. I am not needed here as urgently as before."

Eyerly glanced at Benwick and nodded. "Aye, his spirits seem to be risin.' There'll be another lady along soon enough."

He had told no one on *Laconia* of Benwick's loss. "You continue to astonish me, Eyerly."

"It's the scuttlebutt, sir, the most notorious source of intelligence known to man." He touched his forelock and descended into the boat.

Benwick joined him watching the boat become part of the hubbub of the harbour. "I have decided to forgo the dinner tonight."

Wentworth continued to watch the boats. "I would beg you to go with me. These are perilous times for a captain, James. Like it or not, you must keep your ear to the ground and keep abreast of the news."

"You can keep me apprised of all the news."

"I suppose I could, but I will not always be here. Moreover, you must realize there are officers who will speak freely to you who will have nothing to say to me. These epaulettes can be as much of a disadvantage as an advantage."

"Will Danforth be present?"

"Aye, as far as I know."

"The poor unfortunate fool is usually amusing," Benwick said. He could feel him move away. "I shall go down and prepare." His voice was pure resolve, no anticipation to speak of. Nevertheless, he was moving under his own power, and there had been no having to wheedle him to change his mind. It was heartening to Wentworth. He would be forced to leave soon and was relieved that Benwick might truly be on the mend.

Six were invited for dinner, but before the meal was begun, several others joined them and the party was moved to a larger private room. It was only a bit larger with just enough room to allow the keep to attend to the table but none for milling about by the patrons. The forced inactivity allowed Commander Danforth to quicken the usual pace of his drinking. The man was in his cups and quite amusing by the fish course.

Wentworth took part in one or two conversations but had taken care to put himself out of the way by posting in a corner. From this vantage, he was better able to observe Benwick, who had taken the one opposite. The meal progressed and at the end, he hoisted his glass and drank to the king. It pained him to see his friend's expression when the glasses were then raised to wives and sweethearts.

As the bumpers of port and walnuts made their way around the table, the course of the conversation turned to Napoleon. The group divided the tablecloth into various bodies of water, representing various parts of the world. They availed themselves of cutlery, saltcellars, nutshells and bits of bread to re-fight innumerable battles.

This behaviour was not unusual for a naval gathering. The keeper of a drinking establishment near a port was accustomed to glasses broken and silver bent in the heat of re-enacted or invented battle. Moreover, in such times as these, it was not so unusual a diversion to ward off the apprehension of being thrown ashore. It was a comfort that, with each battle, every captain and commander became more skilled, more brilliant, and quicker to subdue his foe. Wentworth applied himself to his port and considered how much life and property such imagined speed would have spared. He considering as well how much wealth he would *not* have gained were wars so swiftly ended.

The afternoon became evening and the room grew more crowded as one would leave and another two would enter the snug. Thinking it time to take his friend back to the ship, he changed his mind when he found Benwick engaged in conversation with a Lieutenant Moon. If Wentworth was not mistaken, Moon had also lost a wife recently. Perhaps there were words of solace and experience passing between the two–

"Wentworth, don't be coy; only you can adjudicate this matter between Beresford and me."

Putting Benwick and his troubles aside and focusing his attention on his tablemates, he looked from one to the other. Both men were bright with wine and good-natured debate. Knowing Captain Beresford well and Commander Paul by reputation, he knew the controversy would involve either dogs or guns or, God forbid, the fairer sex.

"We are divided, Wentworth. Paul here says you hate women. I say you are merely afraid of them. Which of us is right?" The two men giggled as he imagined young girls might when they were being deliberately naughty.

For a moment, he contemplated telling them God's truth on the matter. However, they were too drunk and he was feeling too low to revisit the past.

"Gentleman, this is a question that has been debated by finer minds than yours, and still there is no understanding." The men laughed too loudly and Beresford punched Paul, causing him to totter in his seat. "But I think you would be better served applying to Danforth. Perhaps this is the night you all will solve this perplexing conundrum." They laughed again as he rose and left the room.

Settling on a crate around the side of the inn, he watched the fragrant cloud of the cheroot float away and wondered what there was about his romantic attachments or, more precisely, the lack of them which fascinated Beresford. The man was like a dog worrying a bone. He was married, though unhappily, if one believed the rumours. So perhaps it was just his wish that everyone would share in his misery.

Wentworth dropped the cheroot and ground it out. There was no understanding the perplexing nature of humankind.

This thought brought him to Edward's sudden defection from the unmarried state. He was astonished and dismayed. Edward's determination to remain unwed was something Wentworth had been certain would never change. However, it was no different from his certain knowledge of always having a ship under him, a rock solid belief that was crumbling all too quickly.

He moved closer to the lamp outside the doorway of the inn and read the letter fully. The new Mrs. Wentworth was born Catherine Keye and was from a large and prosperous family in Glencoe Parish, the next one over. She had taken the liberty of writing a post script which led him to think she was sensible and good humoured Her invitation to come to stay with them at the rectory of Crown Hill Parish was warm and genuine. There was little to indicate how old a woman she might be. Not that he should concern himself with such things. Circumstances were working furiously to make their meeting sooner than later a certainty.

He was being petty he knew, feeling nettled that Edward seemed happy. He decided it had more to do with the fact that he had ignored his brother's advice concerning Anne and the engagement and that he could have been happy years ago rather than alone and–

"Enjoying a word from home?"

He started. Benwick apologized. "You interrupted nothing," he said, folding the paper and tucking it in his pocket. "Just a word from my brother, Edward."

"How is the Rector? Still in the country?"

"Yes. Shropshire now." His friend had never met his brother, but Benwick's father was a religious man and he knew something of the life and its ways. "He has married. I am surprised." It occurred to him that Benwick was not the one to tell about a new marriage.

There was no smile, but Benwick raised his brows, nodded and said a genuine, "I wish him joy." He walked away slowly. Wentworth followed at a distance. They were not moving towards the docks, and he wondered if he should leave him to think his own thoughts.

"I spoke at length with Lieutenant Moon this evening. His wife died of a putrid fever early in the spring. There was nothing to be done. It was a terrible suffering for him and the family." He rested against a cart loaded with empty barrels.

Wentworth chose a short stack of crates and took a seat. "That must have been an agony for them."

"It made me grateful that Fanny was spared such a fate."

Wentworth looked at his friend. There was still something of the morose about him, but there was also an air of normality. As if the real world was beginning to take hold again.

"I hope the conversation was useful to you, James—that Moon was able to offer you some comfort."

Benwick turned. "Oh, he did. His counsel was most welcome. His best bit of advice was that I should, as far as possible, get on with my life. He said I would never forget her, but that I must go on."

"He sounds quite wise. Are you not glad I coerced you into having dinner tonight?"

"I am, sir. Moreover, I am determined to take Moon's advice." He looked quickly at him, then away.

"I have tried to reconcile myself to the fact that Harville was not able to come and bring the news himself." He paused and looked at Wentworth. "I know it is a ridiculous point, that I am meditating on the insignificant, but I cannot get it out of my head that he should have come. Then when I think of you telling me, it all becomes a rush of feelings that I am unable to keep in check."

"That must be terribly difficult." He knew Benwick was not finished, but he was uncertain as to what he might be leading up to.

"This being the case, I think it would be best that you should leave as soon as can be arranged."

He was neither shocked nor saddened by this statement. His only concern was the condition of their friendship.

"*Grappler* is so small, and it is impossible for either of us to escape the other." His expression showed he thought himself unkind. "Captain, it is like being in a storm and falling into the trough of a huge wave every moment. I don't want you to think—"

"Benwick," he said a little sharply. "I understand. Would you rather I stay ashore tonight?"

"No, certainly not."

"Then I shall make arrangements to leave in the morning." He started to the door of the inn to see about transport.

Benwick hurried to his side and took hold of his arm. "Please know that I am grateful to you for all you have done…staying with me through this. I would not have survived otherwise."

"There is nothing that needs saying about this." His frame of mind was not such that he cared to call up these fears.

"I shall overcome this and everything between us shall be right, Captain. This is just something I must do alone."

He looked at his friend and knew he was correct. It was becoming more evident to him, moment by moment, that all difficulties in life are truly borne alone.

Chapter Six

It took a month of false starts to move *Laconia* from the side of the
ledger declaring her fit for duty to the side that made her a
prisoner of the Plymouth shipwrights. Wentworth rose each day
dreading word from the Port Admiral. He was almost glad when
it came, not in a letter, but in the form of a little man surrounded by red-
coated marines carrying the sealed box containing the money to pay off
the crew. The ensuing chaos was a relief. Once a man received his pay,
he would hare off below, gather his few possessions, and do whatever
was necessary to place himself on one of the three small boats running
back and forth between *Laconia* and shore. Wentworth's last night on
board was quiet; only the superior and warrant officers remained, along
with Eyerly and some of his handpicked mates. The next morning he
turned her over to a crew of lubbers who would determine her fate.

He was now installed in Mrs. Bale's boarding house. Mrs. Bale was a
quiet woman with an odd assortment of relatives who depended upon
her biddable nature and open door. Her rooms were clean and the
house was off the beaten path and quiet for the most part. However, he
was not certain whether they would remain so this particular evening.

"Thank you ever so much, sir, for not cuttin' up Jack as much as I'm
fearin' you might have liked."

He looked at Mrs. Bale's pallid face in the mirror of his shaving
stand. The entire situation was his own damn fault, though he never
thought giving her young nephew an opportunity to hone his skills as a
manservant would leave him in such an absurd predicament.

"I know ya only wanted ya hair trimmed up a bit; it was certainly
needin' it; but he got holt of an old pair of scissors I shoulda throw'd
out, and they's not sharp, ya see. Had he'd'a asked, I'd'a give 'im my
good barberin' shears, ya see."

Her mangled statement seemed to accuse *him* for his growing hair,
the dull scissors, *and* her nephew's propensity to take things without

69

asking.' Perhaps it *was* entirely his fault. It was only right that this, his last official day of duty to the Crown, should be marked by calamity. However, must it be one of such a ridiculous nature? Thank God he insisted the boy cover his uniform before proceeding to cut his hair!

On the few occasions a stay off-ship had been required, Wentworth had always been able to find a room with Mrs. Bale. She liked him and, without exception, complimented his manners and his tidy ways. He was certain she also appreciated the extra shillings he was careful to leave on the dresser when he departed. By way of polite conversation, he had been told endlessly of her nephew, Jack, a young man of brilliant potential if the lady was to be believed. There had never been an opportunity for them to meet until earlier that week. Unclenching his jaw, he made a mental note to forgo the shillings.

"It's good that these sorts of difficulties are worked out before Jack goes out and finds hisself a position with a *real* gentleman."

Wentworth turned, and looked eye-to-eye with Mrs. Bale. Was he not a "real gentleman?" His behaviour to this point was most gentlemanly, considering that he desired nothing better than to flog her dear Jack, the aspiring gentleman's gentleman, within an inch of his wicked life. Mrs. Bale's simple brown eyes kept him from launching into the greatly desired tirade.

"I merely said what I felt needed saying under the circumstances." He turned and rose, beginning to unbutton his dress coat. *I should have known better. I was practically out the door. What ever possessed me to be manoeuvred into this wretched scheme?*

Wentworth was a soft touch for a young man trying to improve himself so that he might make his way in the world. As a man of experience, part of him was loath to admit his share of crack-brained blunders. He had come to understand that mistakes were only useful in what they taught. While errors could not be avoided, the challenge was to only make small ones that left no one harmed. The only thing worse, in his mind, than committing a blunder, was to repeat it. He feared that Jack hadn't the brain for either of these lessons.

Resigning himself to the situation, he said, "Please, Mrs. Bale, go down and get your barbering tools." Her face brightened, and with a whoosh of skirts, she was out of the room.

He sat before the shaving stand to await her return and strove to adopt a philosophical turn of mind. As his career was ending, he could see an eerie sort of harmony in this whole bizarre business. His posting to the *Laconia* had been the event that shifted his youthful ideals concerning himself, love, and his career. It was the point in time he last seriously gave thought to Anne Elliot and how she had played him for a fool. He had marked the event by rekindling his dedication to becoming successful...and wealthy.

Stepping into the command of *Laconia* was an accomplishment of which Frederick Wentworth could be rightly proud. His elevation had been preceded by the capture of a French frigate he'd longed to engage. After taking her into Plymouth, the *Asp* had dropped anchor in the Sound and been promptly battered by a four-day blow until she sank. The naval proceeding following the sinking of the *Asp* cleared him of any carelessness, or wrongdoing. He had, in fact, been commended for keeping the whole of his crew alive when, after two days of the hellish blow, he had been obliged to order his men to risk their lives to dismast her. Afterward, the Admiral of Plymouth had installed him as the captain of HMS *Laconia*, and he made the momentous shift of the epaulette from the left shoulder to the right. Only personal happiness could have added more joy to the greatest accomplishment of his career.

Wentworth stood and walked to the window. The weather outside was dry, and a soft breeze blew through the lacy curtains. It was impossible not to notice a number of couples making their various ways on the streets and sidewalks. "Where is Mrs. Bale?" he said aloud. *Probably comforting dear Jack with the news that I will not flay him tonight.* The laugh of a woman echoed over the street.

~ ~ ~ ~ ~ ~ ~ & ~ ~ ~ ~ ~ ~ ~

After the celebrations of his promotion and new command were finished, he noticed much of the sting of the past was gone. The events of the summer of '06 were still fresh and vivid, but the bitterness and the anger they once produced had eased. Several times he had taken pen in hand with the intention of writing to Anne Elliot. However, he found he had had little to say that wasn't accusatory towards her or her family, and his own desires were not precisely formed. He had put the pen away and, again, thrown himself into his career. He hired a genuine steward, had new uniforms made, began building a reputation as a captain with one of the finest tables in the fleet, and set about keeping himself and his crew employed relentlessly in seeking prize. For six years, there had been no time to consider his appearance. When an occasion requiring him to be decent presented itself, he put full faith in the capable hands of Michaelson. And all told, this had worked well while at sea. But now, everything was changing. Anne Elliot's ghost seemed to be everywhere he looked, his career was in the doldrums, and it would seem that he was not even capable of keeping himself properly rigged without getting into a ridiculous scrape. The door opened, and Mrs. Bale entered the room, taking care to immediately comfort him with the statement that she rarely bloodied or maimed any of her regular patrons.

"This won't take more than two shakes, sir. Don't you just see if it don't." The scissors took their first cut and a large wad of hair fell down the frills of his evening shirt.

~ ~ ~ ~ ~ ~ ~ & ~ ~ ~ ~ ~ ~ ~

Again the evening's breeze annoyed him by caressing his bare neck. His collar stood high, but gave little comfort. He determined to buy a scarf against the colder months ahead. Wearing a scarf like a little old man would insure that he never forget this day's events. As he approached the Guild Hall the sound of music grew louder, spilling out of open windows. This meant the place was already a crush.

Do the polite and get out before it's too late. The Admiral of the Port was sponsoring the party as a celebration of the ending of the war. And, he could not help thinking when he opened his invitation, the end of so many careers. Nodding to several fellow officers as he made his way in, he chided himself for being in such a disagreeable frame of mind. After making an inventory of his grievances, he left off, determined to keep to himself for as long as he was in a position to inflict his mood upon the others. Within minutes a man took his coat and another saw that he had a glass of wine. The atmosphere was gay and loud. It seemed there was a tinge of hilarity, almost hysteria, which was not generally present at such a gathering. He was not the only one sensing the changes in the wind.

"Well, it is about time you joined the rest of civilized mankind!" A voice from behind and a hand clapping him on the shoulder startled him. Turning, he faced Gilmore Craig. "You have finally decided that being in fashion is not a sin, eh, Captain?"

Wentworth frowned a moment, then understood of what his friend spoke.

"Ah, yes, well," he absently brushed at the newly exposed skin of his neck and cringed. Craig was rosy with wine and Wentworth had little appetite for derision.

Gilmore leant and looked him over, one side to the other. "Well, I must say, it is a bit short, but that is the miracle of hair is it not?"

"How so?"

"Well, one may groan over a bad haircut, but given a fortnight, there is no reason left, for it is all *grown* out." He smiled at his pun and giggled a bit as he took a drink of his wine.

Wentworth forced a smile. It was to be one of those nights. Craig's tongue was loose enough to make him think such a play upon words funny, and that meant he would not guard himself in the least. Without thinking, he reached up again and touched his freshly shorn neck. *So this is the fashion.* His hard feelings towards dear Jack were not assuaged.

Taking a drink, Craig looked over the crowd. "Everyone seems to be quite lively. The last hurrahs, as it were."

"To be sure. I have no scruple in thinking that most are smiling through the agony."

"Ah, I must ask, how was that last case on the docket settled? Some fellows at the warehouse are interested."

The docket was the courts martial board, and Wentworth suspected Craig and his fellows had monetary interests rather than those of justice. "And why would that be? It was merely a case of self defence."

Craig frowned. "I thought it was unquestionably murder. Letters from the unfaithful wife to the lover and then the cuckold flattened with a belaying pin. Hardly sounds like self defence." His eyes were wide with certainty as he exchanged his empty glass for a full one from a passing tray.

The courts martial had been an endless affair that seemed to create its own set of difficulties rather than solve those presented to it. Just as one affair would be laid to rest and the officers bound to the court close to dismissal, another set of unfortunates would be hauled before them and another set of pitiful stories would unfold. The six officers sitting in judgment were all acquainted and on good terms. This was fortunate, as they saw more of one another than they could have anticipated.

The Admiralty Secretary warned that there might be more cases found as new ships came in port and officers took the opportunity to rid themselves of dead weight in their brigs. This would necessitate lengthening their commitment. They christened the secretary a prophet when the second week began. By the third week, they cursed him as the Magistrate of the Devil Himself and were more serious than not about jumping ship rather than sit the last round of cases.

The final case was one of the worst. A carpenter on the sloop *Reliant* and the ship's purser hailed from the same town near Manchester. They were mates from previous cruises and on good terms. When it was discovered that a bit of criminal conversation had taken place between the carpenter's wife and the purser, a fight had broken out and the carpenter was killed.

When the evidence was presented, the purser was portrayed as a vicious man, bent on ridding himself and his married lover of their mutual impediment. However, witnesses to the fatal fight told a story of the carpenter enraged, embarrassed, and bent on doing the purser a permanent injury. The brawl took place outside the purser's locker, and a lucky blow with a prying tool used to open casks of beef felled the carpenter. The purser was eventually judged to be not guilty of murder and acquitted of the charges; but all knew him to be guilty of another sort of crime.

After explaining the finer points to Craig, Wentworth concluded, "So the purser will not swing. How much did you lose on it?"

Looking disappointed, Craig replied, "Enough! I should have known better. I just returned from London and had not enough time to cast about for good intelligence concerning the matter."

Wentworth emptied his glass. "All I can say is I am happy the thing is over. The Captain of the Fleet discharged us and that is that."

"So when did *Laconia* go into ordinary?"

"Nearly a month ago. The wrights sat on their haunches and dragged us pillar to post as to when they would take her. I finally knew when the Admiral's clerk appeared with the money for the pay-off."

"That's cutting it fine."

"It surely was. They were paying off one watch while the other was rowing their dunnage ashore." Paying off after a fine cruise was a bitter-sweet event, and this being the end of *Laconia*'s career, and perhaps his own, it was even more so.

"So what of the half-wit giant case? I still have a place for him if he's not being used as bear bait somewhere."

"No, no need. My coxswain took him to Cornwall. He's to pull a plough for an old auntie there. But I thank you." Taking a glass from another passing tray, Wentworth took a drink and continued, "Those are the ones I hate seeing off; the mind of a child residing in a giant's body, alone in the world to be abused by God knows who, only God knows how."

"There's only so much you can do for the world, Wentworth. You are a captain of the navy, not a reformer. That's your brother's line, is it not?"

He smiled. "Yes, it is."

"Well, then, leave it to the likes of him…or join him." Craig raised a brow in jest.

Wentworth shook his head, and laughed quietly. Frederick Wentworth, a parson! Such a thing would shock even the archangels.

Craig took another glass as a footman passed. "Look, we both know you will not be joining any religious communities any time soon, but I do wish that you would give more thought to my proposal."

At their first dinner, after the peace was declared, Craig had asked that he take command of his few lumbering merchantmen making their regular run to Ireland and Scotland. It was sailing at its most mundane;

only piloting a mail packet could be worse. The ships were inelegant barges, the men were infinitely worse, though the peace would put decent hands within reach. It was still a sop and though he knew he should be grateful for it, he was not.

"In fact," Craig continued, "I think I might be able to make the offer a little more tempting."

"How so?"

"While I am as patriotic as the next man, and I am glad to see that pox-ridden despot put away for good, my war has always been much larger than just dealing with the French. My bigger fights have always been with jumped-up yokels who have boats big enough and friends sober enough to take to the water with sufficient guns to scare my not-so-gallant captains. A few of my colleagues and I have talked about creating our own little cartel that would include the beginnings of a tidy private navy."

This idea intrigued him, and he encouraged Craig to continue.

"The word is that the Navy will be selling out of service several very nice little ships. It is our hope to buy a brig, perhaps even a sloop, and outfit her to shepherd our ships up north and back. With the peace, all of us are feeling the pinch, and we have to turn our attention to markets farther from home. Guns, shot, and powder take up space better dedicated to cargo; but it would leave us too vulnerable to privateers and the usual pirates hoping for easy pickings to go without them."

"A sloop you say?"

"Perhaps, if we can find one for a bargain and in good enough shape."

"Shepherding, eh?"

"Yes, I'm afraid that is all we could offer you. No letters of marque. No prizes to be had, or five pounds per head for live prisoners. Taking off on a chase would leave our wares vulnerable and defeat the purpose of the entire affair. Though, when last I talked with the gentlemen, I laid down a hint or two that it might be a fine idea if, rather than a straight commission per trip, we paid the captain a percentage of the cargo. They are mulling it over. But if I can convince them, you could pay out a bonus using that Byzantine formula the Navy favours."

It was not very tempting. He had risen above commanding a sloop. But there were no opportunities on the horizon that were in any way superior.

"Besides, you might then be able to take a few of your more deserving mates and give them employment."

Wentworth considered whom he might seek out were he to take up Craig's proposal.

Noting the hesitation, Craig continued, "Listen, there is no hurrying on this. Beezel and Hedridge are out of country until after Christmas, and I doubt anything will be done before the end of January. Take a few months and make the rounds of the family. Then, when you all are thoroughly sick of one another, you can give me a decision."

The idea of being a private captain had some appeal but not enough for him to make an immediate commitment. He decided to turn the conversation from himself to his friend. "Perhaps I will return and find you married." A dark look came over Craig. He took a drink of his wine and stood silent as he studied the crowd. For the past weeks, his friend had been away to Bristol and London, and all Wentworth knew of the romantic intrigues concerning Miss Hammond was that her uncle was still reluctant to have her marry a man in trade. The effect of his quip on Craig's countenance was profound, and though he was not precisely in the mood to enquire further, he felt obliged to offer up a sympathetic ear. "The Admiral has been gone for over a fortnight. Did he find a fitting situation for his niece?"

"Yes, it was the very situation he took her from when he brought her to live in his house. She is back with an aunt outside of town."

"Then you are able to see her frequently?"

"No, the old man was pointed that I should stay away from her." He nodded to someone across the room.

Looking over, he saw Miss Hammond return the acknowledgement.

Turning to Craig, he said, "She seems not to be abiding by her uncle's wishes."

"It would seem not. But I do not wish to bring her any grief concerning her family."

"So, how does her aunt feel?"

He frowned. "What does it matter what the aunt feels? It's the Admiral who has laid down the law."

"True, but it is not unusual for men and women to feel quite differently about matters of the heart. The Admiral is on the other side of the world. There is little consequence if his wishes go unheeded."

Craig turned from watching Miss Hammond. "I am shocked, Wentworth. Here you are, a man who depends upon strict loyalty and discipline to maintain order in life, advising me to boldly disobey. Again, I must say, I am shocked."

Taking a drink, he realised he, too, was a bit shocked. He had not realized that Gilmore Craig's affections for Miss Hammond concerned him enough that he would give any sort of opinion, much less advise his friend to disregard the old man. But as he found another glass, he determined that Craig had nothing to lose, not being beholden to the Admiral for his career or anything but an occasional dinner. Moreover, her being forced to await her uncle's approval while sitting cloistered with her aunt was, most likely, not enjoyable for Miss Hammond. Let them be together and happy was his only thought on the matter.

"I would agree that obedience to authority is vital, but genuine affection is difficult to come by. While Admiral Hammond is an admirable seaman, I think that you are far better suited to make her happy than he suspects." Wentworth's heart was pounding, and he could feel his short hair prickling with sweat. If only someone had been available to persuade him to work at his own happiness with such vigour.

The room was growing hot, and the women's voices were suddenly sharp and grating, like the close-quartered hens kept in coops on the quarterdeck. He was about to say they should step out onto one of the terraces when Craig grimaced. "Sorry, old man, but I must fly!" He disappeared in the crowd instantly.

"Captain Wentworth!" A falsetto voice penetrated the noise of the crowd, causing many to turn and stare in his direction.

"Damned coward," he said to Gilmore Craig's back.

Smoothing his lapels and tugging at his cuffs, he made himself presentable. "She can't eat you alive, Captain," he consoled himself quietly. "Her presence merely stops the passage of time." Smiling, he turned to make his bow.

"Lady Grierson. You honour me."

Her curtsey dipped a bit too low, and he offered her a hand. "Sir, the pleasure is all mine." An ivory fan snapped open, and she stood back a little, eyeing him closely. With no pretence to gracious conversation, she said, "Something has changed about your person, but I am at a loss to say precisely what it is."

Her observation was surprising, as he never thought her terribly perceptive. A cursory study of the lady showed that nothing had changed about Lady Mary. She was still a small, rosy dumpling of a woman, cinched and tucked and still threatening to burst any number of her seams. The dress tonight was Turkey red and the turban, extraordinary. The foundation of this edifice was comprised of yards of silk from which several feathers *and* a stuffed robin perched on the left side. While the elaborate headgear was highly entertaining, it was a small gold tassel, hanging just near her right eye, which truly captured his attention.

Forcing himself to look at her face rather than either side of her headdress, he answered, "Any perceived change is not for the worst, I hope."

"No, no never with you, sir." She continued to study him, but after an uncomfortable pause, moved to another topic. "I am endeavouring to recall when last we were in company. Surely, you have not forgotten how you and our fifth daughter, Emily, got on so famously." The motherly glow in her eyes made Wentworth's stomach churn.

"That would have been in February, Ma'am. In Mahon," he answered. The muscles in his face ached, but settled into a pleasant smile that gave the impression of interest. As for Emily Grierson, it had been strictly duty. Nothing resembling affection had put him in the way of Lady Mary's notice in the first place.

Admiral Sir Henry Grierson's ship had been taking on water and victuals one dirty night in Mahon Harbour. The Captain suspected it was the convergence of the facts of her husband finally arriving in port and her daughters having new dresses that had furnished reason enough for Lady Mary to arrange an exclusive supper aboard the Admiral's man-of-war. Between the wind and rain, every surface had been glistening wet and treacherous. As they had proceeded up the gangway, the girl slipped, and it was Wentworth's hand that kept her from sliding into the drink. When later harassed for his gallantry by fellows just as near the clumsy girl, he had battled back by saying it was either keep her dry or wet his sleeves fishing her out.

"It is so crowded this evening. I would have thought the Admiralty would be more select. It would seem that every man with a board on his shoulder is here eating and drinking his fill."

"I suspect that many are taking the opportunity to pay homage one last time before returning to life on land." It was a lie. He knew many were eating and drinking as much as they could hold in hopes of bankrupting the Crown.

Lifting a brow, she said, "Well, that is honourable...if true." The stipulation was insightful and took him aback. Everything to do with Lady Mary was ordinarily fixed on procuring officers to serve as husbands for her seven marriageable daughters. What else was there for her to do? She had the mischance of giving birth to seven girls, and this drove the speculation that Sir Henry kept to sea out of self-preservation. The only decent thing to do was to see them all married and continuing in the occupation of naval wife. She had been heard to say, "I see my girls as the tenders that spread out all over the ports, caring for the needs of the ships that come in to be refreshed and renewed."

When he'd heard it, he'd thought that in a broad, poetic sense that might be admirable, but in a practical comparison to boats filled with the likes of slovenly jobbers, whores, and chandlers, it seemed to him to fall short of a compliment.

The tassel and feathers were bobbing wildly with the beating of her fan. The room was warming and he wanted nothing more than to wipe his brow. But appearing in uniform, he refused to be seen daubing at his face as if he were a swooning old woman. It did not keep him from fingering his sword knot.

"And your daughters are all well I pray, Lady Mary?"

Her fan closed with a snap, and though it seemed impossible, her complexion brightened even more. "They are all very well. Emily is here somewhere and would certainly accept an invitation to dance." She craned her neck, turning to spy out the girl.

Feigning examination of the crowd, he recalled Miss Emily Grierson. The unfortunate girl was reed-thin, horse-faced, and not much for conversation. His usually amusing anecdotes about life aboard a man-of-war had left her unsmiling. He had not thought of her since February.

Just then a midshipman, too drunk for so early in the evening, hurtled himself in their midst and fell laughing at their feet. In seconds another mid broke through the crowd and grabbed him up and away.

Lady Grierson fanned herself more briskly, saying, "I am sure you were not so ill-behaved as a young man."

He thought to disabuse her of such a misbegotten notion but decided it best to keep her good opinion. "And how does Sir Henry? He has returned to the country?"

She cocked her head. "No as a matter of fact, he is not. And now that you bring him into matters, I must say that I am quite put out with you." She lightly tapped his snowy white lapel and continued. "His Lordship was to bring us home from Gibraltar this spring but was ordered west, leaving my daughters and me at the mercy of a terribly graceless merchantman who offered us passage. I was very disappointed to find that you and *Laconia* had preceded us by little more than a week." She tapped him one last time. The ringing of the fan hitting a button emphasized her point. He was sorely tempted to take it from her and break it in two. Instead, he traced the seams of his glove with his thumb and continued to smile.

Finally, he said, "Ah, well, Ma'am, I must plead that time and tide are strict taskmasters, and none of us in service to the King is any better than a slave to them."

Lady Grierson thought for a moment and seemed to find no fault with his philosophical answer. "I assure you, Captain, our hearts were broken after learning that we would be deprived of your *Laconia*'s most excellent accommodations."

Wentworth clapped an even wider smile on his lips and marvelled at the lady's temerity that she would assume a welcome for herself and her gaggle of girls aboard his ship. Custom and duty aside, in the end it would have been a matter of wills and cunning. He surmised she was of strong will, but with so many daughters to see to, her cunning might have out stripped his own. Regardless, his absence had allowed him to avoid any such contest.

"It was undoubtedly our loss, Ma'am."

The fan snapped open again. It began to wave until its wind touched and cooled his brow wonderfully. "Emily," she called out into the crowd. "I see my Emily. I shall just fetch her so that you may have that dance you desire." The red, round figure began to sweep away and then turned suddenly. "It is your hair. You have cut it to be more in style. It is very appealing. Emily will be pleased."

Well, it would seem that dear Jack had landed him in the current of fashion. But he had no intention of hearing Miss Emily's opinion on the matter. Turning in the opposite direction, Wentworth made a determined trek to the supper-room.

The dining area was generously carved out of a corner using screens and tables. The food was adequate, the wines brackish, and the company only able to converse on topics of past glories or future desperation. The table was emptying of his morbid companions when Wentworth decided that Craig showed a great deal of wisdom in suggesting he visit his sister and his brother before making any decision about the future. He considered his family.

Edward was emphatic that he should come and meet the new Mrs. Wentworth. As for Sophia and the Admiral, surely they would be settled somewhere in the wilds of Somerset by now. Compared to some of his fellows, his choices began to hold some promise of enjoyment.

Scrutinizing the room, he saw nothing of Lady Grierson and so signalled for another glass of wine.

He had no sooner raised the glass to his lips when a lumpish form crashed into the seat next to him. This new seatmate stayed his arm and said, "That swill is too vile, better to have some of this." A generous silver flask was offered in the wine's place.

Wentworth recognized the flask, took it, and drank. "So what have you been up to while I dined?"

Craig took the flask back and drank before he tucked it in his pocket. "Oh, not much. I am thinking that perhaps you are right about Miss Hammond. So I introduced myself to her aunt." He tapped Wentworth's arm. "She is a good, sturdy, sensible woman. I think she likes me." He smiled like an earnest schoolboy.

"All old ladies like you, Gil. You remind them of their favourite nephew; oh-so polite but just a touch naughty."

"True. But the like of Lady Mary prizes you for the oh-so upstanding fellow you are."

Wentworth sighed. Taking a used glass, he began to wipe it clean with a napkin. "I wish the woman would find her daughters another objective. I will have no peace now that they all are back in the country." He held out the glass awaiting the flask to be withdrawn from his friend's pocket.

"No, I suppose not. But face it, Captain; you are every Marrying Mama's dream." When he finished pouring the honey-coloured liquor into Wentworth's glass, he took a drink himself. "I hear that, viewed through the female eye, you are a very pleasing sight. Add to that the fact that you are rich and destined to collect other impressive titles aside from that of 'Captain.'" Normally, he looked on Gil's pronouncements as mere silliness, but this particular evening, they seemed more ridiculous than usual.

"There is also the fact that you are the Royal Navy's model of chastity. There are no hints of false wives in foreign ports or rumours of little boys and girls tucked up in far-away places that bear the striking Wentworth countenance." Gil smiled, and thumped him hard on the back. "Face it, old thing; you are precisely the sort of fellow every father wishes his daughter to marry."

His friend's face was open and smiling. The whole rant was meant to be a wry tribute to his uprightness. Instead, the words mocked him, and he felt the weight of his dinner and the sour wine acutely.

He took a drink of Gil's tonic and began to laugh.

"What is so funny?"

"Nothing that you've said intentionally, my friend, but let me assure you that not *every* father would wish me for a son-in-law." The burning in his throat was pleasant and he put the glass down, wishing to savour the rest.

The crowded, noisy room, reeking of perfume and food and bodies faded, and he might just as well be that overexcited and lovesick lieutenant standing face-to-face with Sir Walter Elliot so many years ago.

"*I would find any alliance between the Elliots and...your people to be a degradation intolerable on my part.*"

He felt embarrassed that he could still feel so wounded by this latent memory. The worst shock had come when Anne began to parrot back the old man's objection that the match was improper from the outset. Her protestations of love for him rang as hollow in his memory as they had in her presence. Over time he had come to believe she had played him for a fool, that his attentions had been merely a diversion in the course of the boring summer and that her family's objections were a convenient excuse to be rid of him. When he walked away from her that day, dejected and angry, he had stopped his ears to her declarations of love. The most galling of her protestations was that their parting was for "his good" as much as for her own.

Reluctantly, he struggled his way back to the noise of the present. Fixing his attention on Gilmore Craig and his inanity, Wentworth forced the memories of her fatigued, tear-stained face out of his mind.

"...and certainly there are men who are no better than jackasses! But considering what you have to offer a woman, I cannot imagine any father would be that much of a problem."

"Perhaps. But I am curious. Why have you put so much thought to my *private affairs?*"

"That is simple enough. I have been travelling by post for several weeks and have found that, after speaking about the weather and the roads, all interesting conversation with fellow passengers is exhausted. There has been little choice but to sleep or put my mind to any number of diverse and amusing topics."

Wentworth downed the rest of the drink and again appreciated the gentle burning. "Gil, you amaze me. Even I do not contemplate my own life so closely."

"I have known you for many years now and have seen an interesting paradox which prompted my musings. Shall I tell you my theories?"

The Captain smiled and rubbed his hands together as he turned to face his friend with feigned enthusiasm. "By all means, I am most anxious to hear your theories."

"Well, I have noticed you are not in the least repelled by females; your eyes brighten when you are put in their company. In that, you are no different than most other men. But I have also noticed that you admire but do not pursue them. I asked myself why that might be. Normally, a man who appreciates women does everything in his power to be noticed, but not Frederick Wentworth. And why might that be?" He cocked his head and gestured as though awaiting an answer.

"Oh, no, Gil, you are the philosopher. I sit at your feet awaiting your wisdom."

"I have come to the conclusion that truly, in your heart, you are a Romantic." He pointed his finger at Wentworth and then folded his hands. A self-satisfied look spread across his face.

At the word "Romantic," the Captain bristled and could only picture Benwick's forlorn countenance.

"So, at the core of my being you think I am one of those wretched, dismal fellows who goes about badly dressed and long-faced, spouting turgid poetry? Thank you so much."

"No, no, not that sort of man, but one who believes there can be true and equal love between men and women." He could not help be touched by Gil's expression as he spoke. He had always wondered if Gilmore Craig thought of anything more than his warehouses, contracts with the navy, and his other shipping interests. Now he had his answer.

"I think you will not settle for a sham marriage of convenience, or even companionship, because you know there is something far superior. I believe you have been deeply and completely in love."

The statement was jarring in its perceptiveness. Realising he'd been listening with particular attention, he now had to force his jaw to slacken. The summation left him nearly breathless. It also left him feeling exposed and raw. He was not inclined to have his weaknesses examined so closely.

"So, if I have been, as you say, 'deeply and completely in love,' why am I not enjoying the fruits of such a love?" He struggled to make his voice and manner as unconcerned as possible.

"I thought on that for some time. As I have observed, you are not a man who will let anything stand between you and whatever you desire. That is why I think the woman is, for some reason, unobtainable." The expression on Gil's face testified to his sympathy. "I believe that she has died."

Were his feelings on gaudy display for everyone to see? Or was Gil exceptional? He did not care; all he wished was an end to the conversation. "So you think I have been mooning over a dead woman all these years?"

"Yes, because, as I said, you are the sort of man who would move heaven and earth to make her your wife–if she were obtainable."

This observation felt like an indictment. But there was nothing to obtain. Anne Elliot had wanted nothing to do with him and had made that clear at their last meeting. Clearing his throat, Wentworth said, "I have to say, my friend–"

Craig leant down and hissed, "Two points on your stern. It's Lady Grierson and not one, but two daughters. You'd best fly."

He didn't even look but stood immediately. Bowing slightly to Gil, he said, "Many thanks for the warning." He walked slowly out of the supper-room, hoping the lady's attention would not be drawn by a leisurely exit.

Manoeuvring behind Lady Mary had been easy enough. As long as he trailed in her wake, he could simply keep out of her sight. He'd followed her to an upper gallery and watched her go back down when she found no trace of him. The gallery was full, but not quite to bursting as was the rest of the hall, and he took the opportunity to take up a post beside a column, near the railing. It was here Miss Hammond joined him.

She nodded in acknowledgement but said nothing as she, too, watched the crowd below. Perhaps he could do Gil some good by striking up a conversation with her.

"Your uncle got off without a hitch, I take it?"

"Yes, he did. He was very glad to be going. He has longed for a foreign station."

"Then he should like India exceedingly."

"You have been there?"

"No, I have been to the West Indies and sailed extensively in the Western Islands."

To that point, Miss Hammond had been dividing her looks between him and the crowd below. Now she looked strictly at him, puzzled.

"The Azores," he said.

Miss Hammond's knowledge of things concerning the navy and sailing made it unusual that she would not have known the more familiar term for the islands.

"Ah yes, the Azores. I am sorry. I thought I saw someone I know downstairs."

He glanced over. "Yes, there I see Mr. Craig. He is just coming out of the supper-room."

She stepped closer and followed his pointing finger. "Yes, I see him." There was no attempt to acknowledge his friend.

Just then, Lady Mary stepped into view. Hastily turning, he found himself so close to Miss Hammond that he could smell her scent. It was roses, sweet but not cloying. She laughed, though she continued to watch the floor below. Turning her attention to Wentworth, she asked, "Will you be going back to sea soon, Captain?"

He backed away a step but met with the wretched column. "Uh, no. My ship has been laid up in ordinary, and I am planning to visit my brother and sister for a time."

"Well, that is probably best." She again glanced over the railing. "The weather has been a bit cool, has it not?" Flipping open her fan, she continued to smile while dividing her attentions.

"The weather has been good. But September is usually mild along the coast."

Without a word, Miss Hammond turned away from him and made a very pointed acknowledgement to someone downstairs. He leant over and saw Craig waving at them.

Quickly she turned back and laughed a bit loudly as she asked where he was to travel when visiting his mother. He began to think Miss Hammond had drunk too much wine. Her bright pink complexion and inattention to the conversation was worrisome. He was about to suggest they go down, collect Craig, and find some coffee when someone pecked at his shoulder.

He'd forgotten to look out for Lady Mary and feared he was found out. He set his face in a tight smile and turned. He was pleasantly surprised and said a little prayer of thanks.

"Jack."

"Captain Wentworth." He touched his forehead in a salute to him and then bowed to Miss Hammond.

"How did you get in here?"

Drawing a letter from his breast pocket, he offered it to Wentworth. "Aunt thought this might be important and so sent me to fetch it to you. I just told the footman I had a message of the uttermost importance. He figured it was official, and I didn't set him straight."

Taking the letter he glanced at the return address. It was from Edward and so hardly an official message. "Thank you, Jack." Digging in his pocket, he hoped to find a shilling, but all he found was a five-shilling piece. Far more than the scamp deserved. He gave it over nonetheless.

Stuffing the letter into his pocket, he spoke only a few moments longer with Miss Hammond when she suddenly found it necessary to go below.

Being free of company was a relief. He stepped out on an empty terrace, and lit a cheroot off the torch. The noise of the party had left his ears ringing and gave him all the more reason to enjoy the calm and quiet. He ground out the cigar and drew out Edward's letter. It was, no doubt, another plea to visit which he thought odd. Edward had never been one to ask for his company. His brother never seemed reluctant to have Frederick visit, but when he was a single man, he seemed to enjoy his privacy. Marriage had evidently changed that.

Wentworth took a place closer to the light of the brazier, broke the seal and began to read. After just a few lines he stopped and leant against the wall. "Damn my eyes! Surely the devil himself is in this."

Chapter Seven

After a decent rest the night before and a morning of travel, Wentworth stepped out of the inn and looked around Monkford. The only reason for the village's existence was that it sat at a crossroads. There was neither a moving body of water on which to build a mill nor any natural sheltering geography to keep an enemy at bay. Like so many other places, it had sprung up to suit a need in its time but now had little purpose and resisted the usual withering away to which all created things are prone.

There was very little he recognised. Since none of the buildings appeared to have been recently built, the fault must have been his youthful oversight. A man of three and twenty years had no care for a crumbling village. Now, he wished he'd been more observant. He had only an hour before the coach left in which to find the cottage he had shared with his brother in the summer of '06.

The cottage had been nearly on the doorstep of the church. At times, the bell's tolling sounded as if it was right inside with them. He located the spire and, once more, checked his watch and then began walking in its direction. As he passed through the village, he was surprised that the place was actually rather pretty. He did not recall this from his summer in the area and mused that, no doubt, there were other things he had failed to see back then. Veering from the main street, he took a well-worn path that kept the spire directly before him.

He had been on land long enough that walking any distance on the hard ground no longer bothered him, and this made it pleasant to walk beneath trees again. Though turning russet and no longer green, their rustling in the breeze and fresh scent cheered him. Had it really been so many years since he listened to bird song? In the past eight years, he'd been no more than a mile or two away from the sea and a change of scene was refreshing. It will be good to be deep in the country again, he thought, now that he had come to a sort of peace concerning Anne Elliot.

When he had read his brother's letter a few weeks earlier, he had thought a curse lay upon him. It was difficult not to give over to a sailor's natural superstition to believe all the recent unbidden thoughts of Anne Elliot were some sort of evil omen and that Edward's letter was their confirmation.

His brother's letter was full of irony concerning their sister and her husband's choice of home. Wentworth could not agree more that the Fates had been quite clever in rescuing the despotic Baronet's fat from the fires of financial embarrassment by way of a simple sailor's desire to live a genteel life in the country. Kellynch Hall. Having heard none of this previously from his sister, the letter was a terrible shock and assumed that he already knew about the letting of Kellynch Hall. His sister's letter relating the Crofts' new living arrangements had arrived the following day and filled in blanks spots left by Edward's.

When he arrived at the church, Wentworth surveyed it with dismay. The faint breeze ruffled disorderly shrubs while in a nearby flowerbed the dead heads of some sort of yellow flower bobbed. Cobbles leading to the door were ringed with tufts of grass that pushed them this way and that. Splits in the door's black paint showed the silver grey of long exposed wood. It was disappointing to see the once tidy place in such a slovenly condition. It caused the same little ache he felt viewing an old ship that he had known in better times. A tidy expanse of lawn, which had separated the church from the cottage, was gone and replaced with a lush green field of knee-deep grass. There was no cottage in sight.

"What do you want?"

Wentworth was startled and annoyed that he had not noticed the older gentleman approaching.

"I was looking for a cottage that stood here some years ago." Observing the collar, he added, "The curate at the time lived there. Edward Wentworth."

The man paused, leant on his cane and began to think. Shaking his head, he said, "No, no Edward Wentworth."

"Perhaps he was before your time."

The bent body straightened as much as possible and a defiant look came over him. "I will have you know, I have been the vicar of Monkford for twenty-seven years." The rheumy eyes of faded blue were as fierce as such an old man could muster.

"I beg your pardon, sir. I meant no offence." That summer, he'd only put himself in the way of meeting the vicar once and that had come just after his arrival. To his embarrassment, this man did not seem in the least familiar, and he could not for the life of him remember his name.

The wrinkled face softened at the apology. "Ah, I am sorry. This morning has been far too rushed and has put me in a bad humour." A bit of smeared egg on his cassock seemed to confirm the statement.

The vicar began to walk awayand then turned. "Regardless, I remember no curate, no Wentworth."

"He was here in the year '06. I stayed with him for a summer and was curious to see the place."

Nodding, the vicar said, "Him, I have no memory of, but the cottage I remember." Pointing towards an overgrown thicket, adrift in the field, "It stood over there. It was the primary residence for the incumbent, but my wife disliked it being so close to the wood. We moved closer to the inn." As an afterthought, he said, "And now we live with my daughter."

Wentworth surmised that living with the daughter might explain his bad humour. Before he could ask what happened to the cottage, the old man continued. "The place was falling down, but there came a fellow one day and wanted to buy it. No one was occupying it, so I sold it to him. He come and took it down and away bit by bit." The old man was still for a moment, looking over the field. Wentworth imagined the far away look was his mind's eye observing the area's alterations.

"I remember a small orchard. There were several apple trees."

"Aye, the fruit was very good, particularly after the gardener pruned them properly. Older fellow, now he did live in the cottage. As I recall, he stayed for a quite some time."

Wentworth smiled. He suspected "the gardener" to be Edward. The whole of that summer, whenever he had wanted to speak with his brother, the man was out-of-doors if there was daylight or a strong lantern available. He had worked up a small vegetable garden to which he was always amending the poor soil with various sorts of manure lugged in by wheelbarrow. Armed with leather gloves, he would endeavour to resurrect some bedraggled rose bushes with judicious pruning. His proudest accomplishment had been the apple trees.

The tiresome story went that early in the year, during an icy rain, he had carefully pruned every one, and during flowering, he had carefully chosen only the choicest blooms to remain on the limbs. Then, when the Captain was visiting, they were setting their fruit and every walk through them was full of plucking and snipping and lopping. It was under one of them that he told Edward he had proposed to Anne Elliot.

Edward had escaped to the sea when Frederick was only a baby, returning over a decade later when their parents died. On that return, the differences in their ages being significant, Edward assumed the role of father to his younger siblings. They had only two years of this arrangement until Frederick was taken aboard a King's ship at fourteen.

The two never played or fought as ordinary brothers, until one particularly hot, emotional night.

"Is there anything else I can do for you? I have my duties in the church." The vicar looked perturbed, as if he might have repeated himself.

"Uh, no," he said, a little startled, but grateful for the interruption. "Though, might I stay and have a look around?"

The old man turned to go to the church, nodding his assent. Wentworth held his breath as the man tottered up the stairs, took forever to unlock the door, and then disappeared into the gloom of the building. As he looked back over the field, the warm autumn sun urged him to remove his coat. Carefully draping it over his arm, he realised, with an unexpected sadness, that everything to do with the cottage and that summer was gone.

A wall separating the property from the next house was broken down in places. All the trees were gone, leaving little hillocks where they were pulled out of the ground. The weeds were higher in a rectangle of ground. He suspected this to be the place where the garden had been. The only thing left was a large flat stone he decided was what remained of the entry.

Standing on the stone, he remembered feeling quite smug when he had entered the cottage for the first time. It was small and he felt quite large from his foreign victories. Everything inside was shabby while he gleamed in his new uniform and polished Hessian boots, all of which had taken up no little sum of his prize money. All that was left now was a faint outline of the foundation and fading wildflowers that dotted the overgrown grass. A mouse darted away, emphasising the neglect. The only ones inhabiting this place now were those who used the web of animal trails running through the space.

He walked over to the wall. There was a stile, indicating that at one time there had been good relations between the neighbours. He replaced one of the steps that had broken lose and counted the bell tolls from the church. There was still time to look around before walking back to the inn. Lightly tapping the step into place, he tried to remember a story Edward had told him about the stile. Something about a slow-witted fellow in the neighbourhood raiding his trees. Wishing now that he had listened more closely, he made his way through the deep weeds to where the apples trees had once stood.

He had been grateful for the vicar's intrusion, but without trying to divert it, his mind went easily back to the argument. There wasn't much to it in reality. As it came more clearly to his mind in the very spot where it took place, he owned his share of the harsh words. But it was Edward's superior insight that dogged him this afternoon.

"...I think Anne Elliot is a splendid young woman..."

"...have you stopped to consider how the Baronet will react to this proposal..."

"...of course I think you worthy of her..."

"...you have undervalued the power the Lady Russell exerts over the entire Elliot household..."

"... I do wish to see you happy..."

Wentworth had been in high spirits when he confided the news to his brother, and he had expected Edward's unqualified joy. When he received words of caution instead, he become angry and took the words of warning as interference. As the conversation continued, he had even accused Edward of caring more for his living and position in the community than Frederick's future happiness.

"Living and position in the community," Frederick said under his breath. Leaning on an undamaged portion of the wall, he was embarrassed to remember his ridiculous behaviour. "The dear man had every right to point out my rash expectations and the reality of the situation. He had every right to fear for his position." The stones of the wall began to shift and he stood.

Certainly he loved Anne in a way he'd never cared for a woman before or since, but honour now compelled him to admit that, before he even set foot in Kellynch Hall to talk to her father, he had gotten a perverse pleasure from the notion of forcing that preening peacock to acknowledge his position, his worth, and his excellent prospects.

Catching a head of the ripening tall grass, he began to pull off the seeds. "Edward's biggest offence was offering me nothing to feed my vanity." He tossed the stripped stalk. "What headstrong dolt wants a liberal dose of practicality and good sense?" he asked the field.

In the beginning of the conversation, there had been only one attempt to dissuade him.

"Of course I consider Anne Elliot to be a splendid young woman, but good God, Brother, can't you fall in love with a woman of your own class? We have nothing as a family to recommend us to anyone of their station." When that had been answered with a vigorous rejection, the curate had done his best to warn of the obstacles that would be placed in his way. "I don't suppose you have stopped to consider how the Baronet will react to this proposal. Her best interest is the least of his worries. I am sorry to say that you are not important enough for his tastes..."

At that point in the conversation, for some inexplicable reason, he put forth that Lady Russell would champion him and his suit. Edward looked astonished and said, "...you need only enter the room and the woman is agitated. You have refused to go out of your way to curry her favour, and I think you perhaps enjoy shocking the old girl. You have

put aside her opinion at your own peril, Frederick. You have undervalued the power the Lady Russell exerts over the entire Elliot household,
I'm afraid..." Edward had been right and he knew it. He had nursed a
hope through the night that it was, indeed, his brother who had miscal-
culated things.

The final word had been about Anne herself. "I know I am merely a
curate, but I am no fool. I have observed these people for nearly a year,
and I think I know them and their ways a bit better than you. I have no
doubt you love her, Frederick. I also do not doubt she has feelings for
you. I do wish to see you happy, but Anne Elliot is not the sort of
woman who would be coaxed into an elopement. Nor should you try."

The argument ended there. He had thought Edward was being a
coward, a man ridiculous and afraid to reach out for happiness. He, on
the other hand, had proven that risk and satisfaction went hand-in-hand.

Saying nothing to Anne about the miserable reaction of his brother,
he had decided to wait a day or two before going to Sir Walter. Meanwhile, their time together was a wonder to him. Never before had
anyone placed him so high in his or her regard. Never had anyone
stirred in him such feelings of attachment and devotion. All her looks
and words enforced the belief that she loved him and that nothing could
come between them. He would move heaven and earth to keep her by
his side—and he was just arrogant enough to believe he could.

"Ah, there you are, Captain," the driver called from the edge of the
field. "It's a good thing somebody saw you head off this way. We need
to be pushing on now. The weather's been a bit cool at night and the
snakes come out from the tall grass right soon after the sun's up," he
added.

Wentworth waved an acknowledgement, and the driver started back.
"It's only fitting," he muttered, as he made his way along. "A garden.
Apples. Snakes." His longer strides caught him up to the driver in short
order, and he was informed that he would no longer be alone in the
coach. "Two local ladies. They're harmless enough." The remark struck
him as less than promising.

If he was to be in the presence of ladies, he thought it best to appear
clothed properly and he slipped on his coat. Involuntarily, he reached
back to flip his clubbed tail out of the way. *Blast, will I never learn it's
gone?*

"Mrs. Chawleigh, Mrs. Crow, this here is Captain Wentworth. He'll
be travellin' with you to the area of Kellynch. We're a little late, so don't
be alarmed as I try to make up the time." The driver slammed the door,
and the coach shook as he mounted.

The ladies smiled as Wentworth nodded an acknowledgement. The
older of the two ventured to speak: "Well now, a captain. That is a rank

of real responsibility. I have a nephew in a regiment in the north, and he is forever sayin' how the captains are the backbone of the army."

The younger woman leant close and spoke to the other. Wentworth was certain she said something to the effect the nephew had said "backside." While he loathed agreeing with a lobster on any point, it was an opinion of which he could find no fault.

"I'm sure your nephew would know better, for I am a captain in the Royal Navy."

Each lady's eyes widened and he anticipated the usual naïve questions that, as a rule, followed this disclosure. When each emitted an "oh" that was less than enthusiastic, he was a bit shocked. It was not the customary response of those on land, particularly ladies.

"Well, I suppose riding in boats is enjoyable enough, and that the navy has its compensations." The ladies smiled and nodded in unison. Then the younger offered, "I am sure it was exciting to see the Emperor."

Again, he was puzzled, and just as he was about to ask for an explanation, the elder said, "The papers say he is amazingly short. Is he really such a little man?" Both leant slightly forward in anticipation of his answer. He had seen this before in those ignorant of the Navy. Many had a notion that the entire Navy sailed the seas as one large armada and that they all took part in every battle and hence, knew every bit of gossip.

"Uh, I have no idea. I have never seen the Emperor Buonaparte. I was on a mission far west in the Atlantic when he was captured." The information excited nothing more than a glum, "Oh," from each of them as they sank back into their seat. It was time to retreat to the safety of his newspaper. "If you ladies will excuse me, I think I will catch up on my reading."

Reading turned to dozing, and he awoke to: "...and so I set her straight, I did. A rector's wife's got no business puttin' on airs and suchlike. 'Another new dress,' I said. And her reply was that her mother had sent her enough for the dress and the bonnet as well. I told her, bein' the wife of a deacon myself, that her lack of humility was a bad example and that it would reflect poorly on her husband should word get back to the bishop."

The conversation between the two women had obviously carried on without pause for breath since Monkford. Returning to a story in the paper concerning a local trial, which was characterized as sensational, he determined that life in small English villages was no different from life aboard a King's ship. Both societies featured gossip and backbiting, merriment and times of crisis. The only difference seemed to be the lack of women on the one.

The carriage jostled to a stop. "Crewkherne," called the driver. The riders up top hallooed those come to greet them and removed themselves. The thudding of crates and bags hitting the ground mixed with the calls of the carriage crew as they took on freight and new customers. The ladies kept talking. The door opened and he expected that they would be admitting someone new, but it was merely the driver.

"We'll be takin' a detour to Uppercross. Picked up a package for Mr. Robertson and need to see it in his hands right away." Without waiting for a response, he slammed the door.

The name of the village rang familiar, and it immediately raised a feeling of unease. Sophia had mentioned it in her letter. Cudgelling his travel weary brain he tried to remember what she had said.

"Well, I never! Let the apothecary see to his own packages, my daughter is expectin' me at the fingerpost. Her husband won't like her havin' to wait alone. Course if he'da come with her..." After savaging her son-in-law, the woman turned her kind ministrations on the local poulterer's sad lack of knowledge when it came to cutting up game birds. Wentworth pulled the letter from his pocket, determined to know what his sister had said about the place.

> Dear Frederick,
> In my last letter I told you of our search for a home in the country of Somerset. You will be glad to learn we have found the most perfect place. The countryside is beautiful and the house is, I am almost embarrassed to say, truly a mansion. It is the family seat of a Sir Walter Elliot...

He could never get past this line of the letter without recalling the day he had gone to request the honour of Anne's hand in marriage. The first reaction of the prating, preening fool had been shock. It was never clear whether the Baronet was surprised Wentworth would dare ask or that *anyone* would wish to marry his second daughter. When the shock was passed, the older man had taken the time to explain to "Lieutenant Wentworth" that if he cherished hopes of "profiting" by marriage to an Elliot, all that should be put aside. Nothing monetary would be done for the pair. The silly ass did not even have the common courtesy to face Frederick like a well-bred gentleman but spent the whole of the insulting harangue preening before a mirror over the fireplace.

It had never occurred to Wentworth that there might be a financial advantage to marrying Anne. His only idea had been to have her for his own. There was nothing that she could bring to him that would please him more than herself. Clearing his throat, he continued with Sophia's letter:

The family is quite prominent, and I would imagine you
know of them from your time with Edward. I wrote to him as
soon as the deal was made and his reply was full of stories
about the surrounding area and stories about the Baronet in
particular. They all were in agreement with matters disclosed
to us in Taunton, and if we had been dealing strictly with the
Baronet, I think we would not have troubled ourselves with
the place. The Admiral sees no harm in him, but the man is
over scrupulous about various, nonsensical things, even going
so far as to wish the pleasure gardens being made off limits.
He is worried about the "approachableness" of his shrubber-
ies! Thankfully, he has a man of business who is more interested in his good than the man himself. We were able to
come to very fair terms and we take possession on Michael-
mas. The family is moving to Bath for reasons of economy.
Now, I am not one to crow over the misfortunes of others,
and I do feel somewhat guilty in benefiting from the Elliot's
circumstances, but our brother's letter has been some solace
by explaining that the family has a reputation for being
proud. As he said, "Pride goeth before a fall..."

Again, there was talk of financial embarrassment and that the Admiral's taking the house had actually been a godsend. He could not imagine being any matter fraught with more personal irony than that of the
Baronet's straitened circumstances.

When he had first received his sister's letter, he had felt anger that
Kellynch Hall and its attendant ghosts were to be foisted on him, and he
had vowed that he would not visit. Indifference was the mantle he chose
and buttoned close to his chest when he finally accepted the invitation.
While he prepared to leave Plymouth, he had come to agree with his
brother's observation of irony in the fact that its new inhabitants were
those the Baronet had found so distasteful in the past. With perverse
satisfaction, Wentworth imagined the once grand Sir Walter Elliot
handing over the keys to those so lowly as to make their living by the
sea.

Throughout this journey, he had clung to that vision of the ruined
Baronet, fleeing to the faded watering hole of Bath. However, reluctantly, his own temperament eventually smoothed the jagged bitterness
he allowed towards the former occupant of Kellynch Hall. He was
certain the silly man did not even comprehend his predicament. The
rest of the letter bore even more interesting news:

The eldest daughter will accompany the Baronet early in the month. A second lives in the nearby village of Uppercross and is married to the son of another prominent family. They are not of any rank, the Baronet assures us, but they are worth knowing. I expect we will be in company with them quite often. The third daughter will stay behind and see to the house and then remove to Bath herself...

So, Anne was married and living in Uppercross. It was not as if he thought she would cease to live after his departure, but he had assumed her well-settled and faraway from Kellynch. It had taken several years, but eventually he had pronounced himself to be free of any lingering emotional attachments to Anne. All this changed in the months since his return to England. After his sister's letter arrived, his days had been filled with unbidden memories of her. More than once his wool-gathering had earned him a hectoring when meeting with fellow officers, and several times he had found himself midway through dressing for dinner only to discover it had taken him ten minutes to do nothing more than mutilate his neck cloth.

Their courtship had lasted only a short time, but now there seemed to be no scarcity of searing memories to torment him. As the time to leave Plymouth neared, he had been forced to take hold of himself and banish her again. When he felt himself slipping, he would reel off lists of chores that must be done, the steps for taking the noon reading, or the progressions of especially complex manoeuvres. If those strategies failed, he enlisted anything mundane to divert his mind and emotions.

To his relief, the past week had elapsed in welcome peace. There had been few flights of fancy. But now, it appeared, irony had dealt him a more complete hand than the Baronet's humbling. He was also to begin his stay in Somerset in the very town in which Anne lived. He fervently hoped that, should they meet, there would be nothing more than a polite introduction that would progress to gracious avoidance. The anxiety of the past few months would end. He could view her safely married and let the past die quietly.

The carriage stopped and swayed as the driver jumped down. Glancing out the window, he could see that Uppercross was typical of the small, old-fashioned villages of Somerset. He guessed they were delivering the package to the apothecary's home. The laugh of a child caught his attention. Looking out the window and up the street, he saw a cottage set back from the road and a woman with two little boys sitting on the steps of a small veranda. The boys seemed to be tussling over something. Suddenly, the shorter of the boys hit the other. The woman took the boy's arm and was in the process of scolding him when the driver returned. He thought it amusing that he had come all this way to be an observer to the little domestic drama. One never knew what would catch one's attention on the road.

The countryside was still brilliant with turning foliage, and the drive, once out of Uppercross proper, was pleasant enough. He began to recognise houses, fields, and local landmarks. It struck him as strange that he should recognise the area here but not in Monkford. The carriage drew near to Kellynch, and Wentworth was determined to put aside the oppressive feeling concerning the past. He reminded himself that to be with his sister and her husband would be an enjoyable time.

It suddenly dawned on one of his travelling companions that they had left the main road. She was vocal once again about the inconvenience to her and to her daughter awaiting her at the Misterton fingerpost. They drew up before the door of the great house of Kellynch and the Wentworth prepared to exit the carriage. "Well, sir, I hope you know this side trip is a great inconvenience to us." The woman was quite displeased and not unwilling to make him know it.

Before he could think of a polite response, the door was wrenched open and the driver announced in a voice of mock importance, "The Great Hall." The laughter from above that accompanied the proclamation had an edge, and the Captain surmised the coach crew had been none too impressed with the its previous occupant. "Your bags are down, and it looks like the drones are here to fetch 'em." The driver turned his bright eye on the two women. "And since the Captain was quite generous when he made the special arrangements, I'll see you and the other lady clear into Misterton."

"But what about my daughter? She's to be—"

"At the fingerpost. I know, I know. *Everybody* knows." He stepped aside and allowed Wentworth out. "Out of the kindness of my heart, I'll pick her up and take her too."

He could hear the ladies shrill, delighted voices through the closed door. "Sir," Wentworth called, "this is for you." Handing the driver some silver, he added, "You and your man have a drink on me."

"Thank you, sir. And you have a good visit at the palace." He winked and went to his seat.

As the coach drove off, he studied the entryway of Kellynch Hall. It was neither as imposing, nor large as he remembered. There was little of the grandeur of the past. It would seem that eight years had brought many changes, but was it the place that had changed or he?

"Sir, this way." A footman dressed in loud brocade and a crimped wig indicated the open door.

Wentworth smiled as he entered. From somewhere inside, he could hear his sister. "Hurry, Admiral. Frederick had finally arrived!"

Chapter Eight

Frederick, it has been an age." Sophia held him close, and he could not help but return the gesture. Not wishing to seem aloof, he waited for her to break off the embrace, but she did not. As they grew older, their times together were less frequent and of shorter duration. Propriety in their greetings was less and less important.

"I have missed you so, Brother," she whispered. The emotion in her voice was unmistakable, and she let him go.

Now it was he who held on. Grasping her shoulders, he looked at her closely for the first time in nearly six years. The hair was dark as always but now shot through with a few strands of silver. Her face had the ruddy hue of one who lives at sea. The lines around her eyes had grown deeper, and her skin, while not precisely coarse, was no longer smooth as it was in her youth. Over the years, everything had changed except her eyes. They were the same hazel eyes that looked back at him in the mirror. They were their mother's eyes. Whereas Sophia's were sharp and perceptive, their mother's had windowed the melancholy and anxiety of her weak constitution and feeble disposition.

When comparing his sister to himself, he'd always thought them different and quite separate; but today he could not help but recognise the close familial bond they shared.

Gently, he kissed her cheek and, pulling her close again, he said, "I think I missed you more."

The Admiral joined them at the door; she let him go and turned to dab at her eyes. Wentworth put out a hand. "Admiral, thank you for inviting me."

"It is our pleasure, Captain." He winked. "You always liven things up when you visit." Sophia tucked her arm around his and the Admiral took her other.

"I have tea or something stronger, if you wish, in the sitting room. Or I will show you to your room and you can freshen up, if you'd rather." Not wishing to part just yet, he accepted something stronger.

"I wonder you brought no one from *Laconia* with you. I would have thought Michaelson and particularly Eyerly would be in your wake."

"Yes, well, Michaelson has taken up with some bad habits and bad company and finds them preferable to the country." He chose not to say he'd not even considered bringing his steward, allowing him to follow his interest in brawling and gaming to their logical conclusions. "And Eyerly was headed south to an aunt. My normally stalwart crew has abandoned me," he laughed.

"I am just surprised that you've no one to valet for you."

"I have learnt to shift for myself, Sophia. I suppose it was inevitable that, once put ashore, I would have to learn to live like ordinary folk."

"Perhaps Lowell might recommend someone to look after you." She rose. "And now I must go down and speak to Mrs. Wallis about dinner. You'll want to neaten up, so I shall have hot water sent up to your room."

He watched her bustle out of the room. As was her custom, Sophia was in charge and seeing to the needs of others. He saw the same confident, capable woman who asserted authority, in her proper sphere, on board her husband's ship and was now in command of a great country house. Sophia remained the same whether on land or at sea.

"We're both glad to have you here, Frederick, but Sophy in particular," the Admiral informed him.

"I am glad to be here, sir."

"When we didn't hear right away, she was worried that you might avoid coming. She feared the country might not be lively enough for you."

This made him feel guilty that he had thought so long about dodging the visit. "I was delayed with standing the courts martial board, and paying off, and all the other petty concerns of finishing out a commission." He relied on the Admiral's understanding of how slow was the climb of any action making its way up the Navy chain of command.

"It worked out well. After signing the lease here, it gave us time to go north and visit Edward…and meet his new wife."

"Ah, yes, the new wife. And what is she like?"

The Admiral laughed a bit. "I knew not what to expect. Sophy is the one who generally has opinions on such things, and she was prepared to dislike her. But to our great surprise, the new Mrs. Wentworth is quite a nice woman. No art, no pretence."

"The tone of Edward's letters has been different. More at ease, I think." Wentworth did not say that he expected that tone would change as soon as the newness of the marriage wore away.

"That is no surprise. She is a lovely woman." Croft poured himself more tea and continued. "I have always liked your brother. Though he and I are not of the same philosophical bent, I have always considered him a good friend. We have shared many a glass and many an interesting conversation. I was very happy to find him so...happy. More than once I walked in on him, book and glasses in place, not reading but staring out a window and grinning like a fool."

Wentworth compared this statement with his own relationship with Edward. There was little resemblance. Edward was always a genial host, but distant. When they shared a glass, it was at dinner, and there was little in the way of conversation. He reckoned it was his lack of religious sensibilities that put them at odds. In the same way that sailors found it difficult to converse on subjects not related to the sea, perhaps the religious knew little of the world outside the church. And there was never a time he had found his brother smiling for no apparent reason. He was hard-pressed to remember his brother smiling at all.

Almost to prove him wrong, the Admiral said, "He introduced me to a friend of his, a physician, I believe, who raises horses. He has hopes of one day winning a cup or two."

Wentworth could not help but remember lectures on the useless pursuit of gambling. Edward had droned on about how casting your bread upon the waters of vice was a wasteful and faithless act. Finishing his sherry, he wondered if his brother had changed his opinion or if the price of friendship with the physician was moral silence.

"I suppose you noticed that Sophy was rather enthusiastic in her welcome."

Lifting his glass to be filled, he said, "I could not help but notice. I've never been greeted in such a fervent manner." Leaving it at that, he chose to not to say that it lifted his spirits more than anything had in an age.

"You may notice that she's a bit changed. Much more sentimental than before."

Not by nature, and certainly not by upbringing, had the Wentworth siblings been sentimental. But it would seem that time was making changes. By the Admiral's accounts, his brother's marriage might have transformed him into a more sympathetic human being, and his sister, while not previously a cold woman, was willing to toss propriety aside and leave no one doubting her love for family.

"Has something in particular happened?"

"She lost a dear friend this summer–a very dear friend. The woman was a widow in Deal. She befriended Sophy years ago, before she started coming to sea with me. They remained close over the years. The woman was an amazing correspondent. No matter where we were, her letters found us. While we were on our way home, a letter from her daughter arrived saying she had died. Sophy had been very much looking forward to seeing her again after so many years in the east. The letter crushed her. After a week or so, she finally began to be herself. She told me one day that no longer would she take it for granted that those she cared for most in the world would always be waiting ashore to receive her. It had come to her that there was no way to know when you were seeing someone for the last time. That's why she was so anxious to see you and to visit Edward."

It was interesting that both he and his sister would have such philosophical revelations thrust on them by untimely death. In the same way, there had never been an expectation he would return to this part of the world and certainly no expectation of ever seeing Anne Elliot again. Clearly, the future was the province of God alone.

"So, if she seems a bit overwrought, you'll know why."

"Thank you for telling me, sir. It will be my first consideration."

"Precisely what will be your first consideration, Frederick?" Sophia had entered the sitting room without either man noticing. Standing, he downed the rest of his sherry and said, "My behaviour while I am here. I will always consider that I represent Kellynch Hall and all the nobility for which it stands." The words sounded ridiculous even to his own ears. Hoping to end the questioning, he came to her, took her arm and said, "Now, I would like to go up and wash away some of the dirt of the road."

"Certainly. Lowell says that one of the footmen, Harkness, would be a good choice to valet. I have instructed him to bring up hot water and anything else you might like." After the stairs, they walked down a long corridor and turned down another. "I didn't put you in the family wing with us. The daughter's rooms are in sore need of attention and are far too feminine for you. You will be in a guest room. It is smaller, but nicely furnished."

She led him to an open door and followed him in. A man in livery was pouring steaming water into the basin. He looked up at Sophia and the Captain. An unmistakable frown crossed his face. Just as quickly, the typical bland expression of a house servant replaced it.

Putting aside the man's greeting, he said, "I've been closeted in a rooming house for the better part of a month, Sister, and accommodations on *Laconia* were not spacious. I am sure this guest room will be more than adequate." In his heart, he was glad to be in another wing from the family rooms. To be placed in the family wing and endure the endless wondering if he might be in the very room which Anne had occupied would carry the irony of the situation to ridiculous lengths.

"...yes, the accommodations of a fifth-rate are a bit snug indeed. I already have plans to redecorate, and if you grace us with your presence long enough, you can be moved to a larger room." She did not wait for an answer. "Captain Wentworth, this is Harkness." She turned to face the servant. "Lowell has said you are the best choice to valet for my brother." *Ah, Sophia, energise the man's pride. He'll break his neck to turn me out well now.*

"Yes, ma'am. Sir, I have taken the liberty of unpacking your case. When you are ready, I will see you prepared for dinner."

He wanted to laugh at the interesting turn of phrase. For a moment, he wondered if there was a serving platter large enough to accommodate his tall frame. "That will be quite all right, Harkness. I will need very little in the way of assistance, but I would have you brush and lay out my blue coat and my best trousers." The man bowed and disappeared through a side door he assumed was a dressing room.

Sophia went to the basin and checked the water. "And how do you find the place? Has it changed much?"

"Changed?"

"Edward said the summer you stayed with him that you visited here some few times. I wonder if it has changed."

Shaking his head, he said, "I would not know. I noticed the place little then."

Turning one of the curtains, she looked at the reverse side. "We have noticed quite a lot of wear since moving in. We thought we had looked it over carefully when the Baronet showed us around, but, well, you know it is rather embarrassing to scrutinise anything very closely with the owner standing over you."

"Do you think he meant to cheat you?" He wouldn't put it past the blighter to engage in that sort of trickery.

"No, no. I just think all the best carpets, curtains, and furnishings were put in the rooms we toured. The family rooms, excluding Sir Walter's of course, are so worn it is more from pride than not wanting to damage your male sensibilities that I put you up here. Those poor girls put up with quite shabby surroundings for a long time."

While he was relieved to know he would not be sleeping in a room once occupied by Anne, he was curious about her reaction to the Baronet giving up the Hall. Perhaps having an establishment of her own had eased the blow.

Pulling the drapes open wider, she said, "I think I told you that I do not revel in benefiting from the family's difficulties. We are determined to do what we can, and if in a few years they might return, we will hand Kellynch back in better shape than they left her." She continued to fuss about the room until Harkness entered with the coat and trousers.

"I will leave you to freshen up. Dinner is not for an hour, so take your time."

As she approached the door, she touched his arm and said, "I am happy you are with us, Frederick." Not waiting for an answer, she left. He was glad to be alone. Although he hadn't remembered particulars of the place, he was beginning to feel the tone of the grand house.

"Sir, ya water's ready. I set out ya shavin' gear."

He'd forgotten Harkness. "Yes, thank you." He mumbled his thanks as he applied soap to his face. He finished the first stroke and then glanced at Harkness in the mirror. The man's hands were flexing, and he was a study in disapproval. Taking another stroke, he watched the man's reflection. It was comical. Obviously, Harkness would have liked nothing batter than to snatch the razor away and take matters into his own hands.

Concentrating on his chin, Wentworth considered that servants could be a double-edged sword. They had a clear, practical purpose at table and there they were quite welcome. It was much more convenient to have them fetch the wine than try to move about the cramped and sometimes heaving cabin. When they were not serving, they stood behind, well out of the way. However, this room was small and he could not help but hear Harkness's muted sighs of frustration.

Wiping the blade in preparation to shave his throat, Wentworth decided to divert the man's attention with conversation.

"So, Harkness, how long have you been with the Elliot family."

"All my life, sir. I was born on the estate."

He could not imagine what his life would be like if he had remained in Liverpool for the whole of his thirty-two years. Would he have become bitter and vicious like his father, perhaps, or withdrawn and miserable like his mother?

"I was being groomed to tend the gardens, but the Baronet liked my looks and brought me into the house."

He studied Harkness' reflection. The man may have been under the thumb of Sir Walter for all these years, but he still had a mind of his own. Wentworth determined it was prudent to cultivate such a long-serving and talkative fellow.

"Then you have seen many changes over the years, I presume."

"Oh yes, sir. Especially lately."

Nothing more was said while his valet saw him dressed. As he brushed down the Captain's coat, he said, "I think it safe to say the opinion below stairs is that the new master and his wife are most worthy and a pleasure to serve." He came around Wentworth's shoulder, brushing as he went. "There are also several that hold to the opinion that Mrs. Croft is quite like her brothers, very good-natured and a quick wit." He gave a final smoothing to the lapels and asked, "Will that be all, sir?"

Wentworth watched the man leave the room. Surely, neither Sophia nor the Admiral had volunteered anything concerning the configuration of the Wentworth family! It would seem the servants possessed an extraordinarily long memory. The question was how inquisitive were they and precisely what did they remember?

~ ~ ~ ~ ~ ~ ~ & ~ ~ ~ ~ ~ ~ ~

Dinner was enjoyable and plenteous. Wentworth wondered if his sister was stuffing him with his favourite foods and wines to prove her ability as a hostess or show off her competent staff. The meal more than accomplished both ends.

"Unless you and the Admiral wish to be formal, I thought we could spend the rest of the evening upstairs."

Looking at Croft, he saw that there was really no choice. "I think adjourning upstairs would be perfect."

As they ascended the stairs, the Crofts pointed out several of the Elliot family treasures. The little sitting rooms, ball rooms, dining rooms and libraries provided the space in which to stuff all the *object' art*, pretentious furniture, and hanging monstrosities they imagined showed off their rank to best advantage.

"There is a large tree outside the window," Sophia explained. "It gives one the feeling of being perched on the limbs of it." The footman opened the door, and they stepped into a smallish, but exceedingly comfortable room. Sophia directed him to a chair. "Would you prefer sherry or something stronger, perhaps?"

"I think he would enjoy a glass of that whiskey Musgrove sent over."

"Thank you, sir. I believe I will stay with sherry."

Sophia said, "We have come to enjoy this little room a great deal. Unless we have a visitor, we generally use this room rather than the sitting room downstairs."

As soon as the chair accepted his body, he was reminded of two days worth of hard seats and ill-tuned springs. It was not long before he had found the perfect spot against the pillow-like headrest and the perfect angle to watch the cosy, warming fire. It was easy to understand why this room would attract his sister and brother. Unlike much of the rest of Kellynch Hall, this room was restrained, restful both in style and colours. The muted green walls and brown patterned rugs were very much in keeping with the notion of being surrounded by the boughs of the tree outside. The furniture was just a little worn, enough to allow one to relax and find peace and respite when the remainder of the house proved too busy.

Another footman brought him the sherry and a plate of assorted sweets. This would round out the meal nicely, and after a bit of polite conversation, it was his intention to heap loads of praise on his sister, thank the Admiral again for his invitation, and then excuse himself for the evening. Leaning back, he closed his eyes and thought of a comfortable bed.

"Now, don't go to sleep, Captain. I've been looking forward to playing chess. Your sister is an excellent player, but she lacks your killer instinct."

Wentworth opened his eyes to look at Sophia's reaction to this pronouncement. "Admiral, you know I play a strategic game. I like to win based on skill and cunning, not on thuggish tactics as you employ." She smiled at him over the rim of her glass.

He wasn't really feeling up to chess, but he knew there would be no putting off the Admiral. He stood. A jarring clank at the fireplace drew his attention. Harkness apologized for his clumsiness as Fredrick's eyes followed the flame up to the mantle then to the portrait hanging above it.

At first he noticed nothing more than a typical portrait of a young woman at her sweet and beguiling best. Further study proved a stunner. The face was indeed sweet and beguiling, and to his shock, it belonged to Anne Elliot.

Chapter Nine

W ell, what do you think of her?" Sophia asked.
What did he think? He stood looking into her tender brown eyes, and his mind was at sea with no lists or manoeuvres to save him. Months ago, he would have laughed and said something to the effect that he thought nothing of her. But here, now, with the heat of the fire rising oppressively, Harkness standing silently by, and his sister awaiting an answer, he could only feign composure and ask where the portrait had come from.

"I found it in the attic. There was a mirror above the fireplace, but–"

"There are so blasted many of them in this house, I begged her to find something to replace it," the Admiral said, tapping his king on the board.

"The housekeeper said I should look in the attic, that the Baronet had stored several pictures up there. She is Elizabeth Stevenson. Just a few months after this was finished, she married the Baronet and became Lady Elliot. That is her father standing behind her."

Of course, this was not Anne. What an idiot he was! He could now see that nearly everything about the picture argued against it being her. The eyes had played him a trick. They were the same warm, intelligent brown that first attracted him. And they were surrounded by the same fresh, pink complexion, but the chin was a bit more angular and less pleasing to him. The woman's hair also should have hinted at the difference. This young woman sported a mass of tiny curls that created a cloud of deep chestnut about her face and shoulders. While the colour was the same as Anne's, he'd never seen her with her hair down. And the clothes were another clue that, had he been more observant, might have saved him from diving headlong into a panic. The dress was not at all in the style of '06. It was more like something his mother wore, though finer in cut and quality. And the man, while having fully the air of Sir Walter, was balding and not very handsome. Moreover, his frock coat and breeches were of an era long past. It was now easy to see this was a portrait accomplished years earlier than Anne's time. Nevertheless, the eyes would not release him.

"Well, now that we've introduced Frederick to the late Lady Elliot, might we get on with this game?" The Admiral rose and took the opposite chair. This left Wentworth squarely facing the portrait. "That corner is a bit dark, and your eyes are younger than mine. Besides, it's only polite that I give you the first move before I blast you out of the water." He laughed and Sophia scolded.

After making his first move, Wentworth downed the last of the sherry. Sitting in the presence of the disquieting picture required fortification. "I've changed my mind, sir. I think I will try your much touted whiskey, if you don't mind."

"Certainly. A man needs a good few drinks to be set right after a day or two on the road," he said with glee. The Admiral was generous and enjoyed having a drinking companion. "Harkness," he called over his shoulder, "don't be mean with that now. There's plenty more to be had." He turned back and made his first move.

The footman offered the drink. Though he gazed placidly only at the salver and glass, Wentworth could swear the man watched him. Had Harkness seen the expression of shock when he first viewed the painting? How much did might he remember of his previous visit? That his old and personal business might be known by anyone connected with Kellynch was unsettling, but that a servant might bandy it about below stairs was particularly repellent.

Though the corner was dark, the cut crystal tumbler spread the liquid into an amber rainbow. The heat of the drink traced a path from his lips straight to his gut. He could not help but appreciate the distiller's art. This was the smoothest, most mellow fire he'd ever swallowed. "Thank you, sir. That has, indeed, set me right." The statement was a lie. All his careful avoidance of thoughts, memories, feelings, and truth concerning her was blasted apart the minute he looked up into the face of the portrait.

With his next move, he left his knight vulnerable. The Admiral would certainly see this and capitalise on it, but Wentworth could not lose the game and get out of this room fast enough. He could tell that the Admiral was growing impatient with drawing his attention back to the board to accomplish another move, but he was powerless to keep his eyes from drifting. The woman's gaze had followed him to his new seat. In no time, Croft was claiming victory and demanding, with a hint of disappointment, that Sophia should take her brother's place.

"Have another drink, Captain. I think you need it."

To his dismay and despite all reason, he took the drink and returned to his first seat. The desire to leave the room was indeed strong but not nearly as strong as his unwilling fascination with the portrait.

"You said this is Lady Elliot." It was a disjointed statement, said less for response than to assure him it was not Anne.

Sophia looked up. "Yes. I believe the housekeeper said it was painted in early '84 ."

"Is there a family resemblance? You said there are daughters."

"Certainly with the eldest, she was here when we toured the place. Miss Elizabeth Elliot is very much like her mother, but has traces of him as well." She and her husband exchanged looks. "If Miss Elliot is the image of her mother in other ways, this was not the happiest of homes," she continued. "Of the remaining two, one very much has her mother's looks and the other her father's, and that's all that should be said on that subject. We don't want to be accused of gossiping." They laughed together as a sailor's major source of sustenance was the hearty fare of gossip.

To his relief, the chess match was heating up and each one's attention was on besting the other. He was free to examine the portrait at his leisure. Scrutinising the canvas, he realised the painting drew him because his memories of Anne had faded. Now, to see even a close approximation of her youth and beauty was at once disconcerting and a lovely and enjoyable study.

As he reflected, it irritated him that all his pretensions of safety were now vanished. It was a fool's notion that her wounds to his heart were no longer open and that her marriage to another man freed him of her influence. It would be impossible to remain unconcerned and indifferent while standing in her presence. He saw clearly that he was a damned fool if he thought they would be introduced and he could quietly go about his business.

Tapping the glass, he signalled for another whiskey. It was excellent stuff, and he could feel the effects of it acutely. Partaking of a third was to indulge perhaps to embarrassment. Harkness filled the glass and retook his post near the fire. What did it really matter? His new valet was there to attend to his needs and, if required, his mortifications. Glancing back at the painting, he wondered how large the portion of his future mortification. He looked deeply into the bright brown eyes, so like those he was coming to remember, and he cursed his weakness and the fact that he was now at the mercy of this scrap of painted canvas.

~ ~ ~ ~ ~ ~ ~ & ~ ~ ~ ~ ~ ~ ~

107

The next morning, Wentworth woke early—even the fires were not yet started. It was too early to be active, and he was in a decidedly brown frame of mind. He'd done nothing to embarrass himself the night before. The obligatory sherry and a fourth whiskey had given him the perfect excuse, He'd pled fatigue after the day's travel and fallen asleep quickly but woke often throughout the night. With every bout of sleeplessness came a desire to walk the few steps down the hall and look at the painting. If the temptations grew worse, he mused, perhaps it would be necessary to lash himself to the bed as Odysseus was lashed to his mast.

Turning from his stomach to his back, he closed his eyes and found her face before him. With each review, the features became more alive. All the thoughts that naturally followed came alive as well. Aggravated beyond endurance, he threw back the bedclothes and stalked to the washstand. As he poured, water sloshed over the edge of the bowl, wetting the tops of his feet. The first splash took his breath away and drove all thoughts of brown eyes and achingly sweet lips out of his head. He wondered if it might be better to await Harkness and hot water.

Wiping drops from the mirror, he looked at his smeared likeness. In seconds the water beaded and his reflection became somewhat clear again. He watched a drop of water appear on his chin and drip to the basin below.

"It's not even Anne," he lectured. "The woman in that picture has been dead and mouldering in the ground for years." Towelling his face and chest, he laid last night's bout of sentimentalism to fatigue and surprise...and too much drink. While he dressed, he reproached himself. "You spent a most unpleasant week closeted away with a man who threw himself head-long into his grief and depression. You shall not allow yourself the luxury of pity. Those eyes overwhelmed you, but only for last evening."

Suddenly, a new energy filled him. The maudlin thoughts and memories were a sort of traveller's hangover, the product of bad food and endless pounding of the body. Now that he was well rested and clear-eyed, he would see things plainly. Pulling on his boots, he predicted, "In the cold light of day, this portrait will not be half so seductive."

Walking down the hallway, he reminded himself that, while it had taken some time, he'd grown quite used to the sight of blood on the deck of the ship and that he'd become hardened to the cries of pain from his own men. His life's experience proved that constant exposure and repetition wore away natural fear and loathing. Therefore, he would confront the painting at every opportunity. Its repeated presence would deaden this reanimated attachment to its subject.

He opened the door, purposely avoided looking over the fireplace, and went straight to the window. Grasping the curtain, he swept it open so that sunlight flooded the room. Stepping back, he looked up and said quietly, "Do your worst, Lady Elliot."

There was no sense of anything of significance occurring—neither did he turn to stone nor the portrait burst into flame. The room remained cool and quiet. The only sound was the whisper of his boots on the carpet as he went from chair to sofa to table, her eyes fixed on him. Her gaze was fully as warm and inviting in the early morning light as it had been the night before. To his dismay, it did not matter that this was not the woman he had loved, and it did not matter that the portrait was not an exact copy of Anne. It had given her substance and returned her to prominence in his mind. Though it was not she, the eyes mocked him with their quiet assurance that he was a lost man.

Wentworth had no idea how much time he'd spent before the portrait. He left the cosy room and re-entered his own, slamming the door and a uttering a string of curses to the Hall. A clattering at the fireplace startled him. A tiny young serving girl stood amid a cloud of scattered ashes on the hearth. She was obviously terrified at his display.

"I'm sorry, sir." Her eyes studied the tips of her shoes peeking from beneath her over-long apron.

For his part, there was little he could gracefully do but mutter, "Carry on," go downstairs, and endure breakfast with his sister and the Admiral.

Sophia was surprised to see him up and about so early. "You needn't be so quick to the table you don't finish dressing. We are in the country, but we are not savages, Frederick." She winked in punctuation.

To his chagrin he realised he was sans waistcoat or coat. Without missing a beat, he took his chair and apologized. "I've had some business on my mind, Sophia. It will not happen again."

It was now Mrs. Croft's turn to apologise and explain that she and the Admiral would be out for the morning. The gamekeeper was anxious to show them several spots where the shooting was excellent. Though the Admiral took out a gun only as an excuse to walk the countryside and run the dogs, he wished to offer profitable day's sport to any visitors they might have. Their hasty finish and departure did little to help divert him. After a second cup of coffee, Wentworth dismissed the idea that he needed to go upstairs again and sent Harkness to fetch his coat so that he might take a turn in the garden.

~ ~ ~ ~ ~ ~ ~&~ ~ ~ ~ ~ ~ ~

The sounds of digging drew Wentworth's attention. He kept to his side of a large hedge and listened. Mackenzie, the head gardener, was delivering a rather convoluted explanation to his underlings concerning which plants were to remain and which plants were to be taken to the Lady Russell. Evidently, she still resided at the Lodge, but was not in residence at the moment.

"Now be careful with all of 'um. It's a bad time of year to be doin' this, and if they dies, I'll have that harpy from Bath down here seein' that I swing." The sound of a shovel commenced. "Oh, and don't go sayin' anythin' about things from the Hall bein' give away. I don't need the other one from Uppercross marchin' down here, nippin' at my heel, claimin' 'er share. There's only enough of these here ones for the Lodge."

An irreverent snort was the assistant's only reply and the shovelling started again. Mackenzie's tone left no doubt that he cared neither for Miss Elliot, who he wished to remain in Bath, nor "the other one." Since he had mentioned Uppercross, Wentworth assumed this must be Anne. It surprised him that anything to do with her would be connected with disdain or contempt. As far as he remembered, her attitudes towards all were caring and fair. Was it possible that she had changed fundamentally? He supposed it would be unjust to decide until he had an opportunity to observe her. Though more curious, he still fostered hopes of avoiding a full out introduction.

Moving around the side of the Hall, he stopped and looked at the prospect. It was a lovely view of the lawns and the drive. The old grey walls shone clean, almost new, in the morning sunlight. He watched the under gardener lug a full wheelbarrow out the main gate, heading to Kellynch Lodge no doubt. In the weeks of preparation to leave the service, the anticipation of returning to Kellynch Hall and dread of the inevitable meeting with Anne Elliot, he'd given no thought to Lady Russell.

Though not mentioned by his sister, Lady Russell was only half a mile away and, therefore, a close neighbour of the Hall. Such proximity would, were her ladyship home, require that proper introductions be made and that they socialise together. Were the gods not smiling on him, he could, even at this moment, be breaking bread with her, all the while deflecting glares and veiled insults no doubt. But, as luck would have it, Mackenzie had mentioned she was out of the neighbourhood until Christmas. He was safe from that hazard at least.

Turning to the rear of the house, he considered the intelligence of the morning. If the gardener were to be believed, time and marriage had caused Anne to become grasping and demanding of her due. *No different than the rest of the family!* Any sympathetic feelings spawned by the portrait or regrets from the same source were a waste. Lady Russell would not be returning to the area until he was safely installed in Shropshire, enjoying the company of his brother and new sister-in-law.

Wentworth was congratulating himself on a successful reconnoitre when Harkness announced that Squire Charles Musgrove was come and wished to meet with the Captain. The name Charles was certainly not extraordinary; there were Charleses enough to man the entire fleet, though the name Musgrove rang a distant, but distinct bell. Following Harkness, he said, "Tell me about the Squire."

It was obvious the man did not leave the house often. He was careful in picking his way through the wet lawn and occasionally shook his foot to be rid of the excess dew. "He's from Uppercross, sir. The family is quite as old as that of Kellynch. He is second only to the Baronet in land and prominence," he added. "His eldest son is married to–"

"That's enough, Harkness. I remember my sister mentioning him now," he said, passing the man his coat, hat, and gloves. "In the drawing room?" Harkness nodded and another footman dashed to announce him.

A white-haired man rose from the chair near the fire. Wentworth suspected his rosy cheeks and sincere smile were permanent fixtures and not due to the warmth of the room or social expectations.

"Captain, I have been most anxious to meet with you again." He bowed and made his way to shake hands.

They were obviously acquainted and, while the man had the air of familiarity, thousands of faces over many years of commissions made it impossible to place him. He was comfortably stout but not fat, and though his attire would be considered old-fashioned, it was clear he was a proper and prosperous gentleman. Perhaps he was a fellow officer, like the Admiral, retired to the country. Looking closer at his face, Musgrove had the ruddy, weathered look of one who makes his living at sea, but he did not think him of the officer ranks. It was possible he was an inferior officer, or had held a warrant at one time. In any case, the man's open manner did not make him think an admission of ignorance on his part would give offence.

Before he could ask about the particulars of their previous meeting, his sister and the Admiral entered. They explained that the gamekeeper and his men were hot on the trail of a poacher and would have to give a tour of the prime pheasant cover at another time. Both were pleased that the unhandy turn of events now meant they could entertain their neighbour.

Sophia was about to order tea when a cart appeared with all that was necessary to make their impromptu assembly enjoyable. After she poured and passed the cups, Mrs. Croft said, "I am continually amazed.

The servants here are a joy and a wonder. Before one even asks, everything is brought just to your liking."

Mr. Musgrove laughed. "Well, ma'am, I suppose that's what comes of being so familiar and close. They see a certain one coming, and they know right away what's expected."

"The families bein' so close, I suppose you were regular visitors here at the Hall," the Admiral said.

Wentworth could easily see that Mr. Musgrove was not an artful man, but his right eyebrow raised and he took a sip of his tea before saying, "Not as much as one would think. It's actually not often that I get out of my own neighbourhood. Just now, the harvests are finished, but I can't say I saw the Baronet above four or five times this year. It was only by Mrs. Charles that we knew of the removal." It was clear, as he took another sip, that he was giving a good face to an intricate association.

Offering the Captain a plate of biscuits, Sophia directed the conversation to a different topic. "On our first visit to Uppercross, Mr. Musgrove said he thought he knew you, Fredrick—that you had met some years ago in Clifton—just a few months after you were made into the *Laconia*."

Clifton. The Bristol Channel. Perhaps the man was a pilot or even a sailing master. He recalled that they had used no pilot on that commission. Eyerly had been sailing the Channel since he was a sprout and proved himself indispensable to the Laconia's coxswain. No, he had no notion as to why the man looked so familiar.

"And Mrs. Musgrove has found that to be true, Mrs. Croft. She went back through the letters from our boy, and just as we thought, your brother here was his captain."

Now he had something to go on! He had met the man only in the course of commanding the son. Wentworth watched the man over the rim of the cup, cudgelling his brain. The name was now maddeningly familiar...

"...as I was sayin', Richard was never so happy as when he was with your brother, ma'am. It was only six months and there were only two letters, but they are Mrs. Musgrove's favourites, I can tell you that."

Good God, this is the sire of Damnable Dick!

"I recall you sayin' your son was a midshipman. I've always impressed upon my brother-in-law that bringin' the mids along is one of the most important responsibilities of a captain. When they rise up in the ranks, they can be the very thing that saves you in a pinch."

Mr. Musgrove had no response to this piece of nautical wisdom. Turning back to Wentworth he said, "It was spring and we were returning from Clifton and decided to make a visit. You were ever so good to allow us a little time with our boy."

He smiled politely to cover the realisation that this Mr. Musgrove was familiar only because he had the nerve to beget a son who, by every measurable means, was the most useless, profligate, and troublesome wastrel ever to buy his way into the service of the King. A prudent captain, by and large, turns a blind eye to the petty frolics of the Boys-Who-Would-Be-Officers and allows them to settle the scores of any within their ranks that brings them undue attention. But the antics of that particular young man came to his first-hand notice too often to be ignored.

There had been times during that six-month commission Wentworth was quite certain he saw more of that particular heathen than all the rest of the Young Gentlemen combined. Musgrove's propensity for trouble kept him the lowest ranking midshipman of the several assigned to *Laconia*. Wentworth decided that any knucklehead thick enough get himself disrated for fighting the very day a new captain took command deserved to be on the bottom of any pile. It was only a happy accident that six months later Midshipman Musgrove was again disrated and ripe for removal when Admiral Pontus Lugg was demanding men from him just as both were beating out of Ponta Delgada, Saint Michael, in the Western Islands. A happy accident indeed!

The mantel clock announced the half hour, and Mr. Musgrove made noises to leave. It struck Wentworth as odd that a man who, by all accounts, had been anxious to meet with him, had conversed almost entirely with his sister and brother and done little more than shake his hand.

"I don't mean to take advantage of your hospitality and then hurry away, but I am obliged elsewhere. And if you will do us the pleasure, my wife is determined that you all will dine as soon as can be arranged." He stood and extended a hand to the Admiral. "She'll accept no excuses."

Sophia smiled warmly. "We are honoured by the invitation, Mr. Musgrove, but I am afraid that we will not be able to satisfy immediately. The soonest would be Thursday week."

Mr. Musgrove was disappointed by the delay but accepted the compromise gladly. Turning to the Captain, he put out his hand and said, "I am pleased to be reacquainted, sir, and look forward to introducing you to the rest of the family, particularly my son, Charles. His wife is a daughter of this house. That should give you all something in common."

All the proper leave taking was accomplished, and Mr. Musgrove was shown out. Wentworth stared at his form following the footman. He was now obliged to visit Uppercross. A meeting with Anne Elliot was fast approaching. At every turn he was coming closer to her: the painting, the servants, and now the fact that he must pay a call to the very family into which she had married. There was nothing to be done for it. They would meet soon and that would put an end to the writhing. Or would it?

~ ~ ~ ~ ~ ~ ~ & ~ ~ ~ ~ ~ ~ ~

To his surprise, he slept well. He woke feeling rested and on good terms with the world. The days of travel were behind him and his normally sanguine temperament was once again in command.

His fire was tended a bit early, and Harkness arrived accordingly with steaming hot water for his morning shave. Those below stairs were learning his ways. This was another item to add to his cheerfulness. Living so many years onboard ship, he had taken for granted that observation of the captain and adjusting to his ways and whims, as far as tradition and life lived by the bells would allow, was customary. After his sojourn at Mrs. Bale's, he feared he would go quite unnoticed in a great country house. At first, he had found it tiresome to be watched and measured and conjectured upon, particularly when considering that some of these people were watching and measuring and conjecturing upon life at Kellynch eight years ago. But there had been no further veiled comments from his valet, and he had no reason to think the servants knew more about his private matters than his sister or any other person in the neighbourhood.

It occurred to him that he did lead a rather cosseted life. In all his years in command, only twice had his quarters, along with most of his books, clothing and important papers, been blown to bits. While it was true that occasionally he had had to endure stitching up after an injury inflicted by an enemy blade or flying splinter of oak, he had had a remarkably easy time of it.

Filling his plate with another round of eggs, ham, sausages, and potatoes, he thought how he should best enjoy himself. He knew that once he was installed in the second-best bedroom at his brother's, all these luxuries would change. While his standing as a captain in the Navy might at first impress his new sister-in-law, she was certain to take her lead from Edward. He would be treated no differently than any other younger brother. There would be little to set him apart from any other poor relation come to beg a room. He took up a newspaper from the sideboard and continued to stuff himself.

Just as he thought he would pass the morning without seeing the Admiral or his sister, Sophia entered. Her face was high in colour and she seemed out of breath. Folding the paper, he rose, waved off the footman, and put her in her seat. "Let me get you some coffee, Sister. You look as though you've run a race."

114

"Thank you, Frederick. It's not me; it's the Admiral. He was up all night long with his legs."

As he poured, he could not help seeing a preposterous picture of the Admiral and his torso in one chair, calmly chatting with his legs in another. He took hold of his thoughts and set the cup before her. "It's being on land. I was wondering if he might not have trouble." After months at sea it was difficult for a sailor to accustom himself to the hard, inactive ground. For older men, it was nearly impossible. "What has been done?"

She savoured the first drink and set the cup down wearily. "Last night, just after we retired, he said he had some pain and that he was glad to go to his bed. But in the middle of the night, he woke and was beside himself. Right now I am rotating hot and cold cloths on the legs."

"Will you bother with a doctor?"

"Not likely. What would a landsman know about a sailor's complaints? No, I shall see to nursing him." She filled a plate and began to break her fast. He was glad to see that being put ashore and living in a fine country house had done nothing to dull her good sense. If her husband was down for any length of time, she would need to keep up her strength; starving herself, either because of affectation or neglect, would do him no good.

"Is there something I might do to help?" He certainly was not fond of the sick room, but if the Admiral needed company, his might serve.

"No, he's sleeping now, dear man. I think the pain is easing up. If that's the case, he will be sleeping for some time."

"Well, if I can be of no use here, I thought I would repay Mr. Musgrove's visit. We hardly spoke, and I am curious about him."

"Why is that?" He explained about Richard Musgrove and that he was curious to see what sort of family could breed such a man. "I think you will find them rather ordinary. Perhaps even common. I have observed nothing that would lead me to think there is anything about them that would mould a man in such a way. Some men are bad for their own reasons, Brother."

"True, but still, I am curious…and a little bored."

"Ah, that is it. Well then," she said, finishing her coffee, "I shall drive you over myself."

"With the Admiral down, do you think it wise to leave him?"

"I will check him once more before we set off."

"I am content to walk."

"Nonsense. I will send word for the gig to be readied."

"As you wish, ma'am." He knew from experience it was useless to argue with Sophia when she had made up her mind.

Setting him down before the Great House, she asked again if she might not send a groom back with the gig. He refused her kind offer, and before she drove away, he teased her saying he did not wish to hear tales of her racketing about the countryside and bring censure upon the good name of Kellynch Hall. At this, her smile eased the lines of worry. Promising her best behaviour, she tapped the flanks of the horse and was off.

The announcement of his visit brought a welcome worthy of someone very grand indeed. Upon his entry, the servants fairly exploded with activity. Mr. Musgrove was happy to greet him, explaining that his wife was visiting her sister nearby and his daughters were make morning calls, so the Captain found him alone.

After the third plate of sweets was brought, along with coffee, tea, sweet wine, and a crystal pitcher of water, Mr. Musgrove finally determined there were refreshments enough for a simple morning visit. Such a welcome was gratifying. As Wentworth related the Admiral's condition, feminine voices in the entryway roused Mr. Musgrove. "That will be my daughters. Girls!" he called out. "Come and meet our guest."

Wentworth heard the voices cry out, then silence for a few seconds, followed by laughter. Mr. Musgrove had said they all were looking forward to his visit and that the girls were particularly looking forward to meeting such a distinguished servant of the Crown. It was a bit overdone, but he supposed children isolated in the country would be excited to meet anyone not from the area. The giggling and such was natural.

Setting down his cup, the Captain stood in anticipation of the introduction. To his surprise, it was *not* two little girls that entered the room, little girls at all. He wondered where on earth he'd acquired this notion of the Musgrove daughters. "Captain Frederick Wentworth, I would like you to meet my daughter, Miss Henrietta Musgrove."

When she raised her head, it was plain to see she was very excited to meet him. The fresh, round face was all blushes and dimples. Her eyes sparkled, but he perceived shyness kept them from looking directly into his.

"And this is my younger daughter, Louisa."

Miss Louisa was as excited as her sister, but the only time her eyes left his was when both nodded in introduction. She was flushed, but there was little he could see in the way of shyness.

"Girls, Captain Wentworth is Mrs. Croft's brother and the man who helped make Richard's career such a success."

He noticed a slight glance between them as their brother was mentioned. Perhaps they knew him better than their parent.

Settling themselves on either side of the Captain, the girls began pelting him with questions. How did he like the neighbourhood? Was he comfortable at Kellynch Hall? Did he like to ride? How long was he planning to stay?

Mr. Musgrove laughed at the Captain's indecision as to whom he should answer first. "This is why you must come to dine. Perhaps you could stay today. I'm sure it would be no trouble."

The man's kind expression and the attentions of the young ladies made the invitation enticing, but he was somewhat concerned with his brother-in-law's condition and could not disappear for the entire day.

"I would be honoured to dine with your family, sir, but, I must beg your pardon for today. My brother..." Mr. Musgrove nodded, quieting the disappointed noises of the girls. "But if I might be so bold, perhaps tomorrow would be a better day. Besides, I am certain Mrs. Musgrove would appreciate a little notice of guests."

"Papa that would do wonderfully! Then we might invite Charles and those at the Cottage," Miss Musgrove said, glancing at the Captain, then away.

"Yes, for you know how *Mrs. Charles* will be if she is not included, Papa," Louisa said, ignoring the shocked look of her sister.

"Uh, well, that is best left for later, Louisa," was all Mr. Musgrove said on the subject. "It will be an honour, Captain. I know you and my eldest son will get on very well. He is not much like Richard, but I know you will like him just as well."

The girls began to lay before him their older brother's sterling character. The prospect that the elder son was nothing like the second did wonders to lighten his growing dread of meeting the younger Charles Musgrove.

The time was set and the Captain prepared to leave. The girls were delighted to find that he was to walk home and offered to accompany him. He was a bit disappointed to find himself manoeuvred into accepting Mr. Musgrove's firm offer that he be driven to Kellynch in his own carriage. The prospect of a leisurely walk, on a lovely autumn day, with such lively young women for company was quite appealing.

Chapter Ten

Returning to Kellynch Hall, Frederick wondered what sort of spell he'd fallen under. There must certainly be an enchantment about the mansion of Uppercross for him to accept an invitation to dine with the family of "Damnable Dick" Musgrove, scourge of the *Laconia* midshipmen's berth. However, that was the past. Who would have guessed that he haled from a warm and welcoming family, not to mention that he had such pretty and amiable sisters?

Considering the merits of the girls, he judged the elder to be the prettier of the two. He also speculated that the younger, Louisa, though charming enough upon a first meeting, had a spirited looked in her eyes that promised a bit of mischief as well. He was surprised how much he anticipated the next day and meeting the Musgroves again. It was particularly surprising when remembering this was Anne Elliot's new family.

The Admiral was up and around in the morning, and he and his wife returned to their regular daily habit of riding out together. At breakfast, Frederick was glad to see Sophia's face was relaxed and not drawn and pale as it had been the previous morning. Her improved state of mind affected the cheerfulness of the entire household, he realised, as well as his own.

After their travels around the neighbourhood, they returned with news that one of Mr. Musgrove's grandsons was injured the previous day in an accident. The Captain reasoned that such a crisis would, by necessity, postpone that evening's dinner. "It did not sound as if the boy was too badly hurt," Sophia said, "but perhaps you should send a note, enquiring after his condition. Then you will have the latest report. If they have forgotten to cancel, it will remind them, and it can be done without any embarrassment on their part." He proclaimed his sister a genius in manoeuvring the complicated waters of country society. "No matter the locale, Frederick, it is always best to make allowances and give others the chance to save face," was her advice.

A note was sent, and within the hour, came a reply that, while there had been some concern the evening before, the child was doing very well, thanks in particular to the ministrations of his capable aunt. It went on to say that the dinner was not in any jeopardy of being cancelled, but that the boy's father would not be joining them. The note closed with fervent thanks for his most kind enquiry.

Sophia remarked that he and his initial note would be talked of with the highest regard around the social circles of Kellynch and Uppercross. "You are giving yourself an excellent reputation without much effort at all. You have always been lucky in that regard."

"Well, in this particularly, I did have some help."

"You have always had help, Frederick. It is just that you are wont to take all the credit for your own." He puzzled over his sister's words for a little while, but then put his mind to dressing for the evening.

~ ~ ~ ~ ~ ~ ~ & ~ ~ ~ ~ ~ ~ ~

"My sword, Harkness."

He stood with his hand out. When the sword did not cross his palm, he glanced behind. Harkness was buffing a spot of plate on the scabbard. He cleared his throat.

"Sorry, sir. Below they missed a bit of polish." One last swipe and he handed the sword over.

Wentworth took it and secured it around his waist. It had been weeks since he'd worn the presentation sword. In fact, not since the Plymouth Farewell Ball had he worn his dress uniform. He preferred the undress uniform, with its longer coat and less fussy lace decorations. But, now that he was at half-pay, he would dress in his finest costume and take upon himself the part of The Dashing Captain in order to justify decent invitations to dinner. Besides, he anticipated the justifiable reaction the uniform would coax from the young ladies Musgrove.

"Your waistcoat, sir."

Slipping into the garment, he began buttoning before Harkness could come to his aid. From the corner of his eye he could see the man fidgeting with desire to take over the task. In these moments he missed the casual, rather slipshod ministrations of Michaelson.

"My coat."

The man jumped into action, and in a trice, the coat was behind him, open to accept his arms.

As Wentworth adjusted his cuffs and Harkness brushed, he said, "Sir, might I ask a question?"

"Go on."

How is your sword kept in such immaculate condition? I mean, it is perfect. No evidence of abuse at all."

"It is in perfect condition because it rarely sees the light of day, Harkness. It is a presentation sword. It was given to me by the Merchants Alliance of Bristol. I captured a clever smuggler who was particularly adept at taking their goods and, by various means, sinking their ships." He chose not to share that the middling pirate and his crew were captured when all were drunk as lords and, after falling asleep, had drifted into the side of the *Laconia* where they were simply plucked up and piled in the brig.

Taking the sword from the scabbard, he held it for Harkness's examination. "There is no cutting edge. Were I to use this in battle, I would be hacked to ribbons in no time." Regardless of the weapon being useless, he took satisfaction in the fact that the blade rang nicely when removed and had a fine heft to it. "That is why I keep it wrapped in my sea chest. I take it out only on special occasions."

"Ladies must find it very impressive."

He would allow Harkness the indiscretion. "I can't think that any ladies have paid it any mind."

"Well, I can see that it could easily turn the head of a country miss."

"Perhaps, if a man was inclined to boast." The man was at once a puzzle and an annoyance. Could he be referring to Anne and their past or was he alluding to the Miss Musgroves? In either case, his statement was bordering on impertinence. He thought it best to ignore it.

"Well, I must say, they was impressed below."

No doubt. As he studied the effect of the entire uniform, he decided it would create more trouble manoeuvring through people and furniture than could be worth any amount of awe generated by the ladies. "I have changed my mind about the sword. This is but a simple dinner party; I doubt there will be any need for arms."

"Most likely not, sir. The Musgroves put on a good party, but nothing close to a brawl."

Handing the sword back, he instructed the man to wrap it well and place it back in his sea chest. "That will be all." Harkness nodded and headed to the door. "And you needn't wait up. I shall see to myself when I return." The man nodded again and disappeared.

Turning back to the mirror, he again measured the effect. The blue wool was brushed to perfection. He reconsidered his missing Michaelson; the sailor never did so well banishing lint from his coat. The gold threads of the braid gleamed in the candlelight. Though daylight was still abroad, Harkness had pulled the curtains and lit the candles, claiming it easier to see the offending lint on the dark field of his uniform. At least Michaelson had the presence of mind to keep this coat wrapped well against the salt air. Perhaps after his travelling when he had determined where he might settle, he would have another made. Since he would be caring for himself, it would be wise to have two. With the occasional tug here and there, he finished the inventory of his gear.

Glad to be living in a more modern time, he thanked the gods of fashion that he did not have to wear a wig. He was pleased to note that Harkness had put his all into tying the neck cloth and seeing that his breeches and stocking were sparkling. The only thing he could wish for was a better shine on his pumps. Settling on the bed with the cloth, he thought of Anne as he worked at bringing the leather to a high gloss. If the younger Mrs. Charles Musgroves made an appearance, he would be ready to meet her on equal terms.

Since accepting the invitation to Uppercross, he had given some thought to their respective circumstances. In terms of family and fortune, she had made a comfortable marriage for herself, but certainly not one of the level aspired to in the past. Though the Musgroves were second only to the Elliots in position in the area of Uppercross and Kellynch, they had no title to bestow. When she broke their engagement, her reasons seemed to be his lack of rank in the Navy, his lack of standing in the world, and fear of being left ashore destitute while he pursued his career. Her sudden placement of importance on marrying a man of greater consequence than even her father had dismayed him.

In the beginning of the relationship, all that had mattered was their enjoyment of one another's company. Even after he proposed, for two glorious days they made plans with little consideration of wealth or position. But after his disastrous meeting with the Baronet, her aims for the marriage seemed to change drastically. It was hinted that a marriage of equals would be accepted, but certainly no one inferior to the baronetcy could be seriously entertained. When asked why she had played him along, the tears had begun and the name of her godmother had come out. Once that occurred, he lost all sense of reason, and she had changed her tack, insisting that she was giving him up for his own good. In hindsight, neither of them had been at their best.

By marrying the son of a squire, she was, no doubt, well off; but without the distinction of a title, there was no elevation that would be acknowledged by her socially conscious family and friends. Now with the Baronet retrenched, their impeccable standards would, no doubt, be expanded to allow for their change of address. He reasoned that, among those who put stock in such things, perhaps it was he who had advanced the furthest, and had best elevated himself.

Studying the pumps and buckles, he was satisfied and took his place before the mirror once more. He had risen above all the insults hurled at him. No longer was he merely keeping body and soul together. He was a man able to chart his own direction. His labours had been great, as had been the rewards. His accounts grew with each prize sold off and now were earning a comfortable interest on their own. To ask a wife to live on that interest and his half pay would be short of lavish but no martyrdom either.

No, she had chosen to marry a man who could give her a home and children. He'd not heard how long since the deed was done. Perhaps she'd wed soon after his leaving, or she had waited as long as she dared for one with better prospects than him to come along. When none appeared, she'd accepted Musgrove. His being a first son was certainly to her advantage. Even if Damnable Dick had survived, all the Musgrove holdings would come to her husband. When the older Musgrove copped it, she would be the mistress of the mansion. While it was old-fashioned, and certainly no Kellynch Hall, it was a comfortable home to further a successful family line.

~ ~ ~ ~ ~ ~ ~ & ~ ~ ~ ~ ~ ~ ~

A knock on the door and a footman's message that the Musgrove carriage was waiting prompted him to finish. He smiled as he considered that though Anne might not be in attendance, it was still vital that he make a presence this evening. His uniform, his bearing, and conversation must be of quality in every way. This evening would be a rehearsal. He would use all the props and costumes so that when he was finally in the company of Mrs. Charles Musgrove, she would have the most advantageous view of the future she rejected. He gave another cursory inspection to his uniform and then gathered his greatcoat, gloves, and hat.

It was his intention to head down the stairs, obtain a compliment or two from his sister, and be on his way. But, without really thinking about it, he found himself standing at the threshold of the door to the small sitting room. There were no candles lit and the portrait was in deep shadow; but he needed no light. The face he saw wasn't that of Lady Elliot. The features he envisioned were the genuine, animated, provokingly pretty features of the woman's second daughter. He turned and left the room knowing that these forays were only hurting himself. Meeting the real woman would happen soon enough, and he was merely torturing himself beforehand.

He was gratified when Sophia was all compliments and did her share in fussing over his appearance. The Admiral, completely recovered from his bout of pain, assured him that he would have a marvellous evening at Uppercross. "They are a family that knows about having a fine time."

Over his objections, Mr. Musgrove had sent his carriage, but now he was happy to be travelling the three miles in relative comfort. Smiling to himself, he mused that the carriage possessed the same, slightly worn cheerfulness as Uppercross mansion.

He noticed something in the shadows and, leaning down, recovered a child's toy from under the opposite seat. A knotted string was attached to a horse on wheels. A yarn tail was down to only two strands, and he observed with a bit of alarm that the nose was distorted by many sets of tooth marks.

"You must feed them, Anne, else they resort to eating their toys." He tossed it on the seat next to him where the gentle bounce of the carriage caused it to slide into the corner. Out of boredom, he righted it and pulled it close to him with the string. Giving it slack, he allowed it to roll back into the corner. The child's toy brought the present into sharp relief.

In the intervening eight years when he had allowed thoughts of Anne, he saw her as a nineteen year-old girl, full of the bloom of youth and love for him. Occasionally, he saw her at their parting, but rarely could he stomach the scene. There was no thought that her life had continued on. He considered now and then that she would no doubt marry, but that coupling never took any form in his mind. He would soon see her with her husband, possibly her children, and her husband's family. The Bower Room portrait came clear in his mind. Instead of Anne's mother and grandfather in the frame, he envisioned Anne smiling and surrounded by her plump, rosy children. A husband smiling down on her with love and satisfaction replaced the older man. To his horror, his imagination supplied even a bit of wicked delight in the man's smile.

He flipped the toy's string away. *What in the name of Jove induced me to entangle myself with this family?* The answer was simple—curiosity…stark, human curiosity. The carriage jolted to a halt and the door opened. He dismounted the coach, the door to the mansion opened, and he propelled himself into the midst of the Musgrove clan.

After divesting himself of his outer garments, he chanced to hear ladies' voices drifting from the sitting room. The footman showed him past the sitting room, however, and through a door leading to a dim, little hallway ended at another door. The man announced him, and he was greeted by an exuberant Mr. Musgrove.

"Captain Wentworth! Welcome, welcome." Mr. Musgrove was as enthusiastic with his greeting as if they had not met for months.

"Sir, I am very glad to be amongst you again. I am looking forward to a splendid evening."

"I told Thomas to bring you in here to start. The ladies can talk of nothing but little Charles and his accident and will not miss us. I hope you do not think me unfeeling, but the boy is on the mend and I find all the stewing to be a bit much. This is why I thought to have you brought in here where we may converse in quiet."

The room was clearly dedicated to the gentlemen of Uppercross. Across one wall was a fireplace with three rifles and a heavy shotgun arranged above. A desk with papers hastily gathered and stacked, supported innumerable ledgers and even a map half-folded to the side. Rods for cleaning pistols and long rifles leant against the wall with a pile of used and clean rags nearby. Two chairs in the corner spoke to Mr. Musgrove and his son's use of this refuge.

Noticing the Captain's inspection, Musgrove said, "The room catches everything that my wife will not allow elsewhere." He smiled and handed Wentworth a glass. "Wives are funny creatures, Captain. They greatly enjoy the fruits of their husband's labour, yet they resist there being any evidence of that labour anywhere in the house." He indicated one of the chairs and took the other.

"I was glad to hear your grandson is doing well. I was concerned that his condition might be grave."

"Oh no, the boy just took a bad fall. Mr. Robinson, the apothecary, replaced the collar-bone, but other than a few cuts and bruises, Charles is quite well." He hesitated, and then took a drink. "My son should be here soon."

A tremor of apprehension shot through him. "I thought he was obliged to remain at home, on account of his son's injury." With the son could possibly come the wife.

"Aye, I spoke with him just above an hour ago, and he was determined to come and meet you. There is really no reason for a man to kick his heels about the house when a child is ill. Women know how to care best for them, and it only makes a man irritable to be cooped up. Yes, I know when the children were younger and would all be down at the same time, it was best that I just go out and attend to my business and leave the nursing to Mrs. Musgrove and Old Sarah."

The conversation was waining when the door opened and a red-faced man, approximately his own age, entered. By his familiar greeting, it was clear he thought to find his father alone. He started when he turned and found the Captain alongside the older man.

Mr. Musgrove smiled and rose. "Captain Wentworth, my I present my son, Charles. Charles, this is Captain Fredrick Wentworth."

Wentworth bowed, then stepped forward and offered his hand. To his shock the man offered not a hand but a pistol. Perhaps he had been a little hasty in leaving his sword. He stepped back and wondered if, perhaps, Charles Musgrove had discovered and highly disapproved of his wife's past romantic attachment.

"Oh, sorry," Musgrove said, pulling back the pistol, juggling it, then finally jamming it in his pocket. He offered an empty hand to Wentworth. "I left my files here somewhere, and the trigger needs a bit of attention. Captain, it is an honour to meet you. My family has been anxious to extend its hospitality." Musgrove's handshake was crushing and hearty.

"I had a taste of that hospitality yesterday and am glad to receive it once more." When Musgrove released his hand, he flexed it to relieve the soreness.

"And how do you find Somerset? Is it to your liking or would you rather be at sea?"

"Most sailors would rather be at sea, but I believe I am developing a taste for being ashore. That is a fine pistol," he added, indicating Musgrove's pocket.

"Uh, yes. A good piece, if I am able to put things right. Do you shoot for sport, sir?" Musgrove asked, shuffling through papers, ledgers, and trash on the desk. "Ah," he said, pulling a small pouch from under a mass of hand-written receipts. Leaning against the desk, he pulled out a file and began working on the metal around the trigger. "Because if you do, I have found several spots that are prime for pheasant…and quail if your taste runs that way."

"I have had little opportunity to shoot of late, so I should be pleased to avail myself of your offer."

"Good. I have several young dogs I'm training. If we go out tomorrow morning, I can take out that dun-coloured one, Father. I think he's ready."

"Yes, certainly old enough." The older man approached his son. "So you were able to leave the house with little fuss?" the elder Musgrove asked quietly.

"Oh, sure. As I said earlier, the boy passed a peaceful night. Besides, there's nothing I can do for him. We decided that we'd both benefit from an evening spent with family."

"So, Mrs. Charles is here."

"Yes. I left her with Mama and the girls. They're going over all the bumps and bruises, one-by-one."

Mr. Musgrove lowered his voice, "Do you think it wise to leave Jemima in charge of the boy. His condition is not serious but still…"

"You needn't worry yourself, Father. His aunt has stayed with the boy. I tried to entice her to come after dinner, so she could meet the Captain, but she thought it best that she stay home the entire evening."

"Well, if she is with him, I will not fret." He returned to his seat and his wine.

So the younger Mrs. Musgrove is not exactly a dedicated nurse. He understood her motives. Her curiosity about him equalled, perhaps surpassed, his own concerning her. Accepting the challenge, he would do his best to see that he did not disappoint.

"So, Captain, have you come armed for the country? If not, my father has that Beresford hanging over the mantel. A fine weapon." He looked at it with longing.

Mr. Musgrove laughed. "It is a fine gun, and one day it will be my son's. Until then, he must satisfy himself with his own collection."

Charles and his father exchanged looks that said this was an amusing debate of long-standing. Awaiting the answer, Charles's face twisted as he attacked the trigger mechanism. "Unless Wentworth hunts with a blade, I would appreciate the loan, Father."

Studying the man at the desk, Wentworth was amused at his own energetic preparations to dislike the fellow. Disliking Charles Musgrove was quite impossible. God love him, Wentworth thought, as he watched him buff the barrel of the gun with the lining of his dress coat. Charles Musgrove was the son of a prosperous farmer and a man of simple tastes. And this was, no doubt, Charles on his best behaviour after a few years of wifely improvements. Trying not to smile, Wentworth speculated how he might have been greeted before such changes for the better.

"I suppose we should join the ladies," said Mr. Musgrove. The unavoidable meeting was upon him.

~ ~ ~ ~ ~ ~ ~ & ~ ~ ~ ~ ~ ~ ~

The ladies were clustered at one end of the sitting room. Mrs. Musgrove's ample frame dominated the small circle. Miss Musgrove's more rounded figure and Miss Louisa's tall slender one stood to either side of a fourth figure. The woman was obviously the younger Mrs. Musgrove; a small fountain of feathers sprouting from her hair set her apart from the maids. Though her back was to him, he could see that, depending on how you measured such things, the years had been either kind or cruel to Anne.

To some, heft equated prosperity. And since it seemed, looking at both elder Musgroves, this was the fashion at Uppercross, then time had indeed smiled on Mrs. Charles. Her figure was matronly and showed the world that there were children about the cottage and that there was plenty of cream and butter on the table. But, if in quiet moments of girlish reflection, the loss of a slender figure was to be lamented, this woman was in a state of mourning. He, too, felt a twinge at the passing away.

Mr. Musgrove cleared his throat to announce the arrival of the gentlemen. Miss Louisa turned and smiled when she caught sight of him. Her gaze quickly passed over him and her eyes communicated a respectable amount of esteem for the uniform. Leaning into the circle of ladies, she said something that brought an appreciative gaze and shy smile to Miss Musgrove's face. The Captain moved to greet the elder Mrs. Musgrove, while the younger ladies discretely primped.

As the lady of the house drew them into the room, he could not help but notice that Mrs. Charles Musgrove had not turned, but still faced away. Perhaps she was just as reluctant to meet again as he. With each step he drew closer and with each step he reproved himself for allowing the portrait to trick him into thinking of Anne as unchanged. The fault was not hers, but his alone for indulging in such foolishness. But, the truth was inescapable. Though he could discern little change in himself over the years, she was certainly altered.

Just a few steps closer and it would all be over. Why did she not turn and face him? Along with her figure, had her manners had fled as well? No matter, once the introduction was made, they both would be free of any personal expectations.

"Captain, I would like to introduce you to my daughter-in-law, Mrs. Charles Musgrove." As the words were said, she finally turned. He could not help notice Miss Musgrove and Miss Louisa watching with inordinate anticipation.

"Mrs. Musgrove." He was well into his bow when he realised the face was nothing like the portrait. If he were not mistaken, the woman was even a bit taller. Straightening, he tried not to stare.

"We are quite lucky that Mary and Charles were able to come and join us, Captain. But Mrs. Charles's sister was so kind as to take charge of little Charles," the elder Mrs. Musgrove explained.

The explanation was garbled; too many Charleses, and no mention of "Anne." He heard it, but was still captured by the woman. Her nose, chin, lips, eyes, and hair bore no resemblance to Anne Elliot. But of course, the original owner of these features was alone, nursing her nephew at the Musgrove's cottage.

Mary Musgrove curtsied. "Captain, it is a pleasure to meet the brother of my father's tenant." She looked at him expectantly.

The woman's voice brought all his confusion to a halt. It was rather too high, a bit thin. Certainly the portrait had no voice, but his memory informed him that Anne's tones were smooth and warm and a delight to the ear. Though he was not terribly interested in the subject, one afternoon, all those years ago she had read him poetry. He could not

127

remember any titles or authors, but he remembered the voice being hypnotic when combined with the heat of the summer and the charm of her company.

Someone cleared his or her throat, and it brought him out of his ridiculous trance. He noticed everyone looking at him, and he realised the woman expected some sort of reply. Of course she would, she was the daughter of Sir Walter Elliot and must be given what was due her.

"Mrs. Musgrove, the pleasure of calling the Hall my home, even for a short period, is one I shall remember for many years to come." He knew he was laying it on rather thick, but nothing he said was a lie; and he wanted no room for misunderstanding.

A footman entered and announced dinner. Mrs. Musgrove had directed everyone to his or her place, when Mrs. Charles expressed her opinion that it was only proper that Wentworth be seated next to her. The others' looks of unease and exasperation, particularly Louisa, were impossible not to notice. He took his new seat in hopes that this would be the last time that evening that he came under the scrutiny of the younger Mrs. Charles Musgrove.

Chapter Eleven

The dinner was satisfying. The food was plentiful if unimaginative, but the conversation was lively. Each Musgrove had an opinion on every topic, except the elder Mrs. Musgrove. She followed the various conversations around the table, giving proper attention to each participant, smiling and nodding at the appropriate times but adding nothing of her own. The younger Mrs. Musgrove seemed to be above every issue, only adding her usually contrary opinion when a subject was nearly exhausted. Again, he spotted private, knowing looks between the sisters.

Wentworth could not help noticing that most of the opinions voiced, while morality correct and staunchly patriotic, were quite provincial in their scope. He thought it strange that his own physically limited world, encompassing only a few square yards of deck and a few tons of wood, metal, canvas and men, had broadened his attitudes, opinions, and aspirations so that they outstripped all others at the table. This made it very gratifying when Mr. Musgrove and his son deferred to him in any matter not related to sheep, hay, and vermin. He expected such deference from his crew, but from freemen, under no threat of the Articles of War, was very agreeable.

After the meal, the gentlemen withdrew and planned for shooting the next day. Over glasses of the same excellent whiskey he'd sampled before, Wentworth was made privy to all the best locations for hunting birds and trapping rabbits, foxes, weasels, and the occasional badger offered by the hills and fertile fields of the countryside. Amusing hunting stories of huge successes and colossal failures were related. When all the enjoyment was wrung out of the topic, Mr. Musgrove proposed that they adjourn to the sitting room.

When the gentlemen returned, the sitting room was set up for an impromptu concert. A quick survey of faces made it clear that Mrs. Charles was not altogether happy with the arrangements. After a bit of conversation he learned that the seating failed to measure up, as did the pieces offered by the musicians. Even the selection of refreshments was lacking. In hopes of smoothing the waters, Wentworth asked if he might take the seat nearest her.

"Certainly, Captain. Though this small sofa is rather hard and placed very awkwardly for listening."

He wasn't sure how the location of the furniture could affect the clarity of the music, but he deferred to her opinion on the matter. Normally he enjoyed music and welcomed even the most amateurish efforts by any man who brought a pipe or fiddle aboard, but he began to consider the ratio of enjoyment to be had compared to the company he was obliged to keep. It appeared that his good manners would likely do him out of a relaxing evening of entertainment.

When Miss Musgrove began to play the harp, accompanied by Miss Louisa on the piano, everyone settled down to listen. Even Mrs. Charles was attentive and still. They were surprisingly good, though he would have to give higher marks to Miss Musgrove for her musicianship than to her accompanist. None of that mattered to their parents who lavished the praise equally. Looking at the shining faces of the girls, he wondered what it was to be possessed of parents who praised, patted, and bestowed genuine adoration on their children. Perhaps Anne and he were mutually attracted because they had seen the results of grim family circumstances stamped on one another.

"If they practice, they may eventually become quite good," Mrs. Charles said.

Clearing his mind of niggling thoughts, he attended to Mrs. Charles's comments: "You would certainly know that better than I." Her looks of supreme satisfaction made him suspect that she'd taken his statement entirely wrong.

"My sister and I are *quite* as accomplished as the Miss Musgroves," she said.

"Yes, as I recall, your sister plays the pianoforte very well." The room and all its activities came to a halt and grew silent.

The elder Musgroves both were sitting, heads cocked as thought they'd not heard quite right. The young ladies stood still, posed like statues in the midst of exchanging sheet music. Mary Musgrove shifted in her seat to face him, a frown growing deeper across her forehead. To the other side, Charles Musgrove was completely still, but he was quite certain he could feel the man's eye's boring a hole into his skull. The silence was unnatural as all waited for an explanation of how he might know of Anne's musical accomplishments.

Mrs. Charles met his gaze with a steely determination to ascertain any and all of the facts. "So, Captain Wentworth, may I know how you are acquainted with my sister?"

He looked about and all the faces bore expressions of acute interest and patience. Shifting in his seat, he cleared his throat. "Well, ma'am, it is no secret that many years ago my brother was a curate in these parts."

Her lips tightened and a brow rose. "Yes, I remember your brother." Her tone let it be known he was not remembered with any great esteem on her part.

"He was the curate at Monkford. When I needed a place to stay for a while, I came and was with him for a summer. That was the year '06—"

"I was left at school that summer or we would also have met."

He nodded and continued. "We met at a party, Miss Elliot and I—or Miss Anne, precisely. However, I did meet your eldest sister and father as well. I was nothing more than an inferior officer, thrown ashore and praying for another commission. We moved in quite different circles."

His choice of words was specific and not by accident. After the engagement was broken and a short time of reflection, he could not help but believe that Anne did think him inferior. The pain of it had fuelled a white-hot passion to shake the dust of Somerset from his shoes and never return. Even now, with circumstances so changed, he felt the sting of his own words.

"We were no more than nodding acquaintances. It is very probable she would not remember me if you were to place my name before her." He could feel every muscle in his face as he worked to keep his expression unguarded and sincere. There was something like a release in the room, and everyone smiled and went back to what they were about. Mrs. Charles mentioned nothing more concerning her sister and, thankfully, asked no more questions. While she remained silent, he could see her mind was active and her curiosity aroused.

As Miss Musgrove played a solo and Miss Louisa turned her pages, Wentworth considered that there was nothing like a gigantic falsehood to lay a really good foundation for forming a new acquaintance. He could only hope that when Anne was confronted with his recounting of their relationship—and he could not imagine Mrs. Charles would pass up the chance to hear the other side of the story—she would not take too much pleasure in exposing him for a fraud. He would deserve it, but he hoped her quick mind would see that to set the record straight would open her to questions that she herself might not want to answer.

Eventually it was Mary Musgrove's turn to entertain the party. He was hard pressed to keep his countenance as she painfully made her way through a piece he could not recognise. Thankfully, she did not sing. As his wife accepted the enthusiastic applause of the family, Charles Musgrove leant close and said, "I know it's not the best, but she does try." He rose to go to her.

Wentworth guessed that a great portion of such enthusiastic praise for such a poor performance was to ward off a fit of pique that would, no doubt, follow an under-appreciated response. The inhabitants of Upper-cross knew that in order to keep the peace, they must sometimes sacrifice their own opinions. He could respect this, since it was no different than aboard a ship. He stood to receive Mrs. Charles back to her seat and give her his congratulations.

When it was proposed that Mrs. Musgrove play for her daughters while they sang, her son took great pains to distract his wife with a plate of sweets and a cup of lemonade. The trio finished to light applause.

~ ~ ~ ~ ~ ~ ~ & ~ ~ ~ ~ ~ ~ ~

"So, Captain, are you interested in thinning my pheasant population?" the elder Musgrove asked.

"Certainly, sir. I should enjoy that above all things." The musical entertainments were finished and they were gathered around the refreshment table. "As long as your offer of a weapon still stands."

Musgrove thought a moment. "Now that I think about it, the Beresford is a bit heavy for pheasants. But not to worry, let me think—"

"If it is a gun you are in need of, Captain, I am sure Charles could loan you one of his." Mrs. Charles looked to her husband. "He has ever so many gathering dust all over the house."

Again a silence seemed to fall over the small group. This silence he understood perfectly. In offering him one of her husband's guns, Mrs. Charles exposed her husband as a man who was loath to have another touch his weapons. Wentworth was certain Musgrove was as conscientious a husband and father as any man, but when it came to his collection of guns, all measures to protect them from the hands of Philistines were employed.

"That is a very kind offer, ma'am, but I have no scruple in using the heavier weapon—"

"No, Captain," Charles said, putting down his glass a bit hard. "I have the perfect double-barrelled and there is no reason you should not use it. In fact, come to the Cottage for breakfast, look 'em all over and take your pick." A curt nod said he was pleased with his generous offer. His wife smiled and made assurances he would be quite welcome to share their table in the morning.

The Cottage was a little out of the way to the best hunting, but the Captain was interested in looking over Musgrove's collection. Breaking his fast with them seemed the perfect way to kill two birds with one stone. The private quip brought a smile but, as he was about to accept, the spectre of Anne Elliot rose in his mind. He was not sure sitting down to a genial pre-hunt breakfast with the woman who broke his heart a desirable beginning to a day of shooting.

Before he could voice a doubt, Mrs. Musgrove interrupted: "I think it would be best if you were to come an' dine in the morning with us, sir. The Cottage is in a bit of a jumble these days, I think." A careful glance at Mary came from her mother-in-law.

"Aye, with the boy on the mend in the sitting room and all, it would be better, I think, to come here—you too, Charles—and dine at the Great House," said the older man.

"But I am perfectly able to see to a guest even when taking care of little Charles. I can wake him early and see that he has his breakfast before the rest of the house is stirring—" Mrs. Charles explained.

Looks were flying between little Charles's aunts and his grandmother. Wentworth felt a bit guilty that the situation was working so much to his benefit. The child's health and comfort certainly was more significant that his pleasure, but he thought it best to take the advantage while it was on hand. "You honour me with your very gracious offer, Mrs. Musgrove, but I would not wish to add to your already sizeable duties just for a simple meal. I would not feel right in taking you from your son's side." He was again laying it on doubly thick, and while there was no discernible response to his fawning, the younger ladies moved away from the table together.

"Then it is settled, Captain. You shall breakfast here, and Charles can bring one or two of his best pieces so that you might choose between them." He sensed it was not often that Mr. Musgrove made his authority as the head of the family evident, but he did on this occasion and it ended all further discussion.

The remainder of the evening was taken up in making the Captain aware of all the neighbourhood gossip, familiarizing him with local characters he might encounter, and generally folding him into the community of Uppercross.

~ ~ ~ ~ ~ ~ ~ & ~ ~ ~ ~ ~ ~ ~

The next morning, after a brisk three-mile walk, Wentworth felt energised, keen for his breakfast, and ready to hunt anything the terrain of Somerset could offer. He was announced and found Charles and Mr. Musgrove already at the table emptying plates of eggs and sausages and racks of toast. It was also a surprise to find Henrietta and Louisa at the table as well. Both were dressed for walking. He watched the sugar disappear into his coffee and wondered if, to bring luck to the hunt, some arcane family ritual compelled the women of Uppercross to accompany their men into the fields. He sipped his drink and listened to

133

the conversation. It was soon clear there would be no ladies trailing behind them after all. This was a relief. He did not relish the idea of being vigilant over his tongue when he stumbled into the inevitable rabbit hole.

"Charles must go to the Cottage and get the dogs, so we thought we would take advantage of the beautiful day and good company to walk over and visit Mary and little Charles," Henrietta said.

"And Anne," added Louisa.

The younger lady's smile disappeared behind her dish of tea as she drank, leaving only her bright eyes for him to study.

He raised a glass of water in a little salute to her. "I, for one, shall enjoy the company."

After setting off, the ladies walked together, leaving the gentlemen to plan the course of their attack. When they fell silent, the ladies joined on either side and brought the conversation around to their nephew.

"Both Charles and Walter were very excited to meet the Admiral. Henrietta and I think a visit from a much-lauded captain of the Navy will cheer our dear, injured nephew," said Louisa. She now walked beside the Captain.

"And you must be sure to properly greet his mother as well," Henrietta added. A muffled snort came from Musgrove's direction.

"I am quite certain Mrs. Charles would not appreciate an unexpected guest so early."

"Oh, sir, please? He is just a little boy who needs some cheering up," Louisa implored Wentworth.

"All right, I shall go in for just a moment, but Musgrove, you must go ahead and warn your wife. I'll not take responsibility if she flies at you for being unprepared to receive company."

"A capital idea, Wentworth." He touched his hat and trotted ahead.

"Anne will no doubt be attending Charles," Louisa informed him.

No doubt. It was now clear that their desire to get him in the house had little to do with comforting a sick child. His admission of a prior acquaintance had piqued their interest. How could he blame them? It was amazing that, in this small, unvarying neighbourhood, two such unconnected people as himself and Anne Elliot would be found to know one another and now be meeting after so long.

He steeled himself to see her, but then he realized that this unforeseen meeting was not something to be dreaded, but embraced. The situation was all to his advantage. His hope was that with Musgrove's warning, she would make herself busy elsewhere and there would be no meeting at all. Barring that, meeting Anne in this way, early in the morning, without anything but a moment's notice and in the presence of her family, was perfect. It was not a proper morning call where suitable conversation would be expected. It was not a dinner or party where people would be at their leisure to observe their recently discovered acquaintance. And at no other meeting would he have the most excellent excuse of Charles Musgrove, impatient to set loose the dogs and hunt. The whole silly venture was brilliant. "All the more reason to do this now," he said under his breath.

"Did you say something, Captain?" Henrietta asked.

Looking from one sister to the other, he said, "No, nothing really; just something about the season. Here we are."

Louisa opened the door and he followed her in. The entry emptied into a small dining area that was flooded with morning light. Crumbs and dishes and steaming cups testified to a meal interrupted. He greeted Mrs. Charles, taking care to say everything that was due her, all the while searching out Anne.

"Our little Charles is in here," Louisa said, gesturing towards a doorway.

Mrs. Charles hurried to precede them into the room. He heard, rather than saw, toys being moved aside. As the lady of the house roughly opened the curtains, she said, "May I present my sister, Anne. But then, you two already know one another." She continued to fuss with the curtains while motioning her sister forward.

The light was a bit bright, and perhaps that accounted for the fact that Anne did not look directly at him. "Yes, Miss Elliot. Good morning." He bowed and she curtsied, murmuring something appropriate. She looked past him and took a blanket from the back of a chair near the sofa and began to fold it. Never did their eyes meet.

Speaking a greeting to the boy, he wished him a speedy recovery. The boy said nothing but nodded vigorously and smiled widely. He glanced over at Anne. She had come to sit on the edge of the sofa and was smiling and nodding along with her nephew.

"There, you have made a little boy very happy," Louisa said, tilting her head in a very pleasing way as she looked at him.

"It is my aim to make as many happy as I am able."

Before he could feel completely the fool, a knock on the window reminded them that Charles was waiting. "I must be off for the hunt. Ladies, Mrs. Charles; a pleasant day to you all." He glanced at Anne. She was busy attending the boy and said nothing. As he was going to the door, Louisa announced it was her intention to follow the hunters to the edge of the village, and Henrietta agreed.

Immediately they joined him, Musgrove began talking about guns and dogs. There was no need for a response other than a well-placed nod or murmur now and then. This allowed him to consider Anne. He could not help being shocked by the alterations time had made in the woman he'd once held so dear. Her person was always slender, but now he would call her thin. Her youthful complexion was now drawn and pale. This made her eyes more intense, but they were no longer the bright, sparkling windows of curiosity they had been. She would not look at him, though he admitted he gave her little chance.

"So, what did you think?"

Obviously Musgrove was finished with him and Henrietta was now seeking his opinions. "Pardon me?"

"What did you think of Anne? Has she changed much since you knew her?" Both she and her sister were looking at him with expectation.

He could not bring himself to speak the truth, so he instead replied, "Time makes many changes, and I think it would be foolish to expect none over so many years. I will freely admit she is altered. Were she to go by me on a busy street, I dare say I would not have known her. And I hope I would not be offended when she passed me by as well."

He was grateful that this answer pacified them and there were no more questions. The ladies left them to return to the Cottage and the gentlemen began to cross a field heading to the hunting grounds.

"Thank you for doing the polite and paying your compliments to Mary. The boy was carrying on last night and this morning. It's put her in a bad mood. Having people stop by helps lift her spirits."

"Well, I hope I should know what is due, particularly when one considers the generosity of your family."

Musgrove brightened at the mention of his liberality, then set down his pack, and declared this the spot where the finest hunting was to be had. Wentworth was offered the choice of several shotguns. After hefting and looking down the barrel of each, he realised he much preferred the heavier Beresford. He chose one that was the most similar. While taking a few practise shots to acquaint himself with the piece, he considered the morning visit to the Cottage.

He felt natural sympathy when he thought of her standing there, studiously looking away from him. The feeling angered him and he shoved it aside while he took aim on a withering apple hanging from the limb of a wild tree. As bits of fruit and leaves settled to the ground, he thought she had no right to look so worn and used up. It was the first thing in the morning, and housebound women, in particular, had no reason to look as though they had worked the night through. What could be her excuse? Even the mother of the child looked remarkably well rested. If the mother could look so well when the child was in a bad way, what was the excuse of the aunt?

The groom handed him his weapon reloaded.

She stood there doing nothing but tidying up, folding a blanket. Her hands so sure in the task she barely looked at it. Sighting in another apple, he then saw clearly the truth of the scene. Mrs. Charles looked well rested since she had passed the night in her own bed, while Anne had used the blanket as she sat the night by the side of her sisters's injured son.

He pulled the trigger and recovered his sight in time to see bits of apple raining down onto the brush below. Handing his gun to the groom, he saw the beaters were in place and the dogs were restless and ready for employment.

"Musgrove," he called out, "I am quite ready to kill some birds!"

~ ~ ~ ~ ~ ~ ~ & ~ ~ ~ ~ ~ ~ ~

The Kellynch residents were arranged comfortably in the Bower Room after a fine meal of pheasant. He took a drink and waited for his sister to continue the genial harassment that had begun at the table. "So how are you when it comes to hunting rabbits, Frederick?"

He thought a moment. "Not good at all, Sister. Birds we have at sea, and I enjoy the occasional practice on them; but rabbits are another matter entirely."

"I was just thinking that since you seem to be making yourself at home, perhaps you could hunt to help divert the costs of feeding you and supplying you with wine."

"Ha! In the last two days I have only eaten twice at your table. At this rate, you should be sending a little something to the Musgroves for my care and feeding."

She smiled in a way that made him nervous. A low snort from the direction of the Admiral told him he had reason. "Yes, that is precisely my point. I think Mrs. Musgrove sets a very interesting table to entice you away from us." Her face was fixed with a slight smile, and her eyes were trained on his with brilliant intensity. His sister was doing a little hunting of her own.

The day had been a long one. Having begun with such an emotional scene and the physical exertions of hunting with a stranger on unfamiliar territory, he was drained and suddenly his stock felt like a noose. He got up and went to the window. For all the world, he wished he could look out and see the churning wake that was his accustomed view from the stern windows of *Laconia*.

"Frederick, did you hear me?"

"Yes, Sophia. I heard you." He found himself resting his hand on the mantel, his fingers excruciatingly near the portrait.

"Well, tell us Brother, what is being served up at Uppercross that is so appealing?"

He glanced up at Lady Elliot as he turned. Pulling back his hand, he leant against the mantel and said, "Mrs. Musgrove offers simple country fare. Good and wholesome, nothing exciting. But it is always in good quantity." He turned back to the window, hoping the interview was ended.

"Well, yes. There are two of them after all."

It was clear to him now what she wanted. Before he could answer, the Admiral interjected. "Leave the man be, Sophy. He has a right to make up his own mind without any interference from his older sister."

Yes, he needed no interference from anyone. The last time he was interfered with he had lost quite a valuable prize. He was determined that should never happen again. There was no reason he should not take advantage of the peace and marry, and there was no reason that either of the Miss Musgroves should not make settling down a pleasant proposition. There was no reason almost any young woman in the area could not do so. And there was no reason his sister should not know it.

"Yes, here I am, Sophia, quite ready to make a foolish match. Any body between fifteen and thirty can have me for the asking. A little beauty, and a few smiles, and a few compliments of the Navy, and I am a lost man. Should not this be enough for a sailor, who has had no society among women to make him nice?" He ended his farcical speech with hands open wide and an expression of pure innocence.

Her good-humoured look faded quickly and she said, "I shall not take your bait, Frederick. You and I both know you are good. You are in fact too good for some women. Do not allow haste and desire to drive you into a union with someone you will find unsuitable."

"I am not foolish, Sophia. I know what I want in a wife. A strong mind and sweetness of manner is what I want. Either of the Musgrove girls is strong-minded and sweet enough for the likes of me."

"But, Frederick, they are not the only young women in this neighbourhood."

He wondered if she had any notions of presenting Anne Elliot as a candidate for his approval. Before she could say anything of the kind, he concluded the discussion. "This is the sort of woman I want. Something less I shall of course put up with, but it must not be much. If I am a fool, I shall be a fool indeed, for I have thought on the subject more than most men." Again he presented the open look of one imparting objective truth. Sophia shifted in her seat and looked at her husband.

He was about to bid them a good night when she asked, "And why is that, Frederick? Why have you thought so much on the subject and yet done nothing about it?"

Though they were only fashioned of paint and canvas, he was acutely aware of Lady Elliot's eyes resting on him. It was as if she too were curious to know his answer.

"It is because I have desired to marry for quite some time, but the proper partner has..." he searched for the correct phrase, "...eluded me."

She may have dismissed him all those years ago, but the damage had been done. The warm attachment he felt for her had never been equalled. He saw no one to equal her now, but he was tired of being alone. If it could not be her in his life, other amiable woman would do.

Chapter Twelve

May I?" he asked, reaching for the *Navy List.*

A gracious invitation to accompany the Crofts and dine again at Uppercross had been issued to Wentworth that morning. Dinner was now over but the gentlemen amongst the large number of Musgrove relatives and guests were reluctant to leave the ladies, and the conversation had taken a most welcome shift to things of the Navy.

"Certainly." Louisa closed it and offered it with a smile. As he took the slim volume, the tips of her fingers met with his. The pleasant tingle made him return her appealing smile with one of his own. Turning his attention to the task at hand, he cleared his throat, fully expecting to read the ship's listing as it had stood for nearly six years:

> HMS *Laconia*; Fifth Rate, 32-guns, At Sea, Frederick Wentworth, Captain.

Previous lists would have included a brief history of his career and a listing of his officers and warrants, but this was a new list published quarterly by the Navy. It was not *Steele's Navy List*, but it was very new, and very up-to-date. For once, the normal creeping nature of the Navy's inner workings had been put aside and the most current information for the quarterly printing was used. He read the listing as it now stood, "HMS *Laconia*, Fifth Rate, 32-guns, Ordinary, Plymouth." There was no hint he was ever connected to her.

"She was the dearest friend a man could ask for." As he looked down at the volume, he thought how good it was that he need not look up. He could keep his expression in check, but he was certain his eyes would give him away. There was no use in being miserable; she was gone from him forever. He did have his memories and those would suffice for the evening. He launched into a short summary of his first cruises with her: the Western Islands with Harville as his first Officer and then his next summer in the Mediterranean.

"And I am sure, sir, it was a lucky day for us, when you were put captain into that ship. We shall never forget what you did," the elder Mrs. Musgrove said.

She had, at various times, been speaking to Anne and to her son as Wentworth praised his *Laconia*, but now it was clear she was speaking directly to the Captain.

"My brother," Henrietta said, leaning close, "Mamma is thinking of poor Richard."

"Poor dear fellow, he was grown so sturdy and such an excellent correspondent while under your care! Ah, it would have been a happy thing, if he had never left you. I assure you, Captain Wentworth, we are very sorry he ever left you."

For a moment, he wondered if Mrs. Musgrove knew all of his dealings concerning her son, would she be so lavish with her praise? He recalled one day coming on the quarterdeck and finding the Officer of the Watch missing. When he'd enquired as to who was standing the duty, his coxswain, Eyerly, had said, "That would be Mr. Musgrove, sir," as he pointed to the mainmast tops. Climbing up the mast, he found the young man writing a letter–to his parents, he claimed.

Wentworth had encouraged the young men to write home with some regularity. It was out of no sense of domestic care, but early on he'd discovered that well-connected mothers felt slighted by their sons if they did not receive regular correspondence. These injured feelings could cause a world of trouble for a captain, and he had determined that, as far as possible, he would impress upon his young men the value of letter writing. All his inferior officers who had dealings with the midshipmen were forever making clear his personal wish–each of *Laconia*'s mids would write home quarterly.

Seeing that Musgrove was actually cooperating, he was inclined to allow him a certain amount of latitude this one time. Out of curiosity, he demanded to read the letter. When he found it to be no more than a slipshod, mewling plea for money, his inclination changed. After that it was a test of wills as to whether Mr. Musgrove could be forced to write a single letter to his family that did not cry poor. In six months, Wentworth managed to force two disinterested letters from the thick-headed laggard.

Though it revolted him that anyone should mourn poor Richard or have any tenderness concerning the blighter at all, he could not deny the woman her motherly feelings. However infuriating Musgrove might have been to him and to every other member of the crew, he was still the woman's son; and by the look of her, she missed him greatly.

Wishing to speak privately with Mrs. Musgrove, he made his way to the sofa where she sat. He'd not noticed her, but Anne sat the other side of the sofa. Their eyes met for an instant. Though he'd looked her way numerous times, he'd never caught her looking at him.

Years before, he would have made his way to the sofa, not to console a grieving mother, but at the enticement of her soft brown eyes and sweet smile. Soon after their initial introduction, her very presence invited him to surround himself in their warmth. Now, with only the formidable frame of Mrs. Musgrove between them, they were as far apart as a man and woman could be.

Taking his seat, he spoke as plainly and sincerely as he could. "Mrs. Musgrove, as the captain of two ships, it has been my grim duty to order men into battle. Part of my penance has been to write the letters informing the families when they are lost."

It was clear that, while Mrs. Musgrove was generally attentive, she was merely waiting for particulars of her son. "I have come to the realization that in war the most arduous task is for those at home."

Mrs. Musgrove began to apprehend his speech. "Those who serve the Crown have their daily duties and the constant preparation for battle. We fight for our lives and then bury our dead. But you at home have no occupation but that of waiting for news. I do not envy you that. Please know that your family's sacrifice is understood and appreciated by his country."

Mrs. Musgrove began to cluck and thank him for his kindness. Anne's expression was troubled. They were all beginning to feel the awkwardness of the close moment, and he was relieved to hear the voice behind him.

"If you had been a week later at Lisbon, last spring, Frederick, you would have been asked to give passage to Lady Mary Grierson and her daughters." The Admiral stood over them, hands clasped behind his back. His smile was a challenge to the Captain's long-standing opinion concerning women aboard ships. A picture of her ladyship's fantastic turban came to his mind, and he said, "Should I? I am glad I was not a week late then."

"Why, Captain, I think that to be glad to leave a lady and her daughters stranded is not very gentlemanly of you." Wentworth noticed the expression on his face and the wink at his sister. When the Admiral felt things turning dull, he always seemed to know precisely how to liven up the evening.

"Sir, I was on a commission for the Crown. I must be prepared for any and all possibilities. To have supernumeraries, particularly of the female persuasion on board, would have complicated matters excessively. Lady Grierson, the wife of a sea-going admiral, would more than understand my feelings. And while I do not mind allowing women, in limited numbers, with limited freedom, aboard for balls or short visits, I stand by my opinion that the best place for them is dry land."

The tone of the exchange, though completely honest, was light and amiable. Those listening raised a good-natured commotion. He smiled and rose. Motioning for quiet, he continued.

"But I know myself, that this is from no gallantry towards them. It is from feeling how impossible it is, with all one's efforts and all one's sacrifices, to make accommodations on board such as women ought to have. There can be no want of gallantry, Admiral, in rating the claims of women to every personal comfort high–and this is what I do. I hate to hear of women aboard, or see them on board; and no ship under my command shall ever convey a family of ladies any where, if I can help it."

With just a few lines, his sister's countenance was becoming rosy and he knew she was preparing to rise to the defence of all women that he would so cruelly snub.

"Oh Frederick! I cannot believe you. All idle refinement! Women may be as comfortable on board as in the best house in England. I believe I have lived as much on board as most women, and I know nothing superior to the accommodations of a man-of-war. I declare I have not had a comfort or indulgence about me, even at Kellynch Hall…"

Comparing the Hall to even a First Rate ship was a gross exaggeration, and when she nodded to Anne, he knew she realised her blunder. Even at this, he knew she would not give up the fight.

"… beyond what I always had in most of the ships I have lived in; and they have been five altogether."

"Nothing to the purpose," he replied. "You were living with your husband and you were the only woman on board."

What one woman would endure for the love of her husband he knew a tribe of them would not countenance for a fortnight. And besides that, one woman uses only a mildly alarming amount of water. In groups, they have no conscience wasting the stuff barrels at a time. She was overreaching, and he could see victory.

"But you, yourself, brought Mrs. Harville, her sister, her cousin, and the three children around from Portsmouth to Plymouth. Where was that superfine, extraordinary sort of gallantry of yours then?"

His sister's exacting intelligence concerning the precise numbers of the Harville party surprised him. The accuracy of the scuttlebutt could never be under estimated. With the winds of the argument backing against him, a hasty change of tack was required.

"All merged in my friendship, Sophia. I would assist any brother officer's wife that I could, and I would bring any thing of Harville's from the world's end, if he wanted it. But do not imagine that I did not feel it an evil itself."

"Depend upon it, they were all perfectly comfortable."

And that was true. Because of time and tide, sleeping arrangements for the ladies had to be worked out. Mrs. Harville and Miss Fanny Harville were quite understanding of the less than spacious accommodations, and, from what intelligence had made its way back to him, the land-loving cousin was made to understand as well. They all behaved themselves perfectly; none expected that anytime they were above deck that they were welcome to wander at will. He suspected Harville had reminded his wife that the quarterdeck was sacrosanct and that it was his soul that would be in jeopardy if they dared to tread its sacred boards without an invitation from the captain.

"I might not like them the better for that perhaps. Such a number of women and children have no right to be comfortable on board."

"My dear Frederick, you are talking quite idly. Pray, what would become of us poor sailors' wives, who often want to be conveyed to one port or another, after our husbands, if everybody had your feelings?"

Curious, to know her opinion, he glanced towards Anne, but her expression gave no hint that she favoured one side of the dispute over the other. He returned to his sister's question. "My feelings, you see, did not prevent my taking Mrs. Harville and all her family to Plymouth." She had him and he knew it; though, looking at the expressions around the room, he saw that the assembly was less interested in the logic and rationality of their contest than in his abundant confidence and eloquent speech making.

He would never admit it, but his feelings had not prevented him from having a boson's chair rigged and arranging for all the children, even the little girl, to be taken into the tops. Their childish wonder of viewing the horizon was a feeling he still had yet to forget. It was of the same pure and unblighted quality as his own. Their questions were mostly silly but occasionally insightful. After he brought them down, he understood a little better why Harville's voice softened when he spoke of his children. When he had offered the boys the use of his second-best telescope, they had gone a little wild. Crouching next to Harville's daughter, he held the scope to her eye; for it was too heavy for her to lift. However, Wentworth's sentimentality was tempered a bit when it took him an hour of polishing to remove the mass of tiny fingerprints.

"But I hate to hear you talking so, as if women were all fine ladies, instead of rational creatures. We, none of us, expect to be in smooth water all our days."

He glanced at Anne. *There was no smooth water for anyone. None of us sails precisely as we wish.*

"Ah! My dear," said the Admiral, "when he has got a wife, he will sing a different tune. When he is married–if we have the good luck to live to another war–we shall see him do as you and I and a great many others, have done. We shall have him very thankful to anybody that will bring him his wife."

"Aye, that we shall."

"Now I have done," Wentworth cried. At this jab, the expressions of the spectators turned to him with great anticipation. "When once married people begin to attack me with–'Oh! you will think very differently, when you are married'–I can only say, 'No, I shall not;' and then they say again, 'Yes, you will,' and there is an end of it." It was best to leave the field with his perceived victory and wait another day to win the war. He got up and moved away, excusing himself to a little terrace he had discovered earlier in the week. It was the perfect place to escape the din of Uppercross.

The evening had started well and was continuing so. The arrival of the Hayters after dinner had made things a bit wild. The parents and the older girls were civil enough, but the younger children were just barely civilized. One of the little barbarians had asked how many pirates he had beheaded. The question itself was not nearly as disturbing to him as the cold-blooded gleam in the youngster's eyes as he anticipated the Captain's answer. When he'd answered that the number was not nearly as many as one might think, there had been a general groan of disappointment from more than just the boy.

Looking through the smoke from his cheroot as it curled and dissipated in the clear, cold air, he watched the servants finish clearing the now-empty dining room. He would have to finish his smoke soon, for when the servants were finished, the lights would be put out. He'd also found earlier in the week that this particular side of the house was confoundedly dark.

The last serving girl left the tidied room, leaving a lighted branch of candles on the table. He relaxed against the railing of the steps, confident there would be light enough for him to find his way back. As he enjoyed the quiet, he stared at the dining room and recounted bits of the meal and conversation. It was disconcerting to find his eyes always straying to one particular chair. Anne had been seated with the Admiral to her right and Charles Musgrove to her left. Their eyes had only met briefly during the introductions. The more dangerous moment had been when Mrs. Charles made mention of his previous acquaintance with Anne. Like a terrier, Sophia had come alive at this bit of news, and he could see there would be questions later about why she was just now learning of it.

During the fish course, the topic of cold-water sailing had come up, and he was quite relieved to bow to his brother-in-law's superior knowledge on the subject. With the Admiral the centre of the conversation, there was no reason he should not freely look to the far end of the table. If his eyes occasionally strayed to her, so be it.

Through dinner, Anne had said little to anyone not immediately near. She was only listening with half an ear to the descriptions of icebergs and seals and snow-covered decks. Her mind was elsewhere, though she put on a good show of listening. What gave her away was the necklace.

It was a simple piece, a few blue stones in silver, and when she was deep in thought, she fingered it. The necklace had nothing to do with him, of course, for he had left her with nothing but memories. He had thought to buy her a token that summer, but he'd landed in Monkford with just a shilling or two above ten pounds to last him until he was called back into service. As he listened to the footsteps of someone approaching, he wondered if her memories of that summer left her as dry and empty as those he kept.

"I thought you might be here." Louisa's voice interrupted his thoughts. She joined him, taking the steps two at a time.

He tossed down the cheroot and ground it out. "I find that some ladies, like my sister, do not care for the smell of cigars." As with his excuses concerning women on ships, he thought the truth was better kept to himself.

Pulling her cape close, she joined him leaning against the stairway. "Well, with deference to your sister, I like the smell of cigars. It is quite different than the scent of ladies and, therefore, more interesting."

He laughed. "My sister finds the scent alarmingly close to that of burning dung—excuse me. She does not like it at all." He was certain Louisa was not offended by such a candid observance, being country bred, but he did not like assuming. Now she laughed. "I respect your sister, but I cannot disagree more strongly. It is quite manly, and I like it." Her tone and demeanour finished the case. They were quiet together for a time. It was pleasant to find another woman who was not compelled to fill every silence with idle chatter.

As if to refute his growing good opinion, Louisa moved closer to him and said, "Captain."

He had no time to answer before another voice called from the darkness.

"Captain? Louisa?"

He scanned the shadows and Louisa sighed. Seeing Henrietta emerge from the dark, coatless and stumbling over unseen obstacles was an inexplicable relief. Coming into the little halo of light from the dining room, she joined them on the steps and said, "Mama missed you, Captain. I was determined I would find you."

"Are you certain it was Mama who missed him?" Louisa asked. The sisters looked at one another for a moment. They were remarkably good tempered with one another, and even now, though some tension was passing between, them they were not obviously angry.

Henrietta broke the gaze and said, "It is awfully cold out here." She chaffed her bare arms.

Louisa began to unfasten her cloak. "Here, take this…"

He touched her hand, and said, "No, keep yourself warm. Allow me." Pulling his coat from his shoulders, he placed it on Henrietta's shivering frame. She pulled it close and thanked him sweetly. "No matter who noticed my absence, I am now found out. Let us head back and join the party." Offering each lady an arm, they began to pick their way through the darkness.

The evening was beginning to lose momentum, and the young ladies debated how it might be saved. The Miss Musgroves suggested an impromptu concert, all the ladies presenting an entertainment.

"Very well for you, Henrietta and Louisa, for I am sure you have done little but practice," one of the Hayter ladies said. The scheme was roundly rejected, and it was made clear that they wished more of the evening than singing the occasional song and making up the audience. The elder Mrs. Musgrove agreed that compelling the Captain to sit through a second concert in just a handful of days would be very bad manners. The alternative she suggested was dancing.

This was greeted with a great deal of enthusiasm from both families. Wentworth enjoyed dancing and looked forward to the activity. Even before the men were called to move the furniture, nearly the entire assembly turned, *en masse*, to the sofa where Anne sat.

"You will play of course, Anne?" asked Mrs. Musgrove.

A faint smile came to Anne's lips. She nodded and went to the piano. As he watched her take her seat at the bench, he knew everyone was quite accustomed to this arrangement. With her tacit consent, the room burst into a flurry of activity. Footmen gathered vases, candlesticks, and glasses while others moved furniture, and a third group rolled up the carpet.

"Sets me to mind of a well-ordered clear-for-action," the Admiral said, as he, too, observed. Sophia joined them, reminding her husband that the last time they had danced was on board the ship leading the convoy from the East Indies.

"Remember, dear, there was a storm coming in and the deck was pitching more and more as the evening progressed."

"Aye, one had to be careful, else you wound up with the wrong partner."

"Or worse, a broken leg," she said, a bit of fun in her voice.

"And such proves my case concerning ladies on ships. No woman should be expected to dance in the midst of a blow." Wentworth smiled at his sister, and before she could respond to the jibe, he walked away.

A table with refreshments had been tucked into a far corner. He worked his way through the crush of aunts, uncles, cousins, sisters, and brothers to pour himself a cup of punch. He helped himself to a biscuit. The slightly bittersweet tang delighted him. Finding any sweets made with arrack was always a pleasure, but especially so in the wilds of Somerset. Dipping another in his punch, he enjoyed the commingling of tastes and softening texture of the crumbs. His enjoyment was cut short when he realised he was staring at the piano, and that he had no other desire but to watch Anne.

The young ladies were crowded around her, making their requests for particular pieces of music to be played. One or two of the young ladies merely thrust sheets at her, while others casually dropped them on the keyboard. The party expected her to play, and she would accomplish it well. Wentworth knew her talent was more than up to the task and that her keen sense of responsibility would not allow her to disappoint. Anne would play and comfort herself with the notion that she was giving pleasure to everyone—if not to herself.

In the summer of the year '06, as they were becoming acquainted, it had pleased him a great deal to see that Anne was most accomplished on the dance floor. She knew all the steps perfectly, and she had the ability to make even an unsure partner feel extraordinarily confident. Besides, she was the most beautiful woman any man could partner with. He could not help being aware that when they danced, people were drawn to watch. The envious looks of other men had given him immense satisfaction.

The party had been dancing for nearly an hour when a break for refreshments was called. Standing near the punch bowl, he again watched her. She stood there amidst the younger women, speaking only when spoken to, which was very little. He could tell she was observing them over the rim of her cup, not joining them in the spirit of the evening. When she moved to join his sister and Mrs. Musgrove, again she was amongst them only in body, not in mind or spirit.

"You are a very good dancer, Captain." Louisa joined him at his little outpost.

"Thank you. I enjoy dancing. It is one of the few civilized pleasures sailors might indulge onboard ship."

She laughed heartily. "But, since you allow no ladies on your ship, do the men dance with one another?" Her eyes were full of mischief and begged him to join her in the fun of the tease.

"Certainly not, Miss Musgrove. We have instruments—tin pipes mostly—but the occasional fiddle comes along. And in the evening, the men gather on deck and take their turns at jigs and fancy steps from whatever part of the world they hail from. Again, Miss Louisa, I must remind you that we are not savages."

"And you drink your tea in a fine bone china cup and watch your men. Do you ever dance, Captain?"

It was her audacious question that made him picture himself on the capstan, like one of his men, dancing a jig. It was vulgar and hilarious at the same time. "No, Miss, I do not dance onboard ship, aside from the rare ball. And that is why I am enjoying myself so much this evening."

"What sort of music do the men play?"

"Canty tunes and shanties. Sometimes hymns. But they do not, of course, dance to hymns."

She caught him by the sleeve. "Show me," she said, taking him to the piano. He glanced about and saw that Anne was occupied with his sister and Mrs. Musgrove.

After a few moments of trying to hum a tune for her to pick out on the keyboard, he took the seat himself and plucked at the keys. When he looked towards Anne, she looked on the whole scene with what seemed to be amusement. It was then he noticed that her sister and the young Hayters were joining them.

The tune was quite familiar to him, and he wondered why he was having difficulty with it. After several tries, he succeeded in remembering the fingering and played the short tune completely. The ladies applauded and proclaimed him a wonder. It was ridiculous that such petty accomplishments were greeted with such adulation. It was also ridiculous that he enjoyed the attention so much.

"Perhaps we should have you play for the next set," Henrietta said.

Turning to answer her, he could not help but notice Anne standing off to one side watching them. Her colour was much improved and her posture indicated that the weariness had lessened. There was an obvious softness about her face. Her eyes were brighter than earlier in the evening, and a trace of a smile graced the once pale lips.

Glancing about, the young ladies were awaiting a clever reply. "I don't think that wise. Only one music teacher has ever been able to penetrate this thick head of mine. The time was short and these, unfortunately, are the only bits of music I am able to play." It was all he was able to muster under the circumstances.

Her smile had grown a bit and he thought he knew why. His reply came extraordinarily close to telling the group that it was Anne who had taught him how to play the selections in the first place.

That summer, it had taken some time for them to become acquainted. After being introduced, they gazed at one another across one or two crowded rooms. Finally working up the nerve, he approached her to ask for a dance. Her warm acceptance bolstered his opinion that she was quick and intelligent and a good judge of character. After that first dance, her attentions were paid to others only as far as it would keep the two of them from being the topic of gossip in the neighbourhood. He cared nothing about such trivial matters but figured she knew the lay of the land and was determined that nothing untoward might travel back to the ears of her father.

The acquaintance between them grew quickly and, he was certain, becoming more serious. It was only a fortnight or so before he was speaking of their association extending beyond his time in Somerset. While she was always quick to point out the difficulties and dangers of carrying on such a relationship, her expressions all said that she looked forward to it.

Nothing was yet declared between them, but he was continually feeling the tug. Every meeting was sweet and anxious at the same time. Every meeting was an exercise in strategy. The problem was age-old: how to be as close to her as possible without rousing the suspicions of the entire neighbourhood.

It was a happy accident that brought the two of them to the piano bench. She had been curious about a tune he occasionally hummed. He told her as much as he knew about its origin, and it was she who suggested an experiment. For some time, at a party much like this, they sat side-by-side while he hummed to her various snatches of songs; and she transposed them to the keyboard. Her natural talent and acute ear for pitch could not help but impress him.

But it was more than her musical talent that had excited his feelings for Anne Elliot. The room had been warm with early summer, and it was then he first noticed her scent. Like most proper young women, she smelled of roses or lavender. When they passed one another while dancing or walking together, he would catch the occasional whiff of sweet flowers. As the night went on, he still noticed the occasional scent of lavender but fused with something richer, deeper; something not born of flowers. Whatever it was, he knew it was a little wild and conjured in him both desire and attachment. There was a creeping certainty that he would do whatever was necessary to have her for his own.

Laughter and a gentle nudge to his arm brought him back to the present. Looking about, he saw Ann standing closer, just outside the little circle of young ladies. He had to leave. He stood and said, "I beg your pardon, this is your seat." It had been a delicious torture to be seated next to her on that bench long ago, but now the stark recollection threatened to sink him.

Stepping back and motioning towards the bench, she said, "Please, Captain, continue with your songs."

To remain in her presence and continue at a diversion that started with her years ago was, of course, impossible. Taking a cup offered by one of the Hayter ladies, he said, "No, Miss, this was just some idle foolishness, nothing serious at all." Without looking back, he walked off to search out something stronger to drink.

In short order, the next set began. Anne was again back in her place. The particular dance was neither long nor very interesting and when they had finished, he asked, "Will Miss Elliot play the entire evening? Surely she will want to dance as well."

Henrietta answered: "Oh! No, never; she has quite given up dancing. She had rather play. She is never tired of playing."

As kind as the Musgroves were to him, it was obvious they were caught up in their own enjoyment. To anyone really looking at her, Anne was, indeed, tired of playing. The colour and softness of the previous hour was gone. In their place was a pale fatigue and discrete stretching to loosen tired muscles. She began again to play, and he turned back to his partner and the dance, hoping to put away stray thoughts of her aching muscles giving way to the gentle pressure of his hands.

Chapter Thirteen

Frederick Wentworth had little use for dreams. Neither grand aspirations of future accomplishments nor meddlesome, fantastical visions that deprived one of needed sleep. Of the first he thought very little. Having your head in the clouds and wishing for a brilliant future would never replace personal exertions, sacrifice, and the willingness to shed blood when necessary. Of the second, he considered them to be no more than a variant of the first, run riot. He had come to this opinion shortly after taking command of the *Asp*.

In a brilliantly coloured, heart-thumping dream of facing a frigate treble *Asp*'s size, he manfully climbed to the tip of the foremast, boarding axe in hand, dagger between his teeth, and jumped onto the deck of the enemy ship. He no more hit the boards before he was on his feet, hacking and slaying everyone in sight. It was a laughable idea that after such a momentous leap he would have possessed fewer than a dozen uncrushed bones and killed over a hundred men single-handedly. Having sole command of a ship and working through the mundane and tiresome chores connected to that responsibility soon pounded out of him such romantic notions. The only other dreams he had involved the opposite sex. He never saw their faces, but more often than he cared to name, these cunning and provocative sleep thieves caused him to awaken frustrated and angry.

This morning he woke with neither pleasant visions of the future or decent night's rest. The dancing at the Musgrove's had gone on very late. The elder couple had retired at an early hour, but not before ordering that a generous collation be served so that all might renew themselves. By the time he and Sophia and the Admiral had reached Kellynch, it was nearly two in the morning. After turning in, he had dozed lightly and dreamed constantly.

In the first dream, all the ladies of Uppercross were dancing but none of the gentlemen. In fact, he was certain he was the only gentleman present and that he was merely an observer. This seemed to go on for a long time, but when he woke and looked at the clock, barely an hour had passed. The next dream began the same way, but this time all the ladies were Louisa or Henrietta Musgrove. There seemed to be dozens of women, but no matter which face he looked into, only the younger of the two smiled back at him. This dream did continue a while. Upon awaking, he saw that the hands of the clock had moved an hour and a half. The most exasperating part of these dreams was that Anne Elliot played the music he heard in the background.

In life one could suspect that a certain thing was true. In dreams you knew to the core of your being that something was true, even without the slightest bit of support. He saw no face, he saw no instrument, but he knew the fingers that played the notes. After putting some order to his scattered thoughts, he got up, looked out the window, took a drink of water, and returned to his bed. "Enough of this," he muttered. His body cried out for real sleep, and as he settled himself, it was with the consolation that he was not required to rise early to duty, or shooting, or anything of consequence.

Out of the blissful nothing, he sensed her presence. His dream eyes were closed, but he knew there was no one else to see. She encompassed him little by little—a laugh, the thrill of her hand in his, the warmth of her next to him when they rode in his brother's gig. He gave in to the sights and sounds and sensations of their short, barren engagement.

Her kisses were insistent, though soft and gentle and he could not help but respond in kind. His lips were equally resolute in their exploration. He wished to reach out and touch her soft cheeks and neck, take her hair down and feel the silken strands caress his hands. Most of all, he longed to take her in his arms and, pulling her to his chest, make her part of himself. But, there was no holding or touching save the kisses.

The sweetness went on and on. The frustration went on and on as well. She was just out of his grasp and there was no relief. Each caress of her lips became its own delightful, taunting agony. Feeling her move away, cool air troubled his lips left warm by her touch.

He could now, in the dream, open his eyes. The scene that greeted him was of Anne, moving farther and farther from him. Her expression was passive. She was neither glad to leave him, nor did she plead to stay. He could not even be sure her look was directed at him. Soon, she vanished completely into whiteness, and he awoke.

He stared at the gathered fabric forming the canopy over the bed, their orderly, symmetric folds stood in stark contrast to his ragged breathing and blighted pleasure. It was not the physical discomfort that bothered him most; it was the deep and abiding disappointment that greeted him. He'd not felt it so deeply in years, and this morning he felt for all the world as if he'd had the breath knocked out of him.

It was not the first time this spectral Anne had visited him. The very first time he fell asleep after she broke their engagement, this was the dream that haunted him. The first few months after leaving Somerset, the dream had followed him. It diminished with time, but regardless how few the occurrences, it caused a bitter waking.

Closing his eyes, he allowed himself to drift back into the dream. No sooner was the delight of her re-established, than the door opened and the smell of coffee told him Harkness had arrived.

She vanished immediately and, though the scent of the brew was delicious, he considered whether a simple flogging or the more barbarous keelhauling would be an appropriate punishment for the interruption.

The sounds of water pouring into the basin and a tray being set on the table, told Wentworth that Harkness had a helper this morning. The sound of the strop was overlaid by the sound of the curtains sliding open. The room brightened noticeably. While Harkness was proving to be an accomplished valet, the open curtains would never do.

"Leave them," the Captain said. The clink of the rings on the rod accompanied the returning darkness. There was a moment of silence.

He heard the distinctive ting of crockery touching. Hushed whispers followed. Footsteps to the door could be heard.

"Shall I pour you a cup, sir?"

"No. Not now."

"Shall I leave, sir?"

"Please do."

There was more silence after the door clicked shut.

Try as he might, the dream and the agreeable feelings it had engendered would not return. Just as she invaded his mind and upset the peace he worked so relentlessly to maintain, Harkness had broken the spell with his coffee and hot water. The dream was depressing for it was a vivid reminder of how she had used him and then moved coldly away from him. It would seem that in nearly nine years, nothing had changed.

He rose, determined to be doing something. Brooding was not his way and would not become so now. Fastening his stock he lectured himself on self-discipline and the importance of taking command of one's mind. He suspected the lecture would become a regular part of his dressing regimen. The small and unvaried society of Uppercross and Kellynch would afford him no means of avoiding her company. Suddenly, he was famished. The late dinner and the collation at midnight convinced his stomach that it should be full constantly.

Over breakfast he considered how life in Somerset had acquired a pleasant regularity. The Admiral and his sister took advantage of every morning to walk and ride over the territory that was theirs by lease. He thought it amusing that two people who so loved the sea could suddenly become expert in sheep and trees and broken down fences. On mornings when they took out the gig, they cut an even wider swath.

As for himself, he was invited to Uppercross often, and he took advantage of it. Kellynch Hall without his family was a gaudily furnished mausoleum full of anger, resentment, and regret. There were spectres at play, and it was clear one of them could harass him anytime she chose. During his waking hours, the portrait presented him with a thorny reminder of Anne in her prime and the recurring dream brought her near even in his sleep. Uppercross was free of such troubling associations. Its only connections to him were of good meals shared with people who respected him for his accomplishments and demanded nothing of him other than his company and stories of the wider world.

A few mornings after the dinner, Wentworth waved away his brother-in-law and sister and headed to the Great House. The lane to Uppercross was becoming quite familiar to him. Already he was marking trees and bushes changing colour or losing more of their leaves from day to day. Soon the weather would turn cold, but he thought walks would not be complicated by snow before the new year. This reminded him that he had made no plans to visit Edward. It would take several days to travel to Shropshire, and he should at least make inquiries about transportation. He was looking forward to seeing his brother after so long and curious about his new sister-in-law, but the pull to stay at Kellynch went deeper. He knew he could stay as long as he liked. The Admiral and Sophia were glad of his company, and he enjoyed them as well.

He was sure Edward would understand if he were to put him off for another fortnight or, perhaps, another few months. How anxious could the newlyweds really be to have a bachelor brother insinuating himself into the midst of their marital bliss? He could think of very few things that would be less appealing.

The old-style house came into view, and all the previous thoughts left him. At one of the windows, surrounded by the sweep of the brocade curtains, he could see Louisa watching for him. Her pleasant face widened into a welcoming smile when she saw him. She waved and then disappeared. He had to admit that it was nigh on impossible for his vanity to resist the lure of Uppercross and his easy acceptance into their family life.

Returning to Kellynch after dinner with the Musgroves was not quite the chore it usually was, for that day he had been introduced to Charles Hayter, the much-spoken-of but never-before-seen cousin from a nearby property called Winthrop. The young man was civil enough in the beginning, quiet but polite when introduced. Henrietta informed Wentworth that he was a curate and that it was his family's fondest hope that he would be offered a curacy in Uppercross Parish. There was something of embarrassment in her manner when the young man said nothing for himself and left Louisa to relate his present circumstances.

Wentworth spoke to the young man, saying his brother, once a curate as well, was now a rector in Shropshire and seemed quite content in his parish. This brought no reply from Mr. Hayter. The conversation carried on apace between the other three.

When his brother-in-law inquired what he thought of the much-lauded cousin, Wentworth replied, "The young squeaker has nothing to recommend himself to me. He had nearly nothing to say, and that which he did say seemed particularly contentious when directed toward Miss Musgrove. I realize they are family, but even a blood connexion does not excuse such bad manners." His relief at leaving the presence of Mr. Hayter was tempered by having to take his port and a game of chess in the Bower Room.

His sister stood behind her husband, and as the Admiral made a move for his bishop, she touched his back with her fan. His hand floated above the board for a moment until it hovered over the most advantageous move. She then said, "All the Hayters seem to be a bit odd and quite unfashionable. From what I understand, he is the most liberal of them all. He is a scholar and has quite ambitious plans for himself, or so says his aunt."

With the two of them on one side, the Captain knew he was dished and began to hasten the demise of his little black army. "Even so, I had the distinct impression that he was angry with me. Why, I cannot say, as this was my first meeting with him."

"Too many women," said the Admiral. "There are so many women in those two families that a man can't be certain when he'll say something that will ruffle all the feathers and he's in the soup. Never good for a man to have to watch his words so carefully."

"I cannot believe that you truly think that." Sophia tapped him smartly on the shoulder with the fan and took a seat by the fire. "I think that most wars prove it is men who would do well to be more circumspect in their utterings." She looked first at the fire, then back to her husband.

The Admiral winked at him. "Oh, now my dear, you just proved my point exactly."

Wentworth laughed quietly. Were he to say such a thing, his sister would cheerfully throw the fan at him, most likely hitting him with it. She had a deadly aim. It mattered not, as the two of them were now bantering gaily without a hint of rancour. It went on for a moment more when she noticed her brother's amusement.

"And why do you laugh, Frederick?"

Sliding his queen to a vulnerable position, he said, "If I observed the two of you, without knowing you as well as I do, I would be amazed. How you progressed past mere acquaintance, I shall never know." The Admiral checkmated him.

"Yes, that is a very old puzzle, Frederick," she replied. "Why is it only certain men and women, when becoming acquainted, chuze to become more deeply involved?"

There was something about her words and in her tone that unsettled him. He watched as the chessboard was regrouped, listening to her shift in her seat. It seemed that sleeping or waking, speaking or keeping silent, it was impossible for him to avoid being hounded.

"We have no more than to look right here in this very house. Perhaps you can say why it is that, upon meeting not one but two good humoured, unaffected girls, you have obviously chosen to pursue knowing them better. But, when it comes to being *reacquainted* with a superior young woman such as Miss Anne Elliot you show not the slightest interest. No interest at all on your part." She finished her speech and he realized they were locked in a stare.

The exchange put him in mind of his boyhood when she'd asked why he had taken a biscuit without permission or if he had hidden the pieces of a broken bit of crockery. However old they were, he always played the little brother to her older sister. He marvelled how she was able to take a man who skilfully commanded other men, fought bravely for his King, and possessed an independent fortune and reduce him to a boy not yet out of leading strings.

When a ready answer was not at hand, he had learnt it was best to keep quiet and buy some time. He rose and refilled his glass, waving away the footman. Feeling an answer resolving, he took a drink. The words began to order themselves as he put down his glass. Now that he knew his tack, he took his time drawing a chair closer to his sister's side. It was almost a pleasure to think of laying it all out for her.

Stretching out his legs, he balanced the heel of one boot on the toe of the other. "Well, my dear Sister, are you now ready to hear the sad business that led up to my *reacquaintance* with Miss Elliot?"

"Certainly, Frederick, we would be most interested in hearing about this affair from the very beginning." Both their expressions agreed with her statement. He could not be certain whether her choice of the word "affair" was an unfortunate mistake or a calculated turn of phrase. For a moment, he considered laying out the whole truth of the sad business.

In the day-to-day business of living, particularly on land, it was his sister who saw to the mundane practicalities of the Crofts' joint life. If asked, she would surely know, to the last penny, how much the butcher was owed, which of the servants were to be trusted, and how much they were to pay in taxes for the year. Above that, in her knowledge of sailing, she was capable of taking command were the unthinkable to happen to her husband. And yet, though she was as practical as any man, she possessed the tenderest of hearts. She had often lamented Edward's single state and wished that he would find a good woman to share his life. He assumed that she stated the same to Edward concerning himself. In the Admiral's opinion, there was no finer material for a husband than a good, decent man of the sea. *To have had the support of two such people would have made the initial blow more bearable. To have their support now...* Rather than entangle himself further, he gave a brief sketch of the meeting between Anne Elliot and himself in the year '06. It was matter-of-fact and to-the-point.

When he finished, she asked, "And there was nothing more to it? A few dances and then a loss of interest on both your parts?" He was not certain she believed him.

"It is difficult to lose something you never had." He wondered what Edward would say about the guilt of sins of "omission" and those of "commission."

"You were not interested in Miss Elliot? Not in the slightest?"

"Sophia, I was staying with the curate of a parish smaller than that of Kellynch. She was the daughter of the manor. The hand was dealt before I came to the county."

"But as I recall, in the year '06, you were fresh from Domingo and all over the papers. I'm sure that counted for something with the ladies," the Admiral offered.

Frederick nodded. "It did indeed, sir—with some." Oh that he'd set a better watch over his words that evening with the Musgroves. This slip of the tongue was growing into a monster, and he would be glad when he finally hit upon the excuse that would slay it once and for all.

"You are sure there was no interference from anyone? Edward perhaps?" He thought it odd, not to mention troublesome, that she would think to name their brother. To date, the good reverend had said nothing significant about that summer, but would he withstand questioning? A little truth would sound plausible just now.

"He was not pleased with any ideas I might entertain in her direction. He thought it overreaching my station."

"So he *did* think there was something developing."

The woman was relentless. She should sit at courts martial. It was certain that neither the cleverest pickpocket nor the most heartless murderer could withstand her questioning. "He did not express it in so many words. It was more his looks and his tone when I would enquire about certain young women. The man can say a lot without uttering a word."

Her doubtful look induced him to continue. "There was nothing to it, Sophia. You know how it is! We were introduced as a matter of form, and then I went my way and she hers. You can't really think that any Elliot would pay serious attention to a lowly lieutenant, even in the wilds of Somersetshire."

"Certainly not the eldest daughter, but the second is a different kind of woman all together."

"Yes, she is, and I think you can see by her behaviour that she has no desire to see the acquaintance elevated to its former intensity. She is civil and no more." He turned away and cursed his own choice of words. If God were smiling that evening, she would not notice them.

"What I see is grave civility on both your parts. It strikes me as odd how two former acquaintances, no matter how insignificant the association might have been, are both so disinterested when you yourself say there was an 'intensity' to the relationship."

Turning back, he said, "To be quite honest, I did have a little more to do with Anne Elliot than I let on to the Musgroves." Before his sister could ask any questions as to how much they had to do with one another, he continued. "We were acquainted over some time. The usual things—cards, dances. We got on very well it seemed."

"And you came to care for one another very much." It was not a question. To tell her would be a relief. To tell her would be to admit his failure in love.

"Early on in the acquaintance, I had an opportunity to dine here at the Hall, and there was a neighbour in attendance. She took an immediate dislike to me. As Anne Elliot's godmother, she used her influence and saw to it that I was not welcome after that. As you can see, things are little changed."

"Might that be Lady Russell?" she asked. "She's the woman who lives in the Lodge," she explained to the Admiral.

"Ah, I see you know the lay of the land. Yes, that neighbour would be Lady Russell." The name still could not be said without a tone of derision.

He could see his sister thinking. The Admiral interjected: "Well, then the woman did Anne a great disservice. There would have been nothing unequal about such an alliance. You came out of Domingo quite well as I recall. The payout on your prize was handsome. The girl could have done much worse than what you had to offer."

He had come out of Domingo well, but by the time he had landed under his brother's roof most of it was gone. He had little to show for it besides two newly made uniforms, one dress and one undress, and the custom made boots he wore that very night. Shortly after, when he'd made commander, it had been a trick to trade the uniforms around for just one proper outfit of that rank. Anne could have done worse, but the cold light of his foolishness was difficult to avoid.

"That is true, dear. But I think we should put ourselves in the place of our neighbour. If she is the godmother of a girl with no mother, she has to be extraordinarily scrupulous in looking out for her interests. While you and I might be amenable to a young lieutenant looking in the direction of a young woman we have interest in, someone not familiar with our ways might not be so broad-minded."

It was nettling that his own sister seemed to be taking up for the woman who was chiefly responsible for ruining all his hopes. In addition, he could see her mind was at work on questions of the past. The present would just have to sort itself out later. He determined that a calculated retreat was in order.

Rising, he stowed his glass and approached his sister. "I am tired and off to bed, Sophia." Kissing her cheek, he nodded to the Admiral. She caught his hand as he moved away.

"Frederick, might there be some chance?" Her sympathy was there in spades. She chafed the top of his hand while she grasped it with the other. "Anything?"

He knelt by her chair and spoke from his heart. "Sophia, I think it best that Miss Anne be the one to determine what she feels about the past. Thus far, I think it fair to say she thinks nothing of it."

Her smile was taut as she patted his hand. Again, the "good nights" were said, and he left them. The door closed and he stopped in the muted light of the hallway. He hadn't meant to, but he thought how he might have stumbled on the absolute truth. Anne's scrupulously proper dealings with him, the dream, his partial confession to his sister—all served to convince him that she did not care.

~ ~ ~ ~ ~ ~ ~ & ~ ~ ~ ~ ~ ~ ~

Wentworth rallied in the morning and, giving a last thought to the evening before, consigned it to the dust heap. He enjoyed the walk to Uppercross and was not bothered in the least when to that walk was added another half a mile to meet the Miss Musgroves, who were visiting their sister-in-law at the Cottage.

"I will show myself in, thank you," he said to the maid. He was becoming as much a fixture at the younger Musgrove's home as at the Mansion-house and was treated nearly like the family.

Entering the drawing room, he anticipated the ladies and Mrs. Charles but found only Anne tending the boy, who lay on the sofa.

160

When she saw him, she stopped in the midst of the room. To be in company with her, alone, with no one but the boy, was startling. He paused in the doorway. "I thought the Miss Musgroves were about. Mrs. Musgrove told me I should find them here."

"They are up stairs with my sister, they will be down in a few moments, I dare say." She motioned towards the stairway and gave him a vague curtsey. He nodded and decided to take up a post at the nearest window.

"Aunt Anne, I want you."

Her shoes tapped across the floor to her small charge. Wentworth leant against the window's frame, turning slightly that he might watch her. She sat on the sofa and helped the boy with a plaything that was not working. She struggled with it for a moment, and he thought to approach and offer his assistance. But whatever the malfunction, it righted itself, and she handed it back. The child was talkative and she stayed close, taking the opportunity to pick up blocks and play figures that littered the floor. As she was about her work, she glanced up and caught him watching.

She stopped and looked at him as well. For a moment, there was no little boy, no young ladies upstairs, no time between them. There was only a kind young woman who once loved him. Her cheeks reddened and she went to a small box and emptied the toys from her apron.

Quickly, he regained his composure and said, "I hope the little boy is better." Turning back to the window, he heard the child summon her back to his side. Again he watched as she knelt beside the sofa.

She talked quietly but with energy, occasionally reaching up to brush aside a stray lock of his hair or straighten the blanket covering him. It was clear she cared greatly for him. This is why she stayed home the night the boy was hurt, and this is why she had sent his mother on to the Great House. She, unlike her sister, cared more for him and his injury than she cared for meeting a newcomer to the neighbourhood. Since he was really no stranger to her, the child's well-being had naturally outweighed his presence. At this revelation, he could not be but a bit ashamed of his grand notion that she used the boy as a convenient excuse to avoid being in company with him.

There were voices at the door and the sound of steps. Turning fully, he saw Charles Hayter.

"How do you do? Will not you sit down? The others will be down presently," Anne said, getting to her feet. The younger man merely nodded and motioned for Anne to remain next to the boy.

Wentworth was determined not to allow their meeting the previous day to be his sole impression of the young man. Louisa, and particularly Henrietta, had taken great pains to explain their cousin's rude behaviour. "He works so hard to improve himself that I fear he pays attention to nothing but work and study," Henrietta had said.

The man was young and had acted imprudently. Certainly, Wentworth could understand the desire for improvement. From Edward's descriptions, he knew Hayter had chosen a difficult occupation. The Church was a place where one misstep with the wrong person could demolish any hope of increase. He stepped forward and was about to greet Hayter when the fellow placed himself next to the small table in the chair furthest out of the way and promptly opened a newspaper. It was clear he wished no conversation or anything else the Captain had to offer.

Returning to his post at the window, he listened carefully, hoping to hear the sound of footsteps on the stairs. It was clear the only relief from this awkward company was either to make his excuses and walk out or hold fast and pray a swift completion of the ladies' business.

He had just put aside his serious consideration of flight and was removing his gloves and coat when the door from an adjoining room opened. Through the opening, there appeared a boy a bit shorter than little Charles. *And this would be young master Walter.* The little man planted his feet solidly and looked very pointedly at Wentworth for a second or two. The door behind him closed by an unseen hand and the Captain could not help but suspect that the boy had become a nuisance elsewhere in the house and was being sent off to the only person who could make him behave.

He smiled, and gave the boy a demi-salute, but the child's expression changed not a whit. Walter looked towards his cousin behind the newsprint curtain, then to the sofa. Deciding that the company of his aunt and brother was the most favourable source of amusement, he charged towards the sofa.

"What is he eating?" the boy asked, even before he reached his aunt.

"Charles has nothing to eat. Besides, you just finished breakfast, Walter."

Wentworth was somewhat baffled by the child's unfriendly response since he was usually a favourite with children. While he was not precisely "Uncle" to Harville's children, they were not in the least hesitant when it came to sitting on him or fingering his gold braid or stretching the bullions on his epaulettes. More than once Mrs. Harville had taken his coat away and returned with the tiny golden cords put back in fine naval order. Visiting with Harville's family was a pleasure, though it never failed to remind him that he had no wife and children of his own.

"But he has something there," Walter said, as he began to pull at his brother.

Anne took the boy's hands and placed them at his side. "Charles has nothing. But you may play with the blocks or perhaps the little boat." She reached into the box where the other toys had been placed and took out a little wooden ship with two masts complete with small sails. The boy grabbed it from his aunt and held it out to his brother, but snatched it away before Charles could take it. Then, with no provocation, Walter threw it to the floor.

"Walter. You are being very unkind to your brother." On her knees, she made her way to the boat and took it up. She glanced his way, and then went back to the boys.

The child's obvious lack of enthusiasm for things naval reinforced Wentworth's dislike. He earnestly hoped he was not so petty as to despise a child merely for bearing the name of a buffoonish grandsire, but he suspected that he was burdening the child with the sins of the Baronet.

Just then, the little urchin turned his attentions away from his brother. He first took his aunt's arm and kept a tight hold of it. When she extracted him, he encircled his arms around her neck. He got away with it for a moment by placing a fat, wet kiss on her cheek. "I love you Auntie Anne," he said.

She smiled and replied, "I love you too, Walter, but you must let me go. I can't tend your brother like this."

Wentworth, too, smiled. It was easy to see this was precisely the child's plan. The little beggar was giggling with delight. He knew he'd hit upon a winning strategy to have his brother's share of his aunt's attention. She nearly got him away when he then managed to climb onto her back. The child was of a fair size and Wentworth could see that his weight bowed her down.

"Walter, get down this moment. You are extremely troublesome. I am very angry with you." Reaching back, she tried to grasp a hold of him, but his plump legs bent and flexed just out of her reach.

It was apparent that little Walter Musgrove neither cared about being troublesome nor that he was making his aunt angry. Fortunately, he was too young to purposely intend Anne any harm. Glancing at the cousin, Wentworth saw little activity. The paper was moving, but it seemed there would be no assistance from that quarter. Though it was none of his affair, he was about to intervene when the paper rattled to the table and Hayter said, "Walter, why do you not do as you are bid? Do you not hear your aunt speak? Come to me, Walter, come to Cousin Charles."

And why do you not take some decisive action to make the little blighter mind? The child was deaf to the voice of his cousin and continued tormenting his aunt. Before giving it any real consideration, he stepped into the fracas.

At first he thought it a simple matter to scoop the child up and take him off to the far side of the room, but when the boy realized what was happening, a struggle began. Sliding his hand under the boy's belly and gently grasping his shoulder, Wentworth lifted. In all the shifting, his fingers caught in Anne's apron strings, and to make matters worse, the little squeaker refused to let go of her neck. Disentangling his own fingers, he reached around to Walter's little hands and, with a little prodding, unwrapped them from around her neck. To his dismay, the chubby little fists were sticky. Moreover, he couldn't help but touch the soft skin of Anne's face and neck as he worked. A lock of her hair went astray in the tumble. Finally the boy was loose, and he was able to grasp him by the trousers and lift him away.

Walter made a lunge, but Wentworth held him more tightly to his chest. Twisting, he tried to struggle down, but Wentworth's strong arms trapped him and he quickly surrendered.

He looked over at the sofa where Anne bent over little Charles, speaking to him softly. She seemed unhurt but in need of assistance to stand. Just as he was about to offer his hand, his little captive, still struggling, kicked him. Any aid would have to be left to Hayter but the curate offered nothing save a mild scolding. "You ought to have minded *me*, Walter; I told you not to teaze your aunt."

Wentworth turned his attention to the boy. "You are a naughty one, aren't you?" The child was not too young to understand that grasping a man's neck cloth and giving it a ferocious yank was not to be tolerated. *I cannot determine whom you most favour, your puffed-up grandfather or your embarrassment of an uncle. I see them both so clearly?* "Oh, isn't that wonderful? The Captain is becoming acquainted with little Walter." Mrs. Charles's voice carried over all the other sounds in the room. He looked over to see the ladies coming to him and the boy.

"Charles, you are come too," Louisa said, noticing the man at the table. Henrietta looked at him and then quickly away.

"Excuse me, Mary," Anne interrupted, "but you will have to see to little Charles. I must fetch something from my room." Her expression was indiscernible to him, and she moved away without looking to the right or left.

Mary glanced back at the boy on the sofa and then took the hand of her youngest son. Quickly letting go, she said, "I am not in the least surprised, Captain, that you are drawn to little Walter. I love my children equally, but I must confess I see much more of the Elliot character and countenance in my youngest."

A clattering sound drew everyone's attention to the door. Anne knelt to pick up a wooden toy that blocked her path. There had been no thanks when he rescued her from the child. No words of credit or appreciation had passed her lips, not that he wanted or expected any. But now, as she knelt, her eyes looked nowhere but to him. Her look of gratitude was inescapable. Giving the toy a gentle push, she rose, passed into the next room and receded into the shadows as she pulled the door closed.

So, this was her life—caring for the children of others while they carried on unencumbered, playing the tune so that others might dance. Anne Elliot was bound to her family and those around her by a strong sense of duty and obligation, and as long as she kept to these duties and obligations, she was assured of the good opinion of all in her circle. It was fortunate there was no interest on his part, for he could never persuade her away from her slavish existence. Yes, he was fortunate indeed.

Out of the blue, the boy lunged and cried, "Mama," distracting him from his thoughts. Glad to be rid of his squirming burden, he said, "Madam, I assure you that I see not only yourself in the boy, but a great deal of his Musgrove forbearers." As he spoke, he hoisted the child over to his mother. She had no choice but to take him, sticky hands and all. Fetching his gloves and coat, he looked around and was glad all the ladies were occupied and had not paid any heed to his comment. He could not escape the thought that, had she been present, Anne would have understood his allusion perfectly.

Chapter Fourteen

The days settled into a regular pattern of shooting in the morning with one or both of the Musgrove men. After hunting, he would join the family at Uppercross for elevenses; the ladies were always accommodating and quickly came to expect him as though he were one of their own. Eventually he would return to Kellynch and make inquiries, hoping that some mail might have followed him from Plymouth. After a bit of a rest, he would change for dinner and, when not promised to the Musgroves, join his sister and the Admiral for a quiet evening. While he did enjoy the company and sporting pursuits of the country, the unvarying days were wearing; and he longed for the activity and excitement of his former life.

Coming down the stairs this morning, he could not help but feel it was a repeat of all the days that had gone before. Though Musgrove had promised him the use of a particularly fine weapon for the day's hunt, he mused it would have to be a fine weapon indeed to set this day's shooting apart from the rest.

Breaking his fast, the Captain exchanged a few words with his brother-in-law and began the walk to Uppercross. While there would be no chance meeting with Anne today, the small society of Uppercross had forced their meeting on several previous occasions. There was the morning he came upon her when the shooters returned to the mansion for much needed refreshment. They found Little Charles, whose health was improving daily, had made the walk from the Cottage to visit with his grandparents. Since his mother was feeling under the weather that morning, his aunt had accompanied him. Her greeting to him was, as usual, proper in every way. Another evening they had dined together at the Great House. Again, her greeting was efficient and brief. It mattered not if their meetings were expected or casual, her duty to him was dispatched with the utmost civility and calm indifference.

The previous morning, Musgrove had indicated more anxiety than usual to be out of the house, promising to meet him at the edge of the village, guns and dogs at the ready. It was a relief to know that, today, there would be no surprise meeting with Anne and no need to rescue her from the tortures of the *enfant terrible*, Walter.

As he drew near the Cottage, he could see Musgrove, true to his word, trying to control a young hound he insisted would be a champion one day. The dog put Wentworth more in mind of the man's unruly brother than a well-trained hunter.

The dog, unfortunately, ruined the hunt; and as the sportsmen returned there was only light conversation. "So what do you think of the Harrington? I prefer it to father's Beresford; it's so heavy you have to hit just right or you'll have nothing left to bring home." He walked on a moment and then added, "You seem to do quite well with it."

"It is a wonderful piece. Its beauty alone is enough to make me like it." He saw beauty in many things, but when it was present in weapons, he was especially appreciative. He owned several edge weapons that were finely crafted for precision and, in his opinion, as lovely as any jewellery. He could fully appreciate this shotgun's ivory inlaid stock and engraved barrel. Perhaps when he was settled, he would expand his own collection to include shooting weapons.

"And it's handsomely crafted, along with the balance of the barrel. She is a prize."

"Now perhaps you understand why I can be so tight-fisted about her. I'm sorry about the dog. He's got all the breeding of a first-rater, but he just doesn't seem to get the hang of fetching back the birds."

For the third time that morning, Wentworth assured Musgrove he was not disappointed in the least by the dog's antics. He said nothing about being sick to death of pheasant and the many other winged creatures they had shot and eaten in the last week. "In fact, as the season will be ending soon, I am thinking of buying a horse so that I might go riding. I am no shrewd judge of horseflesh, Charles. I wonder if you might recommend a trustworthy dealer."

Now that they were in view of the Cottage, Musgrove untied the dog and watched him dash towards his food and water. "Well, there are none here in Uppercross, and the fellow in Monkford is not to be trusted. I would say a man named Hugh Benedict, in Crewkherne, would be your best bet. His grandfather was a Frenchy, but he behaves himself like a proper Englishman."

Before he could ask whereabouts in Crewkherne Mr. Benedict did his business, Musgrove's sisters and his wife met the gentlemen. Bringing up the rear came Anne. When asked about their destination, Louisa was vague concerning the locale but replied they were for a long walk and invited the Captain to join them.

Mr. Benedict was forgotten, and Wentworth consulted with Musgrove as to his desire for a walk. When the gentlemen accepted, they returned their hunting gear to the house and the miscreant dog to its kennel. Upon rejoining the party, Wentworth noticed a look from Anne that went from him to each of the young ladies. She was interested in something concerning them, and he was curious to know what it might be.

As they left the village, it was clear that the sisters were the guiding force behind the walk and so took the lead. As with most things involving the two, Louisa appeared to be more the leader than her sister. She set the direction and pace and seemed quite content to divide her attention between him and, occasionally, her sister, leaving Mr. and Mrs. Musgrove and Anne to fend for themselves.

The conversation was easy and lively. Once the subjects of the weather, cold nights, clear and sunny days, and shooting were exhausted, the talk turned to the health of those in the neighbourhood, his family in particular.

"And how is the Admiral? Mamma has been concerned about his legs. Your sister says he has been down with the gout," Henrietta observed.

"I'm not sure it is gout, but he has been well enough to take her out in the gig the last few mornings. He was suffering terribly, but it seems to have passed."

"Is it true that sailors, who have been at sea for some time, can barely walk on land for days, even weeks?" Louisa made a hasty survey of his legs.

"It can be jarring, reacquainting oneself to dry land. Walking on a constantly shifting, wooden deck is much different than the hard, unyielding ground."

"Then I am surprised you would come on a long walk with us. To walk into the fields and hunt is one thing, but to take a walk with no purpose seems fruitless."

Louisa was young but clever. She knew very well how to fish for a compliment. And he decided he would rise to her bait. "Ah, but the real purpose it to have good company. Good company is difficult to come by, and that makes any discomfort worthwhile. Besides, I walked miles a day on board my ship. I find it helps to clear the mind."

"And how can that be? How can you walk for miles when you are so confined?"

"Simple. When a man strides approximately three feet per step, and that is multiplied by the circumference of the quarter deck and the length and breadth of the ship, it makes for a great deal of walking in a day."

There was always more to say about very little, and he was just in the mood to do so as they made their way across the open fields. Narrow paths made staying all together impossible. He could not help but notice that Anne was saying nothing but keeping dutifully to her sister and brother-in-law.

Louisa, on the other hand, had many observations of the changing countryside, and the glorious crisp, clear weather. "Although, I do so look forward to the snug evenings when the days are short and much colder. It is really like life, is it not? Time passes more quickly and the outside world grows less and less tempting."

What she said had truth to it, if one cared to view the world as something that diminished over time. But this was the view of a person who rarely travelled more than one hundred miles in a lifetime. He had travelled thousands in a few short years and hoped to travel many more. The topic of shorter days and cold nights conflicted with his mood just then. He decided a change was in order. "What glorious weather for the Admiral and my sister! They meant to take a long drive this morning. Perhaps, we may hail them from some of these hills. They talked of coming into this side of the country. I wonder whereabouts they will upset today. Oh! It does happen often, I assure you, but my sister makes nothing of it. She would as lieve be tossed out as not."

"I am sure you do not intend it so, but that seems a harsh thing to say of the Admiral's skills with a gig," said Henrietta.

"Ah, you make the most of it, I know," declared Louisa, "but if it were really so, I should do just the same in her place. If I loved a man, as she loves the Admiral, I would always be with him, nothing should ever separate us, and I would rather be overturned by him, than driven safely by anybody else."

The sentiment was quite perceptive and full of feeling on her part. While he was fully prepared to poke fun at his sister's warm-hearted, though potentially injurious constancy to her husband, he could not help but admire it. He could not stop wishing something like it for himself.

"Had you?" he said, matching her high, romantic tone. "I honour you." The walk in general was giving him glimpses of a depth of perception in Louisa, until now unseen. Perhaps there was something to be said for physical exercise and the beauty of the countryside when it came to increasing the attraction of young English women.

The group continued for a time in silence. When they came to diverging paths, the girls consulted no one but confidently led the way.

An extended conversation between the Miss Musgroves allowed him an opportunity to slip from their sight and, setting his own pace, observe the day. Through an odd chain of divisions necessitated by the freshly turned field, he found himself bringing up the rear, following behind

Anne, who had chosen to allow a separation between her and her sister. At a clearing overlooking a valley, she stopped for a moment, looked over the scene and asked, "Is this not one of the ways to Winthrop?" Not even her brother-in-law, who walked directly ahead and might hear her, paid heed to the question. The group moved on.

Looking again over the valley, she sighed. When she noticed that she blocked him, she coloured, gathered her cape about her and, murmuring an apology, hurried to catch the rest of them. He was caught up to her in just a few strides.

The walking was slower through another freshly tilled field. It was customary for the farmer to leave a narrow strip along the edges so that travellers might have a path that would keep them from trampling the growing crop. The owner of this field had ploughed right to the fence line, leaving no place to walk save through the small ditch left after the last pass of the plough. A large clump of earth had fallen in the trough, and when Anne stepped on it, it collapsed and she stumbled. In an instant, he caught her and, before thinking, said, "Steady on. It won't do to have you hurting yourself."

"Thank you, sir." There was no telling whether the high colour of her cheeks was from exercising in the brisk autumn air or because he held her so close." I am quite sound now," she said, barely above a whisper. Glancing to the group disappearing around a bend, she moved to join them. He did nothing to stop her. His heart was pounding, and now *he* was not certain whether it was from the exercise or the nearness of her. It did not matter and he applied himself to studying his surroundings.

On the whole, the change of seasons had little meaning to a sailor. The sea and sky changed as the weather gods saw fit. Days could go by with only the slightest variance in shades of blue and grey. Certainly, he had been fortunate in that his assignments were all in warm weather climes. He had avoided many English winters altogether. Thus, the autumnal foliage was a treat. Its riot of colour was breathtaking, and the brilliant sunshine which accompanied the cool air made a delightful juxtaposition. Regardless of the novelty of his surroundings and his enjoyment of it, he longed to be back at sea. An existence on the water was as natural to him as the turning of the leaves from their supple green to brittle gold or the fading of the verdant grasses to straw. Autumn on land was a glorious sight, but it was one he would happily forego for the white crests of the sea.

For some time they had been climbing a considerable hill. Everyone saved their breath for the trek, and so, all were silent until they reached the crest, whereupon they all exclaimed their relief. A breeze touched Wentworth's brow when he removed his hat. It was cool and sweet and nearly as refreshing as those which made the tops of the masts his particular haven. In that moment, he determined that if he were forced permanently onshore, he would build a house on the highest point the territory could provide. If he must be a land creature, he would do as other sea-going refugees and mount a scope on his "Olympus" and spend all his time looking over the countryside.

"Bless me! Here is Winthrop—I declare I had no idea—well, now I think we had better turn back. I am excessively tired." Mrs. Charles announced, her voice high as she turned her back to the view of the valley and stalked away. "Come, girls. We should start back now."

Wentworth stepped to an opening in the shrubbery. It revealed a worn path and a clear view of a farm sitting at the bottom of the hill. The collection of buildings looked old and undignified, the arrangement of them giving the impression of being carelessly scattered. There seemed to be no grace or order to any of it, but he was no fit judge of the affairs of landlocked farmers.

Musgrove joined him. "Well, looks as if Charles has done some clearing away." He turned to his wife. "Mary, we have come all this way; we might just as well pay a call on our family."

Henrietta looked anxiously to her sister and then walked cautiously to her sister-in-law. As she joined Mrs. Charles, she, too, turned away. Shortly, she pulled a kerchief from her pocket and began wiping her eyes.

Stealing a glance at Anne, he saw her dividing her looks between Mr. and Mrs. Musgrove and some far off scenery. Her colour was higher than he remembered seeing it the whole course of the walk. It was clear she wished to be elsewhere, as did he.

"No, no," cried Louisa. She flew past him to her sister. Catching up to her and taking her hand, they began a warm discussion that soon took on all the features of an argument.

Charles, with a tussle of his own to settle, said to his wife, "Mary, you have an obligation to your family. You say you are tired from walking; we shall go down and you might rest a quarter hour in Aunt Hayter's kitchen. A cup of tea and a little rest will set you right."

"Oh, no, indeed! Walking up that hill again will do me more harm than any sitting down could do me good." It was obvious from Mrs. Charles's vivid expression and intractable manner that she would not be moved from her opinion.

Musgrove coloured and the muscles in his jaw flexed at his wife's refusal. Turning away from her, he moved over to confer with his sisters who seemed to have settled things between them. The trio stood together, but it looked as though Henrietta had little or nothing to add to the conversation. It took some time, but eventually the three began to walk towards the path leading to Winthrop.

"Henrietta and I shall go down. I assure you that we shall not be very long," Musgrove explained to Wentworth and Anne. "We shall stay long enough to prevent any insult to our uncle and aunt." This was meant for his wife and no other. Taking his sister's arm, they began down the hill. Louisa held her sister's other arm and went a short distance down the hill, talking to her all the way.

"It is unpleasant, having such connexions! But I assure you I have never been in the house above twice in my life." Mrs. Charles glared at the three as they moved farther away.

Wentworth's eyes met hers. It was all he could do to manage a civil smile. When she gave him a pert nod, presuming his agreement, he was angered even more. Gritting his teeth, he turned away to keep from making a malicious observation. In turning, he was eye-to-eye with Anne. She said nothing, then looked down and away from him.

There was nothing he could say with Mrs. Charles standing so close. But why should he apologize for his silence? Certainly, Anne knew better than most what her sister was and how this outburst proved her to be as prejudiced and ill mannered as their father. He had said the same sorts of things in the past; there was nothing new to discover concerning the arrogance of the Elliot clan.

Louisa returned, her eyes bright and her complexion flushed. "They are well on their way," she breathed with a wave of her arm in the general direction of the descending pathway.

Mrs. Charles made a noise of contempt, and then began making a fuss about finding a place to sit. In short order her hunt became ridiculous. One place was too damp, another too shaded, this one too high, or another too low. Finding a stile in a sunny spot, she finally sat herself down on the second step, looking to each of them as if congratulations were in order.

This is the typical Elliot attitude, Wentworth snorted to himself. *Not only is she contemptuous of her husband's family, she expects me to congratulate her on such despicable opinions. What could have induced Musgrove to marry such a woman.*

Through all the excitement, Anne stood silently by, her attention conscientiously fixed away from them all. Her embarrassment was palpable. To have such relations must be a trial. He repented his harsh attitude and could not help feeling pity for her. But pitying certain of the Elliots would do nothing to improve them. Pride was in the blood and ingrained in their behaviour, as Mrs. Charles was proof. Though Anne did not show it overtly, she was still an Elliot; and there was no doubt that her true colours would be hoisted at the proper time.

A tug at his sleeve brought him to the present. "They shall be gone for a little bit. Might we glean some hazelnuts? There are some growing wild in the hedgerows," Louisa pointed out. It was a better plan than paying homage to Mrs. Charles's grievances and her sister's mortification.

"There is a gate just over there," he said, taking her arm.

As they entered the heart of the hedgerow, he found a tree that bore a decent number of nuts. Jumping up, he easily plucked down a fat cluster. While pulling the browned, frilly husks away from the small rounds, Louisa laughed and bid him to listen. He could hear Mrs. Charles's voice as she moved closer. They stood silently and then breathed in relief as she moved away again.

"Poor Anne," she said. "I don't know how she manages to stay civil when Mary is in such a mood."

He followed her down a rough, natural passageway that cut through the hedge. The ground was thick with leaves. The browning carpet crunched under their feet, beneath which reposed spongy layers of leaves from past autumns. At times, the track narrowed so that passing through was difficult. The hedge was shot through with rambling holly, the spikes of their glossy green leaves adding to the difficulty. Occasionally, he found it necessary to reach out and around Louisa to force the limbs from her path. As they made their way, she informed him of the importance of the walk that day.

"Henrietta and Charles Hayter have cared for one another for a long time. Our mother and father are not against it at all. It is just recently that she has become muddled as to her feelings. But after a long talk, she has come to know her own mind concerning him. I told her I thought it best that she should make her thoughts known to him as soon as possible, and when she agreed I said we should set off for Winthrop the very next thing. There is no reason to put off that which must be done." She stopped in the shade of the path. Her satisfaction at mending her sister's relationship was quite visible in her expression.

Tossing a branch she had plucked bare, she continued, "When I have made up my mind, I have made it. Henrietta seemed entirely to have made up hers to call at Winthrop today, and yet, she was near giving it up out of nonsensical complaisance."

They arrived at a wide spot in the channel and happily found a small tree full of the nuts they sought.

"She would have turned back then, but for you?"

"She would indeed. I am almost ashamed to say it."

This confirmed his earlier observations of Charles Hayter. The country seemed to breed men and women who might be fit in body but were weak in temperament and lacked strength of mind when it came to getting and keeping what they wanted. He told her this. She listened intently as she crumbled the frills from the nuts he gathered.

"If you value her conduct or happiness, infuse as much of your own spirit into her as you can. But this, no doubt, you have been always doing. It is the worst evil of a too-yielding and indecisive character that no influence over it can be depended upon. You are never sure of a good opinion being durable. Everybody may sway it; let those who would be happy be firm." Checking the tree, he saw a large nut he had missed. He jumped up and snagged it. Pulling away the ruff, he said, "Here is a nut." He held it up between his fingers for examination. "To exemplify, a beautiful, glossy nut, which, blessed with original strength, has outlived all the storms of autumn. Not a puncture, not a weak spot anywhere." He raised his arm slightly to elevate the nut to its rightful place. "This nut, while so many of its brethren have fallen and been trodden under foot, is still in possession of all the happiness that a hazelnut can be supposed to be capable of."

He was about to add that the poor wretched thing, while escaping the ravages of the weather, would not escape having its shell ruthlessly cracked open and eaten by the hungry pair. He glanced her way and, to his shock, saw that she was taking his silly drivel seriously! She stood in the midst of husking a handful of nuts, her gaze riveted on him. He had seen this look before on the faces of those under the spell a captain firing up his crew as they prepared for battle. His own pride allowed him to admit that he could produce such results under the proper circumstances. A part of him wanted to laugh and teaze her for being so gullible, but a better part went ahead and finished, though with moderation, in the vein in which he had started.

"My first wish for all whom I am interested in is that they should be firm. If Louisa Musgrove would be beautiful and happy in her November of life, she will cherish all her present powers of mind." He presented her with the nut and quickly turned to look for more.

They moved along quietly for a short time. He felt like an idiot and considered several ways he might open a less enthusiastic line of conversation. There was no need, as Louisa rendered him that service.

"Mary is good natured enough in many respects, but she does sometimes provoke me excessively by her nonsense and her pride—the Elliot Pride. She has a great deal too much of the Elliot Pride. We do so wish that Charles had married Anne instead. I suppose you know that he wanted to marry Anne?"

He stopped for a moment to take a jab at the hole of a mole with a stick he'd just collected. *Why in God's name would I know such a thing?* He stepped on the mound to flatten it.

"Do you mean she refused him?"

"Oh, yes, certainly!"

"When did that happen?"

"I do not exactly know, for Henrietta and I were at school at the time; but I believe it was about a year before he married Mary. I wish she had accepted him. We should have all liked her a great deal better. Papa and Mamma always thought it was her great friend Lady Russell's doing that she did not. Charles was not learned and bookish enough to please Lady Russell, and therefore, she persuaded Anne to refuse him."

So, there was a time when being Mrs. Charles was a possibility! In quick order he thought it a shame she had not accepted him. By her very nature, the improvements to the family would have been great and brought much credit to her...to the Elliots as well, in a round about fashion.

The voices of Mrs. Charles and her sister were quiet but close as he and Louisa emerged from the hedge right alongside the stile where they had left. There was no more time to think about Charles and Anne. Thankfully there was no time for conversation or questions from anyone, for Charles, Henrietta, and Mr. Hayter joined them at the top of the hill.

Wentworth knew that he was no romantic, but one would have to be blind in one eye and wearing a patch over the other not to see the happiness and scarlet of embarrassment on Henrietta's cheeks. Even the dour curate was beaming with delight.

Hayter joined the group for the return to Uppercross. In light of the way he took the young lady's arm, there would be no need for the Captain to divide his attentions between the two sisters—now or ever. When the path allowed, natural groups formed again, the most natural being the lovers, who led the way, speaking only to one another. Charles had the pleasure of offering each arm to a lady, though his wife was not acting the part. Louisa and Wentworth were left to bring up the rear.

He was anxious to hear more of Louisa's opinion concerning Lady Russell's second interference in Anne's personal affairs. To his own shame, he felt a sort of satisfaction that he was not the only man to suffer from that woman's superior and meddlesome nature. It was dismaying, though, that Anne should still be so biddable when it came to her godmother's judgments. Not that it mattered in the least, but he would like to know if at any time in the preceding eight years she'd ever got up the courage to tell the woman to mind her own affairs.

"As I said, they have liked one another for a very long time, probably from their childhoods. Do you not think that romantic?"

"Ah," he hedged. He'd been caught off guard by her question. "It is most romantic. More romantic than anything I have heard all day." It seemed that to agree would be the best course.

"They will be very happy; I just know it. He will have the curacy of Uppercross soon, and they will make a home for themselves in the village. I am certain Mamma and Papa will insist on that."

Though he cared little about the marital felicity of the Hayter lad, he was aggravated by the assumption that elders had the right to inflict their wills upon their young. Let the young make their own decisions. When mistakes were made—and there would be mistakes—they would learn their lessons more thoroughly by muddling through them. And when the successes came—and there would be a few—the enjoyment of them would be all the sweeter and the dependence, one upon the other, more lasting.

"But this is not one of those times," Louisa whispered, leaning close.

"Eh?" As he was very close to appearing a dunce, he would have to leave off the philosophising and pay his companion closer attention. "Sorry, I was distracted by the beauty of the day."

The girl smiled, and continued, "I said before that Mary is good-natured in some respects," she pointed ahead. "Not in this one," she laughed.

The trio before them proceeded, but there had been little conversation. Mrs. Charles had certainly talked a lot, but there had been no replies. Musgrove had more than once released his wife's arm to slash at weeds along the path's edge. This in turn made the lady angry, and she told him so…repeatedly. Now, Musgrove simply let go of both his wife and sister-in-law, taking after something in a clump of grass.

"Charles, it is bad enough that you embarrass me by favouring my sister with the easiest path, but now…"

As Wentworth and Louisa prepared to overtake the group, he could not help but notice Anne's demeanour as the Musgrove's domestic drama played out. Staring at the ground, one hand resting on her shoulder, the other tucked into the crook of her arm, she looked like a statue. A statue that cried of unrelenting endurance of a world she did not like and could not change.

They passed and he thought to offer her his arm when he heard Henrietta call, "Admiral, Mrs. Croft! We have been on the other side of the hedge, but heard you approach." She and Hayter were at the gate, waving to his sister and brother. When Mrs. Charles understood there was a fresh audience, she abandoned her railing and moved off, leaving Charles to take Anne's arm and follow.

Wentworth stood back while the other gentlemen saw the ladies in their charge through the gate. "And where have you been on such a fine day, Frederick?" his brother-in-law asked.

"Clear to Winthrop and back, sir," he answered, pulling the gate tight behind him.

"Well, that is an ambitious walk. Even we in the cart didn't go that far." The Admiral whispered something to his wife.

"Certainly, dear. We are going right through Uppercross on our way home, and if any of the ladies is particularly tired, we would be delighted to give her a ride," Mrs. Croft said.

"It will save full a mile of shoe leather," added the Admiral.

Henrietta clutched Mr. Hayter's arm and smiled widely indicating she would not be separated from him. Louisa stated she was not tired in the least. Wentworth knew this to be true; she was having no difficulty in keeping pace with him. Both politely refused and made it clear that to finish the walk was the most desirable thing in the world. The words from Mrs. Charles were all civil refusal, but he noticed her expression was one of offence. No doubt the idea of being seen in the company of her father's tenant, being drawn by only one horse, was a mortification she would not entertain. Anne, too, refused, but he suspected it was not for her pride's sake but for the inconvenience of his sister and her husband.

He thanked them for the offer and followed as the group crossed the lane. He went first over the stile to receive the ladies.

"It is a lovely day, and the view is magnificent," Louisa said, standing on the top step.

"I'm sure the view is not nearly as magnificent as that we just left up the hill," he responded, offering her a hand to hurry her along.

"I think I could fly," she cried. Without warning, she jumped.

For a slender young woman, she hit with surprising force; and he took a step back as he caught her. He held her for just a moment. She laughed, saying, "That was magnificent as well." Pushing away, she turned to talk with her sister.

Wentworth looked to see how her brother took the antic. Musgrove either did not see, his attention being taken up with coming over the stile and assisting his wife, or he did see and did not care. Either way, Wentworth was relieved. Then he saw Anne. She stood a little apart, still in the lane. It was not clear by her expression whether she had seen or not, but it was clear she was exhausted. Her whole being cried that relief could not come soon enough. With no thought, he hopped the short stone fence, intending to see her over the stile himself. Before he could say anything, he noticed the Crofts were not yet away. He halloo'd as he crossed over the road.

Sophia smiled as he approached. "Don't tell me you are suddenly in need of a ride."

He motioned for her to come close. "She may not agree, but I think Anne is fatigued. Please, insist that she join you."

She straightened and studied him a moment. His request had deepened an already intense curiosity, but he would deal with it later. Without another word, he crossed over to see Anne into the gig.

Mrs. Croft called to her, "Miss Elliot, I am sure you are tired. Do let us have the pleasure of taking you home. Here is excellent room for three, I assure you. If we were all like you, I believe we might sit four."

"Thank you very much, but–" She hesitated, but he continued his approach. He wished to leave her no doubt of his intention to see to her comfort.

"You must," Mrs. Croft said. "Indeed, you must."

He did as he should have done earlier and offered her his arm. She laid her hand upon it and followed him without a word. Though she no longer thought well of him, at least she would allow him to do her this service. He was glad of the slight pressure on his arm as they walked.

The few steps to the carriage had given them time to make room for her. He turned and, as she reached for a handhold, put his hands on her waist and lifted her. She was lighter than he remembered, smaller too, if that was possible. It was disconcerting to think that her slight weight included the bulk of her heavy cloak. For a moment, he thought of her as fading away. His memories of her had dimmed over time but being back in her company had recharged them and made them vivid again. It hurt him to think the woman herself was less than she had once been.

His hand rested on the back of the seat, and he could feel her settle in. He could not bring himself to look up for fear of her looking right through him. A gentle hand patted his. For a moment he felt a wild hope it was her thanks.

"We will see you soon at home?" The hand shook his a little more vigorously. It was Sophia.

He looked in his sister's direction, but not closely enough to see her expression. "Certainly. Very soon."

"Walk on," the Admiral instructed the horse, and the seat slid out from under his hand. He stood watching the gig drive away, wishing that his brother-in-law's carriage seated four.

Chapter Fifteen

Wentworth watched the fire through the ends of the towel flipping around as he dried his hair.

"Sir, your small clothes are laid out along with the black trousers and grey wool coat."

"That will be all. I shall call you up later." Harkness bowed and left.

Poor man, he wished so much to be a genuine valet and all Wentworth required was a glorified washerwoman. Dropping the towel to his shoulder, he went to the window. A blanket of cold air came over him when he opened it. Pulling the dressing gown closer, he revelled in the briskness of it.

Soon after his return from his walk with the Musgroves, the sky clouded and turned an alarming iron grey. It would rain later, he was sure of that. Considering the season, this might have been the last dry day for some time. The walk to Winthrop had been interesting. One thing was clear–from now on the attentions of Miss Henrietta Musgrove would be directed only towards her cousin, Charles Hayter. She had stayed strictly by his side during the return to Uppercross, and there had not been even a hint that she'd ever shown interest in Wentworth.

It was for the best, he thought, folding the towel. Henrietta was an amiable young woman, but she never put forth an opinion that was not an echo of an earlier sentiment, and even then, she seemed unsure of what she thought. She might be the prettier of the two, but she was too mild to suit his taste.

As his sister had pointed out, the Musgrove girls were not the only young women in the area; there seemed to be female Hayter cousins by the dozens. But while he was willing to accept a woman less than his ideal, he was not willing to take one who must be completely built from the ground up.

Taking the stairs two at a time, Wentworth shrugged into his coat then began the ritual of tugging the shirtsleeves into place. Absently counting the steps across the entryway–five long strides in total–he hurried to the dining room, hastily cramming the long ends of his unevenly tied neck cloth into his waistcoat. Catching the footman unawares, he took his seat; and placing the napkin in his lap, nodded for his fish to be served.

"We are glad you could join us, Frederick," Sophia said, smiling.

"I am sorry, Sister. I dozed off."

"Did Harkness not wake you?"

"Yes, he did as a matter of fact," he said taking a drink. The fish was always a bit dry at Kellynch Hall. "But I sent him away with orders not to bother me until I called. The man takes orders beautifully." He had not actually slept before or after Harkness's wake up call. He'd been contemplating all that had passed during the walk, particularly whether anyone had noticed what an ass he'd made of himself bounding the fence to see Anne into the Croft's gig. For a man who wanted to stifle curiosity concerning their past alliance, he seemed to be unable to keep away from the woman and leave her to fend for herself.

"I will speak to Lowell. The man should know better," Sophia said, interrupting his thoughts.

"He should know that I wish him to do as he is told, Sophia. I am a grown man, and if I am late, it is entirely my fault, not the servant's." The words were harsh, and this was not his home. "Sister, please, as a favour to me, let the man alone. I will do better in allowing him to do his job."

"The man is under your control; use him as you see fit." She pointed her fork, "Just see that you come to my table on time."

As usual, the Admiral chose not to insert himself into domestic affairs, but he did comment, "I don't wonder you wanted a bit of rest, after that walk. All-in-all it was above six miles, was it not?"

"I suppose it was. All I can say is that it felt wonderful to rest after I returned home."

"Well, I am glad that you insisted Miss Anne allow us to bring her home," his sister said. "I could tell when we set her down before the Cottage that she was quite exhausted."

"The situation was simple enough. I merely did what anyone else would do."

"Well, no one else did anything, now did they?" His sister paused as the footman served her. There was something in her tone he wondered at but she continued.

"Anywise, we took great care in bringing her home. She was very lavish with her thanks for our trouble."

He took great care in mutilating his fish, waiting for any further revelations, but, evidently, there had been no lavish praise concerning him.

"The only difficulty in the entire ride was when the Admiral came close to shocking her with the details of our very short courtship." She winked at her husband, and he lifted his glass to her.

The tale was not terribly shocking when one is acquainted with the quick and decisive ways of sailors when it comes to ordering their personal affairs. But she always enjoyed making reference to it as though it were the scandal of the world. As he recalled, when it was all swirling about the household, he was more interested in returning to sea rather than hear about the embarrassing details of his sister's romantic entanglement with a "significantly" older man.

"Did you bore her with Edward's outrageous behaviour? How he nearly called out Captain Croft when he found the two of you in the sitting room together...alone?"

"No," she laughed. "Since she does know our brother personally, I decided not to mortify him in her eyes. Who knows, perhaps he will visit one day, and I would not wish her to have a picture of our dear brother as a raving madman."

"He was seething, was he not?" Wentworth remembered being alarmed to hear raised voices in the house. There hadn't been any yelling or fighting since the death of their father years before, and for a moment, to his shame, the sixteen year-old Frederick was afraid again. Sneaking past the loudest of the squeaking boards in the hallway, he had crawled to an advantageous place behind the railings and eavesdropped. He was amazed to see his normally dour brother, dressed all in black, wagging a finger in the face of then Captain Croft, magnificently attired in his blue and gold dress uniform.

The young Frederick had been a midshipman more than long enough to know that a full captain was the most godlike creature on the face of the earth, next to an admiral. And here was his brother, risking life and limb to explain how Captain Croft would never hurt his dearest girl and what grievous tortures awaited him if he had the misfortune to stumble in any way.

Edward's tenacious protection was now very understandable to him. Even so, he and his sister laughed at their brother's expense. The Admiral did not join them, but said, "The two of you say what you will. Though I never went in much for dandling with the ladies, Edward's outburst made me know you meant a great deal to him and that I would see Hell's fire if I so much as made you uncomfortable. Sometimes a man must make a fool of himself to show how much he loves those in his sphere."

Sophia thanked her husband for the warm sentiment, but Wentworth was uncomfortable with his words. What might his recent behaviour hint about his own emotions? There was no need to reply, and he was thankful that the footmen were swarming the table to serve the next course. Later, as they were going up for coffee and chess, the butler entered and announced that a marine was in the library and had an urgent communiqué for the Captain.

"Ha, you lucky dog, Frederick! This is orders, no doubt." The Admiral and his sister both smiled their congratulations.

A palpable sense of relief set in as he rose. This was just what he needed. To be doing something useful would set him free from all the mundane worries that were beginning to choke his days. As a matter of form he mouthed nonchalant words that he hoped would disguise the excitement rising in him.

The crimson-coated marine stood in bold relief against the ancient elegance of Kellynch Hall's library. It seemed to be the ultimate of ironies that his haunted past was being eclipsed by his burgeoning present. He said a little prayer of thanks that he was about to be sent back to the life he loved so well.

The marine saluted smartly and handed him a sealed packet. He was struck by the fact the packet was too light, wrapped in paper and not sailcloth, and not nearly thick enough to be official orders. There was not even any string encircling it, and turning it over, he saw that the seal was not of the Admiralty.

"These were found in the posting office. It was thought you should have them immediately." The man threw him a second precise salute and left when absently dismissed.

Holding the packet, he stared at the seal. It was not the elegant seal pressed deep into the glossy black wax customarily used by Plymouth's Port Admiral, but a thin, sloppy red splash of some inferior secretary in an unimportant office at the port. Whatever was contained in the packet was definitely not his salvation.

Crossing the hallway again, he told the butler to inform his sister that he would be occupied for the rest of the evening. Once in his chamber, he tossed the packet on the table, lit a cigar, and took a seat by the fire.

He was a fool to feel so hopeful concerning orders. If a packet of old letters could stir such deep anticipation in his breast, it proved he was not cut out for living quietly in the country and that it was time to find something more substantial than shooting and walking to occupy himself. Cracking the seal on the packet, he pulled out two letters. One was from his brother dated just after he left Plymouth. He'd heard from him since, making the letter of little value. He tossed it on the table to be read later. The next did nearly as much to excite his interest as the notion of receiving orders had. It was from Timothy Harville.

He read through the letter a second, then a third time. Along with the news of a move to the small coastal village of Lyme, there was also news that the *Grappler* was decommissioned and James Benwick had been thrown ashore by the same wave of peace as himself. This cruelty of Providence angered him. To nearly crush James with the sudden death of his fiancé was harsh enough, but then, to further press him by taking away the man's only source of pride and livelihood was enough to make Wentworth question the very idea of a generous God. The fact that Benwick had landed on Harville's doorstep seemed to testify to a need on both sides. He decided that a visit to both friends was his duty.

Setting the details of the visit aside, he took up the letter from his brother. The address was in his brother's hand, so he was surprised to find the opening paragraph in one unfamiliar to him. Introducing herself and apologizing for taking up his time, Mrs. Edward Wentworth opened saying she looked forward to his arrival, as did his brother.

> He misses you greatly and wishes you to come as soon as possible. He will not ask it any more, fearing you will grow weary at his nagging. I have no such scruples and so will take it upon myself to beg. Please, come to us at your earliest convenience, Captain. The Rector is very excited to have you under his roof again. I, too, anticipate your coming and am looking forward very much to putting a face to all the stories I have heard. Again, please come when you are free of your obligation to our sister and her husband.

"What a singular woman," he said, scanning her part again. Her hand was compact, without much flourish, but strong and neat. Though the wording possessed a certain charm, between the woman's script and having some knowledge of the sort of lady who marries a religious man, he began to think the letter less an entreaty than a summons.

"If my brother has been telling her stories, she should be in mortal fear of the sort of family she's got herself into," he said, scratching at the wafer which had kept it closed. Putting aside his speculations about his new sister, he continued on with Edward's part of the letter.

To begin, the Rector apologized for his wife's familial intervention. The words alone were pettish, but when read with what he knew to be his brother's occasional dip into sarcasm, they were almost endearing.

> Though she has me dead-to-rights on this, I do wish you to make haste and give your old brother some of your precious time. I must tell you, Frederick, I am the most fortunate of men. I had grown very accustomed to the knowledge that my past almost certainly predestined me to dying alone. I may very well yet do so; no one knows the future except God, but

I will not live my entire life alone and unloved. I now know love and that I was but a shadow before my dear Catherine's touch.

The letter closed with another invitation and the desire to be remembered to their sister and brother. He was puzzled by Edward's reference to his past. His brother never spoke of any part of his life that happened before returning to England the year their parents died. Once, he had mentioned sailing to New Holland and having been in Barbados but nothing more.

Edward's recent letters were the most cheerful he'd ever received from his brother, and there was nothing to account for it aside from his marriage. No matter what sort of woman she turned out to be, she made him happy; and that was really all that mattered.

"I was but a shadow before my dear Catherine's touch..." It was common wisdom that the touch of a woman could make all the difference in the life of a man, and his brother's marriage certainly bolstered the case. Was Wentworth's life but a shadow? He did not think so. His life felt as substantial as Gibraltar, yet, like his brother, he too longed for the love and companionship of a woman worthy of his affection.

"...it was her great friend Lady Russell's doing..." He could not help despising Lady Russell for making Anne the shadow she had become. It did not seem, at least, that the woman had gone so far as to poison her goddaughter against Musgrove the way she had poisoned everything between Anne and him. Before he could stop himself, he again saw Anne's face as she protested his insistence that she accept the Croft's offer of a ride. It had been the briefest of looks, but it spoke volumes. She wanted nothing from him. The flesh and blood Anne of his past had disappeared and, like a shadow, was beyond his touch.

The final meeting between Anne and him was a muddle. When he saw the scene in his head, it was all tears on her side and anger on his. Her first argument had been that for him to succeed in the Navy, it was best he be single and have no worries about supporting a wife and household. It had taken no time to smash such a weak line of reasoning, and, to his shame, he ground her down until the true reasons were revealed: connexions, fortune, and his very temperament. He had not enough of the first two and far too much of third. Anne had spoken the words, but he knew who had placed them in her mouth.

Musgrove, on the other hand, had more than enough of fortune and local connexions to satisfy the most fastidious concerns for security, and the man's temperament was just the thing to suit a woman like Lady Russell–just enough push to meet the barest requirements of being a man but biddable enough to manage easily. If Charles Musgrove was the perfect match according to Lady Russell's previously stated qualifications, why had she sunk him in Anne's eyes? Was she so cruel as to want the girl to live out her life single, perhaps dependent upon her and her beneficence? Was she grooming a companion for her old age?

He had to laugh at himself. He was becoming ridiculous in his mental wanderings. At one time he'd thought the meddlesome harpy had been placed upon the earth to be a thorn planted firmly in his side. Age and time forced him to see that being at cross-purposes with someone did not necessarily award virtue to one and evil intent to the other. The woman was Anne's godmother and saw everything from that vantage. She had seen nothing in him she liked and had told Anne as much. Regardless of the lady's opinion, it has been Anne who made her choice.

Now there was no Lady Russell to be seen, and though Anne was her own mistress, she still chose to have little to do with him. Their past was obviously nothing to her. A knock on the door interrupted his thoughts. Harkness entered, bearing a tray of spirits.

"Mrs. Croft thought you might care for something as you read, sir." Given leave, he poured a glass and handed it to the Captain.

"How far is Lyme from Kellynch, Harkness?"

"About fifteen, sixteen miles, I believe." *Excellent! You settled in a very convenient spot, Timothy: not too long a ride, but far enough to get the blood moving.*

"Do you know anything about horses, Harkness?"

The man capped the decanter and frowned. "Other than they always smell, no sir, I do not."

Wentworth rose and went to the desk. Dashing off a quick note, he said, "I wish this to go to Crewkherne. Wait for a reply."

"That might take above two hours, sir."

"That is quite all right, Harkness. It seems I have nothing but time."

~ ~ ~ ~ ~ ~ ~ & ~ ~ ~ ~ ~ ~ ~

Many men would not have chosen to buy a horse and take the opportunity of a long and unknown ride to familiarize themselves with their newly acquired beast, but Frederick Wentworth was not most men; and he was pretty certain that nearly all things would go his way. Again, he was right. He took it as a good sign when his note was answered double quick that the horse-coper in Crewkherne had two animals fitting the Captain's requirements. He told his sister his plans to buy a horse and travel to see his friend, begged a ride to Crewkherne from his brother-in-law, and packed his bag in anticipation of the journey to visit his good friend, Harville.

Coming to an agreement on a horse had been simple enough; he paid the man what he asked. The melancholy of the previous evening lifted with the sunrise, and he was determined that such a trifle as haggling for a horse should not invite it back.

Setting off from Crewkherne later than he cared for, Wentworth decided to push on to Lyme though it was late afternoon and he was sharp set. There would be time to refresh himself when he arrived.

As the steps of the horse drew him closer to his destination, his thoughts were of the beautiful countryside. Several large hedges entangled with hazelnut trees reminded him of Louisa's unquestioning acceptance of his flippant rhetoric of the day before. His previous experience of bright, nineteen-year-old women obviously could not help him understand Louisa Musgrove.

Of course she took his banter seriously. That's precisely what he liked about her. She gave him her undivided attention and hung on every word. Just as it should be. He laughed. This was the sort of thing his brother had scolded him about years ago. Edward had seen Frederick's good opinion of himself galloping out of control and warned him to rein it in. He had not then. Little, it seemed, had changed.

Such sinking thoughts could not be born, and to banish them, he dismounted and allowed the horse a short graze. Taking a post under a tree, he removed his gloves and fished in his pocket for a bag of peppermint candy the coper had given him for the horse. "She likes her sweets," he told Wentworth. "You rattle a twist of peps and she'll be at your side in a flash." He found it, and the man was right; the mare was snuffling at his pocket immediately.

"Back, you greedy beast," he muttered. In her excitement, she pinned him against the tree as he tore open the paper. "Damn, you're heavy," he said, offering her a sweet as far from him as his arm would allow. Taking one of the candies for himself, he gave her two more and put the others away.

It would take time to get to know her eccentricities. Horses were little different than people, he suspected. It struck him as ironic that the mare was not the only female in his sphere that he was coming to know better. He recalled Louisa and her somewhat changed manner as they had returned to Uppercross.

After seeing Anne away, he had returned to the field, and the six remaining walkers continued on. Again the natural groups formed, but now the conversation between Louisa and him became more personal, more intimate. He learnt even more about the immediate Musgrove family and their dealings with the vast Hayter clan and other families in the area.

At first, he was uncomfortable with being drawn into such matters, and when he voiced his concerns to Louisa, she laughed. She was surprised, she said, that he was not aware of it all by now anyway, considering how much a part of the family he had become over the past weeks. It was a claim he could not deny. He spent far more waking hours in the company of the Musgroves than he did his own flesh-and-blood. What a shock it would be when they discovered he was gone from the area without a word. The thought caused a twinge of guilt.

He remounted and continued on to Lyme, but it was not long before his thoughts returned to their previous subject. Besides the intimate family knowledge being imparted to him, Louisa's dependency on him for a hand or an arm was becoming more pronounced. Again and again, she wished to be jumped down from the top step of a stile or stone wall edging a field. He deemed such familiar behaviour was generally accepted by the Musgrove family. And accepted is certainly how it would be if he were to continue things on their present course. Nothing would be said, the calm waters of this country life would easily drift into marriage. Louisa would obviously not object to it. The family would welcome him as another son. He chuckled when he thought of claiming the spot left vacant by the lately lamented Richard Musgrove. The irony of such a thing was too amusing.

Checking his watch, he was happy to know the ride to Lyme was neither extraordinarily long nor taxing. Setting up house in Uppercross would keep him close to Harville and the sea. There was no telling how long he might be without a posting. Once thrown ashore, it was not unheard of for a Post Captain to go years before getting another ship. Unless another war was declared or a fever thinned out the Admiral's List, he could be on land for some time. Moreover, when he did resume his life at sea, escaping occasionally to the country would be a welcome change. There would be no worries of leaving a wife at the mercy of a squalid port city. She would be under the protection of her family and his while he was away. All things considered, an alliance with the Musgroves was most advantageous. There was nothing about marrying Louisa Musgrove that he could see would be a hindrance. Nothing except Anne.

"...I was but a ghost..." The phrase from Edward's letter resurfaced. Anne was herself little more than a ghost. Each day that passed, her cool manner made it apparent she had no interest in him. Perhaps, she was merely counting the days until she could join Lady Russell at the Lodge, and he would be out of her sight. This made all the memories he carried in his mind and heart no better than ghosts as well. The spectre of Anne Elliot had kept him single and alone for too long. Dropping down a little hill, he decided that when he returned the next day and rejoined the

Musgroves, he would more carefully consider Louisa in light of his future.

Descending into Lyme was as challenging as the ride got. The mare did not appreciate the cobbles, but she had a tender mouth and responded well to his gentle management of the reins. There was no traffic to speak of, and it seemed he would have his choice of accommodations. It appeared that all the inns carried names relating to the sea, and he chose The Binnacle.

While tying up his mount, the stable boy told him that he could have nearly any room in the house and that a little haggling might just get it at a bargain price. It was well past his customary dinner, and he was not after a bargain, only a hot bath and a little something to pry his stomach off his backbone.

"You come just at the end of the season. There's not much on right now and not many to watch." Despite what the stable boy thought, the innkeeper seemed little interested in trying to squeeze him for a room. He had asked to be placed on the highest floor so that he might have a view of the sea.

"Sure thing, sir," he said, sliding a key to him.

"I would like a bit of bread and cheese sent up, along with small beer. And might you have paper and pen?" The keep again obliged him. Folding the note he'd written, he said, "I need this delivered to this address." He showed the direction to the keep.

"Sorry, sir, I don't read myself, but if you just tell me the place, I'll see it gets there." Wentworth read off the address. "Don't know just the spot, but the boy I send will. I do know it to be close to the oldest part of the pier. Not the best of places, mind; but you'll know it right off. Just ask around. Most anyone down there could tell ya right where ya need to go."

"Thank you," Wentworth said, pocketing the much-read letter.

"By the way, sir. Will ya be needin' a meal tonight? We serve until nine. Things is a little sparse 'round here and me wife, she takes care of the cookin', needs to know much she should get ready."

"Uh, yes, for three in fact. And might I reserve a private dining room, if you have one."

"Yeah, I gots a small one. Cosy as you please."

The extras were agreed upon and paid for; then, he was able to set his mind to relieving his hungry belly.

~ ~ ~ ~ ~ ~ ~ & ~ ~ ~ ~ ~ ~ ~

It only took asking once and he was directed to Harville's new home. He made his way off the beaten track to the small row of houses crammed under the decaying pier and was moved with compassion for his friend. When first they met, Harville was doing quite well and living in a small but respectable house on a decent street in Portsmouth. This new place was a great reduction indeed.

He knocked and was greeted by a slight young woman drying her hands. He introduced himself and she brightened. He was gratified that his message had been delivered, and his appearance was not a complete surprise. Repeating his name to make sure she got it right, the girl announced him.

"Captain Wentworth, ma'am."

He was brought into a small room where every bit of space was occupied. A quick glance about the room told him the place was no different from most other rooms or houses to let. It had suffered or prospered under the carpentry skills of numerous previous tenants. It was easy to recognise pieces of good furniture from better times; they were highly polished and glowed with care. A few things he recognized to be foreign and, no doubt, from Timothy's many voyages. Crammed into the remaining space were extra bits and bobs that seemed to have no purpose whatsoever. Across the room a small, blond woman he suspected to be plump with child rose from a chair in the corner nearest the fire. She had a little blond girl in her arms.

"Captain. It is so good of you to visit us." With her greeting, he was reminded how strange Elsa Harville's accent always sounded to his ear. Her family was Norwegian, and even though she was born in England, her accent was an odd amalgam of highs and lows.

She let the girl down, and both came to him. As she drew closer, he noticed the age that just a few months had drawn on her face. Despite this, her smile and words were genuine. He bowed and she scolded, "You know there is no propriety here, Frederick." It amused him the way she always called him, "Free-rich." He leant down to receive a kiss on the cheek.

"I just received Timothy's letter. I fear it went astray and ran aground in Plymouth after I left."

"But it has reached you now. Timotee is resting. I did not wake him when your note arrived, but I think he's rested enough." She held out her hand for the little girl to follow her up the stairs. "Come Fanny."

The little girl was staring at the Captain and continued to do so even as she shook her head no.

"Fanny, come with Mama."

He'd forgotten her name, but now remembered her from their short voyage in the spring. "I think the young lady and I will be alright, Mrs. Harville. We are old mates, aren't we Miss Fanny."

She gave him the barest of nods.

"Alright, but I shall be back right away." She moved to an open stairway. She took the first step, turned, and said, "Oh, my manners. Please have a seat."

"Remember, there is no propriety here," he said. She smiled and left.

He intended to take the seat vacated by Mrs. Harville and so moved to the fireplace. The chair's upholstery was familiar, but now shiny and threadbare. The slow decay of his friend into poverty was difficult to see. Why should Harville have been the one to have his leg crippled and his career torn from him and not Wentworth?

He took a seat and tried to coax Fanny to him. She continued to stare but would move no closer. Before long there was a low murmur of voices up the stairs, and soon someone was coming down. Expecting Timothy, he rose and said, "I know there was no fair warning, but–" When he looked up, he was looking not into the eyes of his friend Timothy, but those of James Benwick. He felt again the hurt and anger under which they parted, but he still had perfect understanding, and compassion for his friend. He hoped that Benwick felt the same.

"Captain, I'm pleased to see you again." The words were measured and polite. Coming down into the room, he held out his hand and said, "Elsa said you were in town for a visit."

There was still an air of suffering about him. Wentworth wondered if his coming was not a mistake and if his presence might not inflict upon his friend the burden of past, painful memories. "I, too, am glad to see both my good friends on this visit."

The handshake began as perfunctory, but as it continued, Benwick's grasp became stronger and more genuine. Little Fanny came up to Benwick and raised her hands to him. Without hesitation, he took her in his arms. It was odd to see his friend holding a child, particularly as she snuggled herself in the crook of his neck. It was clear both were comfortable with the arrangement.

"How is Timothy?" he asked.

Benwick looked away. "Not as well as we would like. The infection is always there, never quite leaving his system. He's just gotten over a cold and rests several times a day. It is my responsibility to entertain you until he comes down." The young woman he'd met at the door entered, and Benwick asked that refreshments be brought.

"Mrs. Harville looks well."

Benwick smiled. "Yes, she is as ever, and she proves that Timothy is not *always* under the weather." The breath required for the statement no sooner passed his lips than he realised what he'd said. Lightly putting his hand over Little Fanny's ear, he said, "That was quite unforgivable, Captain. I'm sorry."

The comment was completely out of the bounds of good taste, but he was not shocked. "It is forgotten. Just pray Mrs. Harville never gets wind of it. Besides, it is good to hear something of your old, wry self."

"Elsa is convinced I shall overcome these blows. I am not so sure."

Wentworth hesitated to respond. He did not wish to aggravate emotions that he was certain were healing but still obviously tender. "You are resilient, James. I believe she is right. How do you like Lyme?"

"It is a scruffy little place that suits us just fine," a voice from above them said. Timothy Harville, with the help of his wife, descended the stairs and joined the two men.

"Captain," was the call of children's voices that accompanied loud thudding descending the stairs.

"Careful, boys," Timothy said holding on to his wife and the railing.

In an instant, two small boys stood before him, staring as their sister had. "Nearly every other day I hear about your taking them up in the tops. I have also hidden my best telescope, as someone took the time to show them how it works." Harville winked, and then continued down the stairs. "There is never a time this place does not reek of fish, but there is a small shipyard and so lots of rumours of the navy. All in all, it will do until better things come along." The boys were mindful of their father's condition and gave him a wide path to his friend. He took Wentworth's hand and then pulled him close. "I sent the letter and when I heard nothing for so long, I thought you'd probably got a ship and were headed for open water."

"No, nothing so exciting. I merely put *Laconia* in ordinary and then travelled to Somerset to visit my sister and her husband, Admiral Croft."

Harville was glad to hear that they were practically in the same neighbourhood together. "Then perhaps we shall see one another often."

"Count on it."

"You will stay for dinner, Captain," Elsa Harville insisted.

It had been his intention to invite the Harvilles and Benwick to dine with him. He was about to extend the invitation when Elsa helped Timothy to a chair. He sat heavily and leant his head back looking extraordinarily tired. It was clear that going out in the night air, much less making his way up to the inn, would be impossible. "I was hoping you would offer, Mrs. Harville. I have missed your cooking." The innkeeper's wife would just have to endure four too many plates of roasted beef.

"Good. Then I will go and see to things in the kitchen, and the three of you will entertain yourselves."

As she left, she stopped by her husband's chair and spoke to him. Wentworth could not hear their exchange, but he noticed that her hand rested just atop Timothy's. Before she walked on, he took two of her fingers and held them. A little tremor was noticeable. It was nearly nothing as gestures go, but perhaps, in his weakened state, it was the best they could manage. She laughed, patted Harville's shoulder, and left them. Her husband watched her until the door was closed.

It was clear that had he not shown up, the evening would have been quiet but no less meaningful to them. Even with Benwick present, the Harville's were closer than he could remember them in the past. His embarrassment was so profound that he might just as well have spied on them in their bedchamber. Why did he feel so strongly? The gesture was brief, barely noticeable.

"So, Wentworth, what are you up to, now that you are without a ship?" For nearly two hours, the men traded stories about their new neighbours, fashioned solutions to all the nation's ills, relived the glory days of their youth, and saluted the future with relish. All the while, the two boys sat quietly, listening or playing with small, carved toys. Miss Fanny had taken up a sentry post by Wentworth's knee. Occasionally, she leant against him, but always her hand rested on him, now and then patting him.

When Mrs. Harville called them into dinner, she directed the children upstairs to their tea and bed. He watched the nurse take them up and felt a little touch of sadness. Never before had he been so aware of the warmth children brought to a home. Mrs. Harville called to him particularly, and he was reminded that he was famished and ready to wipe the boards clean.

The young girl, named Mary he soon discovered, did her best to serve with grace but was hard-pressed to carry the steaming dishes and remember which side to serve. Each place at the table seemed to be an entirely new circumstance and the steps re-learnt every time. Elsa bore it remarkably well and, with just slight tilts of the head, tiny movements of a finger and the occasional click of the tongue saw the course served without any disasters.

The soup was thin. It was followed by a small piece of bony fish which heralded a beef filet tougher and thinner than the soles of his much-loved but well-worn Hessians. Two of the side dishes were generous. The first was a bowl of potatoes of intricately shaped pieces, indicating that whoever pared them was a dab hand at avoiding bruises and worms. The second, a brimming bowl of sauerkraut, sat alongside a bowl of bitter greens barely covering the china's pattern of a mill wheel, stream, and fishing party.

The fare was scant and far below the quality of former days, but as he observed both Timothy and Elsa, there was never a break in the cheerful conversation to indicate embarrassment. It was his observation that in times of degradation, some felt a need to call more attention to the circumstances by begging pardon. All this accomplished was to bring discomfort and awkwardness to the entire party. But that was not the case with his friends; the conversation never lagged and the small beer flowed freely.

Mary brought out a tart that looked to be the heartiest course of the night. It was cut and the plates passed round. Everyone waited for Elsa to have the first bite. The graceful smile froze on her lips and she reached for her cup. After draining it, she said quietly, "Please forgive me, but there has been a little problem with the sweet." In an instant, her plate and those of the others were whisked away to the kitchen. Timothy covered by passing a decanter of sherry, but the low hum of Elsa's voice could be heard, then a small cry and a slamming door.

The door from the kitchen quickly opened and Elsa appeared with a board bearing a small wedge of cheese and some interestingly cut apples. "Mary is a bit overheated at the moment, and it seems that somehow the salt was taken for sugar. Much to my shame, we will just have to finish our meal like the French." The men laughed and Wentworth helped himself to an apple. Despite all its defects, it was the best meal he had had in weeks.

In the past, he would have stayed until the sun rose the next morning, drinking and talking with his friends. But the past was as far from them as the other side of the world this night, and early in the evening, Harville was near the breaking point. He insisted on seeing his guest to the door and was only made easy about the party ending on account of him when Benwick promised to walk the Captain to his inn. "Now I will not feel like such an old maid," he said as the two set off. The cold night air insured they had the streets to themselves.

After greeting the watchman, Benwick said, "I hope you do not think ill of me for attaching myself to Timothy in this way."

"And what way might that be?"

"Well, Fanny and I did not marry; I have no claims on her family. Much of the time I feel as though I should be exerting myself more, making myself available for another position. Instead, I remain here, quite out of the way."

Knowing precisely how Benwick felt, he considered the agony of grinding upon the rocks waiting for orders. He could not help but laugh at himself and how the arrival of Harville's letter had caused such brief but intense joy in his own bosom. But self-flagellation was rarely useful, and in Benwick's weakened emotional state, it could prove fatal.

"I think the times are against you, James. All of us are looking into a very dark glass just now."

"I know, I just did not wish you to think me some sort of leech on them. I have done what I can. More to the point, what Timothy would allow me to do. You know how he can be. But your visit has cheered them both more than I have seen for some time."

"All men are proud that way. I suspect the reduction has been much more difficult for Mrs. Harville. I still remember their pretty little house in Portsmouth. Living under a pier in Lyme is quite a come down."

Benwick laughed a little and Wentworth asked the reason.

"A few days after I moved in, I stated something to that effect to Elsa. I was trying to be careful not to mention anything of the past or better times. She sat me down and told me that, while Fanny's death was a shocking tragedy, it had taught her a very important lesson." Benwick fell into silence as they walked on.

"And that lesson would be?" Wentworth prompted.

"Ah, yes, it taught her that each day should be praised for the joy it brings since there is no profit to be had in regretting the past. Worry for the future is fruitless as well. There is no guarantee that there will even be a tomorrow, as Fanny's illness proved."

He remembered Edward trying to make him understand such a notion when he spoke of the success and riches he would have one day. It had all been wrapped up with platitudes about chicken counting and green grass. All such philosophising struck him as ridiculous when he was in his twenties, and he had deemed it as little more than excuses for failure. He still felt that a man, through exertion and intelligence, made his own end; but he was beginning to see that life was a hard prospect and that circumstances sometimes dictated striving for only what was barely possible.

"I know that it wears on them both, Elsa especially, but we all manage to go on."

Wentworth was grateful that they reached the door of the Binnacle before he had to reply. Bidding Benwick goodnight, he confirmed his plan to visit again tomorrow. They shook hands, and he watched Benwick disappear around the corner. The inn was quiet, though there were a few tables occupied in the open dining room. The keep noticed his arrival and indicated that he should wait.

"You didn't come to dine."

The man's expression was serious; so serious that Wentworth found unwittingly amused. "Uh, no, my plans changed."

The man scowled and he wiped the bar. "My wife was more than a little put out, I can tell you."

Keeping his amusement severely in check, he said, "I am sorry for any inconvenience I may have caused her. Any compensation that you think adequate, I shall gladly pay." The man's expression lightened at the prospect of money for uneaten food. Wentworth added, "Speaking of your good wife, is she still about? I would like a word with her."

The man's face was serious again. "Oh, I don't think you want to be talkin' to her. She's still put out with your not showin' up."

"Better still. I can make amends and avail myself of her *expertise*."

The man's face turned and he said, "Now, wait there. I don't know what you think, but I run a respectable establishment here."

"I meant that I would like to ask your wife to help me. I would like to ask her advice as an innkeeper's wife."

"Oh now, that's better. There's no one in this town who is more willing to give her advice, whether asked for or not, than my wife."

The woman was indeed put out with him. He was not certain she might not reach over the counter and demonstrate to what degree. In spite of this, when he began to share his brilliant plan and the part he wished her to play in it, she began to look on him more and more with a friendly eye.

Chapter Sixteen

The grey waves and their relentless heaving distracted Wentworth from his packing. He wondered if the same waves of fate that washed his friends onto their present, humble shore might not sweep him along to a similar destination. Years ago when he and Harville and Benwick were new to the service, there had never been a second's doubt about wealth and glory. But now, with his friends laid low, he could not deny the uncertainty of his own future. Taking another look out the window, he was thankful the weather would be dry, though cool, for his ride home.

Forcing himself to look away, he closed his bag and resolved to apply the advice Mrs. Harville had given Benwick about being grateful for the day and nothing more. He gathered his hat and gloves, took a last look around the room, and headed downstairs. There he spoke with the keep's wife, arranging for his horse to be ready at one, and set out for the pier.

Before dropping down to the shingle, then to the pier, he stood at the end of the Cobb and took in the whole of the view. No matter where he was in the world, his mistress, the sea, was ever glorious, mysterious and seductive. No matter how uncertain, his life with her was superior to any other he knew and a part of him would like nothing more than to jump ship after ship and stay as close to her as any lover. But now it no longer seemed enough.

He was ashamed to admit that, although Harville was a prisoner to straitened circumstances, the family's happiness gnawed at him. He was tired of being alone. He was tired of fretting about the past and planning for a future that was uncertain at its best. What had happened to the jumped-up lieutenant who knew no better than to strut his imagined consequence on the rustic gentry? A chastened man had taken his place and now was faced with life as it truly was. For the marital happiness Wentworth had seen and felt, he would live under that pier. He was certain it was the woman who made the difference. He resumed his walk to Harville's house, setting a small flock of shone birds to flight. He envied them their uncomplicated lives.

Again, the boys greeted him heartily, and Miss Fanny stared. Again, he felt disappointed when they disappeared up the stairs. He came late enough and assumed breakfast would be over, but Mrs. Harville had planned for him to join them for elevenses, which today was slightly more than a light meal. It seemed there was no getting around his being fed, and he tucked into the stew and hot bread accordingly.

"After you left us last night, we realised you'd managed to remain quite silent about your future plans. Elsa is always concerned that you are unattached." Harville glanced at his wife, who was blushing furiously. "She feels that every man needs a good steady woman to care for him."

"Timotee," Mrs. Harville cried. She frowned and nodded slightly towards Benwick.

"That was Fanny's philosophy as well. She always said a man without a woman is like a ship without a rudder." James paused a moment and Wentworth expected his moderately cheerful countenance to darken, but instead, he hoisted his glass, "To Fanny. May her wisdom guide us all."

The three glanced one to the other in surprise. "To Fanny," they cried, raising their glasses as well.

"So, when shall the repairs be finished?" Harville asked.

Wentworth hesitated. "If you mean *Laconia*, she is in Ordinary. The crew has been dispersed, and I am no longer her captain."

"No, I meant your rudder," he gestured towards Benwick. "Surely you've been in the country long enough to find a beautiful girl anxious to be a sailor's wife and ready at a moment's notice to take on the next adventure the Crown tosses your way."

Wentworth smiled, intending to refute his friend's claim, but no words formed in his mind. The quick wit that had rescued him out of a thousand awkward situations was silent. Laughing a bit, he shook his head and continued eating.

Harville halloo'd and slapped his napkin to the table. "There *is* someone. Look at him, Elsa! He'd blush if he were able. I knew you could not be on land so long and not fall in love."

The accusation put starch in his spine. Carefully wiping his mouth, Wentworth turned to Benwick. "Now see here, James, do you believe this bilge Timothy is spilling?"

Looking from Wentworth to Harville and back again, he broke into a grin. "Yes, yes, I believe I do." He barely got the words out when he began to laugh.

His only hope was to divert them away from the subject of women altogether. "You are right, there are pretty enough girls in the country, but that does not mean–"

"Excuse me, ma'am, there is something you really ought to see out back," Mary said, smiling as she peeked from the doorway.

The interruption could not have been timed more perfectly. If he didn't fear it would frighten the poor creature to death, he would have kissed her on the spot.

"I wonder what the poor wretch has done now," Mrs. Harville sighed, leaving the table.

Harville looked at Benwick, who smiled. "I hope it's not the fellow in back of us. He has been known to do something he likes to call, 'air bathing.' The last time Elsa caught him at it, she took a broom to 'im." The gentlemen laughed and Wentworth anticipated a return to the previous ridicule.

"But then it could be something Mary has done herself. My wife truly has the patience of a saint. I tried to persuade her that after last night's catastrophe, it was clear the girl has no talent for the kitchen. She said it might look as if she has no talent, but she's sure she can find something the girl can do well."

Wentworth took the last bite of his stew and said, "Your wife might very well be a saint, and that would make me the devil for I would have put her adrift after the first bite of salted tart."

Heavy footsteps and loud thumping from the kitchen interrupted them. All eyes went to the door, and Harville called out, "Elsa, are you all right? What was that?" Wentworth took a deep breath and made a study of folding his napkin. If the noises proved to be what he feared, what would he say upon its discovery?

Soon, Mrs. Harville, breathing quickly and eyes bright, poked her head out the door, saying, "We are fine. Just a little rearranging. I'll be out in a moment." She disappeared back into the kitchen.

"Huh, I wonder what she might be rearranging? There's not much out there as I recall."

"You know how ladies are, Timothy," said Benwick, "They can always find something to put their hands to."

The loud noises stopped only to be replaced by feminine voices, the sound of wood being dragged on wood, and the occasional gentle thud. After another quarter of an hour, Mary came out, said her mistress needed a man of stature to reach a canister from the tallest cabinet, and requested particularly the Captain's help. After the message she dropped a curtsey and disappeared into another part of the house.

With both the gentlemen looking at him, Wentworth shrugged and rose from his seat. "After all these years of bashing my head on the beams of my cabin and cursing my height, it seems there is a use for it."

Timothy, in particular, looked suspicious. "I can't understand why she'd ask that you assist her. I've done well enough over the last few weeks."

Getting into the room was difficult, and he had to push something standing in the way of the door. After closing it quickly, he took a survey and was reminded of his father's warehouse, or even more, the bedlam of the purser's locker onboard ship. The long counter against the outer wall was crowded with oddly shaped bags, crates of various fruits and vegetables, and large bundles wrapped with brown paper and twine. Nothing stood close to the hot, ramshackle stove, but the rest of the floor was crowded with small barrels, large and small sacks, and more bundles. In the midst of it all stood Elsa Harville holding a brightly wrapped bundle that marked it as something from a confectioner's.

"It seems that today is the day Providence has chosen to answer my prayers." Her eyes were shining with unshed tears. For a moment she looked nearly as young as she did when he was first introduced to her. Along with happiness, he thought he saw no small amount of relief. "There is easily three months worth of food here. Longer if I am careful"

He would not admit his part in this unless forced. "My brother preaches that God owns the cattle on a thousand hills. I don't suppose this little bit will be missed."

She held up the bright bundle. "He even saw that the children have some sweets."

The stove, inadequate as it might look, was throwing off enough heat to make the little room oppressive even on a dreary November day. He would help reach whatever she needed and then be gone. "And where is this canister?"

"Up there," she pointed. Clearing a spot on the counter, she took it from him. "Not only was there food," she said, opening the canister and dumping out the contents. He suspected this was her way of indicating how close to the edge her family was treading. "The driver made sure this was delivered straight into my hands." She held up a brown paper packet with two wax wafers holding it closed. On it was scrawled, "Mrs. T. Harville."

Lightly touching one of the seals, he said, "Hmm, even God knows that a bit of wax goes a long way to keeping men honest." Their eyes met and he knew she understood.

Opening it, she discovered a small sack tied shut with an intricate knot in the string. He took the sack and expertly undid the knot. As she opened it and counted the bills and coins within, he could not miss her slow intake of breath. Without looking up, she said, "It is exactly a full year's pay for a man of Timotee's rank."

"I imagine Providence knows precisely the wages of His Majesty's officers." He breathed a silent sigh of relief that the innkeeper had trusted his letter of credit and been his bank. Folding the little sack closed, she opened the canister and dropped it inside.

It made a muffled but satisfying thud when it settled. She caressed the canister as she replaced the lid. "Yes, I'm sure He does. But," she said, turning to him, "we both know that all this was not miraculously conjured, that there was a human hand involved."

He did not reply to that, but asked if he might replace it for her.

"No, I will have to find a new place to hide my bank. It would be too awkward to explain to Timotee."

"Yes, I see that could be the case."

"Many years ago, when Timotee first told me he was to sail with Captain Frederick Wentworth, I was ignorant of your reputation and asked him what sort of man you were. He laughed and said that when chasing a prize, you had all the cunning and guile of a Barbary pirate. But the rest of the time you had the heart and soul of a gentleman."

"Well, there are many who would not agree with that."

"No, there aren't. A handful at most, and they are merely jealous of your success. I know there was a mistake and that you meant to be out of sight and sound of Lyme before all this was delivered. You wished to avoid any sort of praise, but that is impossible now. You will have to accept my very deepest thanks." She stood on her tiptoes and kissed him on the cheek. It was a small gesture that left him undone for a moment.

"He cannot know," he said, pulling on the string that hung from a bag of sugar.

She shook the little tin. "He will not know." Her tone was definitive on the point. "Were he a shiftless lout, I would shout of your gift from the housetops, hoping to shame him into action, but he cannot help our condition. I shall move heaven and earth to keep him ignorant." Taking the paper in which the sack had been wrapped, she tossed it in the stove. "This would be the only clue and now it is gone." She stood, "I recognised your hand from the note you sent round yesterday. Timotee would know it for sure."

For all the years he had known Elsa Harville, their relationship had been wholly obligatory. She was the wife of his closest friend who, when he was in the same port, welcomed him to their home, fed him, and offered him a bit of domestic rest. But now he saw her truly.

"Ah, you are very clever, Mrs. Harville, but after seeing all this, I have my doubts that keeping this secret is possible." He waved his hand indicating the bounty. "Things may have been a bit overdone."

"You have done no such thing," she said, holding the candy close and resting her hand on a brace of rabbits. "I can hide all this. He already thinks I am able to feed the multitudes on five loaves and two fish. With all this, the feat will just be a bit simpler." Smiling, she took an orange from its crate and sniffed it.

"I believe you will. Perhaps one day soon, I will find a woman who will be half the wife to me that you are to Timothy."

Her look shifted and she examined him closely. "No, Captain, you are not the sort of man who will accept less than a full measure of anything, particularly not when it comes to the woman who will share your life. But then again, neither should you."

The scraping of chairs in the dining room made them move to the door. "Well, Captain, it is time to go out and say our formal farewells. And, if I might have one more favour from you, please entreat the gentlemen to walk a ways with you so I might put away my prize without fear of discovery?"

"Certainly, madam. Anything for a friend."

~ ~ ~ ~ ~ ~ ~ & ~ ~ ~ ~ ~ ~ ~

The three reached a place in the long street that began the climb out of Lyme. Wentworth felt reluctant to part. They had shared the seafaring life together in many parts of the world. Now, it was clear, one of them would never partake of that life again. Another's future was clouded by grief and uncertainty. The third would return to the sea and, no doubt, wring out of her as much glory as she would ever allow. But, for the moment, they were three friends who must reluctantly part company.

"Now that I know where you are, the letters will not go astray." Harville shifted on his stick and looked out to the Cobb.

"And I shall do my best to be a faithful correspondent, but have a little mercy; I am used to having the services of a secretary. Unless I am able to convince my sister to take the post, everything will be up to me." They all laughed with the dread of the inevitable.

Benwick extended a hand and said, "Captain, it was very good to see you. I shall write as well, I'll but not expect completely equal replies."

"Thank you, James. You will probably not be disappointed with that attitude. Timothy." He touched his friend on the shoulder.

Harville turned and smiled. "Both Elsa and I want you to know that you are welcome here any time. Please, do not hesitate to come to us." He took Wentworth's hand and shook it as firmly as was possible.

"I will not hesitate, I assure you."

"Well, come, James. We shall go back to the house and see what sort of trouble we can stir up." The men waved and watched one another for as long as duty required. Wentworth turned and entered the inn.

All was as he left it. He took one last look out the window. It never stopped, the sea's advance and retreat, but it was soothing to watch and hear. Since his arrival, the company of his good friends had washed any cares aside, and he was feeling a bit morose at leaving. But there were things to do back at Kellynch and, particularly, Uppercross.

Wentworth thanked the innkeeper and his wife in the most appropriate way, collected his gear, and departed the establishment. After he had mounted, he looked over the water and watched the cloud shadows move across the ever-churning sea. Lyme was beautiful in its own way, and he was determined that he would visit again as soon as he possibly could. He urged the horse on, took a last look at the sea, and headed towards home.

~ ~ ~ ~ ~ ~ ~ & ~ ~ ~ ~ ~ ~ ~

His arrival at Kellynch was greeted with a kiss from his sister and an offer from the Admiral of something to "take the edge off a long ride." He welcomed them both. Standing by the fire in the Bower Room, he answered Sophia's questions about Harville.

"I had feared a reduction," he told her. "Lyme is not a place I had ever heard to be popular with well-off sailors. Unfortunately, I was correct."

"Well, one can't blame the Admiralty," the Admiral said. "There are too many healthy fellows wanting ships to consider a man in Harville's condition."

"There is no blame cast on Harville's part or mine. I did what I could, but it is not enough to pull them off the rocks. Something will have to happen eventually."

"So, did you see anything of great interest while you were there?" his sister asked?

"Anything of interest? Not really. As Timothy said, it is a raggedy place that smells of fish most of the time. But the ride there and back was good clearing the head. I have decided to go to Edward's for a fortnight or so."

"Really? By all signs, you were content to stay here. What precisely has changed your mind?" The question was worded to convey disinterest, but Sophia watched him closely.

"I have made him beg my company long enough, don't you think?" He looked at the Admiral and laughed.

"Yes, I suppose you have. He's come very close to accusing me of keeping you prisoner here. When will you leave?" his sister inquired.

"Soon. I thought I would send a letter off today, give it a day or two head startand then be off."

"That is quite soon. Almost as if you want nothing better than get away from us."

"No, nothing of the sort. It is just that the longer I delay, the closer I am to bad weather. Don't the rustics say, 'Make hay while the sun shines'? I think I must make miles while the rains hold off."

"Very wise, if you ask me," the Admiral said.

"Yes, a very wise decision, indeed." Her tone was bursting with insinuation; her look was doubly so.

"Well, you were not the only one busy with friends. Mr. Musgrove came to call yesterday, him and one of his daughters."

"And how are the Musgroves?" he asked. He purposely avoided asking which daughter, as there was no need to guess. He knew his avoidance would smoke out his sister's true intentions.

"They are very well, Frederick, although a little surprised you'd not been around. They worried you might be ill."

"They are very kind people," he said. Taking a drink, he turned away and faced the portrait. He felt the brown eyes scolding him for teasing his sister in such a horrid fashion. "I should go over later and tell them of my plans."

"Yes you should. They have extended to you more deference than politeness would dictate." To the Admiral she said, "Dear, do you remember which of the girls Mr. Musgrove brought yesterday?"

"No, can't say as I do. You know I can't tell them apart. There are such a number of names that I can't remember a quarter of them. Parents would be wise to name their girls Sophy and save us all the trouble." He touched his wife's hand as he rose to fill his glass.

Frederick decided the game was up. "I would think it was Miss Louisa who accompanied him. Henrietta was no doubt otherwise engaged with her cousin."

"So it was, Miss Louisa. She is the talkative one. Anywise, she wanted me to tell you particularly that you have been sorely missed at Uppercross."

There it was. The small nugget she wished to present him. Now he understood her favourable tone concerning his decision to visit Edward. For whatever reason, she seemed to have little taste for the idea of him pursuing either of the Miss Musgroves, and since his own notions were no longer firm on the matter, it would seem that his leaving the area was just the thing to please her.

~ ~ ~ ~ ~ ~ ~ & ~ ~ ~ ~ ~ ~ ~

Dinner with the Admiral and Sophia had been full of her reminders of little chores that needed doing before he should leave. It struck him as ironic that she was now the one who seemed to be hurrying him out the door to their brother. He could not help but wonder how dinner might have gone had he announced his earlier decision to pursue Louisa Musgrove. No matter how he turned it in his mind, the picture was not pretty.

He wrote to the Musgroves later that day and thought how it was a shame he could not thank the Harvilles for helping him to see his error. Aligning himself with the Musgroves would do a disservice to Louisa and to himself. Watching Timothy and Elsa Harville, as anxious as their lives had become, still caring for one another, still reaching out for one another, made him long for that solid, comforting sort of love. It had been his once, and he would somehow find it again.

Dismounting, he handed the horse over to a boy and walked to the door of Uppercross Mansion. He removed his gloves, thinking that had he not changed his mind, the house could have become a fortress where he might have spent a lifetime hiding from his true feelings.

Before he could knock, Louisa opened the door and greeted him with a mild scold. "We were worried when you failed to appear yesterday."

She stepped aside, allowing him in. After she took his hat and coat, he said, "I found I had the opportunity to visit a friend and decided it best to go immediately. It is hard to believe that my absence would be grounds for such concern."

"Oh, but it was! We were desolate without you." Shoving his things into the hands of a manservant, she took his arm and propelled him into the sitting room where the elder Musgroves and her sister were assembled. He was greeted warmly by them and was soon seated in the room's second-best chair and swamped with offers of tea and any other food he might wish. Refusing all but the tea, it was not long before he was relating everything concerning his trip to Lyme.

During the early part of his recounting, the residents of the Cottage arrived and joined the party. Anne, he noticed, disappeared while her sister and brother-in-law availed themselves of the refreshments. When they were settled, Charles asked about the horse he'd seen out front. Once Wentworth laid out particulars of the purchase, Louisa begged that the Captain should continue with his account of his travels. Even so, he was not allowed a word before she saw that his cup was refilled.

While she returned to her seat, he looked past her into a mirror that hung near the doorway and realised he could see Anne perfectly. She was seated on the piano bench and was looking through pages of music. His account of Lyme seemed of little interest to her, but it gave him the perfect opportunity to observe her.

"Never been to Lyme. What's it like?" Musgrove asked through a bite of cake.

He described the bay and the Cobb and the cliffs to the east of town. "It is the sort of coastline that, if one is not onboard a ship of any real size and looking for safe harbour, is beautiful even to the eyes of a sailor. I am surprised Lyme is not more popular. Even at this time of year it has a great deal to offer the visitor. I shall return as soon as I am able." The room remained quiet. Normally, he was not put off by their deference, but now he felt as though he was rambling and wished that anyone else would relieve him. A glance in the mirror showed him that Anne was listening. No one rescued him, so he ploughed on. "It is particularly so if one is inclined towards more sedentary pursuits: reading and writing and the like. I suppose that is why the place seems a perfect fit for my friend."

"So this Harville is a real headpiece?" Musgrove said.

"Harville? A great intellect? No, no, I meant a mutual friend of ours who is living with Harville and his family—a Commander Benwick. He was my First Lieutenant sometime ago, probably my finest. He was engaged to Harville's sister, and they would have been married by now had she not died in June. They had waited for him to gain a promotion, which he received this summer, but it was too late. A sudden fever took her." The faces around the room were sympathetic. "I believe that few men have ever suffered so heavily at such news."

He could not help but remember binding the injured hand of his friend after imparting the news. The tearing of a man's flesh was nothing to the tearing of his soul. Draining his cup, he gathered his thoughts and avoided looking at Anne's reflection.

As the others began to exchange their own ideas on the merits of Lyme, Wentworth made his way to Mrs. Musgrove, who poured him another cup. After refusing, for the third time, anything to eat, he walked to the window. He would miss the lively chaos of the family, but after this visit, he knew more surely than ever that he must go quickly to Edward's. The easy care and affection witnessed between Harville and his wife stood more and more in stark relief against the measured practicality he saw in allying himself with the Musgroves.

"Lyme sounds to be such a lovely place! Perhaps, you would consent to join us in a trip there come summer, Captain?" Mr. Musgrove said, joining his reverie.

"Ah, summer, well that—" he began.

"Papa, why could we not go now?" Louisa's voice raised above all the others. Before her father could answer, she leaned towards the Captain, a very pretty smile spread across her face. "It is only seventeen miles. I looked it up after Mrs. Croft told father and me that you had gone there," she said. "And though it is November, the weather has been very good. I spoke with one of the gardeners, and he said that all the signs are for a very late winter, nothing alarming until after the new year."

"I know that Maddox sets much store by his caterpillars and sheep's wool, but I am not prepared to risk my carriage to a freak rain—or snow, for that matter."

"But, Papa, what is thirty-four miles? We could easily go and return in one day. And if the weather was a worry in the morning, we would not depart."

"Louisa, you do not realise the time it takes to travel so far. Thirty-four miles would mean—what Charles—six, seven hours there and back? The horses would barely be rested before they were summoned into action again. No, dear, I cannot consent to that."

Wentworth watched the back and forth between Mr. Musgrove and his younger daughter. Looking around the room he sensed that only he felt any embarrassment at the scene playing out so publicly. Perhaps as a man of authority himself, he was acutely aware of her father's position. No man relished having his opinion disregarded before the eyes of others.

"Father is right, Louisa. Were this urgent, the risk to the horses would be understandable, but merely for pleasure...well, it isn't worth it." The son's stepping in to aid his father was a heartening sign. Soon the whole matter would be laid to rest. "Besides, even if you were to leave early, the travelling time would leave only an hour or two for the visit. Not worth the effort if you ask me."

"Perhaps not to you, Charles, but there are those in this family who have interests in a wider world," Mrs. Charles said. There seemed to be a little nod of support moving through the younger Musgrove ladies. Stealing a look at the piano, he saw that Anne was puzzled about some-thing, and as best as he could tell, the object was her sister.

He was encouraged to think that they might be in agreement. Per-haps she, too, thought it strange that her sister, a woman who probably gave little thought to anything not directly involving herself, would make such a statement in support of Louisa.

Now, Louisa was on her feet. "Papa, might you consent if we were to go to Lyme one day, stay over to allow the horses a rest, and then return home the next day?" The expression on her face was angelic, and her hands were folded in such a way as to be a model of supplication. He wondered whether, before was all said and done, the girl might not have her father driving the carriage himself. A glance at the piano made him know he was not the only one intrigued.

Though the poor man stood right next to him, in every practical way he was being goaded into a corner. His discomfort was conspicuous. He studied the faces about the room, drained his tea and muttered as though he bore the weight of the world on his shoulders. Old Mr. Musgrove hadn't the stomach to outright deny her, and he seemed unable to find any plausible excuse at his disposal. Were it not a family matter, Wentworth would step in with reasons enough, but his own news had not yet been told; and he wished to leave the area on good terms with the family. Silence was his best strategy.

"Father, that might not be a bad plan," Charles finally said. A smile at his wife made it clear where his central allegiance lay. The son approached and began to outline his idea. Louisa joined him.

Oh, God, now the scheme is infecting the whole bunch of them! He moved away. Standing next to the tea table, he relented and took a piece of cake. Just as he took a bite, Louisa said, "That is not a problem, Father. Surely Captain Wentworth will see to everything. He knows the town well. He would take care to find us the best accommodations and introduce us to the best sort of people. No one would dare to do or say anything untoward with him in our midst. And if that is not enough, I'm sure Anne can be persuaded to accompany us. I know you trust her judgment."

The deed was done. Her father gave his bruised consent and she shifted her gaze to Wentworth. He had to marvel. The girl had beat back every objection and gotten precisely what she wanted. While he was stuffing himself with cake and could raise no objection, she had tidily pulled him into the scheme as well. In fact, he suspected it was on the weight of his and Anne's supervision of the group that the old man had allowed himself to be persuaded. *What a chit! She used me to hoist the old boy.* He had never met a master tactician who looked so innocent and lovely.

Plans were flying fast and furious. He heard his own name and Anne's mentioned together in nearly every sentence. To this point, he had said nothing. There was little left for him to say! He had not been invited; so his consent was unnecessary. Whether he cared to be their guide and protector seemed to matter very little to anyone. So, this is what it is to be a part of the cyclone called the family Musgrove.

He was then engulfed by the group with questions on the specifics of visiting Lyme: how warm during the day, how cool at night? Would the ladies and gentlemen dress for dinner and need eveningwear? Would there be dancing when they visited the Harvilles or merely a quiet card party? Wishing to say there was not enough time in a week to accomplish all they mentioned, he tempered his answers and tried to remind them of the restraints of time and the situation of his friend.

"I know it is wholly unexpected, Anne, but you will not disappoint us," Henrietta asked as Anne abandoned the piano bench to join them. He was curious to hear what she thought of the proposal.

"No, certainly not. By all the Captain has told us, Lyme sounds to be a lovely place. I am happy to be included in the party." Her former puzzlement was replaced with a genuine smile of interest. All of his misgivings immediately disappeared. Now all that was left was to explain to his sister this latest change in his plans.

~ ~ ~ ~ ~ ~ ~ & ~ ~ ~ ~ ~ ~ ~

The night before, in the midst of all the various discussions and all the varied, woolly opinions, he had managed to impress upon them the importance of setting a departure time and sticking with it. They would all meet at the mansion for an early breakfast. While they ate, the dunnage would be loaded. This would necessitate that the ladies be packed and ready by the time they retired. As he studied the nodding, smiling faces, he suspected that only one had any intentions of being ready in the morning.

The first plan had been that the ladies and the gentlemen would ride together in Mr. Musgrove's travelling coach. This plan brought an immediate demand from Mrs. Charles, who declared that she would not only sit forward, a position desired by several others as well, but that she would also be seated on one particular side of the coach and not the other. "The view to the right hand is always more varied and interesting I think."

"You know, the idea of being cooped up with four women for several hours does not appeal to me," Musgrove said to Wentworth, offering him a generous glass of sherry. "We could show our fortitude and ride with the driver," the Captain said. Though, considering the time of year, that suggestion was one he might come to regret.

"Yes, well, since you don't mind the chill air, I shall take my curricle. It will give me the opportunity to try her out full tilt." Musgrove chuckled a little. He was relieved when Musgrove came up with this bit of sense. It was presented as the only means to give the maximum amount of comfort to all parties. All the ladies, save one, were enthusiastic.

The next day the Admiral drove Wentworth to Uppercross and was astonished to see all the preparations. "Whoa." The Admiral pulled the gig to a stop and declared, "Good God, Frederick, you told your sister you would only be gone one night. This looks to be a six-month at the very least. You *did* say you were only going to Lyme?"

The travelling coach was out, with two grooms polishing various bits of brass and inlay. Of the six horses, two were being changed out in favour of two others. He suspected Mrs. Charles was responsible for this as now all the horses matched in hue. No doubt, the polishing was also undertaken at her suggestion since the curricle sitting alongside was being wiped down as well. Its horses looked to be matched already. He was dismayed to see several small trunks strewn about, and a few others going up and down off the top of the coach. The drive resembled the staging area worthy of a First Rate ship, not the preparations for a pleasure trip of just over twenty-four hours. Jumping down, he pulled his battered satchel from under the seat. "I suspect when the Musgroves travel, they like to be comfortable."

"Well, there is comfortable, and then there is comfortable. Remember what your sister said." The evening before, Sophia had listened patiently while he explained how the scheme to go to Lyme had evolved and he had been pulled into the whole affair. He was prepared for some lively discussion and was surprised when all she had to say was, in her opinion, he could not get to Edward fast enough and that he should be careful while travelling, as there were always unexpected dangers away from home.

"I shall be careful, sir. Perhaps you might help my sister polish her crystal ball so that she can see more clearly just what sort of dangers I face." Instead of the customary understated reply from his brother-in-law, he was surprised to see a knitted brow and a thoughtful look.

"She's a woman, Frederick. She sees things that neither you nor I would ever notice." He bid him a good trip and manoeuvred out of the yard.

Entering the house, he had few hopes of it being in any better state. His expectations were well-founded. Servants were hurrying here and there; Mrs. Musgrove welcomed him but rushed on and excused herself quickly. He was taken to the dining room where he found most of his fellow travellers and Mr. Musgrove gathered at the table. He had to admit, in the midst of all this chaos, they were a happy lot. The loud conversations were punctuated with frequent laughter. It was a definite contrast to his own family, now or in the past.

Mr. Musgrove bid him fill a plate and join them. He approached the table to find that the only seat not occupied by a body or baggage for the journey was next to Anne. As usual, her part of this world looked to be calm and quiet. He was glad to share a bit of peace at the moment.

"Captain, you must help me," Louisa said, gently taking his arm so as not to spill his plate and guiding him to a place she had cleared next to herself. She picked up two bonnets so that he might put down his food. "Which of these would be more appropriate for Lyme?" she asked. "I am more partial to the one with the red trim, but perhaps the blue is more the fashion there."

What he knew of the fashions in Lyme would leave a vast wasteland in a thimble. Other than Mrs. Harville, he'd noticed no women on his trip, much less what they chose to wear on their heads. He was partial to blue and said as much. Her frown mystified him, and he was rather put out when she immediately began a long explanation as to why the red would better suit.

"It is obvious that you have more understanding and have given more thought to such matters than I," he said, taking a seat. As he salted his eggs, he glanced at Anne. Before she could look away, he saw a very pronounced smile grace her lips.

Have your fun, Anne. I would see you have a little cheer even at my own expense. He was raising the fork to his mouth when Mr. Musgrove declared the group should be off if they were to arrive in good time. It appeared he would again arrive in Lyme ravenous.

His hopes for a quick remove improved for a few moments, when everyone moved themselves and their belongings towards the door. These hopes dwindled as he stood to the side and watched first one, then another, of the party remember something in the house that must be retrieved. The others had all disappeared except Anne. She stood out of the way but close enough for him to say, "Do the Musgroves travel often?"

Clearing her throat, she said, "No, not really. This is very exciting for everyone." She didn't turn so he could not see her expression, but he thought she was smiling.

"May I put your bag up for you?"

"No, that is not necessary. One of the men can put it up."

"Please, it would give me something to occupy myself."

"Well, if you really need something to do." She handed it to him.

"You travel light."

"It is only overnight. There is no need for much."

"I had thought so myself." He nodded towards the top of the carriage. "There is more than enough dunnage up there to see us through to the other side of the world, I think," He handed up her bag and directed its placement. Returning to her side, he found there was nothing much to say.

The chaotic air and activity, all of which accomplished nothing, was getting under his skin. Checking his watch, he could not help a sigh. It bordered on a growl, and he determined to check himself. Stepping around the carriage, he surveyed the yard, hoping to find Musgrove. He and Mrs. Charles were at the curricle having an animated discussion. Rejoining Anne, he observed, "I cannot comprehend this. The time was set yesterday. All knew it and all agreed to it."

"Perhaps, because you do not suffer women to travel aboard your ship, you do not understand the preparations involved." She was obviously not speaking for herself, as her baggage was perfectly arranged.

"I suppose it is my nature. I am not used to such disorganization."

He heard his name being called, and Musgrove appeared from the other side of the carriage. "Captain, could you hold this brute? He does not like all the upheaval, and he's getting the other all stirred up. And now Mary has decided that she needs me inside." He leant in close, "Were it not for the fact that the shrieking and crying would be so loud as to follow us all the way to Lyme, I'd just as soon we take the gig and leave at once." Wentworth smiled at the thought, but said nothing.

"Charles!"

"Coming, Dearest!"

He turned to make comment to Anne, but she was nowhere to be seen. The horses began a little two-step that demanded his full attention. Walking them, he settled on a nice patch of sunlight for some warmth.

"Aye, if I was captain of this crew I'd be frothing," he said to his equine audience. They bobbed their heads up and down, seemingly in agreement. The encouragement was heartening. "Yes, you understand." The beast nearest him looked to be a fine creature, and he was glad he had asked Musgrove for his advice. It was clear he knew decent horseflesh. "You are no cart horse, are you? No, but in the country one does what one must in order to eat." The second nickered.

"Truly, if this were *Laconia*, I'd have a few in irons by now." The horses stamped their feet and one nudged Wentworth's shoulder. "In sympathy with the common man, eh? Grounds, you ask? Well, there is Article Thirty-six. So broad and deep that nearly anything annoying falls under it. But for this crew, I rather favour Twenty-seven, 'negligence in performing duty'."

One of the pair nodded while the one closest to him swung his head and landed a hard blow on his chest. "Ah well, yes, not her. She's performed admirably. Right on time, gloves on and hat in place, bag packed and stowed. No fault to find with her at all."

"No, no," a voice cut into his peace. "Carry it flat. Please, be very careful with it." Mrs. Charles was evidently annoyed with one of the footman. "Anne, you simply must convince Charles to take me back to the Cottage. I have forgotten my new gloves, and I must have them for the evening."

"Mary, I do not think you will need such fine gloves for the evening."

If he could hear the sisters just around the corner, he wondered if the sound of his own conversation might not drift their way as well. And just what would the daughter of a baronet think when she discovered him talking to two horses?

The conversation about the gloves continued, the elder sister admonishing the younger. "I think it is more important that we get on our way. It is rude that a time was agreed upon and we are very close to missing it. The Captain is very kind in taking us to this new place and introducing us to his particular friend. I am afraid we may be trespassing upon his patience." It was cheering to hear her speak up. Particularly concerning anything to do with him.

"I think it is you who are not patient. You are the one who has been nowhere since returning from school. It is you who is in a hurry to be away. Besides, do you actually believe he does us the favour? Do you not think it will put him in good stead to show his 'particular' friend that he moves in such good circles here in Somerset? Honestly, Anne, you act as if he should not take pride in his alliance with Kellynch Hall and the Elliot family."

Leaning close to his new friends, he said, "My sister and brother save her father from financial ruin, and she thinks the alliance is to *my* good." Moving closer to the corner of the carriage, he leant back to listen again, but the sisters were gone. Ruffling the forelocks of both beasts, he said, "She understands, doesn't she? Never been anywhere in all these years. Perhaps I should take you and her and we all ride to Lyme and leave the rest to ponder the error of their ways." The horses merely blinked.

"Captain, I think I've got the ladies moving towards the carriage. Just another few minutes," Charles said, tapping one of the horses on the nose. "I'm off to herd them this way."

He wondered how Mrs. Charles would take to being herded. "Aye, we shall be right here," he called. To the horse, he said, "Article Twenty-seven it is."

"Twenty-seven?" repeated a female voice.

He started and immediately began cobbling together an explanation to Anne, then was more startled to find it was not her but Louisa who had overhead. "It is nothing. Are the ladies ready?"

"Not quite yet. Anne is to be impatient to be off. She is helping Mary find a pair of gloves and hurrying Henrietta. She sent me out with strict instructions to do nothing more than stand by the carriage, ready to leave." Patting one of the horses with just the tips of her gloved hand, she said, "I was thinking that I could easily convince Charles that Mary would be most pleased if he were to ride with her in the carriage."

Her hand wandered close to his that held the horse's bridle. "Then I could ride with you in the gig. I do adore riding in the open air."

Henrietta's intentions were quite transparent. He began checking the harness for anything loose. "I think it a bit cool and too long a ride for any lady to be in the open air."

"Surely you remember your very own sister saying how women are rational creatures and do not wish to be always in calm waters. I would add, warm carriages."

Admiral Nelson's saying about putting aside manoeuvres and going right at the target came to mind. "Miss Louisa, I think we both know it would be highly improper for the two of us to ride alone all the way to Lyme. Your parents—"

"My parents are very trusting...particularly of you." Louisa smiled persuasively.

"Well, Mary has found the perfect gloves," Charles announced from behind them, "and Anne is doing her best to get her out the door. Henrietta is saying good-byes to Father and Mama, so I would say we are nearly gone, Captain."

"Charles, the Captain and I were just talking and—"

"And if you will take the horses, Charles, I will see the ladies seated. Then we will be off." Taking Louisa by the arm, Wentworth walked her to the carriage door.

"You are quite sure you would not like me to speak to my brother?"

"Please watch your step, Miss Musgrove," he said. She grasped his hand particularly close as she ascended the steps. The last in was Anne. He took care to follow her up and guide her in just the same. He stepped back down and asked the ladies if they were well and settled. Anne's smile of thanks precluded his hearing their answer. Walking back to the gig, he muttered, "I should have charmed Anne, shanghaied the cart, and been done with it."

Chapter Seventeen

The descent into Lyme was as delightful as it had been earlier in the week. The thrill of another's hand at the whip and reins was not lost on him. Musgrove was a decent driver and handled well the changeover from gently graded road to the steep drop into town. Looking behind, Wentworth watched the progress of the ladies' carriage as the driver slowed to a crawl to manoeuvre the slope. He imagined the conversation inside. Mrs. Charles would be afraid and twittering. The Miss Musgroves would be alive with the novelty of the decline, and Anne would most likely be holding her sister's hand, trying to convince her that no harm was about to befall them. He shifted in his seat to ward off the vision in his head of Anne and him, entering the town together, alone, and anticipating the enjoyment of the sights.

The curricle came to a stop and Musgrove looked about. "Not much to catch one's eye here."

Jumping down, Wentworth said, "It is not the buildings that hold the greatest delights, Charles. It is what surrounds the buildings." Giving directions to the inn's stable, he caught glimpses of the sea.

In a true sailor's heart, every yard of coastline was unique. Those tethered to the land by their breeding and occupation rarely noticed the dangers lying beneath a placid shoreline or the skill which made navigating a rocky, frothing piece of coast a death-defying adventure. No, it took a heart willing to accept the sea's risks as well as her few comforts to fully consider her rich enchantments.

The larger travelling carriage pulled up to the doorway of the Binnacle. The feminine voices inside seemed to be playing, to the letter, the parts he had assigned them. Anne's muffled voice could be heard: "Mary, please, the coach has stopped. We are no longer moving." There was laughter in the background. Though impossible to know precisely, he suspected the laughter was borne of contempt and not some innocent amusement. Soon Louisa Musgrove's face appeared at the window, and she made a gesture with her gloved hand, the fingers working up and down as though a mouth was speaking. Her eyes were bright with laughter.

Musgrove passed him and said to no one, "Best let them out." There was a decided air of resignation in his voice. He helped his wife and her sister down while Wentworth went to the other side and helped the driver and man with the bags. He could hear the two girls inside, their conversation muffled. A knock on the window brought a little wave from Louisa. Henrietta looked also, lingered a moment, then an exchange between her and her sister made her disappear.

"Would you please help me, Captain?" Louisa said, through the glass. She pointed to the door behind her. He came around to the door and found the others had entered the Binnacle. Even her sister had disappeared. He stood at the bottom of the step, raised a hand for her aid, and waited.

"I seem to have lost an earring, Captain. Might you come and help me to look for it?"

He leaned in, thinking it would be on the floor. Bending to search under the seats, he said, "I see nothing." Straightening, he was face-to-face with her. The young lady had taken a seat and was not at all engaged in the search.

Her gloves removed, she held up something shiny in her hand. "I found it." Tilting her head a little, she replaced it on her ear. It was impossible not to hear the softness in her voice and observe the becoming curve of her neck.

"We should get inside so we can get settled." He winced inwardly at the statement's cosy sound. Offering her his gloved hand, she rose, came to the door, and stood as straight as she could.

"Jump me." The statement was not a request, nor was it the good-natured plea that had become her custom when they walked together. It had the air of authority. Her voice implied it was his duty to give her satisfaction. The two words made claims on him.

Noting the driver clambering down from his seat, Wentworth said, "Miss Louisa, please, let us go inside." He extended his hand further. Rather than take his hand, she placed hers on his shoulders and stepped out. It was a long step and he unconsciously reached out to lower her down. She was now no more than a hand's width from his face, in no hurry to remove herself from his grasp. It was undeniable that standing with her in his arms was a pleasurable sensation, but he could not help be aware of the driver's nearness–though the man seemed to be loitering on the opposite side of the carriage. This delay did nothing to save Wentworth from the danger of her brother finding them in such a position.

"Please, Miss..." He stepped back.

"Please yourself." She smiled boldly. "I believe we are well enough acquainted that you may call me 'Louisa,' at least when we are alone together."

With her eyes full of nothing but him, her look was entirely appealing. The blush of her cheeks was a prominent and sweet pink that swept clear into her hair. And the hair was falling teasingly from beneath her bonnet. She reached out the short distance between them and touched the button of his blue coat. "I am sure no one in the family would mind."

No one would, and that was the precise reason he must extricate himself from this circumstance immediately. But what was he to say that would not offend the young woman?

"Hobbs!" Charles' call to the driver pre-empted his answer. Thankfully, the moment was broken.

"Let me take you inside. The sooner we are settled, the sooner we can see the sights." Louisa eagerly took his proffered arm, and they entered the inn.

"We are on the first floor, Captain," said Musgrove. "You have a room up top. I thought you would like it as it has a view of the sea."

"Same as the other day, sir," the landlord said to Wentworth.

Taking the key, he nodded his thanks. As the group moved away to their rooms, Louisa turned and said she would be back down in an instant. Her particular attentions to him were becoming embarrassing, but this was soon swallowed up with his pity for Musgrove. When the couple mounted the steps, he heard Mrs. Charles comment that Charles might have considered her wish to have a view of the sea. Her husband's answer was unintelligible. Before going up, Wentworth arranged for dinner and breakfast the next morning.

He stowed his bag without bothering to unpack and savoured a quick look at the view, then went back downstairs. No one else was down as yet, and he decided to take the opportunity to smoke a cheroot. He found the door handle to be finicky and finessed it open. Outside he was met with a stiff breeze and the low roar of the sea in the background. After the rhythm of the curricle and Musgrove's voice, the change was quite welcome.

Catching a whiff of the coming cold weather, he considered a winter spent in Lyme and how Harville would manage. Before long, the door handle clattered. Perhaps the rest of the party was just as anxious to go down to the shingle as he. Reaching over, he held the handle just so and lifted. He waited for the great hubbub that followed the Musgroves, but was surprised to find only Anne looking around the door at him.

"I wondered who to thank. The latch seems quite particular as to how it is handled," she said, stepping out. The breeze surprised her, and she pulled her cloak close.

His natural impulse was to quip that the door's hardware had much in common with most women, but he instead said, "Yes, it needs a gentle hand." He suspected his irony was not lost on either of them. He stepped forward to close the door.

"Pardon me," she said, moving away.

"Pardon me," he countered, dropping the cheroot and grinding it out. She took up a place on the sidewalk and looked around. The way she held her bag and cloak made her seem very small, almost unnoticeable. "So, here we are again; waiting for the Musgroves." It was out and within her hearing before he even knew it.

She thought a moment, and a wry smile accompanied her reply. "Yes, again. It was necessary for Charles to change rooms, and Louisa and Henrietta are freshening up."

No doubt Musgrove changed rooms to keep his wife happy; she would have a room with a view regardless of the trouble. As for the young ladies, they were obviously more concerned with their appearance than looking at the scenery of Lyme.

It occurred to him that he and Anne might start out together, though it was certainly not polite to abandon their party and some might decry two unattached persons strolling alone. To the others they were old acquaintances; he did not think anyone would question their actions. It was still daylight, and certainly they would not get much past the end of the street before the others appeared.

"Since we seem to be the only ones interested in the sights, perhaps we might start–" A gabble of voices just proceeded the jangling of the door's hardware. Before he could reach over and assist, the door flew open and the other four of their party surrounded them. He glanced down at Anne. From her expression, had the others tarried longer, she had had every intention of accepting his suggestion.

There was plenty of chatter about what each wished to see, but in the end, all looked to him to decide the way. They naturally fell into groups of two: he and Louisa in the front, followed by Henrietta and Anne. In the rear were Musgrove and his wife.

"Really Charles, we should not be following behind."

"Mary, this is not a royal display, and I will not leave my sister and yours to walk alone behind."

She lowered her voice, "You might mention to the Captain that Anne is due some deference as the eldest and her father's daughter."

"Just hush, Mary. Everything is well as is. You just don't like the Captain walking with *my* sister."

It was mortifying to overhear them speaking so freely about the two of them. He could only guess what Anne must think about such conjecturing. Pretending to brush something from his shoulder, he glanced back at her. Thankfully, she continued her conversation with Henrietta and showed no sign of hearing them. That was his hope, but he knew better.

The supreme irony rested in the fact that it was he who had pointed out to Sophia that country proprieties were more lenient. He could now be walking with Anne if only he had appealed to stricter convention. He had locked his own shackles in this situation.

The wind rose the closer they drew to the water's edge. The sun was setting behind the hills and the air was cooling. He did not care about the weather, but the murmurings from the others let him know they would only stay a few minutes on the beach and then move on to Harville's.

The ladies stood together in a little knot and discussed how much they were missing by being so late in the season. There might be a better choice of accommodations and more activities and people to see. In all, it was a wonderful excursion, but would be much improved by doing it in the warmer months. Musgrove found entertainment chucking rocks in the waves. Anne, alone, seemed to be content to watch the water lap at the rocks and the sky change and darken with the sun's setting.

He stepped back a few paces, out of the sight of the others, so he could watch her more freely. She removed her bonnet and raised her face to the breeze. Then, pulling her cloak close, she stood motionless. He could easily imagine the two of them alone, he standing behind with his arms encircling her. They had stood such a way once all those summers ago. He could still remember the warmth of her against him, her head resting in the crook of his neck. Her sighs of that summer were still a pleasure to remember.

"Captain–!" Louisa was smiling at him and shaking his shoulder. "Captain, everyone is ready to move on." His gaze had fallen to the stony shingle. Looking around, no one besides Louisa seemed to notice his wool-gathering. It was decided that he would go to the Harville's and announce their arrival. They would see more of the sights from the pier and wait for him.

~ ~ ~ ~ ~ ~ ~&~ ~ ~ ~ ~ ~ ~

The Harville's welcomed him with the same heartiness and cheer as before, and when he told them he had brought friends, Harville, his wife, and Benwick were anxious to meet them all.

"I am sorry to burst upon you completely unannounced this time, but the party was arranged and executed before I had a chance to send word."

"Captain, there is nothing to worry about. Your friends are as welcome as you," Harville said, as Elsa helped him with his coat.

While the three were preparing to go out, Wentworth took James aside and enquired about Timothy's strength that day. "He's very well as he was after you left. Elsa attributes it to your visit. She says it has been a tonic to him."

As they approached the Cobb, Wentworth explained the family connexions between the Elliots and the Musgroves.

"This proves mating rituals in the country are not any different than those of the King's Navy."

"Timotee! That is not a subject for polite conversation."

Wentworth laughed, but since the group was still a ways off and he was intrigued by Harville's conclusion, he urged him on.

"Well, as I see it, the young squire marrying the daughter of the local gentry—a baronet in this case—is not much different than an inferior officer of the navy marrying the sister of his superior officer. Eh, James?"

Benwick looked stricken for a moment, then softened. "Yes, for regardless of the results, such ties strengthen the bonds between brother officers."

Harville clapped Wentworth on the shoulder. "Now, Captain, if you really wanted to do well for yourself, you would marry the Baronet's other daughter. Then you'd have the Elliot's blood and position on one hand and an alliance with the Musgrove's money and land on the other. In no time you would have a little dynasty of your own in Somerset." Leave it to his good friend to navigate straight, albeit blindly, into the mare's nest presently at the centre of his thoughts.

There was nothing to answer as they were joined by the group from Somerset. The introductions were made and, as far as Wentworth could tell, everyone was disposed to like everyone else. Timothy might as well be Lord Mayor of Lyme for his prodigious welcome of Musgrove. Mrs. Harville was gracious to the Miss Musgroves and Anne. Even Benwick put himself out and greeted them all accordingly, though he soon retreated into his customary shell.

"Well, I feel the wind picking up, and that means my wife will insist that I be inside soon. You must all come back to the house. We shall make ourselves comfortable there while dinner is prepared." He raised a brow to his wife, and she took the signal.

"Certainly, the gentlemen can entertain you with all their favourite stories while I see to the meal." Looking directly at Wentworth, she said, "I am anxious to have so many new friends in our home."

"You can't be serious wanting to feed this crew," Musgrove said. "I alone would put you in the poor house." They laughed at his jest.

"I assure you, it is no trouble. And I know for certain, Mr. Musgrove, that your party can do no damage to my larder." Her confidence at making provision for them all gave Wentworth deep satisfaction. He wished more than anything to oblige her, but nonetheless, he had ordered their dinner and it would not due to sour his relationship with the innkeeper of the Binnacle.

"Well, Captain," Harville drawled, "I shall forgive you this once, but the next time you bring such good friends to visit, you will be under firm obligation to dine with the Harvilles. Is that clear?"

Wentworth smiled. "You take a great deal upon yourself for an inferior officer, Captain Harville, but yes, I understand perfectly."

"No matter that you cannot dine tonight, you must all come now and have something to warm yourselves," Elsa Harville insisted.

The visit to the Harville home was brief. The house was so small that there was much moving of chairs and tables and enough upheaval that, when the children joined them, the atmosphere was a bit like Bedlam. It was easy to see the shocked expressions on the faces of those who had wondered about dancing and card parties and splendid dressing for dinner. He wondered if Lyme might not be a great disappointment for some of the party. Standing aside, Wentworth watched the groups mingle. Harville was in his element, excitedly entertaining them all, Benwick directed the serving girl in serving refreshments, and Mrs. Harville took Anne on a tour of Harville's curiosities. He could not help observing that Anne belonged so much more with the one group and not the other. Were she given the time and opportunity, she would be a perfect fit with his friends. Though she was raised amidst the elegance of Kellynch Hall, he saw she was made of finer stuff. Not that the Musgroves were not genuine. But for them, Harville and Benwick and this life was a novelty, somewhere to visit and then return home thankful for Uppercross Mansion. It would stand when the little house under the pier finally washed away. He did not blame them for such feelings; they were understandable for a family steeped in their country heritage. But Anne was a different matter all together.

"Captain, the ladies wish to get back and change for dinner, and I'd like to see to Father's horses before nightfall."

"Certainly, Musgrove." Wentworth paid his compliments to Harville and his wife, thanked them for the hospitality, and made plans to see the gentlemen later in the evening.

It was a relief to be out of the confines of the Harville's home and into the waning sunlight and fresh air. He and Musgrove brought up the rear of the party as they walked back to the inn, leaving him free to watch the ladies. Mrs. Charles and Henrietta walked ahead, arm-in-arm, while Louisa and Anne followed. It was clear the younger woman did all the talking, and he could imagine the elder's patient expression. A bit of the conversation floated back to the gentlemen.

"...their character is beyond reproach and their friendliness is unmatched by any others. Their brotherliness is stronger than blood. They are upright and open as no other men in the world. I believe sailors have more worth than any other set of men in England and that only they know how to truly live. I do not think I shall ever be able to respect or love a man not a part of them."

The statement was breathless and eager, and he knew that, at this moment, she meant every word. Though her judgment was naïve and based on little experience of sailors, he could not help admiring her zeal. Beside him, Musgrove snorted. Giving him a sharper look than was intended, Musgrove said, "Sorry, no offence intended. It's just that all her high blown talk of sailors is a bit ludicrous. After all, 'Poor Richard' was a sailor." They were approaching the inn. Musgrove moved ahead of the ladies so he might open the door for them. There was more to Charles Musgrove than met the eye.

~ ~ ~ ~ ~ ~ ~ & ~ ~ ~ ~ ~ ~ ~

The food was adequate in quality and plentiful in quantity. The service was prompt and respectful. The keep's wife deferred to him in all matters and saw to their every need. There were several apologies for the quietness of Lyme at this time of year. Regardless, nothing could dampen the cheer of the party.

When the meal was finished, the others went to their rooms to make ready for Harville's promised visit. Wentworth had little to do to prepare for his friend and found himself alone with Anne. A serving boy took away the last of the dishes, having wiped the table and refreshed the candles. When he left the room, Wentworth moved closer to her and asked, "And how do you find Lyme, Miss Anne?"

His question brought an expression of thought to her face. As she considered, her countenance lightened and she replied, "I think it is a beautiful place. A winter here might be a hardship in some ways, but in others, it would be a very great pleasure. The scenery is lovely and the sea..." She hesitated and looked the merest of seconds at him. "The sea is beautiful any time, I suspect."

This was an opinion he took much pleasure in hearing. He was about to ask her opinion of his friends when it seemed the room filled with Musgroves returning from their various errands. Louisa entered and looked around the room. Spotting him, she approached and took the seat next to him. Anxious to have her share of the conversation, she asked what was so important that they both looked so serious.

He'd not realized their expressions were out of the ordinary. Would others notice them and question their exchange? Shifting in his seat, he said, "We were merely discussing Lyme and its charms." Turning to Anne, he asked, "And the Harvilles, how do you find them?" Her eyes answered first. In them was expressed genuine affection for his friends.

"I thought they were wonderful," Louisa said, "and so brave to be unashamed of their poverty before strangers. I cannot imagine what I would do if I had so little and were faced with the opinions of so many. Oh, here is Captain Harville," she said, smiling and rising to her feet. "And he has brought poor Captain Benwick as well." Her look and tone were less than enthusiastic. In spite of this observation, she smoothed her gown and hurried to the door.

Wentworth watched her greet the gentlemen, and while he perceived Louisa too capricious at times, she seemed to have taken her own pronouncements concerning sailors to heart. By playing hostess, she was doing all she could to show it in every possible way. Speaking briefly to Harville and Benwick, she pointed to him and Anne.

Benwick shook his head and pointed towards the other end of the table. Louisa's plans were becoming clear; she laughed, shook her head, then took his arm and brought him to the Captain.

"Captain Benwick did not wish to interrupt you two, but I assured him that Anne would much prefer his company to yours, Captain."

He was taken aback at what was surely a muddled phrase on her part. "And precisely why would Captain Benwick's company be preferable to mine, Miss Louisa?"

Urging Benwick to take the seat next to Anne, she replied, "Well, all those books at the Harville's are his, and Anne is a great reader. I am sure they have ever so much in common. I don't believe I have heard you say a word about books or reading since being in our acquaintance, Captain."

Benwick did as Louisa bid and took the seat. His expression was hesitant and Wentworth thought to save them all the embarrassment of the situation.

"My reading habits, or lack of them, are nothing to the point. I am sure that the commander and Miss Anne would be more comfortable joining the rest of us at the other table."

"Pardon, sir, but for my part I think I would much prefer the quiet of this corner," Benwick offered. "I know that Timothy is not in the least sympathetic to the discussion of poetry, and I am sure no one else will care to discuss it either." He smiled at Anne and then Wentworth.

"You needn't concern yourself about us, sir. We shall do quite well here." Anne smiled and made it clear she was comfortable with things as they stood.

"See, everyone is settled. Let us join the others." Louisa tugged at his arm. He nodded to Anne and Benwick and left them.

As they approached seats at the larger table, Louisa leant close and said, "He is so morose; he draws the life out of any room he is in. I am determined to have fun this evening, and I think Anne is the perfect one to entertain him and keep him out of the way." The comment itself was shocking, even more so as she had shown a great deal of sympathy for Benwick's misfortunes earlier. He took his seat and watched her smile as she joined the company, absolutely unconscious of how unfeeling her statement was and how cold it had left him.

Eventually, however, his vexation was overruled by the good company and his own natural cheerfulness. The ladies and gentleman pressed Harville and him for stories of their former days. Each traded turns sharing anecdotes of foreign ports, curious mates with whom they had served, and the good times and bad that left them each changed forever. Their audience was alternately breathless, awaiting the resolution of tense and dangerous circumstances, or caught up in helpless laughter. When he was not the storyteller, Wentworth had a difficult time keeping to the conversation. His eyes drifted away from the faces of his Uppercross companions, and his mind drifted to the two at the small table in the corner.

It appeared, at first, that the conversation between Anne and Benwick was a bit awkward. She spoke more than Benwick at first. Her manner was gentle and her countenance mild, unthreatening, undemanding. On both sides there were occasional smiles, but never anything approaching laughter. He could see Benwick warm to her ministrations, and soon, losing his reserve, the Commander looked most glad to be positioned as he was.

Bowing to Harville's prowess as a narrator, Wentworth waved off his next turn and continued to watch the couple over his pint. It pained him to notice that neither of them wasted a look in the direction of the more animated table. Even at a distance, he could feel the perfect perception growing between them. There was a mutual understanding drawing them closer together. It was difficult to watch Anne listening intently, encouraging Benwick to reveal himself and his grief to her. Years earlier, then-Commander Wentworth, too, had revealed himself. However, his revelations had been of grand future plans and assurances of successes to come once he gained a ship. It was clear the conversation between Anne and his friend was not all Benwick's; she was revealing herself to him as well. To Wentworth's consternation, he could think of no single hope or dream Anne Elliot had shared with him in all the time they spent together. He could not think of a single time he asked; all their confidences had been centred on his prospects in one way or another.

As much as he wished to resent Benwick, he could not stir up the feeling. Knowing how utterly broken-hearted Benwick was left by the loss of Fanny Harville, Wentworth deemed the man to be safe from any affection that might be aroused by Anne's kindness. Such was his one cold comfort in the whole evening.

Harville called to his friend that they must be going soon. Benwick waved an acknowledgement, but, to Wentworth's dismay, instead of rising to leave her, took out a pencil and small notebook and began to write. More precisely, Anne spoke and Benwick wrote. Once she pointed to the page. He crossed out something out and wrote some more. The only thing the Captain could think was they intended to exchange correspondence. Surely the Anne Elliot, who in the past was acutely mindful of propriety, would not now throw modesty to the wind and accept letters from a strange man. Of course she would not! There had to be another explanation. Unable to bring one to mind, he cursed his assumption that Benwick's broken heart was safe.

~ ~ ~ ~ ~ ~ ~ & ~ ~ ~ ~ ~ ~ ~

The next morning, Wentworth dressed while it was still dark. Standing before the window, he watched the sea, the pier, and the shingle appear with the rising sun. Small boats were pushing out to sea for a day's fishing. They joined boats that had gone out earlier under the cover of darkness. He would miss the sea when they left for home, but this time leave-taking could not come soon enough. Abandoning the window, he took a seat on the bed and eventually lay down.

"...he absolutely draws all the life from any room he enters..." Much of his night had been spent thinking on Louisa's interaction with his friends. He knew Harville liked her open ways and quick opinions, but he was still shocked by the girl's lack of compassion. She had seemed genuinely interested and eager to meet Benwick after hearing of his misfortune. That had either been a misreading on his part or, to be fair, in her youth and exuberance she was incapable of comprehending the depths of the man's grief and pain. It still did not excuse her behaviour. This visit had proven his doubts about Louisa's substance and that taking himself off to his brother's for a time was the most prudent course. Despite the manoeuvring on Louisa's part, Benwick had not seemed to mind being passed off to Anne's care. In fact, the more he thought about the pair of them, the more troubling it became that neither had seemed to notice being purposely separated from the rest of the party.

The church clock struck a decent hour, and he decided to go down and see who else might have risen. The one undesirable feature of the uppermost floor was the squeaking floors and stairs. On his previous visit, it had been amusing to find various combinations of floorboards or treads which did not make noise enough to raise the dead. On this visit, on this particular morning, he was not in any mood for games. He supposed himself lucky that Mrs. Charles had not cajoled a room alongside him. He was the sole occupant of the top floor. He tried another combination of stairs as he descended, but it did not matter what he did; they all squeaked alarmingly.

Reaching the lower floor, he approached Anne's door, slowed and listened. He stood motionless for a moment and then scolded himself for being a fool just as the door flew open, and he nearly walked into Louisa.

"Good morning, Captain. It is very kind of you to come for us."

It had certainly not been his intention, but to straighten out the misunderstanding would be extraordinarily rude. "Providence is everywhere." The statement was rather ridiculous on its face, and the idea of blaming God for what, on his part, was an untimely meeting, was surly close to blasphemy. Without commenting, she nodded and disappeared for a moment, returning with her pelisse and bonnet.

Quickly pulling the door shut, she said, "Henrietta is not ready just yet. She will join us later." Taking his arm, she assumed the place she now claimed as her own. They had made their way to the edge of the shingle. "Shall we go down here?" she asked.

"Will not the others be about and breakfast near serving?" They had retraced all the previous haunts on the Cobb, and now she wished to go down to the beach. He would not mind but he suspected that afterwards there would be complaints about sore feet and sand in her shoes—not strident complaints, but merely things said in passing that had begun to grate on his nerves.

"I am sure we have time," she said, with just a hint of a pout. "Besides, you never told me the sea was so beautiful in the morning."

He offered her a hand to come down the steps. He looked into her eyes and beheld a hint of smugness that he'd never acknowledged before. It was clear that, either by art or natural understanding, she was rapidly and precisely coming to know just how to work him.

She came down only a step or two when she stopped. "Jump me," she said, smiling, as she looked him in the eye.

"I think not, Miss Louisa. It is too high. The stones are uneven and make getting a firm footing impossible." He raised his extended hand a bit higher and set his mouth in a firmer line.

"I shall not trot down like a sheep. I like to jump."

Docility was not a trait he would attach to her. "I have already explained about the footing, and you are far too high. It would not do to have you fall."

"I think you very much underestimate your own strength, Frederick. I believe I could jump from the highest point and you would have no trouble in catching me."

For a brief moment he panicked that she might try it. But she stood still, smiling and watching him.

He castigated himself with the realization that he had no one to blame but himself for this. It started it with the stiles and she's taken it to these ridiculous heights. He knew his adjournment to Shropshire was coming almost too late.

"Please, Miss Louisa, come down now." The scene was becoming an embarrassment, for there were a few walkers out; and he did not wish to continue with their test of wills.

Without looking away, she sidestepped down a few of the stairs. "Frederick, it would please me very much if you would call me Louisa."

The game was no longer about jumping down the steps, but their becoming more intimate. He considered walking away; her pettish behaviour was far too annoying at this point, and a couple was standing at the top of the stairs, wishing to come down.

"Please, Louisa." He disliked being blackmailed, but it seemed to be the only choice he had to bring about her compliance.

Hopping down several more steps, she was a mere five steps from the bottom. "I shall never fear as long as your strong arms are there to catch me." Taking his hand, she leant a bit forward and hopped into his arms. "See," she said, "you can do anything." He said nothing as he lowered her to the ground.

It was hardly what could be called a jump, but that had not been the point. She made no move to separate herself and stood oddly poised.

Good God, she expects a kiss!

Were this another time, years ago, there would have been no hesitation. In fact, he had not hesitated and could even be called a thief, having stolen a kiss from another young woman. His pause spoke volumes and confirmed the rightness of his decision. He cleared his throat and stepped back. Laughing, she turned away and headed down the shingle. Wentworth looked around, fearing the waiting couple had noticed her antic. To his relief, they had moved on and there was no one in immediate sight.

They walked the shingle for a brief time and he had been right about Louisa's complaints. They made their way back up to the firmer footing of the Cobb. In the distance he saw two female figures and guessed them to be Henrietta and Anne. He thanked God they were a quarter of an hour late in taking their walk.

Suddenly, Louisa said, "I know Henrietta is having a wonderful time, but I am not certain about Anne."

"And why might you think this," he asked.

"She has had so little to say for herself and is always attaching herself to Captain Benwick. Not that they do not seem very suited."

It was her machinations that had thrown the pair together. It was a clever trick of the mind that she now viewed Anne as 'attaching herself' to his friend. Were she to actually engage Benwick in conversation and see that aside from his grief, she would find him a fine, intelligent man.

Pleasantries were exchanged, and Louisa said, "The Captain insisted I accompany him on his morning walk."

Henrietta's smile widened while Anne looked away from the pair and off to the sea behind them. A gust of wind nearly unseated his hat and caused all the ladies to pull close their cloaks.

"We came to walk until breakfast. Perhaps it is ready and we should go back," Henrietta said, looking to her companion.

"Perhaps you should," Louisa said, "I have some things I must get in town. We can meet you at the inn." She gave him a look that said "we" meant just the two of them.

"We shall go with you, Louisa. We are in no hurry, are we Anne?"

Anne looked from Henrietta to him, then away. "No, we are at your disposal, Louisa." Perhaps he misread her expression, but he was certain he saw again a hint of amusement on Anne's face. He watched her as she turned to walk with Miss Musgrove and was gratified to see the wisp of a smirk bloom into a full-on smile.

Ah, there you are! His suspicions were confirmed, and she was still as much his clever Anne of old.

Coming to the stairs leaving the shingle, he noticed a gentleman at the top who stepped aside to allow them to pass. The gentleman touched his hat to both Henrietta and Louisa. When Wentworth drew even with him, prepared to acknowledge the man, the fellow's eyes were already looking past him, taking in the one who followed.

Turning, he spied Anne. By her expression she knew she was being watched, not only by the stranger, but himself as well. It was impossible to ignore how the sea had brought to life her normally pale cheek and the whole of her pretty face.

Smiling, modestly, she nodded to the fellow as she passed. *Well, well, that man certainly is struck with you, and I cannot disagree; for at this moment,*

I see something like Anne Elliot again. It was good to see her more like her old self, but Wentworth could not shake the thought that a gentleman in mourning, for the man had worn a black armband, should not be quite so open in his appreciation of a strange woman.

As they passed the shops, Louisa seemed undecided as to what she needed until they came to a store with a window full of fabric and ribbons. "This is where I wish to go," she said, waiting for him to assist her.

They could see the shop was crowded. Henrietta had already entered, while Anne demurred and walked on to a bookstall next door. "I think I shall stay out here and wait," he said, holding the door for Louisa.

"That might be best," she said, with an indulgent smile. She entered the store, and he closed the door firmly behind her.

Taking up a post between the store and the bookseller, he enjoyed the warmth of the sun for a moment. He first removed his gloves and checked his watch. Then, quite naturally, he fell into a study of his other companion, who studied the selection of books in front of the store.

As was her habit, she'd not tied the ribbons of her bonnet and left them to arrange themselves over her shoulders. The stiff breeze caught them; first, they waved separately and then together in a staccato fashion. Moving to another display, she turned to read the titles. Again, as the sun touched her face, he could not help but notice her improvement. At first glance, there was a look of health that accompanied fresh air and sweet sea breezes. The pink in her cheeks was more appealing than any rouge could accomplish and there no sign of the customary strained expression she wore at Uppercross. Her appearance was all easy enjoyment. He speculated that, given a few more days, he might even see her laugh again.

Soon, she, too, removed her gloves so that she might touch each book as she read their titles. Now and then she would pick one up, open it, read a bit and then return it to its place.

"Are you looking for something in particular?" he asked.

At first, she looked towards the store. Seeing no one, she glanced his way. "No, not really. I just thought I might find something for Captain Benwick. We talked much of the evening about books."

"I thank you for being so kind to my friend. I am afraid Harville is not quite up to matching wits with Benwick. Intellectually, that is." It was more than he intended to say to her, but there it was and it could not be taken back.

"He is an interesting young man," she said. "Very knowledgeable about many things."

"Yes, James is quite a brain box. Puts me completely to shame."

She did not answer, but picked up a book and smiled. "John Gay."

It was obvious she expected him to know this Gay fellow, but it rang no bells. "Philosopher?"

"Poet." She opened the book and turned the pages without reading. Stopping midway through, she glanced at a page and said, "You do not remember–"

The door to the notions shop opened and Miss Musgrove stepped out, saying, "Captain, please. My sister needs you." He joined her in the doorway, and she pointed to her sister arguing with the man behind the counter. He could hear Louisa's voice over the din the shop. Other patrons were neglecting their notions in favour of the show.

"I have told you, my brother Charles Musgrove will pay. We are at the Binnacle, and as soon as I tell him, he will come and pay you." Louisa held a packet to her bosom, undoubtedly the merchandise her brother was to redeem.

"Well, Miss, if yous all stayin' at the Binnacle, I can't trust that your brother won't decide that he don't need this odd bit of cloth that you've had cut, and head on out of town. And if he don't come, I'll have a devil of a time sellin' it to anybody else."

"They do this for me all the time at home."

"But you ain't at home, are you? Now give me the stuff." The man held out his hand to take the package.

"Excuse me," Wentworth interrupted. Both turned and began to rush him with talk

"Oh, Captain, thank you for–"

"Are you the brother?"

"No, I am not the brother, but how much is the lady's purchase?"

The merchant named his price and Wentworth settled the bill. As they left the store, Louisa thanked him for his thoughtful intervention but was still aggravated that the man could not see his way to handle the purchase as they did at home. He said nothing, but Henrietta pointed out that it really wasn't a purchase since she had no money and that the man didn't know them and, therefore, did not know he would be paid.

Louisa stopped and said, "I understand, Henrietta, but still, it was mortifying." Sliding the bundle into the pocket of her cloak, she said, "And please, don't tell anyone what happened." Looking to her sister and the Captain, both promised their silence on the matter. The little group was all smiles when they collected Anne from the bookseller.

There was little conversation as the group returned to the inn. With nothing to distract him from his own thoughts, he contemplated a breakfast of kippers and eggs. He was adding a decent slab of ham and a generous helping of potatoes, when Anne and Miss Musgrove passed them. It was then he realised that he and Louisa had slowed their pace.

She came to rest against a low wall directly across the street from the entrance of the Binnacle. Slowly she took the packet from her pocket. "Thank you for rescuing me." Her smile was pleasing and sincere. "I really thought I had some money when I ordered the cloth cut. But, as all of Lyme now knows, I did not. It must be in another purse. The sensible thing would have been to leave it and return with Charles after breakfast."

Her frank, openhearted confession was refreshing and intriguing. He wished to hear more from *this* Louisa. "And why did you not?"

"You saw; it became a challenge when he would not do as I wished. I apologise for making a spectacle of us all."

He was glad she could see and admit her folly. "It was nothing. I am glad I was there to help." At moments such as these, he was reminded that Louisa Musgrove was a well-brought-up young woman, intelligent and kind. Her youthful lack of experience and growing need to have her own way overshadowed the good qualities she possessed.

"I suppose I would not have been so stubborn had the materials not been for something special."

She obviously wished him to ask about her undertaking. "And what might this special thing be?"

"I am no seamstress, but I am determined to embroider a pillow or some such memento. It will serve to remind me of this wonderful trip with my family...and friends."

Louisa could be quite charming, and her idea of creating a reminder of the trip was just that. Reaching out to take his arm, she started to the inn. "You are the sort of man who is always at the ready when someone needs help, aren't you?"

Indeed, she was charming, but he would always be a little suspect of her compliments. "I fear you make me out to be more gallant than I deserve."

She laughed, and leaned into his shoulder. "Never."

"And, I assure you, I am the one who needs help just now."

"And what sort of help might that be?"

"Finding breakfast." Their laughter mingled as they crossed the road to the inn.

~ ~ ~ ~ ~ ~ ~ & ~ ~ ~ ~ ~ ~ ~

He'd seen Louisa to her room, and now his thoughts turned to serious considerations about breakfast. Part way down the stairs to the first floor, he heard the voices of a man and woman. Stopping to listen, he assumed it must be Charles Musgrove and his wife, but was then surprised to recognise the voice to be Anne's. There was a disquieting addition of an unfamiliar male voice.

She said, "No, it is quite all right. The hall is a bit dark, and it is easy to stumble. I am not hurt."

The man replied, "You must think me a clumsy ox. I am not usually thus." Wentworth was intrigued. He had seen no other male guests.

"Not at all, sir. You were no such thing earlier. Since we are both safe and sound, I will bid you good morning."

"And I shall do the same, but only after I claim the right to introduce myself the next time Fate throws us together." The sound of steps indicated that they were walking away. There was nothing left for him to do. If he wished to hear the rest, he must follow. Taking a step, the stair tread groaned. He stopped. Refusing to feel guilty about following them, he determined not to sneak about. Let them see that their meeting does not go unobserved.

Making his way to the landing, he trod more heavily than he might otherwise and took a sort of odd pleasure as he scraped and squeaked down the hallway. The pair took no notice of him and his wooden symphony as they continued down to the end of the hall. Here they were forced to part company.

The dining room lay at the end of the right turn, and the stables to the left. Anne pointed towards the right, and when the man turned to point left, Wentworth knew him instantly to be the man from the stairs. This was the poor, grieving man who had taken care to make his admiration of Anne very apparent.

Even as they parted, Wentworth was annoyed to see both were smiling. His feelings of ease suddenly vanished, and his desire for a hearty breakfast turned sour. Miss Elliot, it appeared, seemed to be gathering new gentlemen friends right and left.

Chapter Eighteen

The new acquaintances disappeared in opposite directions as Wentworth continued down the empty hallway. Turning towards the dining room, he thought how the gentleman took a good deal upon himself in assuming that he and Anne would meet again. He also wondered if Anne had referred to their earlier meeting in order to ensure that the gentleman remembered her. Perhaps he should have quickened his pace and provoked a meeting between the three of them. Surveying the dining room, he saw that the only seat open to him was next to Louisa and across from Anne. With this particular arrangement, all he could look forward to was the fresh fish promised for breakfast. Most were already tucking in as he took a seat. Mrs. Charles was the only one who found fish for breakfast not to her liking.

"Fish is not a food one should eat in the morning. I believe it to be upsetting to the humours. I heard of a woman who developed a very shocking case of boils, and it was all due to eating fish in the morning."

Wentworth laughed, amused by the idea that an item he enjoyed with great regularity, and even the time of day he enjoyed it most, should be the cause of such a painful and disobliging malady. "I do believe, Mrs. Musgrove, you can be assured that the eating of fish in the morning hours is rarely the cause of anything dire and is an excellent remedy for an empty belly," he said, taking his first bite.

Mrs. Charles assured him that she would be just as satisfied with a generous slice of good English ham. As he pondered the nationality of these particular fish, Louisa cleared her throat and tapped his ankle with her foot. He did not look at her but was certain the expression she wore was one of derision.

Pots of tea and coffee were being emptied and bone-filled plates pushed aside when the sound of a carriage drew several to the window. "It is a gentleman's carriage, a curricle, but only coming around from the stable-yard to the front door," said Mrs. Charles, the first to the window. At the mention of a curricle, her husband joined her.

"Somebody must be going away. It was driven by a servant in mourning," added Henrietta. At the mention of this detail, Anne rose to see.

Wentworth had his suspicions as to whom the "somebody" might be and stood along with Louisa to confirm them.

"Ah! It is the very man we passed," Wentworth said. He gave half a look to Anne as he regained his seat. Her expression gave no hint that the two were more closely acquainted than a mere nod on the sidewalk.

"Yes, it certainly is. I remember the coat. The very one," Louisa said, taking the opportunity to move a bit closer.

The waiter returned with fresh pots of hot drinks and began his clearing chores. "Pray, can you tell us the name of the gentleman who is just gone away?" Wentworth asked. He was determined to learn the identity of the impertinent man in mourning.

"Yes, sir, a Mr. Elliot,"

All turned when Mrs. Charles cried, "Elliot," but returned their attention to the waiter when he continued. "A gentleman of large fortune came in last night from Sidmouth." A small murmur went up. He was certain it had more to do with the gentleman's fortune than his unremarkable arrival from Sidmouth. "I dare say you heard the carriage, sir, while you were at dinner. The gentleman is going on now to Bath and London."

At the mention of Bath, he looked at Anne. She was apparently too busy rearranging the bones of her kipper to make any comment. Or, he wondered, was she contemplating this very interesting intelligence concerning his destination and their presumed third meeting?

"Bless me! It must be our cousin. It must be Mr. Elliot; it must be, indeed. Charles and Anne, must not it? In mourning, you see, just as our Mr. Elliot must be. How very extraordinary! In the very same inn with us! Anne, must not it be our Mr. Elliot; my father's heir?"

Louisa nudged him, eyes wide, mouthing: "The Elliot Heir." He raised a noncommittal brow and turned back to the pratings of Mrs. Charles. Her observations concerning the Elliot family lines interested him, and he wished to hear more of them.

"Pray, did not you hear; did not his servant say whether he belonged to the Kellynch family?"

Excellent question, madam! Ask as many questions as the poor man will endure.

"No, ma'am, he did not mention a particular family, but he said his master would be a baronet some day."

"There! You see! Just as I said! Heir to Sir Walter! I was sure that would come out, if it were so. Depend upon it; that is a circumstance which his servants take care to publish wherever he goes." Her discovery brightened her look in a way he had never seen before. Taking the seat by her sister, she pulled a plate not her own to her, and began eating the fish. "But, Anne, only conceive how extraordinary! I wish I had looked at him more. I wish we had been aware in time who it was, that he might have been introduced to us."

Even the discovery that she had eaten an entire kipper did nothing to stop Mrs. Charles's lamenting the lack of introduction to Mr. Elliot, and pondering whether he bore the Elliot countenance. Anne listened, looking occasionally at her sister while continuing to pick at the bones on her plate. She was a master when it came to listening, but he was certain she was preoccupied with her own private thoughts.

Louisa cleared her throat He could feel her moving closer, hoping to draw out a response from him, no doubt. Regardless of who might notice, he continued to watch the sisters.

"If the servant had not been in mourning, one should have known him by the livery." All was quiet for a moment. It seemed that Mrs. Charles was finally through with her treatise on the gentleman.

This last observation, again of the man's state of mourning, seemed to be of interest to Anne; and she raised her head. But before she could make any reply, Wentworth said, "Putting all these very extraordinary circumstances together, we must consider it to be the arrangement of Providence, that you should not be introduced to your cousin."

She was obviously puzzled by his remark, and to an extent, he was puzzled as well. His tone had been lamb-like innocence, while in his own mind the words reeked of sarcasm. But really, what right did he have to entertain resentments, even privately, prompted by nothing more than an innocent meeting in the hallway of a public house? It was well he was leaving Somerset to clear his head concerning, not only Louisa, but Anne as well.

Anne made no reply, then turned to her sister and said, "That would be unwise as father and our cousin have not, for many years, been on good terms. It cannot be doubted that an introduction would not be desired by either of them."

So, there is a breech that guarantees there will be *no* third meeting and certainly no cosy family gatherings in Bath where the two shall laugh and reminisce about their fortuitous meeting in Lyme.

Mary's voice cut through his thoughts. "Of course you will mention our seeing Mr. Elliot the next time you write to Bath. I think my father certainly ought to hear of it; do mention all about him."

He was very certain by Anne's expression that, as far as was in her power, the Baronet would know nothing of Mr. Elliot's travels to Sidmouth, Lyme, or any points south and west of Bath.

~ ~ ~ ~ ~ ~ ~ & ~ ~ ~ ~ ~ ~ ~

Breakfast was done and everyone returned to their rooms to prepare for going out. All gathered back in the dining room just as Harville and his wife, and Captain Benwick arrived for their promised last walk about. Such timely preparations made Wentworth hopeful that their departure from Lyme would have none of the confusion and frustration marking their departure from Uppercross.

The wind was cold and bracing as they walked down the street, making for the shore. Harville spoke of the warm breezes of the Western Islands and how he missed them in the fall and winter.

"Yes, but there is nothing like an English spring to waken the heart, said Mrs. Harville. "So, Captain, might we expect another visit from you this winter?" she asked. The two looked at him hopefully.

"I can not say definitely. I have a brother with a new wife in want of a visit." He smiled. "Edward is getting most insistent. And, in truth, I am anxious to be off myself." He looked off towards the others as they followed along after.

"I am surprised at your wishing to be away. I would think there is quite a lot to keep you occupied in Somerset these days," Mrs. Harville said, smiling.

Harville was quick with a word in her ear and then said, "The area, from your descriptions, is beautiful and we are surprised that you would not wait it out until spring."

"While the accommodations with my sister and brother are very elegant, I have a duty to pay to the new Mrs. Wentworth. Besides, I am curious to get a look at Edward's new wife. By his account, she is all charm and perfection."

"She sounds very nice."

"Yes, I am anxious to meet the woman who has my dour brother using such superlatives."

"Captain, I insist you and I lead these landlubbers to the beach that we might all bid a fond farewell to the sea." Louisa joined them, indicating Mr. and Mrs. Musgrove and Henrietta to be the lubbers. The three officers exchanged amused looks at the presumption of Louisa's statement.

Heading on, he noticed Harville dropping back to speak to Anne. Benwick joined Wentworth and Louisa. Again, as on the walk a few days previous, he missed large portions of conversation and had to be urged again and again to the present.

The group began to move towards the pier. He was relived when Louisa chose to join her sister, who walked alone, and turned to Harville. "We are to leave by eleven. After seeing you to your door, if I am able to urge them all back to the inn and see the vehicles loaded, we shall depart on time."

Harville laughed. "Leave it to Frederick to give a pleasure trip all the feel of an urgent mission for the Crown. I suppose if they dally, you will have them up on charges?"

Only Musgrove's horses knew of his earlier grumbling, and he was sure they would be silent. "Certainly not, Captain. You must think me an over-zealous monster."

"No, merely a man who sees punctuality as a near cousin to constancy. You can't help yourself; you are faithful to all you serve and in all you do." A little bow added to the jest.

The group had reformed as they drew nearer the Cobb, and there was a general desire to revisit it before taking their leave of Lyme. Louisa in particular made it clear that one last walk on the Cobb was her fondest wish, and that she would not be satisfied without it. "You must agree, Captain that one last walk on the Cobb will make our trip to Lyme complete. Do you not?" The sweet, contrite girl of earlier had vanished.

"I doubt a quarter hour will make much difference, will it Captain?" Charles Musgrove asked. "Even Father's horses can make that up with no trouble."

Harville made a show of looking away, but Wentworth caught the smirk on his face. Unless he wished to take up the title of Iron-fisted Monster, he had little choice but to acquiesce. It was agreed they would walk Harville to his door and then return to the Cobb. As they were about to set off, he noticed Anne examining him. Her expression was perplexing, and when she realised he saw it, she turned quickly and walked away with Benwick.

"Thank you for bringing us your friends, Captain," Harville said. "Mr. Musgrove, Mrs. Musgrove, it was a pleasure meeting you and your family. Please return to us when the weather is warmer." Harville's expression indicated he regretted their parting as he bid them farewell.

"We surely will, Captain. And if you are ever in the neighbourhood of Uppercross, you are most welcome. We would be insulted if you did not return the visit," Musgrove answered.

Wentworth knew all of the promises and invitations to be perfectly genuine; though it was doubtful any of them would ever be drawn upon. It was odd that his navy life and his life on land should intersect, but it had been done with such ease and cheerfulness that he could not be more pleased about it.

"When you decide to return from the north, come back and reacquaint yourself with the sea," Harville said as they shook hands.

"Count on it," Wentworth's grasp lingered. "Benwick," he nodded to his other friend, "take care. Write me and keep me apprised. If a letter might help, any good word I can give, I will."

"Thank you, sir. I shall."

With all the good-byes finished, the Uppercross party made their way to the Cobb. They stood silently for some time, admiring the sea. Eventually Mrs. Charles complained of the wind, and they made their way towards the steps to the lower Cobb.

Wentworth descended first to receive the ladies. He then noticed Benwick had rejoined them. He saw to Anne and Henrietta; even Mrs. Charles followed without undo ceremony.

"Louisa, go on down, and I shall follow," Musgrove urged.

"No, Charles, you go on." She moved aside, letting him pass. "Captain Wentworth will help me down." Fixing her eyes on him, she said, "Jump me." Her tone was playful, but he knew the phrase was undergirded with rods of iron. Indeed, she looked at him and smiled as sweetly as anything, but the fact was that the indomitable Louisa had returned.

The wind, even on the lower level, was freshening and the other ladies were pulling their cloaks and pelisses closer to ward it off. Looking about, he decided it would be simpler to give in to her whim than to try to reason with her. Removing his hat, he said, "I really must insist this be the last time, Miss Louisa." The act was accomplished with no ill effect. He retrieved his hat in preparation to walk.

"Again, please," she said, making her way back up the steps. The childish behaviour had played out. Any sense of charm or excitement it once elicited was spent. He would not relent and bow to her petulance. A second jump from the steps was completely out of the question.

"Louisa, come back down this minute." Mrs. Charles's admonition was both surprising and very welcome. He could only wish Charles Musgrove would add some brotherly authority. He turned away, and allowed Mrs. Charles her say. "Louisa, stop this. The pavement is hard–"

"Once more. Please, once more. There will be no chance for another, and I do so love the feel."

"We must be on our way, we haven't the time for–"

"Oh, please, please Captain. I am determined I will," Louisa cut Mrs. Charles short.

There was no choice but to relent and be done with it. He stepped back to the place he had caught her before. Remembering his hat, he turned and tossed it onto the pavement. Resentful that it would need a good brushing, he looked up, saying, "You will have to come down several steps–"

She had already jumped.

He heard nothing but his own heart, saw nothing but her fear as she realised he could not possibly catch her. The horror of her expression was heart-piercing. Instantly, everything about the scene slowed. Still he hoped to stop her fall, but even his own response was reduced to a snail's pace. When he did reach the spot, only her pelisse brushed his hand as she fell, crumpling onto the paving stones.

They all stood motionless, gaping as her bright red pelisse settled gently around her in a heap. "Oh my God!" he cried, as he went to her side. "Louisa!" Her eyes were closed, and she did not respond to his voice. Gently he shook her and called her name again. "Louisa. Please, Louisa, answer me." He examined her as much as was proper, moving her pelisse and dress, hoping he would find no hidden blood. Thankfully, there was none, nor any visible injuries, for that matter. Despite these facts, her eyes remained shut. When he leant closer, her warm breath touched his face. There was no sound from her.

"She is dead! She is dead!" Suddenly Mrs. Charles's voice cut through the eerie silence shrouding him and the girl. There was a scream, and he heard Anne call Benwick's name.

"Is there no one to help me?" He felt completely undone. His mind might as well be empty for all the good his swirling thoughts could do him. "Please," he called again.

"Go to him, for heaven's sake, go to him." In this moment of chaos, Anne's voice was sweet relief. "Rub her hands, rub her temples; here are salts–take them, take them." Her voice conveyed intelligence and authority and helped to subdue the agony swelling in his chest.

Suddenly Musgrove and Benwick flanked him. Each helped to raise her and support her more firmly between them while administering the salts and doing all Anne suggested. He could no longer endure being close to her and had to move away. The men moved together, closing the gap he left. Backing away, he crashed into a nearby wall, knocking the breath out of him. This brought him fully into the calamity. "Oh God! Her father and mother!" The realization of the hurt to the Musgrove family burst upon him.

Anne's voice touched him again. "A surgeon!"

A surgeon! "True, true a surgeon, this instant." The timely suggestion might be the saving of him!

"Would it not be better for Captain Benwick?" she said. "He knows where a surgeon is to be found." James looked at Anne and nodded, handing off his share of her weight to her brother. He seemed to vanish from the scene. Without much thinking, Wentworth moved back to Louisa and Musgrove.

Charles, crying his sister's name softly while trying to comfort his other sister, stayed with Louisa even as Mrs. Charles insisted that he must come to her. Wentworth knelt, taking some of the burden off him. He looked again to Anne, and she did not fail to encourage them all that Louisa would no doubt recover, and that all would be well as soon as the surgeon returned. The words did nothing to lift his hopes, but Wentworth fervently prayed that they might prove to be true.

Louisa's bonnet slipped and fell away from her face, and her hair spilled over his hand and swung freely across his knee. The peaceful expression on her face was chilling. Had he not known better, he would guess her dead.

"Anne, Anne, what is to be done next? What in heaven's name is to be done next?" Musgrove's anguished cry for his sister-in-law again drew Wentworth back to the hard cobblestones and the crowd that had formed. Wentworth's resolve was flagging; nonetheless, he looked to her also, hoping she would supply more answers.

"Had not she better be carried to the inn?" someone asked.

"Yes, I am sure." Her voice however remained steady, and her directions certain. "Carry her gently to the inn."

Thank God! Anne had not failed him. Her instructions were all he needed. "Yes, yes, to the inn." Her brother did nothing to stop him as he carefully took Louisa in his arms. "I will carry her myself. Musgrove, take care of the others."

He was aware of the crowd again and that there seemed to be approval of the action on their part. Laughter was coming from some quarter, and voices were yelling but he could make out no words. All he knew was he must hurry to the inn. The inn would bring regulation to the circumstances, and the surgeon would come and make Louisa whole.

Out of nowhere, Harville's voice came to him. "God, man, what has happened? We saw James fly. The fellow never moves that fast for anything; so we knew there must be something wrong."

"She has fallen from the top of the stairs." Again, Anne supplied the answers. "We are taking her to the inn, and Captain Benwick is to bring the surgeon."

As the others spoke, Mrs. Harville examined Louisa closely. A look passed between her and her husband. "Bring her to our house. All of you need looking after," she said, touching Mrs. Charles's hand. The acknowledgement brought her around and salved the Elliot Pride, damaged by her husband's neglect.

"It is very generous of you, but we do not wish to impose upon your family," Anne said. The others added their thanks but raised their own objections as well. Harville put aside every opposition. Meanwhile, all Wentworth could do was look at Louisa, willing her eyes to open.

"There is nothing more to be said," said Mrs. Harville. "Frederick," she touched his arm to get his attention. "Take her to our house." Anne moved aside to allow him by. Even in his state, he could not help notice a look pass between her and Mrs. Harville. There was an understanding there. Harville shoo'd them on while he arranged for a boy to run ahead and tell Benwick where they had taken the patient.

They entered the tiny house, which was growing even smaller in the presence of their crisis. "Hannah," Mrs. Harville called softly, moving to the back of the house. Turning to Wentworth, she directed him to the stairs. "Come, straight to the back and lay her on my bed."

He did not slow and began to go up. The narrowness of the stairs made for difficult manoeuvring. Holding her close to his chest was the only way to take care of her head. Her sister followed close behind, and he heard someone call out, "Henrietta, do you think it wise for you to go up?"

Anne's calm voice added, "Yes, I wonder that you should stay here with Mary."

"She is my sister, and I will see to her." The reply was punctuated by a teary-sounding gulp. There was no time to worry who would attend Louisa, the women and the surgeon would decide those incidentals.

"Here. Lay her here," said Mrs. Harville indicating the low bed.

Where Anne appeared from, he knew not; but he was grateful that she was at his side. As if she knew his arm was weakening with fatigue, her small hands covered his, lifting, guiding, assisting in laying Louisa in the bed. It felt like forever, but eventually their hands met the pillow.

Anne's hands slid away leaving the burden in his alone.

"Captain," she said.

He could not move.

"Frederick," she whispered. "You must move that we may attend her."

Turning, he was surprised to find her face mere inches from his own. There was anxiety in her expression, but he saw something he hoped was sympathy as well. Regardless of her feelings for him, there was no joy in seeing what his weakness and folly had produced. Taking his arm, she eased it from under Louisa's head.

"Louisa," Henrietta cried loudly. She threw herself between the Captain and Anne. "Louisa," she cried again. "Look, her eyes. Her eyes are open!" Everyone turned. They were indeed open, but soon closed again. "No, no, Louisa! No, wake up!" She grasp at her sister's cloak. Her sobbing was pitiful.

"Captain," Anne said, "might you help her downstairs?"

"Yes, Captain," Mrs. Harville helped Henrietta to her feet, "I think Miss Anne and I are quite able to see to her sister." She gently folded Miss Musgrove's hand around Wentworth's arm and urged them to the stairs. He supported her down the narrow steps as best he could, and when reaching the bottom, she ran to her brother.

"Captain, you look a fright. Drink this," said Harville. Handing him a small blue glass, Wentworth drank down the slightly viscous liquid without hesitation. As it burned its way down his throat, he thought it must be brandy, but he could not be sure. "Take a chair," Harville directed. He took the offered seat, joining the others gathered about the dining table.

"She opened her eyes; she looked directly at us! Do you think she will be all right, Charles?" Henrietta said.

"I…I can't say, Etta. I have no knowledge of things in the medical line."

A knock at the door took Harville away for a moment. He returned with a stout, pink-faced man dressed in a red waistcoat, carrying a tattered black bag. Mr. McCracken was introduced as the finest surgeon Lyme had to offer.

"I will be down as soon as I have something useful to tell you." He looked over the assembled group and gave them a confident nod.

With the arrival of the surgeon, Miss Musgrove began to weep. Wentworth despaired that the group's hopes were all pinned on a man who looked no more skilled than the average bookkeeper.

"Come and sit by me, dear," Mrs. Charles said, taking her sister-in-law by the shoulders and moving her to an out-of-the-way seat. He was surprised to find that unaffected kindness was possible in the Elliot family.

It seemed Harville had no more begun reassuring them of McCracken's qualifications than the man reappeared with a confident look about him. He set his black bag on the table and began putting on his coat. "She has no broken bones, but she took a right smart crack to the skull. I think this case is not so grave as first I imagined. Considering the dire nature of my summons, I thought it would be only a few hours before the end." At this, Henrietta muffled a sob with her sodden kerchief.

"It's all right, young lady, the skull is the strongest bone in the body actually. It can take an amazing amount of pounding without death occurring."

"When do you expect that she will be back to complete health, sir?" Wentworth asked, anxious to steer the report away from the shocking and back to useful information.

"Well, that is another matter. The skull is quite strong, but the grey stew within can take its own time to settle. And even then, there's no tellin' whether things will be completely normal again."

A little murmur went through them. It was then he noticed Anne, standing on the bottom stair. She still looked concerned but not nearly as much when they were above in Mrs. Harville's room.

The surgeon continued: "But that bein' said, there's no reason to think that she won't recover completely and be as healthy as she ever was. I've seen much worse, and the patient was eventually as good as new." He opened his bag, shuffled things about and closed it. Harville and his wife appeared from the kitchen, thanked him for his time, and saw him to the door. Looking back at the group, the surgeon said, "Leave her where she is, and time will do its work."

There was no reason to think the man was hedging his opinion. They were strangers, and he had no reason to spare their feelings. At that moment, Wentworth decided to pin his hopes on the surgeon's statement about her being "as good as new." By the sound of it, the others did as well. The first wave of thanksgiving was loud, led mostly by Charles Musgrove. In the midst of the rejoicing, he watched Anne as she embraced each of the Musgroves and accepted as well the good wishes of the Harville household, including smiles from James Benwick. Rapidly, fatigue overtook his mind and body, and all that was manageable for him was a hushed, but heart-felt, "Thank God."

After a little time, Harville said, "A toast to the good news, then."

Musgrove stood and took the glass offered him. "Aye, it is. However, as the man said, she must be left here to heal. I wish that there were some way to remove her to some other place. Even if it were just to the inn—"

Mrs. Harville interrupted, "Certainly not, Mr. Musgrove. I'll not allow that to be risked. Timotee and I have discussed this and—" she was interrupted by the nursery maid, calling her upstairs. "You tell them what we decided." Indicating that Anne should accompany her, the two disappeared.

Picking up a decanter, Harville began to refill the cordials, explaining their thoughts as he went about the room. "My wife is an excellent nurse, as is her nursery-maid, who's been everywhere with us. Anywise, Elsa was pretty certain that Louisa would have to stay put. McCracken tends to be of the mind that one should wait and watch before blundering in. He's usually right. So, we have taken the liberty of removing some of the decisions from your shoulders and making our own plans. Your sister will stay in our room for the duration, and Benwick will find a bed elsewhere. Now, perhaps by putting the children away in the maids' room, or swinging a cot somewhere, we could make room for one or two others, if they should wish to stay."

Musgrove interrupted. "We've cut too wide a swath as it stands. Puttin' a man out of his own bed is the worst I can allow to either of you." He nodded to Benwick to acknowledge his sacrifice as well. "Perhaps this McCracken can recommend to us a nurse. I want her to have the best no matter what time of the day or night."

"I shall see to her. In fact, I insist." Mrs. Harville had rejoined them. "My nursery-maid is as experienced as I, and between the two of us, she will be well cared for, have no fear."

"You've left us nothing to do. I have to say thank you on that score," Musgrove said.

Looking at Wentworth and Musgrove, Harville said, "We've done what we could, but I think you still have some things that can only be decided by the family." He and his wife left them in privacy.

"Someone must return home, and tell Mother and Father," Henrietta said, her voice low and strained from crying.

Musgrove reached for the cordial decanter Harville left on the table. "I must confess that I have no stomach for the task."

Wentworth knew that, short of Musgrove declaring his intentions of being the one to break the news, there was only one solution. "It is getting late. They will worry as it is now impossible to be in tolerable time."

"Dear Louisa. It is usually Henrietta who makes us late," Musgrove sighed.

"We must be decided and without loss of another minute. Every minute is valuable. Some must resolve on being off for Uppercross instantly. Musgrove, either you or I must go." Wentworth dreaded the answer he knew was to come.

"You're right, Captain. Nevertheless, I cannot go. I'll sleep on the floor if need be, but I can't, nay, won't leave her alone."

"And I shall stay as well," Henrietta declared. "She will need me when she wakes up. And that will be at any time now." There was nothing in her voice to hint true belief in her statement.

"Sister, please, I think it best you go home." Mary Musgrove looked her in the eye as she straightened her bonnet. "Henrietta, the Captain practically had to carry you down the stairs for all the weeping. It will not do, in a sick room, to have someone about who hasn't the nerves for it. There are others much better suited to the task."

Miss Musgrove was convinced that her staying was worse than useless, and that she would be much more comfort to her mother and father. Wentworth could see her relief and that now she was anxious to be home.

"Then it is settled, Musgrove, that you stay, and I take care of your sister home. As to the others–" He would tread carefully here. Though Mrs. Charles showed good sense in convincing Henrietta to leave, there was no guarantee that she would do the same when it came to her own leaving. "If one is to assist Mrs. Harville, I think it need be only one. Mrs. Charles Musgrove will, of course, wish to get back to her children; but if Anne will stay, no one so proper, so capable as Anne!"

Musgrove and his sister both brightened at this suggestion. A glance in the direction of Mrs. Charles warned him that these congratulations were by no means unanimous. Nevertheless, as she said nothing, he was convinced she would go along with the plan.

"So, Anne, what do you think of the Captain's proposal?" Musgrove said.

He turned to the doorway, and there she stood. "You will stay, I am sure; you will stay and nurse her." The words were loud and bleating to his own ears; he hoped they sounded less so to her.

Smiling, her cheeks grew pink. He too felt suddenly warm and could say nothing.

"I am most happy to remain. I had been wishing to be allowed to do so. A bed on the floor of Louisa's room will be sufficient for her, if Mrs. Harville would but think so."

Wentworth looked out the window, considering what was to be done next. Upon hearing Anne speak about staying, he could only remember his outrage when he realised she slept on a chair in order to care for her nephew. Now he must own the outrage and direct it where it belonged. If he had the chance, he would speak with Harville and insist she be given more than on a palette on the floor. However, this would have to wait, there was still much to do.

"Musgrove, your parents will be alarmed that we are so late. Taking the travelling coach will only extend the time. I propose to rent a chaise from the inn to take your wife and sister home." Musgrove nodded his agreement. "You can send the carriage home in the morning, along with an account of how Louisa passed the night."

It was all agreed upon, and he left them to see to his part of the plan. The walk from Harville's was his first chance to recount the events of the past few hours. Out of the company of the others, he was acutely aware where the blame for the wretched events should rest.

After a short explanation, the innkeeper gave orders that the blue rig and the best horses should be readied immediately. Wentworth passed the room the sisters had occupied on the way to retrieve his bag. Hesitating, he considered retrieving Miss Musgrove's luggage but soon dismissed it. Musgrove would have ample time to see to such incidentals. Grabbing his satchel, he glanced out the window. The sun was shining, and everything looked distinctly normal. He thought how, thank God, the world does not reflect the individual's calamity. Surely our blood would freeze were we to realise how quickly change can come.

The keep directed him to the yard and the promised blue rig. It was a first-rate outfit, and the horses were, to his inexpert eye, quite fine. As if preparing to make sail, Wentworth walked up and down the carriage, shaking, tugging, wrenching, scrutinizing every bolt, hinge, peg and seam for anything that might give way and slow their progress home. He made his way around the team, keeping a watch for the ladies.

Seeing Musgrove approach, he gave the seat one last shake and waited. As the group drew closer, he could see Musgrove had the arm of his sister. However, to his surprise, following behind was Benwick, not accompanied by Mrs. Charles, but Anne. While shoving a length of rope under the seat, he grew cold remembering Mary Musgrove's look when he made it know that Anne's nursing skills were preferred over her own.

For a moment, he was certain that the plans had changed. But surely Musgrove would not be so easily persuaded when his sister's well-being was at stake. The far simpler explanation was that Mrs. Charles expected him to drive down and fetch her from the house..."Too far to walk for the daughter of a baronet," he muttered. No doubt Benwick had come to assist Anne in retrieving her belongings from the inn. The situation was not so desperate as he first thought. Taking his gloves from his pocket, he put them on and waited.

They drew closer and he could not help but see that all the faces of the party were grim. No one spoke, save Anne. "She will be all right, Henrietta. Mrs. Harville and her nurse will see to it. You and I will be of better use at Uppercross."

"Damn," he said quietly. So much for his feelings of relief. Regardless of the kindnesses he had witnessed earlier, it was clear that Mrs. Charles was fully prepared to put her own desires before the needs of her sister-in-law. He had to wonder what devilry was at work to make Musgrove agree to the exchange.

"Ladies. Benwick. Musgrove. I thought we were agreed that your sister and wife would be returning home—that Anne is the most use to Louisa."

Musgrove glanced to the others, then beckoned Wentworth step away, out of their hearing. "I know I agreed. But after you left, we all got to talking and decided that it would really be better, as Louisa and Mary are family, that she would stay and that Anne would return—"

"You mean that after I left, Mrs. Musgrove made it clear she would stay. Never mind she is no nurse, by her own admission." Glancing up at the rest of the party, he saw them all looking tactfully away. "Never mind it was Anne who nursed your own son." He had no wish to batter the already grieving brother, but such folly made him grow white hot with anger.

"You have no wife and don't understand how things stand. She is terribly grieved and wishes to stay by me. I will send her home tomorrow–"

"I understand better than you know, sir. I understand that you are willing to send away the most capable and practical woman to care for your sister, all to keep peace with your wife." Musgrove looked away in shame. Wentworth cursed himself for his unguarded tongue. In a lower, though forceful tone, he continued. "I shall go to Uppercross and tell your parents the unhappy news. It is my duty to do so, but if there is further mischief because of this decision, you shall have the burden of bearing the message." There were no more opinions to exchange; he was done. Giving the seat a second, violent shake, he said as politely as he could manage, "Ladies, please make haste. We must be off immediately."

Miss Musgrove reluctantly bid her brother farewell and spoke, half-heartedly of remaining.

Glancing towards Wentworth, Musgrove smiled weakly and reminded her that they all had a duty in this and that she would be the best comforter for their parents. She nodded as she hugged him. Trying to maintain a smile of her own, she clung to him and began to cry.

Again, everyone looked away, and it was left to Wentworth to rescue Musgrove. "Miss Musgrove, please come. The sooner we are off, the sooner you can be united with your parents," he said, quietly.

Letting go of her brother, she allowed herself to be handed into the carriage. Musgrove stepped back and Benwick brought Anne forward. "Thank you again for all your help, Commander," she said. He merely nodded, though smiling, and stepped back.

Turning to Wentworth, she took his offered hand. Their eyes met for an instant. While he was angered by the exchange of the sisters, he could not help feeling relief that Anne would be making the journey home instead of Mrs. Charles. Certainly, Miss Henrietta's emotions would benefit from her calm influence. Though, to be honest, he welcomed her comforting presence, too.

When she gained her seat, the mild look of earlier changed markedly. Now, as she looked away, it was replaced with a troubled expression. It took only seconds for him to consider the large number of offences he had committed that day. Any one of them could explain her dismay.

Bidding farewell to those staying behind, he hoisted himself into the carriage, put himself between the ladies, and commanded the horses to walk on. A quarter mile had not been travelled when he knew the journey would be exhausting to them all. Poor Miss Musgrove could not resist indulging in wild speculation as to the condition of her sister. In one breath, she proclaimed a full recovery a certainty. In the next, she nearly consigned Louisa to the grave and crumbled into tears.

Saying little, he kept a close watch on her. When he did speak it was only to bolster her optimism. Aught else only served to remind him of his part in the mischief. While his own opinion was strongly for Louisa's recovery, he knew even robust improvement in the ill or injured could turn bad in just a few hours. There was nothing to be relied upon in this case except fervent prayers to what seemed a distant and disinterested God and firm faith in the medical knowledge of the red-vested surgeon.

~ ~ ~ ~ ~ ~ ~ & ~ ~ ~ ~ ~ ~ ~

He estimated they had been on the road for nearly two hours. His shoulders ached from rigidly holding the reins and avoiding touching Anne. He longed to rest. He was about to suggest they stop when a rut caught the wheel and violently pulled the carriage to starboard. Miss Musgrove cried out as he lurched into her. Turning to see how his other passenger fared, he freed Henrietta by hurriedly reaching out to pull Anne back from a fall.

"Whoa." Bringing the horses to a halt was simple enough. They seemed as anxious for a rest as the passengers.

"Miss Musgrove, are you injured?" She said she was well and set to straightening her cloak and bonnet.

"I, too, am unharmed."

Turning to Anne, he was embarrassed to realise how closely and tightly he held her. Releasing her, he said, "I'm sorry. I saw you falling forward–"

"And I thank you for catching me. It would not do to have another fall." She gave him a nervous smile and slid as far away as the crowded seat would allow. He wondered if she condemned him for not doing so much for Louisa Musgrove. He manoeuvred out of the rut, and they were back on their way.

Thankfully, there was no more conversation. As much as he dreaded the possibility Miss Musgrove would agitate herself, it was better for his state of mind that she remain quiet. Unfortunately, the quiet could only be filled with thoughts of the morning. It was impossible not to relive their final walk on the Cobb. He could not help regretting being angry with Louisa for her insistence on being jumped one last time. It was impossible not to remember her face as she realised he would not reach her in time.

After a bit, he checked his watch and was heartened. By his estimation they would arrive at Uppercross before dark. A glance at the clouds gathering in the sky undid his joy. It was his plan to return to Lyme that night, and he did not relish a three-hour drive in the cold rain.

"I wonder how she is." Miss Musgrove interrupted his thoughts.

"I am sure she is all right. She has no doubt had her dinner and is now resting." The statement rang false even as he said it, but he wished to head off any contrary thoughts that might be forming in her head.

He felt her shift in the seat. She was looking at the sun setting through the clouds. "It is lovely. I'm sure it is very beautiful from the Cobb."

He said nothing at the mention of the wretched place.

"If only we had known what was to happen and never returned. Had we only gone straight back to the inn when we left the Harville's!" In vain he listened to her choked regrets. Every word inched her closer to tears. "Oh that she had not been allowed to jump. Why was she allowed to—"

"Don't talk of it, don't talk of it," Wentworth exclaimed, his guilt rising at her words. "Oh, God! That I had not given way to her at the fatal moment. Had I done as I ought! But so eager and so resolute! Dear, sweet Louisa!"

Miss Musgrove bit her lip and looked shocked. Anne did not look in his direction at all. Though he saw her only from the side, the set of her mouth proclaimed her not in sympathy with him. The only appropriate words were of confession but his guilt was still too new and too overwhelming to allow those words voice. He muddled through an apology then retreated into silence.

The last miles dragged on. In time Miss Musgrove tucked herself into her little corner of the seat and drew her shawl over her face. She cried softly for a while. Before long, she was silent. Asleep, he assumed. Finally, the last hill was before them, and his agonizing duty lay only minutes ahead.

Quietly, he spoke. "I have been considering what we had best do. She must not appear first. She could not stand it. I have been thinking whether you had better not remain in the carriage with her, while I go in and break it to Mr. and Mrs. Musgrove. Do you think this a good plan?"

"Yes, yes I do." Her reply was unreserved, and though he could not look at her, he thought it encouraging.

They drove up to a yard and house lit in anticipation of a merry return. Pulling the horses to a halt, he gave himself no time to ruminate. Stepping over Anne, he dismounted the carriage. He leant over to toss the reins into the seat. Anne reached out and took them, lingering a moment on his hand. She said nothing, but looked kindly at him.

He walked to the door and thought about the numerous letters he had written to families over the years. Over one hundred of them were to tell mothers and father and wives that their loved one was dead. Most of these deaths occurred by accident or illness. Very few of his men were killed in battle. They were not a part of the fighting war, but men died nonetheless. As much as writing those letters pained him, it was nothing to the dread he felt approaching the Mansion-house.

The door opened to him, and his hat and coat were taken. Waiting to be shown to the family, he wondered if he dreaded dealing with their grief, fear, and doubts; or did he fear the accusations that would surely follow when his part in the evil was discovered.

Upon entering, he was seen by the master of the house. "Captain, welcome home." Mr. Musgrove rose and extended a hand. "I hope the trip went well. I was just telling Mrs. Musgrove that she should stop worrying. Whenever a group of young people gets together, there is no such thing as arriving home on time."

"Where is Charles? That is not his curricle." Mrs. Musgrove had gone to the window and seen the unfamiliar chaise parked in the drive. "And who is it that remains in the carriage?"

"Don't tell me there was a problem with the coach?" Mr. Musgrove began to join his wife at the window. "I was hesitant to let it go, and if there has been any trouble, I will certainly regret allowing the scheme to proceed."

There was no way to soften the blow—telling them straight out was best. "There is nothing wrong with the coach, sir. However, I have bad news. There has been an accident. Your daughter, Louisa, has taken a fall and is injured."

Mrs. Musgrove let out a strangled cry, and her husband helped her to a chair.

"How bad is it?"

"A surgeon was called, and he is of the opinion that she will, most likely, be as good as new."

"Most likely. But there is a chance of her not recovering fully."

"Yes, sir."

"Well then, I must make for Lyme tonight." He had already called for a servant by the time Wentworth could say, "Sir, I have brought home your other daughter and she is very much in need of you both. She witnessed the accident and is greatly distressed. I have also brought Miss Anne home. Your son and his wife stayed behind to see to their sister."

He went on to explain that the coach would be sent home the following day with a report on Louisa's condition.

"I realise it is not my place, but might I advise you to stay home for now and wait. It is darkening fast, and it looks like rain tonight. Please, sir, I would beg you to stay home, comfort your daughter, and wait for word from your son."

His natural authority was to his advantage, and he used it. Both parents were pale from shock, and he ordered the servant to bring some brandy. He also ordered that the ladies in the carriage were to be brought in immediately.

Miss Musgrove entered leaning on Anne, but when she saw her mother, she flew into her arms and began to cry. The Captain and Anne stood together, apart from the parents and child mourning for their injured one. He would have given anything in his possession to be in another place just then. There was no comfort to offer. The family was scattered, and there were only the words of a faceless man, in a far-off county, to repeat for hope. Letters were difficult to write but were infinitely to be preferred over witnessing the personal turmoil.

Mr. Musgrove was the first to regain his senses and begged them both to take a seat. "You look weary to the bone. Let me call for some supper to be brought"

"I am sure Miss Anne could do with something, but if you please, sir, I intend to return to Lyme tonight. I will beg some grain and water for the horses and then I shall be off." *Bloody damn coward, be off and leave her to tidy up your mess.*

The feed was called for and he bid them goodnight. Relieved to be departing the scene, he went to see to the horses.

The horses were baited and he again began tugging, shaking, and wrenching the carriage and harness. He worked around a groom removing the feedbags and another lighting the carriage lanterns. As they gathered their materials, one remarked the Captain was fortunate the promised rain had cleared off. Only wishing to be on his way, he bid them goodnight and made another round of the chaise.

The silence was excruciating. This was the first occasion he could remember being anywhere near Uppercross when all around him was quiet. He would give his soul for some of the customary chaos to drown out his nagging guilt. However, all around him was the cold calm of a clear November night.

Taking a last look at the quiet house, he saw Anne standing in the window. The cosy light of the living room framed her, and he took comfort that she was safely home, warm and out of harm's way. He wondered how long she had been watching him. It mattered not, he was certain any accord that might have been resurrected between them was now impossible since she was a witness to his undoing of Louisa Musgrove. She was too good a woman to desire a connection with the man he was proving to be. Her good opinion would never be restored.

He reluctantly looked away as he mounted the chaise. As soon as he took his seat, his backside protested another three hours of the hard seat. Just as he was about to head out, a small, old woman hailed him.

"Sir!" She waddled along, clutching something to her bosom and carrying a small bag. "The lady said to see you had these before leavin'." Straining to lift the items to him, she continued, "The blanket's been warmin' by the fire. Sit on it now, and when it loses its heat, wrap yorn legs good an' snug. There's a jug o' small beer, an' a good slab o' venison, an' some Cheshire an' bread in the bag."

The blanket was the most welcome item. The notion that Mrs. Musgrove would take time from her own sorrows touched him and deepened the already profound guilt. He realised that from this day forward every encounter with the Musgroves would be tainted with self-reproach

The old woman was on her way back to the house. Wentworth called to her, "Tell Mrs. Musgrove all the provisions are very much appreciated."

She stopped, turning to him. "Oh, the Missus is as fine a woman there is, but she's in no fit state to be callin' for vittles to be took to travellers. It were Miss Anne saw you was took care of." With a quick nod towards the house, the woman turned and bustled in earnest to the house.

Looking where the woman suggested, he saw Anne still in the window. Of course, Mrs. Musgrove was grieving for her injured daughter and too consumed to see to the comfort of the man responsible. She met his gaze full on, and he knew she studied him as closely as he studied her.

"God, Anne, what have I done to us?" he said aloud. There was nothing to do but return to Lyme. "Walk on," he urged the horses.

Looking back, he saw that she was gone. No, he would never have her good opinion again, but he would take comfort in the fact that she cared enough to see him warm and fed.

—&—

End of Book 1

—&—

Printed in the United States
200100BV00003B/121-729/A